More . . .

NERD IN SHINING ARMOR

"A sharp, sassy, sexy read. Stranded on a desert island? I hope you've got this book in your beach bag."

—Jayne Ann Krentz

"Ms. Thompson continues to set the romance world on fire and keep it burning."

—WritersUnlimited.com

"The heart of this story is the endearing development of a relationship between Gen and Jack . . . will likely rescue you from reading doldrums."

—*Romantic Times*

"Thompson's fun, sexy island adventure gets points for casting a nerd in place of a Fabio."

—*Booklist*

"A lighthearted and frisky tale of discovery between two engaging people."

—*The Oakland Press*

"Thompson writes cheeky, sexy romance, and Jack is a delightful hero."

—*Contra Costa Times*

"If you're looking for something fun and sexy, this is the book for you, especially if you have a soft spot for nerds."

—*All About Romance*

"Vicki Lewis Thompson has created a fun-filled Pacific adventure for the absolute delight of her readers."

—*The Best Reviews*

"Shades of Jennifer Crusie! I just loved this book!"

—*A Romance Review*

NERDS LIKE IT HOT

VICKI LEWIS THOMPSON

St. Martin's Paperbacks

NERDS LIKE IT HOT

ISBN: 0-312-93908-6
EAN: 9780312-93908-3

Printed in the United States of America

St. Martin's Paperbacks edition / August 2006

St. Martin's Paperbacks are published by St. Martin's Press, 175 Fifth Avenue, New York, NY 10010.

10 9 8 7 6 5 4 3 2 1

To my fellow Bent Quill Posse members (in alphabetical order), Jennifer LaBrecque and Rhonda Nelson, for aiding and abetting . . . just about everything!

And to Audrey Sharpe for providing the kind of assistance money can't buy. ·

Acknowledgments

AS ALWAYS, I'M GRATEFUL FOR THE ENTHUSIASTIC SUPPORT of my editor, Jennifer Enderlin, and the wonderful efforts of everyone at St. Martin's Press. Together, we will bring respect to nerds the world over! I would also like to thank the following restaurants—Pei Wei, La Madrina Pizza, Wendy's, Rubio's, Quizno's, and La Salsa. Without them and my darling Larry, who schlepped home take-out every night, I would have starved to death.

One

"GILLIAN, DARLING, IT'S CORA. FOUR OUT OF FIVE women surveyed say that nerds are *amazing* in bed. You simply must go on this cruise with me. Kiss, kiss."

Gillian erased Cora's voice mail from her cell and picked up her makeup kit. She'd stayed at the studio later than usual to tidy up the makeup room, knowing tomorrow she'd be working on Theo Patterson, who was terminally fastidious. He was also a royal PITA.

Matter of fact, she could hear raised voices coming from his dressing room right this minute, which wasn't surprising. He treated people with all the finesse of a belt sander. Now that he'd landed the Tony Curtis role in the *Some Like It Hot* remake, he'd be worse. Unfortunately, he'd requested her because she'd done a decent job on him for his last film.

Looping the strap for her makeup case over her shoulder and grabbing her purse, she headed down the hall. The argument taking place in Theo's dressing room was partly obscured by the construction noise and laughter of the tech crew hard at work on tomorrow's set. Gillian had an early call in the morning, which meant she needed to stop by Cora's on her way home, bid her friend bon voyage, and convince her that she'd have to go cruising alone.

Times were tough, and if Gillian tried to get the time off, she would be fired. Cora should understand that. She used to be in the business. But ever since she'd heard about this nerd-themed cruise sailing out of Long Beach, she'd been all hot for them to go together. She'd even booked a double in hopes Gillian would wangle four days of vacation time.

But no matter how dateless Gillian felt at the moment, she wasn't desperate enough to accompany an eighty-two-year-old woman on a cruise full of nerdlings of all ages. Cora thought Gillian would find her soul mate, which was more than a little insulting. Just because a girl wore glasses and kept her checkbook balanced didn't mean she was a nerd or that she wanted to date one.

Besides, an August cruise guaranteed that passengers would be running around in bathing suits. Gillian wanted to lose at least ten pounds before anyone, even a clueless nerd, saw her seminaked. Ten pounds weren't going to disappear in less than twenty-four hours, which was when the nerd boat sailed.

As Gillian approached Theo's dressing room, the angry voices became more distinct.

"You have the talent of a salamander!" shouted whoever was in there arguing with Theo. "I was supposed to get that role!"

Neil Rucker? Everyone said he'd left for Barbados in a total snit after losing out to Theo for the role of Joe. Apparently Neil and his snit had returned.

"My dear boy, I have more talent in my left nut than you have in your entire scrawny body."

Gillian knew she shouldn't eavesdrop, but this was too juicy to pass up. Besides, she had a professional interest in the fight. If it got physical, she'd be responsible for covering up the damage on Theo's pretty face in the morning. Maybe she should hang around behind the wardrobe rack in the hall and see what developed.

"Be careful, Theo." Neil lowered his voice. "Remember who you're talking to."

"Hey, Mafia boy, if you're trying to threaten me with your *gangsta* connections, save your gin-soaked breath. I refuse to be intimidated."

Gillian had to give Theo credit. Or maybe his ego was making him stupid. Mysterious accidents still happened in L.A., and Neil's stepfather, Phil Adamo, was a constant shadowy presence in town.

"I don't need my stinkin' stepfather, if that's what you mean. Watch out, asshole. I have a stiletto and I know how to use it."

"Put down my Jimmy Choo this instant. And get yourself a better scriptwriter. That's the worst line I've ever heard in my life."

"May it be the last line you ever hear!"

"I'm so scared."

Okay, that was enough. Gillian moved from her hiding place. Time to intervene before somebody got hurt. But as she started toward the door, she heard a sharp crack, a groan, and the sound of something heavy falling to the floor. Like . . . Theo?

The dressing room door opened. Gillian had a split second to decide whether to confront Neil about whatever had happened in there or slip back behind the rack of clothes. She thought about Neil's stepfather and slipped behind the rack. Once Neil had left, she'd go help Theo.

Neil hurried down the hall carrying a purple pump with a five-inch metal heel. Gillian recognized it as part of Theo's audition outfit. Theo loved those shoes. He would never have let Neil walk out with one of them unless he was in no position to argue, which meant he'd been hit in the head or in the balls.

Gillian crept quietly around the rack of clothes and into Theo's dressing room, all the while trying desperately to recall her first-aid course from high school. She vaguely remembered you were supposed to cover an unconscious person. So if Theo happened to be unconscious, she'd cover him with something, and once she was sure Neil had left the building, she'd sound the alarm.

Neil was more than a little bit scary, and she didn't want some member of the tech crew to act like a hero and try to detain him. The cops could take care of it. Then again, maybe Theo wouldn't even want to call the cops and risk the bad publicity.

But when she stepped inside the dressing room and found Theo lying there with his eyes rolled back in his head and his chest not moving at all, she realized he wouldn't have anything to say about bad publicity ever again.

She lost track of time as she stood there staring at Theo, dead in his purple dressing gown. He'd been naked under it, which left her with a problem as to where to rest her gaze. She didn't want to look at his eyes, which were totally creepy, but the bloody spot on his temple where the heel of the shoe had landed wasn't much better.

That left the rest of him, and the robe had twisted

when he fell, revealing far more of Theo Patterson than she'd ever wanted to see. Well, she had been slightly curious about whether the rumors were true, that his bad behavior was compensation for a tiny dick. Score one for the gossip mill.

Gradually the shock of seeing Theo dead gave way to an icky sense of horror. Neil Rucker had killed Theo Patterson with the metal heel of a purple Jimmy Choo, and she was the only person who could testify to that fact. She was as brave as the next person, which meant not very.

Because she'd seen all versions of *The Godfather,* she knew that a witness to a murder committed by the stepson of a known Mob boss was a marked woman. Gillian had never aspired to that. Her name prominently displayed in the film credits was one thing. Being famous among gangsters was something else again.

None of her first aid would do Theo any good, so why hang around? Let someone else find Theo, someone who would have no idea who had done this thing. Later she could make an anonymous phone call, maybe use a voice scrambler. She didn't know where a person bought a voice scrambler, but that was a minor detail. First she had to vamoose.

Backing slowly out of the dressing room, she turned and ran smack into somebody. She steadied her glasses and looked up, afraid that Neil had returned. One glance at the swarthy complexion of the heavyset man told her that this wasn't Neil. But it might be somebody from Neil's underworld.

"Uh, excuse me, I'm late," she said. Lame, but all she could think of. She was lucky anything came out when she felt as if she'd swallowed a large cocktail olive whole.

The man looked at her closely. "Are you okay? You look upset."

"I'm terrific! Just very late! Bye!" She hurried off, her makeup case banging against her side as she race-walked to the exit.

"Wait!" the man called after her. "I want to ask you something!"

"No time!" She didn't stop until she was out the door and tucked into her Saturn with the locks depressed. The adrenaline rush made her shake so bad she couldn't find her keys, and once she did, she couldn't seem to get the key in the ignition.

She'd finally started the motor when the swarthy guy burst out of the back door of the studio. Gillian put the car in reverse and peeled out. Damn it, somebody had witnessed her being a witness. She'd sat through enough movies to know the solution to that problem. She had to disappear.

"YOU HAVE TO DO MORE THAN DISAPPEAR." CORA paced the living room of her bungalow, martini glass in hand. "You have to transform yourself in the process." She turned to Gillian with a dramatic sweep of her red caftan. Age might have added a few extra pounds, but it hadn't altered Cora's regal bearing. She could pass for a woman twenty years younger. "You realize that you must go on this cruise tomorrow, darling."

"What can the cruise do for me?" Gillian had asked Cora to serve her a martini in an eight-ounce tumbler. No point in messing with classy stemware at a time like this. Her Saturn was parked inside Cora's two-car garage, so unless she'd been followed, she was temporarily safe.

"The cruise is a vehicle to get you out of the country," Cora said. "From there you can go anywhere."

"Like South America." Between the gin and the idea of fleeing to South America, she was getting light-headed. She thought of her mother living back in Trenton. She'd have to visit her in disguise. She'd have to send her coded messages through Cora until the coast was clear, which might take years.

Cora studied her with a critical eye. "You need to cut your hair shorter, go blond."

"Oh, Cora, I don't know. Blond looks good on you, but I don't think that I—"

"Nonsense. You'll look fabulous. With a different wardrobe and contacts instead of glasses, you'll make a perfect Marilyn."

"Monroe?"

"Absolutely, darling. I've thought so for ages. You've been hiding your light under a bushel."

"And I want to keep on hiding it! The Mob wants to wipe me out!"

"All the more reason to take your look in the opposite direction, turn yourself into a blond bombshell. We'll start with your hair."

Gillian stared at Cora. Cora's hair, currently honey-colored and cut in a short bob, always looked salon perfect. "You know how to do that?"

"My dear, I've been doing my own for years. Now go into my bathroom and change into the robe hanging on the back of the door."

Gillian took another gulp of her drink. "Couldn't I just buy a wig?"

"No. Wigs come off. And besides, you aren't leaving this house until you look like somebody else entirely. We're about to make Gillian McCormick vanish into thin air."

* * *

AFTER CORA FINISHED GILLIAN'S DYE JOB, SHE LEFT
her in the bathroom to shower and shampoo. Now was the
perfect time to make a critical phone call. She walked
into the bedroom she'd converted into an office and
reached for the receiver of her retro forties-style phone.
Pulling off her clip earring, she tucked her hair behind
her ear.

A disguise would help Gillian, and the cruise was handy
as a getaway plan, but Gillian could use more than that.
She needed a couple of bodyguards on the cruise. Fortunately Cora knew exactly who to call, two friends who
would drop everything if she needed them.

When she connected with Lex Manchester's voice mail,
she hung up and tried Dante Fiorello's number. Then she
crossed her fingers and prayed that Dante would pick up.
This was no time to play phone tag. She wanted to hire
both men before Gillian had a chance to object.

Gillian probably hadn't thought of the monetary ramifications of this flight out of the country, but Cora had.
She'd dip into her retirement savings to hire the two-man
PI team and pull out another chunk for Gillian to survive
on until she'd established herself in a foreign country. In
order to convince Gillian to take the cash, Cora was prepared to lie about the vastness of her savings.

Ever since she'd met Gillian on the set of a fund-
raising TV special, Cora had felt an affinity with the girl.
There were a million reasons why they'd clicked, including Gillian's inherent kindness. Marilyn had been kind
like that, and Gillian's uncanny resemblance to her made
the connection even stronger.

Gillian was too young to re-create the friendship Cora
had shared with Marilyn, but she was exactly the right

age to substitute for the granddaughter Cora had never had. Cora had always suspected foul play in Marilyn's death. She hadn't been able to save her friend all those years ago, but she would, by God, save Gillian now.

CROUCHED BESIDE HIS PARTNER IN THE BUSHES next to a ranch-style house in Ventura, Lex felt the vibration of his cell phone and ignored it. Instead he concentrated on the three-inch gap in the curtains that gave him a restricted view of the master bedroom. Lucky for him the gap was directly opposite the bed where his client's naked wife lay moaning beneath the sweaty body of the pool boy.

"Fake moans," Dante said under his breath. "Too evenly spaced."

Lex shot him a warning glance. They'd managed to creep up to the open bedroom window undetected, which was a miracle considering Dante had tripped on the brick edging surrounding the flower bed. Lex had counted on a closed window and a working air conditioner, but apparently he had neither, so he and Dante had to be quiet.

Dante wasn't a quiet kind of guy, nor a coordinated kind of guy. That was a dangerous combo when trying to skulk under an open window. Fortunately, the two people on the bed were making plenty of their own noise, but that didn't mean Lex condoned unnecessary conversation.

Dante was all about unnecessary conversation. Consequently, in his school days he'd practically lived in the principal's office. Most times Lex had been dragged in there with him, as an accomplice. Some things never changed.

Lex checked his digital camera to make sure the flash was off before raising it above the window ledge. As he

rested his finger on the shutter button, the Hallelujah chorus erupted from the vicinity of Dante's belt.

Lex's four-letter response was drowned out by the yelp-
ing of the couple on the bed and the sound of feet thumping to the floor. Lex took off, followed closely by Dante
and his musical cell phone, the cell phone he'd forgotten to
turn off before leaving the car. Lex was ready to kill him.

They vaulted the low patio wall and ran to the Toyota
parked at the corner. Lex jumped into the driver's seat and
started the car, not really caring whether Dante was coming or not. But his partner managed to hop in and slam the
door before Lex stomped on the gas pedal and peeled out.

Dante unclipped his now-silent phone from his belt
and leaned against the seat with a sigh. "Cora. Might as
well call her back."

"Might as well. The assignment's totally FUBAR."

"Sorry, man."

"Ah, well. What's a couple grand, anyway?" They both
knew what it was—the difference between paying the
office rent or losing the lease. Theoretically they could
operate without an office, but in Lex's opinion, doing
business in a Starbucks wasn't the best way to inspire
client confidence. Tipping off a cheating wife that she
was being watched wasn't the best professional move in
the world, either.

He should never have let Dante sweet-talk him into
opening their own PI firm. He should have continued
working for Aetna, even if investigating insurance fraud
had become more boring than watching the home shopping channel. At least he'd had a steady paycheck.

Dante had always been his nemesis, and this latest
thing was so typical, Dante treating him to the Hallelujah
chorus in the middle of a stakeout. What a ridiculous

situation. Ridiculous, embarrassing, and . . . more fun than he'd had in years. In spite of himself, Lex began to grin. The missus and the pool boy must have thought the Day of Judgment was upon them.

He glanced over at Dante, who was in earnest conversation with Cora. Good old Cora. She must have been something in her heyday, but at the time she'd moved into the Pasadena neighborhood where he and Dante had grown up, she'd retired from the movies and had seemed content to live on her savings.

Lex and Dante had taken turns mowing her lawn in exchange for stories of Marilyn Monroe, Jean Harlow, and Betty Grable. These days they both kept in touch for old times' sake. Instead of the Pepperidge Farm cookies she'd given them as kids, she now mixed them killer martinis.

Dante snapped his cell phone closed. "She has a job for us."

"A job?" Lex couldn't imagine. "Doing what? Did her lawn guy quit?"

"Very funny."

"Maybe not. At this rate we should probably switch to landscape work."

"Look, I'm sorry about the cell phone thing, okay? Do you want to hear about Cora's job or not?"

Lex sighed. "Hit me."

"A friend of hers, Gillian McCormick, needs someone to watch out for her."

"Gillian McCormick. I've heard Cora mention her. Are we talking bodyguards?"

"Something like that."

"Do we do that?" Lex wasn't clear on what a bodyguard assignment entailed, and he liked to be clear about his responsibilities.

"We do now. I told her we could be there in about an hour, give or take, depending on freeway traffic. We can meet Gillian and work out the details."

"Yeah, but—"

"Look, it's not like we have a ton of clients, okay? So Cora wants us to do this, and I said we would. She's paying well. And we could use the income."

Lex controlled the urge to point out that they wouldn't need to be taking jobs they weren't quite qualified for if Dante hadn't screwed up their latest assignment. "I suppose we can protect one lone woman, with two of us keeping an eye out. Who's after her?"

"The Mafia."

Lex almost ran a red light. In the nick of time he slammed on the brakes. *"What?"* Visions of severed horses' heads danced in his brain.

"Gillian was a witness to a murder. The Mob will probably want to eliminate her to protect its own."

Lex stared at him. "Do you hear yourself? *Murder. Eliminating people.* That's hardly in the same league with taking candid shots of a wayward spouse, now, is it?"

"Are you chicken?"

"Hell, yes! This is way bigger than we are."

"Speak for yourself."

"I'm speaking for both of us, Dante. You're a *very* recent graduate of a crash course in private investigation procedures, which you barely passed, I might add, and I'm fresh from the exciting world of insurance fraud. We don't do gangsters. I love Cora as much as you do, but she needs to hire somebody else. Somebody who has a freaking idea what the hell they're doing."

"She wants us." Dante glanced at the intersection. "Green light. Go."

Lex checked traffic and pulled through the intersection. "You need to call her back and tell her we're not qualified."

"Not going to. We can do this. And we get a cruise out of the deal. When was the last time you went on a cruise?"

"Never. I've never been on a cruise." The idea made him shudder. "They make you play games like bingo and shuffleboard. I would hate a cruise."

"Too bad. You're going. Cora's arranging it. Gillian will be on the cruise, and when we get to Mexico, she'll jump ship and head off to South America, where she'll hide out until the coast is clear. Once she leaves the ship, our job will be over and we can party all the way home. In the meantime, we're supposed to keep her safe."

"On a cruise? There will be a gazillion people to worry about!"

"Did I mention Cora's paying really well?"

"How well?" Lex really didn't want to go back to Aetna on his hands and knees.

"We'll be able to cover our rent for six months. And I know how you hate doing business out of Starbucks."

"Okay, so maybe this isn't such a disaster." The prospect of financial stability eased Lex's panic. "The Mob might not even figure out Gillian's taking the cruise. I mean, there must be a shitload of Mexican cruises leaving from Long Beach these days."

"And we'll finally be on one! All expenses paid! Babes in bikinis, umbrella drinks, limbo contests, more babes in bikin—"

"We're supposed to be working, remember?" Lex sighed. "No drinking, and no babes. *Especially* no babes."

"What detective shows have you been watching? Magnum always had a babe."

"Is that why you wanted to be a private eye?" When Dante didn't answer, Lex groaned. "I should have known."

"I don't see a thing wrong with my motivations. And you need to watch more detective shows."

"I need to call Aetna and get my job back. I've gone into partnership with a nut job who thinks he's Magnum."

"You can't quit now. You promised Cora."

"No, *you* promised Cora. But you're right. We have to do this thing for her. After that, I'm calling Aetna."

Dante smiled. "No you won't."

"Watch me."

Two

NEIL HAD A BAD FEELING HE'D BEEN FOLLOWED TO the movie studio. When he'd come out the back door he'd spotted the black sedan parked next to his Porsche. His stepfather's goons always drove black sedans. It had killed him to leave the Porsche, but he'd had no choice.

Breaking into a run, he'd hopped the first bus that had appeared. He'd been forced to transfer three times, but eventually he'd made it to Nancy's apartment and let himself in. A quick peek through the blinds had revealed a deserted street with no telltale black sedans cruising by. Excellent.

So far nobody, not even his stepfather's henchmen, had made the connection between Neil and Nancy Roth. Nancy's existence was his little secret, and he'd worked hard to keep it that way. She was a total turn-on, the most exciting thing in his life, and he wasn't about to lose her.

He glanced down at the purple stiletto he'd carried all the way here. Great shoe. Too bad he hadn't snagged the other one so Nancy could wear them. Probably too risky, but he would have loved the irony of that. Instead he had to destroy the shoe, which seemed like more of a crime than offing Theo.

Might as well get it over with. He had places to go and people to see. The night was young. Taking the shoe into the kitchen, he flipped on a light and pulled a medium-sized knife from the block sitting on the counter. Then he started hacking.

Ten minutes later, he'd nicked his thumb twice and all he had to show for it was a two-inch square of purple suede grinding away in the garbage disposal. This could take all night, and he still wasn't sure what to do with the metal heel once he'd destroyed the rest of the shoe.

Neil looked at the stiletto with a mixture of frustration and respect. "Damn you, Jimmy Choo! You make one hell of a pump!" Maybe he should try incinerating it, but he had no lighter fluid.

There was a bottle of rum in the liquor cabinet, though. That should work. Soaking the shoe thoroughly as it lay in the sink, he found some matches, struck one and held it over the shoe. The resulting flame was spectacular, so spectacular that he leaped back from the sink.

Was that smell from the shoe burning? Or was he . . . on fire? Shit! A spark singed his scalp as he ran to the bathroom, threw on a light, and looked in the mirror. His hair was burning!

Spinning toward the shower stall, he turned on the spray and stuck his head under at the same time the cell phone clipped to his belt played the tune he dreaded more than any other sound in the world. His stepfather was on the line.

He could let it go, of course. But ignoring a call from

Phil Adamo could have serious consequences, both personal and financial. Mopping his hair with a towel, he put the phone to his ear.

Phil wasn't the kind to waste his breath on pleasantries. "You were seen."

"Seen where?" His heart pounded as he tried to think of how he'd get out of this one.

"You know damned well where." Phil's voice was icy with rage. "I should tell your mother, but I won't, because it would kill her. Now listen, and listen good. I'm ordering you to leave the country. There's no way I can smooth this over. You've gone too far."

Sweat trickled from his armpits down his ribs. "So, one of your guys saw me. What's the big deal?"

"Not one of my guys. One of the studio's makeup artists."

"How do they know that?"

"Enrique bumped into her coming out of Theo's dressing room after you left and she was carrying her makeup case. A couple of phone calls, and we had an ID. So I'm telling you, and I'm not going to tell you again, leave the country. Enrique and Hector are taking care of the body, so the cops won't have evidence right away, but we don't know what the witness will do."

"Who is she?"

"No dice. You get nothing on this."

"Can't you take care of her?"

Phil's voice was calm but deadly. "I haven't decided yet. It would seem like the expedient thing, yet I keep telling myself that she doesn't deserve to die because you are a vindictive little creep. So there's no firm decision on that yet. I want you out of the country, Neil."

"What about Mom?"

"I'll tell her you landed a role in an Italian film and you had to leave immediately. She'll be fine. Give it a year and then get in touch with me. I'll let you know if it's safe."

Neil gulped. A year was like *forever*. No way was he staying out of the country for an entire year. He had a life. He had friends. He had Nancy. And he liked L.A. just fine. No reason to give that up because some makeup artist happened to see him conk Theo over the head. "Okay," he said. "I'll hop a plane for Rio tonight."

"I mean it, Neil."

"Yeah, sure. I'll throw a few things in a suitcase and head out."

"See that you do." The phone went dead.

Neil controlled the urge to throw it. Instead he walked back to the kitchen and surveyed the smoldering mess in the sink. God, it smelled worse than his hair, but it wasn't recognizable anymore. Wrinkling his nose, he pulled the trashcan from under the sink and scooped the remains of the shoe into it. Then he tied the plastic ends of the garbage bag together. Garbage pickup was in the morning. He'd drop the bag in a Dumpster before he went to bed.

Returning to the bathroom, he switched on the makeup mirror and opened a drawer. Several of Nancy's friends at the club worked for the studio. A few drinks, a few laughs, and Nancy would have the information about which makeup artist might have been working late tonight.

Neil took his time shaving, although he'd never had much of a beard. Then he trimmed off the singed ends of his blond hair. Not a great job, but the wig would cover up the damage. Later tonight he'd give himself a buzz cut. After cleansing his face, he began putting on his favorite color of foundation.

Fifteen minutes later, a woman dressed in a slinky black dress that complemented her auburn hair strolled out of the apartment and climbed into a cab. Nancy Roth was ready to party.

MAYBE IT WAS MARTINIS ON AN EMPTY STOMACH, OR maybe it was because she wasn't wearing her glasses, but Gillian thought she looked a teensy bit like Marilyn Monroe, after all. Sitting in front of Cora's dressing-table mirror with a bath towel around her shoulders, she admired the platinum curls and the makeup Cora had expertly applied. Her image was a little fuzzy, as if the cinematographer had chosen a soft lens approach.

After years of putting makeup on other people, Gillian had enjoyed having Cora do the honors. But the longer she sat there, the heavier the makeup felt on her skin. Thank God she wasn't an actor who had to wear this stuff all the time.

"Darling, you're gorgeous. I knew you would be." Cora picked up her martini glass and took a sip as she surveyed her handiwork. "You could win a look-alike contest, hands down. Even that little mole of yours is in the right place."

"I have to admit, I look halfway decent." She took a drink from her tumbler. "But that could be the gin talking."

"Nonsense. You're fabulous. By the way, do you own a pair of contacts?"

"They're at home. I don't really like wearing them."

"Well, we can decide that later, I suppose. But I love your hair this way. You should have gone blond years ago."

Gillian shook her head. "Too much work. My hair grows fast. I'll have dark roots in no time. You know me. I'm all about low maintenance."

"Where's the fun in that?" Cora drained her glass and put it down on the glass-topped dressing table with a precise click. "It's like painting every wall in your house white."

"I like white walls." Gillian glanced around at the pink walls of Cora's bedroom and realized that might have sounded rude. "Not that other colors aren't nice. But with colors you have to bother with a different kind of touch-up paint for each room. With white, you're set for the whole house."

Cora waved a hand heavy with rings. "You're young. You don't have to worry about the ghastly effect of white walls on your skin tones. But I still can't see how you can live with all white. Don't you crave more excitement than that?"

"No." Her father had been the one who'd craved excitement—from climbing mountains to diving with Great Whites. His addiction to thrills had exhausted her mother with worry and frightened Gillian to death.

He'd made quite a name for himself as a daredevil. He'd tried wing-walking one sunny fall day, and the roller-coaster ride had been over, for all of them. "I like things calm," Gillian said.

Cora gazed at her in sympathy. "That's too bad. I don't foresee a lot of tranquility in your immediate future."

"Me, either." Gillian had tried not to think about what lay ahead, but everything about it frightened her. She didn't know the first thing about running off to a foreign country and creating a whole new identity. "Cora, I don't even speak much Spanish."

"You're a smart woman." Cora patted her arm. "You'll pick up what you need. Once you're settled somewhere, you can contact me."

"But won't they trace me through you?"

"Not if we use my lawyer's address. I'll keep you up-to-date on the case. As soon as I think it's safe for you to come home, I can let you know."

Gillian nodded. Cora expected her to be brave, so she'd be brave.

"Right now, we need to get your wardrobe together," Cora said.

"Should I try to go back to my apartment?"

"Absolutely not. You're staying with me until we sail. We'll get someone to sneak in and grab whatever you need, like your passport."

"I actually have that in my purse. I like carrying it as an extra piece of ID, just in case. I wouldn't mind having some of my other stuff, although I don't know who we can send over there. I don't want to risk asking one of my friends, in case someone's . . . waiting." The idea gave her cold chills.

"I wouldn't ask any of your friends."

"Then who?"

"Oh, I have some ideas. Anyway, when I was talking about your wardrobe, I meant it's time for you to choose from what I have." She walked over to a closet and drew back the bifold doors to reveal a long rack of clothes arranged by color. "I don't have the figure for these anymore, but you do."

"I don't know, Cora. I'm not a skinny person."

"You are not a fat person, either. A size ten, right?"

"Yes, I am most definitely a size ten." The booze had loosened her tongue. "And every day I work on women who are a zero! Or if they've retained water weight, they might move all the way up to a two, perish the thought. And then they complain about being a balloon."

"Anorexic, the lot of them. Pay no attention to them, Gillian. Did you know that if Marilyn could waltz back in here today at the age she was when I knew her, she'd wear about a ten or maybe even a twelve?"

Gillian thought of Marilyn stretched out on that red drapery, the famous nude shot. She'd been perfect. "You're just trying to make me feel better."

"I am, but I'm also telling you the God's truth. And it's not speculation. I worked with her. We were friends. We wore the same size and we traded clothes sometimes."

"That's . . . amazing." To Gillian, Marilyn was some sort of mythical creature. She couldn't imagine her as a real woman who swapped clothes with friends. "Do you have something in there that belonged to her?"

Cora nodded. "One dress. After she died, and there was all the hullabaloo about her, I thought of selling it, but I wasn't sure how to authenticate that she'd worn it. I didn't really want the hassle of trying to prove what I knew to be true."

"Which one?" Gillian shouldn't be feeling so starstruck. She worked with famous people all the time. But a dress that Marilyn had worn . . .

Walking to the closet, Cora took out a garment bag and unzipped it. Inside was a silver sheath studded with rhinestones around the scooped neckline. "This one. I think you should wear it on the cruise."

"I couldn't do that." Gillian grabbed her glasses from the dressing table and put them on. Even blurry, the dress looked incredible, but once it came into focus, her mouth watered with dress lust. Mostly she didn't care about clothes, but this dress called to her.

"I'm not offering to let you take it to South America,

but I would love to see you wearing it at the captain's dinner on the cruise."

"I don't think so, but it's amazing of you to offer."

Cora laid the dress, still in its garment bag, on her king-sized bed. "You have until tomorrow night to decide. In the meantime, let's move on to some of the other outfits. We'll start with the basics. I have several bathing suits. Let's see which one shows off your assets to best advantage."

"Cora, in case you don't remember, I'm not trying to attract attention on this cruise. I'm trying to blend in."

"I don't think you understand my strategy. If you try to blend in, you'll look exactly like what you are, a timid makeup artist hoping to be inconspicuous."

"I'm not either timid! I'm conservative!"

Cora looked amused. "Semantics, darling. One person's timid is another person's conservative. In any case, if Phil Adamo's men track you down, I want them to find someone who couldn't possibly be Gillian McCormick. You'll be too flamboyant, too blond, too out there to be the woman they're looking for."

"I may need a personality transplant."

"I'm not so sure about that." Cora smiled at her. "A few months ago, I researched your father, since you've been so adamant about not mentioning him. The Internet is a beautiful thing."

Gillian flushed, as she always did whenever someone connected her with Duke McCormick. He'd demonstrated to the world that he was both self-centered and foolish. "Well, I'm *nothing* like him!"

"You're too smart to believe that. You know there's a part of you that's very much like him, which is what you're so afraid of." Cora's voice softened. "Don't fight that part of you. It may be what keeps you alive."

Gillian didn't want to hear that. She'd tried so hard not to think about the fact that her life was in danger. She held out her glass. "I think I'll have another martini."

"Of course." Cora took the glass, but instead of leaving with it, she reached into the closet and unhooked three hangers. "While I'm gone, try these on."

Gillian had to admit the one-piece bathing suits in jewel tones—one red, one peacock blue, and one purple—had babe potential . . . on someone else. "Thanks, anyway, but I don't want to get into the whole bathing suit scene."

Shaking the hangers, Cora made the suits shimmer and dance. "You might not, darling, but the person you're going to be on the cruise definitely would. She'd prefer the red. Start with that one. I'll be right back with your drink."

Gillian accepted the trio of bathing suits. "Better make it a double."

"Don't be silly. You'll look marvelous. I'll be right back." Cora swept through the bedroom door and closed it after her.

"I'll look like a ripe tomato," Gillian muttered as she dumped the suits on the bed. Then she took a deep breath. Okay, she'd squeeze herself into the red suit to make Cora happy. But there was that silver dress lying there, too, the dress that had once belonged to Marilyn.

She wouldn't agree to take that dress on the cruise, not when it was so valuable. But if she didn't take it, then she'd never have a chance to try it on, because she'd be hiding out in some peasant village in the Andes plucking chickens for a living, or whatever peasants did to earn money in the Andes.

When she thought of what her life might become once she left the cruise ship, she became very depressed. A depressed person who was also feeling a wee bit fat would be crazy to try on a bathing suit in that condition. No, instead she should zip herself into a silver sheath that had once belonged to Marilyn, who had worn her size.

Although Gillian looked for a tag, she couldn't find one. That made sense. The dress was probably custom made. The thought gave her goose bumps. Without a tag, she had no idea what the material was.

Taking off her glasses, she laid them on the table and pulled the dress over her head. As it slid smoothly onto her body, she imagined that the material had been woven from some magic substance that had no name. It hugged her hips as if it had been sewn just for her. She really *was* Marilyn's size, and that thrilled her to her bare toes.

Pulling the side zipper up without sucking in her breath, she adjusted the scooped neckline and walked over to the free-standing floor mirror in the corner of Cora's bedroom. *Marilyn*. She stared in disbelief. She really looked like Marilyn Monroe. Same hourglass figure, same generous bust, same soft blond hair.

Bracing her hands on her knees, she leaned forward so she could see better. Glasses would ruin the fantasy she had going. Puckering her lips the way she'd seen Marilyn do in film after film, she let her eyelids droop in that slumberous, sexy way that was all Marilyn.

Then she ran her tongue slowly over her red lips. This whole gig was turning her on. If a man were to walk in the room right now, she'd put the moves on him, no problem.

Was that Cora's doorbell ringing? Gillian was so fascinated by her new Marilyn persona that she couldn't bring herself to care. When she shifted her shoulders, the dress undulated just enough to show off her cleavage. No wonder Marilyn had been able to transfix every man in the room. In a dress like this, Gillian could, too. She would be unstoppable.

"Gillian?" Cora knocked on the door. "Are you decent?"

Gillian snapped out of her trance and visions of Marilyn disappeared like smoke. "Why?"

"There's someone out here I'd like you to meet. If you're wearing the bathing suit, you can throw on a bathrobe."

"You want me to meet someone?" That made no sense. "I thought I was supposed to be hiding out."

"You are." Cora hesitated. "I've hired a couple of bodyguards to go with us on the cruise. I didn't consult you because I know you wouldn't have wanted me to spend the money, but I have plenty stashed away, and I—"

"Bodyguards?" Gillian began to shiver. "You really think the Mob will follow us on the cruise?"

"Probably not, but—"

"You do!" Gillian walked over and wrenched the door open. "The cruise isn't that safe a getaway, after all, is it?"

Instead of answering the question, Cora stared at Gillian. "My God, you were made for that dress. It's astonishing how much you look like her."

"Do I look enough like her to keep from getting killed?" Adrenaline shot through Gillian's system, making her feel reckless. "Because if you hired two bodyguards, you must think that's a distinct possibility!"

"Not at all. I just believe in covering all our bases."

"Maybe I should forget the cruise. Maybe I should just get in my car and drive . . . somewhere. I could go up into the mountains, or head for the desert. I could criss-cross the country, never staying in one place more than a night."

"Gillian, you—"

"No, listen. On my own, in the car, I could bob and weave like a rabbit. I think this cruise will turn me into a sitting duck!"

Cora grabbed her by the shoulders and gave her a little shake. "Hey! Get hold of yourself. You don't want to take off on your own, with no one to look out for you. That's crazy."

Gillian didn't really want to run away by herself, but what if she ended up trapped out in the middle of the ocean with a hit man on board? "Who . . . who are these guys you hired? Are they any good?"

"They're pure gold. I've known Lex and Dante since they were kids. I would trust them with my life, and you can trust them with yours."

"That sounds better."

"Of course it does. Now come out into the living room and meet them, so we can start making plans."

Gillian glanced down at the dress she'd put on. "Like this?"

Cora surveyed her with a loving eye. "Yes, darling. Exactly like that."

"Let me get my glasses." She started back toward the dressing table where she'd left them. "The better to see them with."

"Humor me, Gillian." Cora walked over and took her hand. "Every time I look at you, it's like having Marilyn back again. Leave the glasses off a little while longer, okay?"

Truth be told, Gillian was curious about what sort of reaction she'd get from the bodyguard types when she walked into the room. Without her glasses she wouldn't have a real clear idea, but she'd hear if anybody gasped. She'd like to make a man gasp at least once in her life.

"Okay." She squeezed Cora's hand. "I'll humor you."

Three

LEX HAD NO IDEA WHAT HE SAID DURING THE IN-
troductions. He was too busy taking in the view of their
newest client, who had actually made him catch his breath
when she'd walked into the room. Lex liked to think he
had better control than that, but not tonight, apparently.

Whatever he'd expected from Gillian McCormick, it
hadn't been a blond-bombshell routine. She was a babe
straight out of the detective shows Dante loved so much,
and Lex was ready to play Magnum to her damsel in dis-
tress. Especially the sexy parts.

He'd always laughed at the idea of instant attraction, but
it wasn't so damned funny right now. She was pulling reactions out of him where he'd never had reactions. Besides
the usual groin-tightening, accelerated pulse, and excess
saliva, the back of his neck felt hot. What was up with that?

Those big brown eyes of hers should be registered as
dangerous weapons. Ditto her cleavage. She was quite
obviously a bottle blonde and he didn't care at all. He,
the guy who had always maintained he liked his women

natural, thought this fake shade of platinum was gorgeous.

The dress, the hair, and the ruby red lipstick all made her seem exotic and slightly dangerous. His fabled detachment crumbled more with every second he stayed in the same room with her. This assignment had the makings of a complete disaster.

Dante was the first one to break the silence. "You didn't say we were guarding a Marilyn impersonator." He sounded pleased as punch about it, too.

Personally, Lex thought Gillian was prettier than Marilyn, but he kept that opinion to himself. "We . . . uh . . . might need to rethink this, Cora."

"I'm not a Marilyn impersonator," Gillian said in a strong, very un–Marilyn–like voice. "I'm a makeup artist, and I don't usually look like this. Cora thought I needed a disguise."

Dante gazed at her with puppy-dog adoration. "I'd say this beats the Groucho Marx nose-and-eyeglasses approach, hands down."

Lex imagined his hands down the front of that dress. He fought for sanity. "But she's hardly what you'd call inconspicuous," he said. "I'm not sure how she's supposed to blend into the woodwork looking so . . ." *Hot*.

"She's not supposed to blend in," Cora said. "Blending into the woodwork would describe her before." She smiled at Gillian. "Sorry, darling."

"That's okay," Gillian said.

"But you blended in a really nice way." Cora turned back to Lex and Dante. "My plan was to go against type. I think that might confuse any pursuers."

"Works for me." Dante's gaze traveled slowly over the silver dress.

Lex wanted to smack him. Once they were alone, he'd deliver another lecture about getting mixed up with clients. Gillian didn't need to have one of her bodyguards hitting on her. *Unless it's me.* He squished the thought the minute it crawled out of his testosterone-soaked brain.

He had a problem, and he wasn't sure how to handle it. Judging from his visceral reaction to Gillian, he should reject this assignment immediately. But if he did, who would watch out for this gorgeous woman?

If he backed out, Cora might hire someone incompetent, not that Lex felt all that competent, himself. The truth was, it didn't matter whether he felt up to the job or not. One look at Gillian and he'd appointed himself her protector. Now wasn't that trite?

"Please sit down, everyone," Cora said. "I'll mix us all a martini and we can talk strategy."

"I don't want to sit down in this dress," Gillian said. "Let alone drink a martini while I'm wearing it. I'll go take it off."

Let me help. A moan of desire tickled the back of Lex's throat. The silver material outlined the kind of curves he'd dreamed about all his life. Women these days were too skinny and underendowed for his taste. Not this woman.

"Must be Cora's designer duds you're wearing," Dante said.

"Something like that." Gillian turned and walked down the hall to Cora's bedroom.

God help him, Lex watched. The silver dress was cut low in the back, and the material stretched lovingly over Gillian's sexy butt. As she walked away, the material shifted in rhythm with her steps, creating a play of light and shadow that mesmerized him. He prayed she wasn't taking that dress on the cruise.

"Relax, boys." Cora headed for the kitchen. "I'll be back in a flash with exactly what you need."

"I doubt it," Dante said under his breath.

"She's off-limits." Lex's statement came out a little more forcefully than he'd intended.

"I know that." Dante sounded insulted. "She's a client, right? I know the drill. We don't get involved with clients."

"Exactly." Lex's head was filled with images of total involvement.

"The thing is, we've never had a client who looked like that. Take Mrs. Hannigan, for example. The pool boy must have been blind as a bat, because Mrs. Hannigan was no prize. She—"

"She wasn't the client. Her husband was."

"Technically, I suppose you're right. And who would want to get involved with him? Blech. But for the sake of argument, I want to point out that Gillian McCormick is the best-looking client we've ever had."

Lex couldn't disagree. He could still see her standing there in the silver dress that nipped in so perfectly at her waist and flared out at her hips. The fact that she'd been barefoot had made the image even more tantalizing. He could weave an entire fantasy around Gillian and that silver dress. There would be music, maybe something Latin, and candles, and—

"Lex." Dante snapped his fingers in front of Lex's face.

"What?" Lex blinked at his partner. "Did you say something?"

"I asked if you owned anything that could be described as cruise wear."

"I doubt it."

"I doubt it, too. Are you okay? Your eyes sort of lost focus there for a minute."

"I'm fine." Lex ran a hand over his face. "It's been a long day."

"Yeah, but it's turning out great. Cora's mixing up martinis, and we're headed out for a cruise with a genuine babe. What could be better? Well, it would be better if we could actually hit on the babe, but you can't have everything."

"Dante, about the cruise, there's something I should tell you."

"What's that?"

"I can't swim."

Dante started to laugh. "We'll be on a boat, buddy. Swimming won't be an issue unless you fall overboard."

GILLIAN HAD WANTED TO CHANGE OUT OF THE SILVER dress before drinking another martini and risking a spill, but changing clothes had also been a convenient excuse to give her some privacy to think about Lex Manchester. She'd distinctly heard him gasp, which had been as thoroughly rewarding as she'd expected it would be. The thing is, she might have done a little bit of gasping, herself.

From the moment she'd stepped into Cora's living room, his lean good looks had seduced her imagination. He was handsome in a careless sort of way, the kind of man who couldn't be bothered to primp. His dark hair was ruffled, as if he'd recently been running his fingers through it in frustration. His clear blue eyes seemed to miss nothing.

Maybe her poor eyesight had given her a false hunk reading, but she was afraid he really was gorgeous. When Cora had mentioned bodyguards, Gillian had imagined a couple of no-neck guys with muscles on top of muscles.

For some reason she'd thought they'd be wearing dark suits and narrow ties, like Secret Service men or the Blues Brothers. She'd even expected sunglasses, although that made no sense at this hour of the night.

Instead these two had arrived in jeans and T-shirts. Lex's was a faded blue UCLA model, and Dante's red shirt said *ITALIAN STALLION* on the front. Although they were both broad shouldered and in good shape, neither man fit her concept of bodyguards. Maybe they were martial arts experts who didn't need muscles. Maybe they were smart.

She'd bet Lex was smart. His blue eyes were definitely analytical, but the fringe of dark lashes added a dose of sensuality that was not lost on Gillian. She'd eased closer to get a better look. Ever since her five-year-old self had watched Christopher Reeve walk on screen as Superman, she'd had a thing for dark-haired men with blue eyes.

Dante was cute, with his Mediterranean coloring and curly hair, but Lex could never be described as cute. Rugged, maybe. Chiseled. Yes, that was it. Definitely chiseled. Plus he could fill out a pair of jeans in a most satisfying manner. Even a blind woman would have been able to see that. To top off the presentation, he had an intensity about him that she found wildly appealing.

That would have to be her little secret, though. In a few days she'd be disappearing into Mexico, on the run from the Mob and bound for South America. Not exactly the time to begin a romantic interlude. That was a shame, too, because her recent transformation had given her new confidence in her ability to snag a good-looking guy like Lex.

That didn't mean she was ready to try on the bathing suits, though. Laying the silver dress on the bed, she started to dress in the outfit she'd worn over to Cora's house, khaki slacks and a shapeless yellow shirt. She couldn't make herself put them on. They didn't go with her new hair and makeup.

Instead she crossed to the closet and found a black tank top and white Capri pants. They fit, although the black tank dipped fairly low in the front. She should probably go back to her yellow shirt. It wasn't as if she wanted to captivate either of the men in the next room.

Liar. In spite of knowing that nothing could come of the attraction she felt for Lex, she wanted to look good for him. Maybe she had some melodramatic idea that he'd think of her with longing after she'd left the country. A girl could be forgiven for melodramatic thoughts when she was running for her life. It seemed to go with the territory.

She wouldn't wear her glasses, either. Leaving her shoes off, she walked back into the living room where Lex, Dante, and Cora were already drinking martinis and talking about the cruise. On the way down the hall she'd wondered if Lex would look not quite so yummy sitting down. But he looked fabulous sitting down, one manly arm stretched across the back of the love seat. She wanted to plop down next to him and snuggle in.

Instead she settled on the sofa where Cora was sitting. Because she felt Marilyn-like, she turned sideways and propped her feet up on the middle cushion. A woman with platinum-blond hair and an hourglass figure could do that kind of thing.

Dante had appropriated the recliner and looked like a man ready to enjoy *Monday Night Football*. All he needed was a remote in his hand. Gillian took in the relaxed posture of both Lex and Dante. They seemed completely at home here. She liked thinking of them as kids living in the same neighborhood as Cora.

Cora picked up a stemmed glass from the coffee table

and handed it to Gillian. Apparently Cora didn't think the tumbler of gin and vermouth fit the Marilyn image. "I filled the guys in on what happened tonight with Neil and Theo," she said.

"Thanks." Gillian appreciated not having to retell it. As it was, she probably wouldn't sleep tonight.

"Anyway," Cora continued, "we were just starting to talk about the cruise. I know the owners of the cruise line, so I can probably pull some strings and get Lex and Dante the cabin next to ours."

That sounded great to Gillian. Protection and eye candy right next door. "But what if the cruise is full?"

"I happen to know it's not." Cora ran a manicured finger around the rim of her martini glass. "Marie and Tom called me the other day to see if I'd recruited anyone else. They let their grandson plan this cruise because he's been begging them to try it. Turns out reservations aren't what they'd hoped."

"Maybe nerds don't like to cruise, after all," Gillian said.

Dante lifted his head from the cushioned recliner. "What do nerds have to do with it?"

"Well, um . . ." Cora glanced at Gillian. "I haven't quite gotten around to telling them that part."

"Oh. Sorry. I thought they knew." And come to think of it, she wondered how two such yummy guys could pass themselves off as nerds.

"Knew what?" Lex looked uneasy.

Cora set down her drink. "Well, this is a theme cruise. And it's a little . . . different."

"Oh, I get it." Dante looked relieved. "It's probably based on something like the Harry Potter movies or *Lord of the Rings*. Am I right?"

"Not exactly," Cora said. "It's more like a, well, a nerd cruise."

Dante looked stunned. "A *nerd* cruise? You mean we're getting on a boat with a bunch of *geeks*?"

Cora picked up her drink again. "Don't look so scandalized, Dante. All you need to do is disguise yourselves as nerds for a few days. It won't kill you."

"So we have to look like geeks, too? Oh, *man*. This is so not going to be the cruise of my dreams. If I'd known that, I would have—"

"We'll be fine with it," Lex said quietly. "The main thing is to keep Gillian safe, right, Dante?"

Dante had the good grace to look ashamed of himself. "Well, sure. Sorry, Gillian. Lex is absolutely right. Gotta put things in perspective. Dressing up like nerds is only a temporary thing, whereas dead is forever."

Gillian choked on her martini. When all eyes turned in her direction, she waved off their concern. "I'm okay. Just swallowed wrong."

"I would imagine so." Cora leveled a stern glance at Dante. "We'll have no more of that talk."

"That's for damned sure." Lex's position had changed from relaxed to extremely alert. "No one is going to die, and that's final."

Gillian's pulse rate slowed as fear loosened its grip. Hearing Lex's confident reassurance helped enormously. "I appreciate you saying that," she said.

"Just stating the obvious." He met her gaze with those startlingly blue eyes.

Even without her glasses, she picked up on the strong sense of purpose in his gaze. And there was something else, something zinging back and forth between the two of them. Her tummy quivered in response. She hadn't felt that kind of sexual tug in ages, and wouldn't you know, she couldn't hang around to take advantage of it.

"I should probably get the brochure," Cora said. "That will explain it better than I can." She got up from the sofa and hurried down the hallway.

"This is totally weird," Dante said. "I've never heard of a nerd cruise before. Who would think of such a thing?"

"I'm guessing the grandson's a nerd," Gillian said.

"Oh, I'm sure." Dante rolled his eyes. "But why would Cora want to go?"

Gillian thought about Cora's latest voice mail. Nope. Didn't want to go there. "I'm sure it's reasonably priced. And she might be trying to do the grandparents a favor."

"Here we go." Cora swept back into the room and handed the brochure to Lex. "Read all about it."

Lex glanced at it and handed it over to Dante.

"Hm." Dante studied the brochure. "It says here, 'the cruise is designed specifically for single members of Mensa who are looking for a chance to meet that special someone in an atmosphere of intellectual stimulation and camaraderie.'" He paused and looked at Cora. "Are you in Mensa? I never knew that."

"No, of course I'm not. That isn't a requirement. The idea is to create an environment where supersmart people, or those who want to hang around them, feel comfortable." Cora sipped her drink. "I think it's a marvelous idea."

"I think it's whacked," Dante said. "I mean, cruises are supposed to be fun, but how can you have fun with, and I quote, 'mentally challenging activities with an emphasis on brain power'?"

Lex sighed. "Dante, we're not there to have fun. We're there to protect Gillian."

"And speaking of Gillian, what's up there?" Dante's appreciative glance moved over her. "She most definitely doesn't look like a nerd."

"That's on purpose," Cora said. "I'm introducing her as my companion, so she doesn't have to look nerdy. There will be two kinds of people on this cruise, the nerds and those who aren't nerds but hope to hook up with one. The second category will be mostly female."

Dante looked confused. "I don't get it. Why would any woman deliberately look for a nerd?"

"Because," Cora said. "All the research I've done shows that—"

"Nerds are faithful." Gillian nudged Cora with her bare foot. She'd rather not have Cora launch into a description of nerds and their superior sexual skills.

Dante seemed to accept that explanation. "Faithful is good, I guess. Especially if you're thinking long-term commitment."

"Or short-term commitment." Cora laughed. "I'm eighty-two years old. At my age, *long-term commitment* is a vague description at best. It could be six years or six months, depending on the EKG."

Lex sat up straighter. "You're really looking?"

"I am, and if I were forty years younger, I'd look no further than you, my darling."

Red crept up Lex's neck, which Gillian found cute as the dickens.

Dante nodded wisely. "So you picked up on it, too, huh? Our Lex has nerd tendencies. I didn't tweak to that until a few minutes ago, but once you think about it, he has all the signs."

"I'm not even going to comment." Lex took a big swallow of his martini.

Dante jerked his thumb in Lex's direction. "He doesn't want to admit it, but I have evidence. Back in high school, before I stopped him, he was going to join the chess club and the Honor Society. I rest my case."

"I was in Honor Society," Gillian said before she could stop herself. "But that doesn't mean I consider myself a nerd. I'm certainly not in Mensa," she added quickly. After all, she was dressed in Marilyn clothes, and she had Marilyn hair. She was—at least temporarily—very cool.

"My point exactly," Lex said.

"But we're going undercover as nerds," Dante said. "How do we do that?"

"I suppose you could start with glasses," Gillian said.

Lex groaned. "Cliché."

"I know, but it'll work, at least for a few days." Gillian hated to think of how short her association with Lex would be. Instead she concentrated on helping these two hotties turn themselves into geeks. "Your haircuts are too good." The thought of Lex's silky dark hair getting massacred made her cringe, but it couldn't be helped.

Dante's eyes widened. "I have to get a bad haircut? Damn."

"You don't really mind, do you?" Cora asked, an edge to her voice. "Compared to saving Gillian's life . . ."

"Of course I don't mind." Dante sounded like a little boy who'd been scolded for leaving his bike in the driveway. "Whatever it takes, that's what we'll do."

"Then get some mismatched clothes," Gillian said. "A discount department store should work." She got a kick out of seeing Dante wince. Lex remained stoic, as if an ugly wardrobe was beneath his notice. Gillian didn't think the clothes had been made that would disguise Lex's innate sexuality.

"And we need you to go over to Gillian's apartment tomorrow and pick up whatever she needs for the trip," Cora said. "Be discreet." She snapped her fingers. "I know! You can disguise yourselves as exterminators."

"Bug thugs," Dante said without enthusiasm. "This just gets better and better."

Cora lifted her eyebrows and gave him a warning glance. "Dante, I—"

"Don't worry," Lex said. "Dante will do what needs to be done. Right, partner?"

"Absolutely," Dante said. "What do you need from your apartment, Gillian?"

"My contacts, and . . ." She wouldn't have been able to mention this if she hadn't been wearing Marilyn clothes and Marilyn hair. "And my underwear."

BY SOME MIRACLE DANTE DIDN'T SAY ANYTHING ELSE that was terminally stupid before Lex got him out the door. Lex had the key to Gillian's apartment and the list of what they needed to bring her in his pocket.

"First stop, Kinko's," Lex said.

"You got a sudden urge to copy something?"

"No. We need to see if they can do a rush order on a couple of magnetic signs for the white van we're going to rent in the morning for our exterminator gig."

"Oh." Dante nodded. "Good thinking."

"Thanks. And speaking of thinking, can you start putting your brain in gear before you open your mouth?"

"Yeah, that was bad when I alluded to her getting dead."

"Did you notice she went white as a sheet? We're supposed to make her feel protected, not scare her out of her wits. For God's sake, Dante."

"I know, I know. I'll work on it." He paused. "You really like her, don't you?"

You have no idea. "That's not important."

"Buddy, it's always important, especially in your case. You haven't fallen for that many chicks in your life. I haven't seen you this perky since Mary Jo Simpson, and that was, what? Three years ago?"

"Three and a half." Lex had dated since then, but nothing had lasted. He guessed the term for it was *casual sex,* which had left him feeling sort of empty. There was nothing casual about his interest in Gillian.

"It's a shame she's a client," Dante said.

"If she hadn't become a client, I never would have met her, so there you go."

"You might've. She's friends with Cora, and we're friends with Cora. If Gillian hadn't had the bad luck to witness this murder, the two of you might have run into each other at Cora's sometime."

Lex would rather not think of that possibility. It hadn't happened that way, so no sense in wishing for things that couldn't be.

Dante was silent for a while. "You really can't swim?" he asked finally.

"Nope."

"How did I miss that in all the years we've known each other?"

"I made sure I always played a manly game of volleyball in the shallow end."

Dante gazed at him. "You covered really well. I never put it all together before. I mean, you were just my friend, and I was saving you from making stupid mistakes, but without me, you probably would have turned into a first-class nerd."

"I wouldn't say that." Lex drove five miles over the speed limit, just to show he wasn't all that geeky.

"I would." Dante looked at his partner as if seeing him for the first time. "But I saved you. I need to give myself credit for that."

"You go ahead and do that."

"The thing is, you being a nerd could come in handy for this assignment. Do you think you could revert back?"

"I'm not, nor have I ever been, a nerd!"

"Thanks to me, that's true. But unlike me, you at least had nerd tendencies, once upon a time. If you could tap into those, you could be in charge of the nerd factor on this gig."

Lex felt a tension headache coming on. Between guarding a woman who looked like Gillian and dredging up his long-buried nerdiness, he had quite a week ahead of him.

Four

GIVE A WOMAN A COUPLE OF APPLETINIS AND SHE'LL tell you anything. Neil had learned that early in his cross-dressing career, and when you threw in the element of dishing with the girls, there were no secrets left after the second round. Nancy, looking extremely trendy in her short black dress, was considered one of the girls. The barflies who hung out at the Swingin' Monkey had never guessed otherwise.

Neil had been careful never to hit on any of the guys here, because this club was his place to gather industry information. Another club, far from this particular Hollywood hangout, was his source of liaisons. Men there appreciated surprises. The Swingin' Monkey catered to a more conservative, definitely hetero crowd.

Thanks to Heather and Joanie, two of the makeup artists working on the *Some Like It Hot* project, Neil had an overview of the entire makeup crew. He'd never paid much attention to makeup artists before, thinking they were beneath his notice. Now he wished he had a better working knowledge of the breed. For all he knew, the person who'd seen him leaving Theo's dressing room was someone who'd done his makeup once upon a time.

At least tonight he'd ruled out Heather and Joanie, who wouldn't be here slurping appletinis and spreading studio gossip if they'd recently witnessed a murder. And one of the crew was a guy. Phil had said the witness was a woman. That left either Eileen or Gillian.

Eileen was an older woman who lived in Van Nuys and supported a disabled son. Gillian lived alone in an apartment in Burbank and hung out with Cora Bledsoe a lot, according to Heather. Cora had been trying to get Gillian to go on a nerd cruise, which told Neil that Gillian might be something of a nerd, herself.

Now that he'd narrowed the field to two, whichever one didn't come to work in the morning would be his girl. To find that out, he needed a reason to see Heather or Joanie tomorrow.

He slipped off the bar stool. "Okay, Heather and Joanie, you're my friends. Tell me honestly, do these shoes look hideous with this dress?"

Heather gave him the once-over. "They look okay."

"I think Manolo Blahniks are a little overexposed." Joanie went back to her appletini. "But if you're a Manolo fan, go for it."

Neil controlled his irritation. The bitches. They wouldn't know a good shoe if it bit them in the ass. But he'd counted on this reaction.

With a dramatic sigh, he propped his foot up on the bar stool. He loved doing things like that, showing off his crotch for anyone who cared to look. They wouldn't see anything they didn't expect. His taping job was always perfect.

"I *knew* these shoes were wrong!" he said. "I want to wear this dress to a funeral this weekend, and I need better shoes."

"Somebody died?" Heather tried to look sad, but she burst out laughing. "I'm sorry. Too many 'tinis, I guess. Of course somebody died, but here you are worried about the right shoes. You must not be all broken up about it."

"Actually, I'm not. The world's better off, if you know what I mean."

Joanie rolled her eyes. "Don't I ever. Isn't there a shoe sale at Nordstrom's?"

Neil closed the trap. "You know, there is! Listen, if either of you could get away for thirty minutes tomorrow and help me pick out something, I'd be so grateful. I'd even spring for drinks tomorrow night."

"It's a deal," Joanie said. "I'll figure out some excuse to leave. I could say that whatever they brought in for lunch made me sick. I need shoes, and I might find something for myself while I'm at it."

"Can't go." Heather rolled her neck. "Joanie can play Russian roulette with her job if she wants, but I'm staying on the job all day."

"Then it's Joanie and me," Neil said.

"Right," Joanie said. "Two girls in search of the perfect funeral shoes."

Neil clicked his glass against hers. "Proving once and for all that mourning and fashion statements are not mutually exclusive."

He wasn't lying about attending a funeral, either. Assuming he took care of his nosy little witness, he'd be attending Theo's funeral and loving every minute of it. Or rather, Nancy would be attending. And she really did need a pair of killer shoes for the occasion. Ha, ha. He cracked himself up sometimes.

BETWEEN TOO MUCH BOOZE AND WAY TOO MUCH stress, Gillian didn't sleep much. Every hour or so, she'd wake up in Cora's guest room scented with lavender and wonder where she was. Then she'd remember Theo and the Mob.

She'd touch her hair to make sure it was shorter. As she lay in the dark she'd think about Lex Manchester and wonder what he'd be like on a cruise. He didn't seem like a cruisin' sort of guy.

But then, she wasn't a cruisin' sort of gal, either. This blond person she'd turned into was a fake. Soon the dark roots would begin to show, and she'd start wearing her glasses instead of her contacts, and the glamour would disappear. Lex had shown an interest in her blond self, but he might not have the same reaction to the real Gillian.

At the moment her life felt more like a movie than reality, but in a movie, she'd end up with the hunky hero at the end. Plus, there would be a soundtrack, and nothing but silence played in the darkness surrounding her. She thought about Cora's security system and wondered if the Mob would be able to get around that. Seemed like they would have no problem with an ordinary security system.

With that she turned on a light and started reading one of the issues of *Variety* Cora had left on the nightstand. That's how she woke up the next morning, with a crumpled magazine under her cheek and the light still on. She'd dreamed of living in a mud hut and plucking chickens. Then the Blues Brothers had shown up ready to haul her off to meet the Godfather.

She was relieved to see sunlight coming through the bedroom window and smell coffee brewing in the kitchen. Maybe the cruise was a good idea, after all. There would be a boatload of people around, and she could take refuge in that. So long as she didn't allow herself to become isolated, she'd be fine.

Feeling a little hungover and a lot decadent in the silk pajamas Cora had loaned her, she walked down the hall, through the Art Deco living room, and into the kitchen. Cora was sitting at the diner booth she'd bought a year ago when they were auctioning memorabilia from *American Graffiti*. She wore a purple caftan this morning as she sipped from her coffee mug and held a cordless phone to her ear. Trip reservation papers were spread out in front of her on the aluminum-edged, white Formica tabletop.

"Maybe I should speak to Jared, then," she said. "Yes, I'll wait." She covered the mouthpiece and glanced up at Gillian with a smile. "Little twerp. I remember when he was still picking boogers out of his nose, but now that his grandparents have put him in charge of this cruise, he thinks he's Aristotle Onassis."

"Are you having trouble booking the cabin for Lex and Dante at this late date?"

"Oh, I can book it, although they said it's the last available cabin. I guess Jared's been beating the bushes for passengers. And the reservations person doesn't want to guarantee Lex and Dante will be right next to us. Help yourself to coffee. I should be through in— Hello?" She turned her attention to the phone. "Jared? Sounds as if you have a hit with this cruise idea of yours! I'm thrilled for you. Yes, your grandmother told me you've been working on the concept day and night."

Gillian found a *Star Wars* mug in the cupboard and poured herself a cup of coffee. Glancing at the clock, she realized that on a normal day she'd be going in to work right now. The rest of the crew would be arriving, and any time now somebody would find Theo. She wondered if he'd look the same, but probably not. Bodies changed over time. She really didn't want to think about that.

She should have called in sick last night. By not showing up today, she might even be . . . yikes . . . casting suspicion on herself! Had she touched anything in the dressing room? She didn't think so. But she wanted Cora off the phone ASAP so they could discuss this.

"Jared, you're a genius." Cora hesitated as the man on the other end responded. "Um, yes, I know you're literally a genius, but I meant that as a casual comment, not an evaluation." She paused again. "You bet. I most certainly did know that you are in Mensa. Well done."

Gillian waited impatiently for the call to end.

"Thanks so much, Jared," Cora said. "I truly appreciate the favor of putting Mr. Manchester and Mr. Fiorello in the cabin next to mine. They're socially backward, unlike yourself, and they'll appreciate having me close by to coach them during the cruise. See you this afternoon by four. Give my love to your grandparents. Bye-bye." She pushed the disconnect button and laid the receiver on the table with a sigh. "Pompous little prick."

Gillian couldn't help smiling. "Not much of a fan, are you?"

"No." Cora left the red Naugahyde booth and walked over to pour herself fresh coffee. "Only child, graduated from Harvard at the age of eighteen, geeky as they come. Even the millions he'll inherit someday haven't attracted any women, so he dreamed up this nerd love boat idea and talked his grandparents into letting him orchestrate it. God knows what we're in for."

Gillian slid into the booth opposite where Cora had been sitting. "I thought you loved the idea."

"I love the idea of a boat full of nerds, especially after I found out that Jared's grandparents had beefed up the passenger list with retired UCLA professors." Cora returned with her coffee. "I'm not getting any younger, you know."

Gillian gazed at her across the expanse of table. "I think you are. I hope that I—"

"If this is the speech about hoping you look as good as I do when you're my age, I'm here to tell you that you can look better. Forget the exciting alpha men out there. They'll give you nothing but grief and wrinkles."

"You're not all that wrinkled."

"Plastic surgery, darling. Take my advice. Once you're settled in South America, find yourself a good nerd and stick with him. I wish I'd been smart enough to figure that out at your age, but better late than never."

Gillian cradled her coffee mug and wished she could make this cozy moment last, instead of having to think about saving her skin. "Do you suppose they have nerds in South America?"

"Nerds are everywhere, but you might not want to stay in South America, come to think of it. I've heard the Finnish nerds are outstanding."

Gillian tried to picture herself traveling the world searching for the perfect nerd. She'd much rather comb the wilds of Southern California, but that option was no longer open. "Listen, while you were on the phone, I thought of something. By not showing up for work this morning, won't I be considered a suspect?"

Cora's gray eyes widened. "I didn't think of that."

"Me, either, until now."

"Call on your cell phone. Tell them you have horrible cramps but you'll try to come in this afternoon. Chances are they won't take much time to listen. Someone's probably discovered the body by now."

The coffee didn't taste good anymore. Gillian pushed her mug aside. "Probably. I didn't like Theo, but I hate that he died."

"And that you had to be right there. That's what I hate." Cora got up and came around to scoot in beside Gillian. She put her arm around her. "You're going to be fine, though. And you'll have resources. I'm giving you money to live on for a few months, until you get settled."

Cora's generosity brought a lump to Gillian's throat. Swallowing, she turned to face her. "No you're not. I'm strong and able. I'll be okay."

"Of course you will." Cora squeezed Gillian's shoulder. "But you need traveling money, and cash to rent a place to live, and maybe buy a car."

"My car!" Gillian had been in such shock she hadn't considered all the ramifications of leaving town. "Okay, you can have my car. I'll sign the title over to you today. You can give me whatever it's worth. And I'll write you a check for the balance in my checking account. I'll accept that much."

"Fine."

"But no more than that."

"We'll see." Cora gave her another hug. "Now go make your call."

CORA STACKED THE PAPERS FOR THE CRUISE AND rinsed out her coffee cup. Let Gillian think the value of her car and the contents of her checking account would equal what Cora would give her. Cora planned to give her ten times that amount and she wouldn't take no for an answer.

At her age, she didn't need much money, anyway. And maybe she'd meet a wealthy geezer on the cruise, someone who was willing to share pleasant conversation, still remembered how to make love, and had a healthy bank account. With Gillian gone, Cora would need someone around to take up the slack. She was going to miss that girl more than she wanted to think about.

As she reached for the dishcloth to wipe the table, the phone she'd left lying there rang. She put down the dishcloth and picked it up.

"Cora, it's Lex. I've been monitoring the news, expecting a report about Theo. Nothing."

"I'm surprised." Cora had left the TV off on purpose, not wanting Gillian to be treated to gory news coverage of Theo's murder.

"Is there any chance he was only knocked unconscious? I can imagine the studio trying to keep the lid on it, in that case."

"I don't know, Lex. She said he was definitely dead. Not breathing. Eyes rolled back in his head. I'll ask her again, but I think—hold on a minute. Here she comes. She just called the studio to report in sick. She should have some info."

"Why don't you put her on?"

"Okay. Sure." Cora thought Gillian looked pale as she handed her the phone. "Lex is on the line. He hasn't seen any news coverage about Theo."

"That's because there's no . . ." Gillian cleared her throat. "No dead body." Her voice quivered. "Heather said the place's in an uproar because Theo was a no-show for his morning call. He's not in his dressing room, and he's not answering his cell or his doorbell. They all figure he took a few days off without bothering to tell anybody. It's a Theo kind of thing to do."

Cora stared at her for a long moment. "Okay." She was very afraid of what this meant. "Tell Lex that."

While Gillian repeated her story to Lex, Cora tried to think like a gangster. Sure as the world, Neil's Mob friends had come along behind him and cleaned up the mess. Once they got rid of Gillian, Theo would become just another unsolved missing person case.

She and Gillian needed to start packing immediately. They'd board the boat early. Cora might have to make another phone call to that obnoxious dweeb Jared to arrange that, but she'd do whatever was necessary to get Gillian out of sight. The boat sailed at six. Cora prayed that would be soon enough.

Gillian clutched the phone. "I understand," she said. "Yes, we can be ready fast. Here's Cora."

Cora took the phone back. "We have to get our butts on that boat ASAP, right?"

"Right." Lex sounded tense. "If Theo's body's gone, that means Neil's friends are on the job. Can you get the okay for all of us to be on board by noon today?"

"Definitely."

"We'll get Gillian's stuff and be there to pick you up in two hours."

"We'll be ready." Cora disconnected the phone and turned.

Gillian stood with her back straight and her gaze determined. Only the slight tremble of her lower lip betrayed any fear. "We'd better get moving, huh?"

"Yes. I'm mostly packed, so we can concentrate on you. So far we know the silver dress fits, but—"

"I'm not taking the silver dress." She gulped. "Something could happen to it."

Cora gazed at her. "Nothing's going to happen to it, and nothing's going to happen to you."

Gillian met her gaze as if wanting desperately to believe that.

"Take the dress," Cora said. "When you had it on last night, you looked as if you could conquer the world."

Slowly Gillian drew in a breath and let it out again. "Okay, I'll take it."

"AFTER THIS GIG I'M GOING TO BURN ALL THE CLOTHES we bought." Dressed in a khaki jumpsuit identical to Lex's, Dante rode in the passenger seat of the white utility van they'd rented a half hour ago.

"I'm just glad we found a twenty-four-hour Wal-Mart last night." Lex wasn't particularly happy with their purchases, either, but he kept focusing on the goal of protecting Gillian, and that helped. Thanks to some discount shopping, they now had nerd clothes, nerd glasses, and something that resembled a uniform.

In the lawn and garden department they'd found a serious-looking tank-and-wand arrangement that would substantiate the exterminator disguise. With the magnetic signs advertising *BOBBIE'S BUG THUGS*, Lex thought they had a chance of passing muster.

Dante, being Dante, was still running his mouth. "And let me go on the record to say that I also *hate* this haircut." He opened the window and leaned out to see himself in the side-view mirror. "Horrible! No wonder that barbershop was open so early. They must need to stay open longer hours in order to get any business at all. I had no idea my hair could look this bad. My stylist is going to shit a brick when she sees this."

Lex had to admit he wasn't all that comfortable with the nerd thing, either, but listening to Dante bitch was cathartic. "I guess when we started this PI firm, you didn't think about going undercover."

"Of course I thought about it! I thought we'd go undercover as international playboys! I can't say that being an undercover nerd ever crossed my mind. I mean, what are the chances?"

"Pretty good, apparently."

"Yeah, well, it's not my dream assignment, okay? Turn here. This is Gillian's apartment complex on the corner. Building B, number 208."

Lex followed the signs and parked in front of Gillian's building. "See anything out of the ordinary?"

"If you're talking about the black sedan with the goon sitting in the driver's seat, yeah, I see something out of the ordinary."

Lex considered the implications. "I don't think we should go in there. They're watching that apartment, and they could end up following us."

"Couldn't you lose them?"

"I might, but he'd alert all his friends." Lex cruised past the black sedan. "It's tough to be inconspicuous with *BOBBIE'S BUG THUGS* on the side of the van."

"But what about Gillian's contacts? What about her underwear?"

"At least she has her glasses, and as for underwear . . . I guess you make a call to Cora's and find out the sizes, and then we go shopping."

"You and me together in the lingerie department?

That'll look weird, buddy. You'd better let me. I'm more of an expert on these things."

Lex had to admit that could be true, but he didn't want Dante picking out Gillian's underwear. "No, I'll do it." The thought made him nervous, but he'd brave the lingerie store rather than have Dante choosing styles and colors, which might give him ideas once they were on the cruise. A guy like Dante didn't need much encouragement to get ideas. Lex had far more control.

Dante shook his head. "I'm telling you, you need to turn that over to me."

"Nope." Lex pulled back on the street and headed for the nearest mall. "Logically it has to be me."

"How do you figure?"

"Gillian should have nice stuff, right? Like from Victoria's Secret?"

Dante blinked. "I'm surprised you know the brand name. But yeah, I guess you're right."

"Then that settles it. I have more room on my credit card." He glanced at Dante in triumph.

Dante opened his mouth, then closed it again. "You have a point," he said, "but I'm still amazed that you worked so hard to make that point." He grinned at Lex. "Want to know what I think?"

"Not particularly."

"I think you *really* like her."

Five

WHEN CORA'S DOORBELL CHIMED, GILLIAN LEAPED up from the sofa where she'd been waiting, a small rolling suitcase by her side. She still couldn't believe she'd given Lex her bra and panty size so that he could shop for her. No use in pretending to be a skinny minnie now. He knew her deepest underwear secrets.

How embarrassing, in an exciting sort of way. If he was to be her bodyguard, he knew exactly the type of body he would be guarding. *Zaftig.* Maybe he was drawn to that type. The sparks flying between them the night before made her think he might be.

But when Lex walked through the door carrying the signature pink and white striped bag from Victoria's Secret, she forgot about the undies. Lex and Dante had a whole new look, and because she'd chosen to wear her glasses, she had a clear view of their transformation. This was serious business, so she shouldn't laugh, but it wasn't easy to keep a straight face.

They'd followed her advice and were both sporting really bad haircuts—super short around the ears and finished on top with a bowl cut. By adding the black-framed glasses, the plaid short-sleeved shirts, and the ill-fitting khaki pants, they'd made the switch from studly to nerdy in a matter of hours. They'd even bought pocket protectors and stuffed them with pens. And all to keep her safe.

She was unexpectedly touched by that. "Thanks, guys. You look really—"

"Hideous," Dante said. "If this is how the rest of the passengers show up, they need to schedule a visit with *Queer Eye.* Are you sure all nerds are fashion challenged?"

"Probably not." Gillian smiled. "But you couldn't have gone the way you were. If you've overcompensated, it won't be a problem." The more she studied Lex, the more she liked the glasses on him. The clothes were ugly and the haircut silly, but the glasses gave him Clark Kent panache.

"Lex seemed to think this was the right uniform. I went along with it, because as we all determined last night, Lex is a better judge of what's nerdy and what's—"

"Give it a rest, Dante." Lex held out the Victoria's Secret bag. "I hope these work."

Now that the attention was back on her underwear, her cheeks warmed. "I'm sure they will. Thanks for doing that." She was torn between chagrin and fascination. No man had ever made such an intimate purchase for her. It had a certain bonding effect.

"You'll like them," Dante said. "I double-checked everything on the way over here."

"Which I tried to prevent him doing." Lex glared at his partner. "But I was hit with heavy traffic."

"It's okay," Gillian said. She thought it was cute that Lex was taking such a protective stance toward her underwear.

"See?" Dante smiled in triumph. "I told you she wouldn't be upset. And let me assure you, Gillian, that's primo stuff. I didn't know the Lexter had it in him to pick something that sex—" He caught his partner's warning look. "I, uh, mean, that *nice*. Really nice. Say, where's Cora?"

Cora bustled out of her bedroom pulling a suitcase that barely fit through the door. "Right here. I see you've been shopping."

"Lex handled it," Dante said. "I would give anything for a video of his shopping experience."

"And we need to be going," Lex said.

"Yes, we do." Gillian stuffed the bag into a zippered pocket in the front of the suitcase. "Tell me how much I owe you."

"It'll be calculated as part of their fee," Cora said. "Lex is right. We need to get this show on the road."

"Yes, ma'am," Dante said. "Just let me get my forklift so we can load your suitcase."

"Smartass." Cora laughed and turned the handle of the suitcase over to him. "You can't catch a fish without bait."

"Then you must be stalking a whale." Dante pretended to stagger as he pulled the suitcase toward the door.

"Hold it." Lex stepped to the window and pulled aside the curtain. "Before we go out there, let's make sure we don't have company."

Just like that, Gillian stopped smiling. She might feel a tingle whenever she looked at Lex. She might find Dante's teasing funny. But the bottom line was that these two hadn't been hired to keep her amused. They'd been hired to keep her alive.

Lex moved away from the window. "Cora, take a look. Tell me if the car parked two houses down belongs to anybody you know, or if the guy sitting in the driver's seat seems familiar."

"Sure thing." Cora edged over to the window and peered out. "I don't know that car or the guy sitting in it."

"Damn. I was hoping you'd recognize him."

"Lex, dear, I wouldn't recognize him if he lived next door. I don't keep track of the neighbors. I have a life to live, you know."

Lex glanced at her in surprise. "You used to keep track. Hell, we had Christmas block parties, trick-or-treating on Halloween. Everybody knew everybody."

"True, when your parents and Dante's parents still lived around here. Everyone got older, grew up, moved. I have a bunch of new neighbors, but I'm not the kind to show up at the door with a welcome casserole."

Dante laughed. "No, I guess not. I remember you used to give out Godiva for Halloween. Which we didn't value nearly enough at the time."

"So we don't know if someone's watching the house or not." Lex moved back to the window. "But I can't imagine why a person would be just sitting there in the car on a hot August day. Looks suspicious to me."

"Let me look." Gillian walked over to the window, which put her in close proximity to Lex. He didn't smell like a nerd. She didn't really know how a nerd was supposed to smell, but she doubted they'd choose such a manly aftershave, one that made her think of dark woods, a secluded cabin, and two people naked on a bearskin rug.

"That's a good idea." Lex's voice sounded a little rough around the edges, as if his vocal cords had been affected by . . . well, thoughts of sex.

She glanced up at him, startled. Was he a mind reader? "What's a good idea?"

"You checking out this guy. You saw the man who was at the studio last night. Do you think that's him?"

"Oh." For a minute there she'd thought the two of them were occupying some alternate universe where they could indulge their passions. "Right." Her senses were on high alert from standing so close to Lex she could hear him breathing. Trying to block his impact, Gillian looked out the window.

The black sedan was two houses down, and the man in the driver's seat had dark hair and sunglasses. He could be the man she'd bumped into, but he also could be somebody's noncustodial father sitting at the curb waiting for his kids because this was his week to have them.

"I don't know," she confessed at last. "It's possible, but then again—"

"Then again, all mobsters look alike," Dante said. "I can say that because my ancestors actually came from Sicily, so it's like a Polish guy making Polish jokes."

"You don't look like a mobster," Cora said.

"That's the point," Dante said. "Mobsters come in all shapes, sizes, and colors. You have your blond mobster and your dark-haired mobster. You even have your red-haired mobster."

Gillian stared at the car. The longer she did, the more nervous she became. "I don't think we should take any chances."

"Neither do I," Lex said. "So let's mix this up. Cora, I think you need to drive your car and leave first with Dante. Take your suitcase and Gillian's. You can act like he's your boy toy for the weekend."

"I don't have boy toys!"

"Nobody said you did." Lex continued to watch the guy in the black sedan. "We're trying to throw this guy off the trail, if he's even on the trail in the first place. So if it looks as if you're going off on a trip with Dante, we'll have more time to see what happens with the sedan when you leave."

Dante nodded. "Good plan. Come on, Cora. We can do this."

"Well, of course I can *do* it. I just didn't want anybody to think I actually operate that way. I prefer mature men."

"Hey!" Dante bristled. "Are you implying I'm not mature?"

"Of course not." Cora patted his arm. "You're mature for your age. You need a little more seasoning, is all. Gillian, let me have your suitcase and we'll be off." She walked over and took the handle of Gillian's small rolling bag. "So you two will follow later?"

"Yeah," Lex said. "But we might give it some time, so we confuse the issue if the guy's still there."

"Don't forget that Gillian looks a lot different," Cora said.

"Oh!" Gillian had been so involved in thinking of the potential mobster who might be waiting to gun her down if she stepped out the door that she'd forgotten about her Marilyn disguise. "I guess you're right. If I take off my glasses, I might not be recognized."

"And you won't be carrying a suitcase, as if you were trying to escape somewhere." Lex nodded. "This might work."

"All righty, then." Dante trundled Cora's big suitcase back toward the kitchen, where a door opened into the garage. "Call us in a little while to let us know what's happening."

"Right," Lex said. "And when you go out there, make a show of it. Let Cora back the car out and then you put the suitcase in while it's sitting in the driveway. Act chummy."

Cora paused at the door and turned. "Which is exactly what you and Gillian should do, too, Alexander. Excellent ploy."

Lex hesitated. "You're probably right."

Gillian's heart rate climbed the charts.

AS CORA BACKED HER MERCEDES OUT OF THE garage, Lex positioned himself about five feet from the window so he could see out without being seen. He also worked hard to ignore Gillian's presence in the suddenly small living room. His plan had seemed like the only logical one, but it had left him alone with a woman with the power to distract him from his job. Just his luck she was the job.

"What's the sedan doing?" she murmured.

The sound of her voice skittered along his nerve endings, setting off a longing he had no business having. "Nothing so far." He took note of a slight scuff mark on the front bumper. That would help him identify it if it showed up again anywhere else.

Changing the focus of his attention, he watched as Dante loaded the suitcase in the back of Cora's car. Cora got out and openly flirted with him. Then she pinched his butt.

Lex laughed.

"What?" Gillian moved up beside him.

"Cora goosed him."

"That would be Cora. Give her a role and she's all over it. The woman has chops, even after all these years."

Lex felt the need to make conversation to diffuse the effect of Gillian's perfume on his libido. Logically it couldn't be her perfume, of course. She had to have borrowed some from Cora.

But borrowed or not, the scent of it made him think of where she might have dabbed it on her naked body. He'd had reason to think of her naked body ever since his shopping trip to buy underwear. That silky stuff with the lace trim would be covering and supporting places he shouldn't think about, but he couldn't seem to help himself.

Maybe discussing Cora would give him some relief. "How did you and Cora hook up in the first place?"

"A TV special about two years ago. She came out of retirement because it was a charity thing for Alzheimer's research."

Lex vaguely remembered it. "Wasn't it a Christmas special?"

"Exactly. She was the heroine's wacky grandmother who was starting to slip mentally. I love her earlier work, so I specifically asked to do her makeup. She seemed pleased by that, and . . . we got along."

Lex felt a stab of guilt. "I'll bet she was lonely. Dante and I should have stopped by more often. She always said we were like the grandkids she'd never had, but . . . life gets in the way."

"She didn't seem particularly lonely or pathetic."

Lex appreciated the protective urge that prompted that comment. "No, I'm sure she didn't. That would never describe Cora. Well, there she goes with Dante, her boy toy."

"And the guy in the sedan?"

"Not moving, damn it." Lex blew out a breath. "I was hoping he'd follow them."

"He's waiting for me, though, isn't he?"

The slight tremble in her voice socked him in the gut. He wanted to put his arms around her and promise she'd be safe, but that would be instant insanity and might not be a promise he could keep. So instead he glanced at her with a smile. "Maybe he's waiting for you and maybe he's waiting for some other reason. Don't let it spook you. We'll work this out."

She responded with a smile of her own. "I'm sure we will."

He would have to armor himself against that smile of hers. "We might as well sit down and relax." He walked over to an easy chair, to eliminate the possibility of them both choosing the sofa. "I'd like to give the guy time to get bored before we walk out the door."

"Boredom would be good." She took the sofa. "I doubt if a person's aim is half as good if he's bored."

He sat up straighter as he realized her fear was far more specific than he'd imagined. "Okay, hold it right there. You're not about to get shot."

"I know you'll try to keep that from happening, but—"

"Correction. I *will* keep that from happening." Somehow. He'd never figured on putting his life on the line when he agreed to be partners with Dante in this PI business, but here he was, in charge of keeping this gorgeous creature alive and well. The challenge of it was exhilarating. And he realized in that moment that if he lived through this assignment, he could never go back to insurance fraud.

Gillian leaned forward, her brown eyes earnest behind her wire-framed glasses. "I don't know what your fee is, but it can't be enough to justify taking a bullet for me."

"It's not always about the money." He loved saying that. The statement made him feel brave and true, a Superman type who stood for justice and the protection of innocent women and children. Insurance just didn't have that kind of payoff.

"But you don't even know me."

"You're important to Cora, and Cora's important to me. That's enough."

She clasped and unclasped her hands in her lap. "I don't want Neil to get away with this."

This was news, and it scared him. It was all fine and dandy for him to make like a hero, but if she tried any heroics, she could get herself killed. "Look, once you're safely out of the country, then you can—"

"What if that's too late? What if he's completely disappeared by then?" She looked frightened, but determined, too. "Instead of heading off on this cruise to try and save my neck, I should go to the police and tell my story."

"And then what?"

"There's always the witness protection program." She didn't say it with much conviction.

"I suppose."

She took a breath and pumped more enthusiasm into her voice. "They could create a whole new identity for me and move me to the Texas Panhandle where I could work as a checker in a neighborhood grocery store."

"I don't think you start out as a checker. There's training and stuff."

"You're right. Plus that's too high-profile. I could be recognized. I'd probably have to get a job on an assembly line screwing widgets into thingamabobs. If it's high tech and I have to wear some sterile suit and a mask, so much the better."

"Sounds sort of grim."

"But not as grim as death. And maybe I could put Neil behind bars."

"Listen, Gillian . . ." He hesitated. He was also a fan of

justice and nailing the bad guy, but he'd be happier if the system worked better. "It's your decision, but Phil Adamo has quite the network."

"Maybe people exaggerate about that."

"It's possible, but I wouldn't want to take that chance. I don't have a lot of faith that the witness protection program would do the trick in this case." As ill-prepared as he felt for this job, he still didn't want to turn her welfare over to some faceless government agency that would relocate her to suburbia and give her a job screwing widgets into thingamabobs. She'd always live with the threat of somebody blowing her cover.

"I'm not too keen on that plan, myself. Too much room for error." She looked down at her tightly clasped hands. "I wish I could be braver, though."

"There's brave and then there's foolhardy. I think going to the police right now, when Neil's contacts know you were at the scene, would be suicide."

She glanced up, her expression bleak. "Yeah, me, too."

"Tell you what. Once you're on the ship and we're confident you're safe, you can use the ship-to-shore radio to call the police. How's that?"

"Better than anything I was coming up with." She stood. "Let's get out of here."

Lex pushed himself out of the chair and moved closer to the window. "Our guy's still parked in the same spot. We should probably wait a while longer."

"I say he's going to stay right there until we make a move. I can't speak for you, but I'm going nuts sitting around, waiting to see what will happen."

He thought of counseling her in the art of patience. They really might outlast the joker in the black sedan. But the longer he stood there looking at her in her slinky out-fit, the more he began to realize that they needed to leave. It was either that or kiss her.

"All right," he said. "We'll go. I'll stay on your left as we walk down the sidewalk. We'll put our arms around each other. Think of me as your shield and keep me be-tween you and the black sedan. We'll be fine."

"Unless he starts to move. Or another one comes from the right, catching us in the cross fire, and we end up like Bonnie and Clyde, our bullet-riddled bodies lying across your white Toyota."

"Good God, woman." The image appalled him. It also made him sweat.

She laughed. "Sorry. It's a bad habit of mine, imagin-ing the worst-case scenario. It eases the tension."

"For you, maybe."

"From now on, I'll try to keep those thoughts to myself."

"I'd be grateful. So are you ready?"

She hoisted the silver leather tote that had been lying on the sofa. "Ready."

"Glasses."

"Oh, right." She took them off and tucked them inside the tote.

Once she did that, the resemblance to the legendary Marilyn was uncanny. Lex did his best not to stare. She even had the trademark mole on her upper lip, which drew his attention to her full mouth with its coating of shiny red lipstick. He'd never been a big fan of lipstick. In general it smeared and tasted funny. So his sudden urge to dive in for some smearing and a taste test was unchar-acteristic and unsettling.

"Going without my glasses is probably better," she said. "I'll never know what hit me."

That snapped him back to reality fast. "Hey! I thought you were going to keep those morbid thoughts to yourself."

"Was that morbid? I thought it was sort of cheerful. If you're going to be gunned down, it's better to be taken by surprise than to see it coming."

"Not in my opinion. I always like to see what's coming." And in the case of Gillian, he could see very clearly what was ahead. No doubt about it, he was in for a very bumpy ride.

Six

DESPITE ALL HER ATTEMPTS TO BEEF UP HER COURAGE, Gillian was shaking as she stepped through Cora's front door. She had more than one reason to shake. The first was the man in the black sedan parked two houses away. The second was the man who wrapped his arm around her waist and pulled her close to his side as they left the small entryway and started down Cora's flagstone walk.

They were pretending, she reminded herself. But Lex's warm embrace didn't feel fake. It did feel incredibly right, as if she'd been waiting all her life for this particular man to tuck her against his side and head off to whatever paradise they could create together.

Lex reacted to the contact with a muffled little hum that could have meant anything from delight to indigestion. Or maybe he was signaling that the black sedan was on the move.

"Is that car going anywhere?" she asked quietly.

Lex leaned down and nuzzled her ear. "No."

She nearly swooned. The warmth of his arm was lovely,

but nothing compared to the velvet brush of his lips against that tender spot behind her earlobe. She wondered if she could get him to do that again. "Are you absolutely sure?"

He dipped his head and repeated the caress, this time adding a flick of his tongue. "Not moving. Wish I could see the license plate. Wrong angle."

"Too bad." Her knees wobbled. If Lex could get that kind of response from her so easily, what would happen if they ever ended up in bed? She wouldn't allow that to happen, of course, but it was mind-boggling to think about the potential fireworks.

"Almost there," he murmured. "And the car's stationary."

Whereas she was in high gear. A simple walk down the sidewalk and her panties were damp. "Maybe he's not who we think."

"Maybe. But I'm not taking any— Hold it. He started the engine."

A thrill of fear shot through her.

"It's okay. We're here." Lex reached for the door handle. "Locked. *Shit.*"

At the same moment Gillian heard the car approaching, Lex shoved her up against the car, bracketed her face with his hands and leaned into her, covering her with his body. "Hold still."

A flush that was part terror, part sexual excitement, spread through her. "I couldn't move if I wanted to."

"Good. Now act as if you like what I'm doing." He kissed her hard on the mouth, somehow managing to avoid poking his glasses into her face.

She'd never considered herself much of an actress, but that didn't matter in this case. She didn't have to act as if she liked what he was doing. She'd rather have Lex smash her up against his car and kiss her like this than win the lottery. And she played the lottery every single week.

Kissing Lex resembled riding the Tilt-A-Whirl with your eyes closed. She would have screamed with delight, except that her mouth was too busy to be bothered. She couldn't bring herself to care about the black sedan, either, and the fear of being riddled with bullets lost its power. Fate wouldn't riddle a person with bullets at such a moment as this.

The kiss went on for a satisfyingly long time, long enough for Gillian to become lost in the heat and the sweet moisture of it. He was good with his tongue, which was an important quality in Gillian's estimation. She also noticed how beautifully Lex's body lined up with hers.

To be more precise, one particular part of his body was in a state of transformation that gladdened her heart. It gladdened all of her, come to think of it. She wiggled with joy.

The wiggle might have been too much, because Lex groaned and pulled away. She would take back the wiggle if she could, but it had slipped out before she could stop it. Lifting heavy eyelids, she watched him drag in air as he looked around.

His glasses were so fogged that he had to take them off. Finally he glanced down at her. "He's gone."

Even without her glasses she could see that his blue eyes were glazed from the powerhouse kiss. She was supposed to say something, but she couldn't think what would be appropriate under the circumstances. He'd kissed her better than she'd ever been kissed, and yet that shouldn't be the primary focus of the conversation.

Or should it? Nothing else seemed important to her, but she thought Lex might want her to acknowledge that his impromptu kiss had apparently helped them get rid of the bad guy in the black sedan. "Nice work," she said at last, hoping that covered everything.

"Thanks." The glazed look began to fade. He cleared his throat and replaced the glasses, à la Clark Kent. "Sorry about the manhandling."

"Womanhandling."

"Uh, yeah." He rubbed the back of his neck and looked at her with poorly disguised longing. "I didn't know what else to do."

"I thought it was brilliant."

"I'm surprised about your lipstick."

She blinked. "What about it?"

"Didn't smear or anything. When I first saw how it looked, all shiny and wet . . ." His eyes glazed over again.

She could see them moving right back into the kiss. She was ready. "You were surprised it looked shiny and wet?"

"No." He hovered closer. "That it stayed that way."

"It's supposed to look wet, no matter what." She slid her hands up his chest. The plaid shirt was nerdy, but the pecs underneath were prime stuff.

"But I kissed you a lot." He cradled her hips in both hands.

"That lipstick stands up to heavy kissing and still looks wet." She wanted to prove it to him. "I'm a professional."

"Kisser?"

She smiled. "Makeup artist. I'm only an average kisser."

"Couldn't prove it by me." His warm breath tickled her mouth.

Sliding her arms around his neck, she waited, heart pounding, for the Tilt-A-Whirl to start spinning again. Nothing happened. The tickle of his warm breath disappeared, too. Slowly she opened her eyes.

Behind the lenses of his glasses, his eyes were dark with concern. "This is not good," he said.

"You don't like kissing me?"

"I like it way too much."

Her ego recovered its balance. "That's not so bad. We have to pretend to be involved. What if you hated kissing me? You wouldn't be convincing."

"That won't be a problem."

"I believe people should be happy in their work."

Lex sighed and backed away from her. "I think you're missing the point. In order to protect you, I have to maintain an aggressive stance."

"That kiss was pretty aggressive. I can still feel the imprint of the doorframe on my back. Your tongue was on the aggressive side, too, which I enjoyed, by the way. There's nothing worse than a man who's tentative with his tongue."

Lex groaned. "Still not the point. That was just my sex drive kicking in."

Yeah, baby. "So? What's wrong with that?"

"Ultimately, sex fosters cooperation, not aggression. If you want to make war, you can't make love."

"Oh." What a disappointing thought. "And I suppose this is war, huh?"

"It is."

"But how are we supposed to pretend to be involved and keep our natural sex drive under control?"

He gazed at her silently for a long time. "I honestly don't know," he said at last.

"When you figure it out, will you tell me?"

His smile was tight. "Oh, you'll be the first to know."

NEIL'S SHOPPING TRIP TURNED OUT BETTER THAN HE could have expected. Although Joanie spent the whole time complaining about Theo's taking an impromptu vacation and ruining the shooting schedule, Neil was able to pull out a couple of critical pieces of information. Eileen had shown up today, but not Gillian. And the nerd cruise left this afternoon out of Long Beach.

Thanks to that information, Neil could plan his next move. A couple of phone calls put him in touch with Jared Stevenson the Third, who seemed to be the dork in charge of this cruise that was supposedly all booked up. Neil would see about that.

"Jared Stevenson, here."

Neil cringed at the nasal twang. Good thing Nancy was on the job. She could charm even the terminally nerdy. "Jared Stevenson. Am I talking to *the* Jared Stevenson?"

"That depends. There are three of us."

Neil controlled the impulse to laugh and ask if the guy had multiple personalities. As for Neil, there were technically two of him, so this conversation could get crowded, indeed. "My name is Nancy Roth, and I'm looking for the Jared Stevenson who organized the brilliant cruise that's sailing this afternoon."

"I'm that Jared Stevenson."

"Excellent! What a cutting-edge concept you came up with!"

Jared's voice filled with pride. "I'm gratified that you recognize the value of my work. Some shortsighted individuals scoffed at my plan, but I'm pleased to announce that we'll sail with a full complement of passengers."

"That's wonderful for you!"

"Thank you. I must say that I'm pleased that so many—"

"And terrible for me! Simply dreadful!"

"Excuse me?" Jared's voice squeaked in surprise.

"I simply *must* go on that cruise, if for no other reason than to meet you!"

"Oh! Well, uh, all the cabins are reserved as of this morning. I'm sorry. Maybe when we get back, you and I can meet for lunch. You sound like a discriminating woman. And I'm a discriminating man. Are you free on Monday?"

Neil deliberately unclenched his jaw and took a breath. "I'm sure that will be too late, Jared." *No shit, Jack. No telling what damage this witness could do in the next four days.* "Some other lucky woman will have bewitched you by the time you dock on Sunday."

Jared cleared his throat. "I, uh, doubt that. But I suppose it's always possible. I can call you when we get back and let you know."

"No fair, you naughty man." Neil injected his voice with exactly the right amount of sexy petulance. "Keeping me in suspense all that time." He decided to take a gamble. "You know how I handle somebody who teases me like that?"

Another geek squeak. "How?"

"I give him a good spanking." In the dead silence that followed, Neil was afraid he'd overplayed his hand.

When Jared finally spoke, he sounded out of breath. "Hold on. Let me make a phone call. Don't hang up."

"I wouldn't dream of it." Neil clenched his fist in triumph. As the theme song from *The Love Boat* played in his ear, he wandered into his bathroom, pulled off his wig, and inspected his buzz cut in the mirror over the sink.

Jared came back on the line, still sounding out of breath. "I've worked it out."

"I just knew you would." Neil smiled at himself in the mirror. Even without the wig, he was a damned good-looking chick.

"You'll be sharing a cabin with a woman named Bernice Thigpen. Her roommate backed out, so this is financially advantageous for her."

"Um . . . great." Sharing could be dicey. Extremely dicey. But he'd take it over missing the cruise completely.

"Don't worry about privacy." There was a funny little tremble in Jared's voice. "I . . . uh . . . have a cabin to myself, if we . . . uh . . . should hit it off."

"You sly dog, you." Neil wondered if he dared take time out of his scheduled plan to seduce the cruise director. Maybe he could work it in, literally, if all went well. A guy who was excited about spanking had possibilities. Not every man who discovered Neil's true sexual identity was disappointed.

Jared cleared his throat again. "We board at four, sail at six."

"I can hardly wait. Until then, Jared. Bye, now." Neil disconnected the call and hurried to pack. Too bad there was no way to take a gun on board, but with security these days there was no way he'd get it through the scanners. He'd have to be inventive, but fortunately, he was good at that. Or rather, Nancy was good at that. Thank God for Nancy.

THE DRIVE TO LONG BEACH GAVE LEX PLENTY OF time to feel guilty. He didn't have to kiss Gillian to protect her body with his. He could have cupped her face in both hands, moved in close, and simply talked to her, making it look like a tender lovers' conversation. An actual kiss had been totally unnecessary.

On the bright side, he now understood how completely screwed he was, in case he hadn't realized it earlier. He would have to fight his desire for this woman during the entire cruise and all the while he was supposed to be clinically assessing the danger she might be in. If he thought turning her over to Dante would help, he'd do that.

Hell, no, he wouldn't, either. Kissing her had been incredible, and he wanted to do it again. And again. And yet again, until they moved to the next phase. Thoughts of the next phase had the material of his khaki pants rising to accommodate his reaction.

"It's probably nothing, but there's a black sedan that's hanging back about two cars behind us in the lane to the right," Gillian said. "I think it's the same guy."

Lex cursed under his breath and glanced in the rearview mirror. Sure enough, it was the car that had been parked down the street from Cora's house. The scuffed place on the front bumper gave it away. Lex had been so busy thinking about sex with Gillian that he hadn't noticed the car following them. But she had.

"Do you think it's him?" she asked.

"Yes."

"Damn it. I thought we got rid of him with that kissing routine."

"Obviously not." Lex checked the position of the sedan, which hung exactly in the same spot. It had probably been there for miles. "I'm beginning to think you'd be better off without me."

"And I'm beginning to think if I didn't have you, Dante, and Cora on my side, I'd be dead already," she said. "I think we have confused him, but he has no other lead, so he's following us. If he knew who I was for sure, he would have tried to kill me already. I don't think he's sure."

"Maybe." But it grated on Lex's nerves that the guy had managed to follow them all this way, and he, the PI guy who was supposed to be up on these things, had missed it. "I'm going to try and lose him."

"In this kind of traffic? And I don't want to insult you, but your car isn't exactly . . ."

"It's nimble." Lex had never told anyone his fantasies about being a professional race car driver. He'd never followed through because he couldn't justify putting that kind of money into something that might never pay off. This PI deal with Dante was about as crazy as he ever planned to get.

But still, his adrenaline spiked as he assessed the situation around him. The semi on his right was slowing a fraction. He came up on the bumper of the van in front of him, hoping they'd be motivated to go faster. When they did, he gauged the space in front of the semi, waited for his opportunity, and cut in front of the big truck.

Gillian yelled and the truck sounded his air horn, but Lex didn't care. He spotted another tiny hole to his right and swerved into it. Then the magic began. The Jeep in front of him tromped on the gas, probably to get away from the maniac in the Toyota.

Exactly what Lex wanted. He followed, swerving into a space to the left that had precisely enough room for his car. No more, no less. Now cars started making way for him. He'd established himself as a player. He swerved right, then left, then right again, stitching a rapid path up the freeway.

"You're going to kill us!" Gillian shouted as he almost grazed the bumper of a Hummer and the driver sounded his horn.

"Nope."

"And . . . and . . . you're *smiling*!"

He hadn't been aware of that. He tried to wipe the grin off his face, but it kept coming back as he charged through traffic. The black sedan, he noted with satisfaction, was nowhere in sight.

But he was having so much fun he damn near missed the Long Beach exit.

Gillian, who was gripping the dash with both hands, kept him honest. "Lex! You're going past our turn!"

"Right. I knew that." He skipped across three lanes while she wailed in protest.

At the first red light, she slumped back against the seat. "Remind me never to ride with you on the freeway again."

"But we lost him!" Women. Why couldn't she appreciate the skill involved in that fine piece of driving?

She gazed at him. "I almost peed my pants."

"We were never in any danger."

"Says you. We almost clipped about six cars during that little demonstration. What if we'd wrecked? Then what?"

He blew out an impatient breath. "I know the exact dimensions of this car and how to handle it. I don't take unnecessary risks." Even as he said it, he knew it wasn't true. Kissing her had been an unnecessary risk, but he'd done it anyway. He'd always thought of himself as a conservative guy, but what if that wasn't everything there was to know about him?

"My father used to say stuff just like that." She folded her arms protectively over her chest. "And then he'd bungee jump off the Golden Gate Bridge."

Lex noticed that she was trembling, and he was sorry for that, but he'd done what he thought was best to shake the black sedan. He pulled away from the light. "Jumping off the Golden Gate Bridge is hardly in the same category as a little weaving through traffic." Then he processed what she'd just told him. "Your dad jumped off the Golden Gate Bridge? Really?"

"Really. He was a certified daredevil. And in case you couldn't tell, I'm nothing like he was."

"Was that past tense on purpose?"

"Yes. He's dead."

"I'm sorry."

"Me, too, mostly because he died doing something reckless. He was wing-walking at a county fair. It wasn't even a very big county fair."

Lex wanted to take her hand, but touching her always seemed to get him in trouble. "Were . . . were you there?"

"'Fraid so."

His gut clenched. "How old?"

"Eight."

He didn't know what to say. In some idiotic quest for glory, her father had traumatized his young daughter. But she might still love the guy, so he had to be careful about trashing the imbecile's memory.

Finally he settled on something safe. "Thanks for telling me." And he was grateful. It helped him understand why she'd freaked out in such a major way. "And despite the freeway episode, I'm not that type of guy."

"I hope not. Cora said she'd trust you with her life."

"That's good to hear."

Gillian sounded shaky. "I'm trying to be cooperative, and I appreciate the effort and money Cora's putting out. But the bottom line is that I don't like the idea of trusting other people with my life. I don't like giving up that kind of control."

"Nobody does." But especially someone who'd watched her father fall off the wing of an airplane to his death. Lex couldn't imagine the scar that would leave.

"I have this urge to get out at the next intersection and just handle this on my own."

That was the scariest thing he'd heard yet, worse than the story about her dad or her urge to call the police. He swerved into the parking lot of a McDonald's and cut the motor. "Please don't do that." He turned to her. "I haven't handled this assignment all that well so far, and I apologize for that. Number one, I shouldn't have kissed you. Number two, I—"

"Kissing me was the best thing you've done so far!"

That stopped him. "It was?"

"Absolutely." She gazed at him with those melt-your-heart brown eyes. "When you were kissing me, I forgot to be scared."

"I can't imagine why."

"Because you kiss like a man who can be trusted."

"That's backward logic if I ever heard it! How can I be paying attention to your safety while I'm busy kissing you? I don't have eyes in the back of my head. Kissing you was reckless, and I pride myself on not being reckless."

She seemed to consider that. "I suppose you have a point."

"Of course I have a point. And there are residual effects."

"Like what?"

He hated to admit this, but she needed to understand the dangers of a physical involvement. "I didn't pick up on the guy following us because I was daydreaming about that kiss."

"You were?" She looked pleased.

"Don't look so happy. That's why I ended up dodging

through traffic to lose him. You hated that part. So kissing isn't the best approach to this situation."

Her mouth curved in a soft smile. "That's a damned shame."

Lex had to agree with her on that one.

Seven

SITTING NEXT TO MCDONALD'S AND TALKING ABOUT kissing had calmed Gillian considerably. Thoughts of fast food and good sex could do that for a girl.

"The cruise is your best option," Lex said. "I'm sorry if I shook your confidence in me with that wild car ride. If I'd been doing my job, it wouldn't have been necessary. But I didn't want that goon following us to the dock."

"No, I didn't, either." And that was a major difference between Lex and her father, she realized. Duke McCormick had taken chances for the hell of it, but Lex had had a reason. Even so, there had been that telltale grin as he bobbed through traffic, and she decided to call him on it. "It's just that you looked like you were having way too much fun."

His expression was classic—little boy caught with his hand in the cookie jar. "It's only natural to feel a little . . . exhilaration."

"Admit it. You were loving that whole thing."

"I wouldn't say that."

"I would, but it doesn't really matter. Once we get on the ship you won't be driving anywhere."

"So you're definitely going?" He looked relieved.

"Yes." Now that the terror from Lex's freeway stunt had worn off, she'd lost the urge to head into the unknown by herself. She'd have to do that eventually once she got to Mexico, but for the time being she had three people who were watching her back. That was comforting.

"Thank God." Lex started the engine and pulled into traffic. "If you'd decided to take off on your own, I don't know what I would have done."

She hadn't thought of it from his perspective. "I suppose Cora would have had your head on a platter if you'd showed up without me."

"It wouldn't have come to that."

She glanced at him, intrigued. "What do you mean?"

"I'd have figured out some way to change your mind."

"That might have been impossible. When a person's operating on emotion, all the logic in the world isn't going to help."

"Okay, then I would have tried something else."

"Kidnapping?" She couldn't imagine him in that role.

"Absolutely not. Wouldn't work, anyway. I seriously doubt they'd let me bring a bound and gagged woman on board."

"Then what?"

He didn't respond.

"Come on, Lex. I want to know your devious plan. I'll bet you don't even have one."

"Yeah, I do. But we don't have to worry about it. We're here." He pulled up to a parking gate and took a ticket. Beyond the lot was the dock where the ship, gleaming white in the sunshine, dwarfed the people loading supplies.

Ordinarily Gillian would have been interested in watching the pageantry of a ship being readied for a journey, but right now she was determined to find out how Lex would have solved the problem if she'd refused to go on this cruise. "Satisfy my curiosity," she said. "Tell me how you would have made me go on the cruise against my will."

"It wouldn't have been against your will." He parked the car, took off his sunglasses, and opened the console. Inside were his nerd glasses and some clip-on shades. He put away his sunglasses and put the nerd glasses and clip-ons in his lap. Then he reached in the back seat and got a folded sunshade. "Can you tuck this under the visor?"

She helped him position the sunshade, but she wasn't about to be sidetracked. "So how would you have convinced me? Get me drunk? I wouldn't have agreed to that."

"No liquor involved." He folded his visor over the sunshade and picked up his nerd glasses and the clip-ons. "Ready to go?"

"No! Tell me your plan. I'm tempted to refuse to go, just to see how you'd work this."

He turned to her. "You have to promise not to laugh."

"I won't laugh." With the sunshade blocking the windshield and the windows rolled up, she felt a certain amount of intimacy inside the car. In a few minutes the lack of air-conditioning would make it stifling, but for now, she felt cozy. And more than a little bit aroused.

Lex cleared his throat. "I would have talked you into having lunch at a quiet little place I know and then I would have seduced you."

She didn't have the slightest urge to laugh, but she had some other urges. The longer she looked into his blue eyes, the stronger those urges became. "In the restaurant?"

"There's a back booth that's very dim. I could have managed it."

She had no doubt. He was beginning to manage it simply by talking to her about this imaginary seduction. Thinking of making out in a dark restaurant booth reminded her of the thoroughness of his kiss when he'd backed her up against the car.

She wanted more of that. She also had a hunch he'd be good with his hands. Sex hadn't been a part of her life in many long months, not since a half-baked affair with a member of the set crew during her last film.

Lex's eyes began to glow with intent as he leaned closer. Then he abruptly pulled back. "We need to go."

She had to believe he'd just invoked his new no-kiss rule. Damn. "What if I said I didn't want to take the cruise, after all?"

"I'd think you were testing me to see if I'd follow through."

"Would you?"

"Nope." He broke eye contact and opened his door.

"Why not?"

"Number one, you said you'd go, and I don't see you as a person who breaks her word."

Gillian sighed. "Low blow."

He turned back to her, and now he was wearing the nerd glasses with the clip-on shades. "Am I wrong?"

"No, you're not wrong, and you look hilarious in those clip-ons. So is there a number two?"

He grinned. "There's always a number two if you start with number one. Otherwise, why say that?"

"Some people do."

"Not me. If I ever start with number one, you can guarantee there's at least a number two."

"That's good to know." She liked that he wasn't care-less with his words. Words were cheap in Hollywood, tossed around with no thought about the repercussions. Lex wasn't like that. "What's number two?"

"You may not have noticed, but this is a most excellent parking spot. We're on the end, so when I come back, leaving the lot will be a snap. I don't want to lose this spot."

First she was sad thinking about him coming back here without her, but as the comment sank in, she began to feel insulted. "You mean you'd give up seducing me for a parking spot?"

"It's only one factor. There's also a third factor. Now that we're in sight of the ship, I could use my cell to bring Cora down here in less than a minute. In other words, I can call for reinforcements. Seducing you would be a last resort."

Now she was really insulted. "A last resort? What's that supposed to mean?"

"Gillian, it's a compliment," he said gently.

"Doesn't sound like one."

"Well, it is. If kissing you messes with my concentra-tion, I can imagine what making love to you would do. I'd be worthless as your bodyguard. Instead of keeping an eye out for the bad guys, I'd want to spend every spare minute in bed with you."

That program sounded good to her, but she wasn't about to give him the satisfaction of knowing that when he was looking for every way to avoid physical contact. A girl had her pride.

She took a deep breath. "Well, then, we might as well get on board, don't you think?"

"Yep." He climbed out of the car. "Just let me haul the backpacks out of the trunk. I have Dante's in there, too."

Backpacks? Gillian got out of the car and walked around

to the trunk. Sure enough, Lex unloaded two large backpacks, but they weren't just ordinary backpacks. "*Star Wars* and *Lord of the Rings*." She shook her head. "I see you took this disguise seriously."

Lex swung a backpack over each shoulder and started toward the ship. "Admit you're jealous because I have these cool backpacks and you don't."

"Yeah, baby." She laughed. "I'm in love with the clip-on shades, but I really lust after those backpacks."

"That's good, because I thought you might like to have one when you make a run for it."

Gillian stopped laughing. Then she stopped walking. She couldn't do this, simple as that.

LEX KNEW THE MINUTE GILLIAN SKIDDED TO A STOP that he'd said the wrong thing. He shouldn't have mentioned making a run for it. What a stupid thing to say. "Listen, forget that. One day at a time. You—"

She was breathing fast—too fast. "You know what? This is a stupid idea. Who do I think I am, a contestant on some reality show? I don't know the first thing about disappearing into a foreign country and living off the land. It all sounded possible after several martinis, but the truth is, I'll never make it."

Lex cursed his loose tongue. "It won't be so bad. The Mexican people are very friendly. My family used to go on vacation down there all the time when I was a kid. You'll be fine."

"You don't understand." She looked totally freaked. "I'm not a risk-taker. I eat familiar foods, drive familiar streets. I choose swimming pools over the ocean because I'm afraid of sharks. I don't even go on Splash Mountain!"

He frowned. "Are there sharks at Splash Mountain? I haven't been to Disneyland in a few years, so I—"

"No, no, there are no sharks in Disneyland. I was making the point that I don't even take the risk of going down that waterfall, because something might happen. I'm a coward!"

Lex came closer, set down both backpacks, and took her by the shoulders. "I don't believe that for a moment." Then, because it had worked to calm her down before, he pulled off his nerd glasses, abandoned his no-kiss rule, and planted one on her.

Just like before, he was swept away to a place he'd never been, a place where a woman with lips like a tropical flower beckoned him deeper into ecstasy. *More,* she seemed to say. *Give me more.* As he began sliding quietly and willingly under the waves of surrender, a piercing whistle brought him back to brutal reality.

He broke contact instantly and looked right and left, heart pounding. If anything was threatening Gillian, and he'd been too busy kissing her to notice, he'd never forgive himself.

"Up here, Romeo!"

Glancing skyward, he spotted Dante leaning on the railing of the cruise ship. "Hey!" Lex yelled. "Don't scare me like that!"

"Me? You're the scary one! I thought you were going to call me and let me know what was going on with you guys!"

Lex groaned. He'd been so involved with Gillian that he'd spaced that request. He remembered it now, when it was too late and he looked like an absentminded professor. "Sorry, man."

"Tell me about it!" Dante seemed to relish the role reversal. Usually he was the screwup. "Cora and me, we've been chewing our fingernails wondering what the deal was. I come out for a look-see and find you playing tonsil-hockey."

"We'll be right there." He glanced down at Gillian. "At least I hope we will," he said quietly. "Are you okay?"

She took a deep breath. "I'm lots better than I was. It's amazing how that works."

He decided not to remind her that those kisses were giving her a false sense of security. He wanted her on the ship, and if a kiss worked to get her there, he'd have to live with the consequences, which happened to be a raging case of hormones at the moment.

Putting on his nerd glasses with the clip-ons, he picked up the backpacks and hoisted one over each shoulder. "Then let's go."

She straightened her spine in a really endearing way. "Okay."

"Like I said. Let's not project too far into the future. One day at a time."

She smiled bravely. "Right."

At the top of the gangplank, Lex turned to scan the parking lot. There were plenty of dark sedans there, unfortunately. One looked familiar, but he might be spooking himself. He'd lost that creep back on the freeway.

That might not mean anything, whispered a voice in his head. This was the Mob they were talking about. By now they had a full description of his car. If he'd lost one goon, another might have picked up the trail later on.

But he couldn't imagine how one of those guys could be on the cruise without Lex or Dante spotting him. No way would a gangster be able to pass himself off as a nerd.

THE MINUTE GILLIAN AND LEX WENT THROUGH THE security check at the top of the gangplank and were given directions to their two cabins, Dante appeared and hustled them down the corridor. Then he unclipped something from his belt and spoke into it. "Screen Goddess, this is Italian Stallion. Painted Lady and Clark Kent are on board. Over."

Cora's voice crackled from the walkie-talkie. "Copy that, Italian Stallion. Screen Goddess, over and out."

Gillian paused to stare at him. *"Painted Lady?"* If she was going to have a code name, she wanted something better than that.

"Yeah. Because you're a makeup artist. Cora wasn't wild about it, but I thought it was kind of clever."

"When did you come up with walkie-talkies?" Lex asked.

"Brilliant, huh?" Dante beamed.

"I'm not so sure it is," Lex said. "Communicating with each other isn't a bad idea, but those things will make us look suspicious."

"Aha!" Dante looked pleased with himself. "Start thinking like a nerd, my friend. Cell phones won't work on the ship, so wouldn't a certain type of geek decide to create his own form of communication?"

Gillian was impressed. "Good thinking, Dante."

"We can talk about it more on the way to the cabin. Cora gave me orders to get you two into her room the minute you arrived. She wants to see with her own eyes that you're okay, plus she thinks we need a strategy session."

Lex inserted himself between Dante and Gillian as

NERDS LIKE IT HOT 93

they headed toward the elevators. "Do we have a schedule for the rest of today?"

"Yep. Plus an overview of the activities for the cruise. It's, uh, different, as promised in the brochure. Oh, and Gillian, I don't know where you're going to put your clothes. Cora's hogged the entire closet."

"That's okay." Gillian couldn't think of anything less important right now than closet space. She'd been given a code name and they were headed for a strategy session, which meant this escape plan was for real.

By stepping onto the ship, she'd left behind her previous life, maybe for several years. She didn't know when she'd set foot in the United States again. Besides that, she'd finally found a man who could kiss like he meant it, and she couldn't have him because she was on the lam.

"I guess the walkie-talkies are a good idea," Lex said at last. "I should have thought of something like that."

"To be honest, it was Cora who thought of them, so we stopped by a Radio Shack on the way here. I was waited on by a genuine geek who thought they were very cool. I thought we should only get one for you and one for me, but Cora wanted one, too."

"I don't get one?" All this spy talk was making Gillian nervous, but if everyone else had a way of communicating, she wanted that, too. The ship felt cavernous and spooky without any other passengers on board. "Someone could get lost in all these hallways."

"That's why you should take one of us with you whenever you go anywhere," Lex said.

"Exactly." Dante led them to the elevator and pushed the button for C Deck. "Normally, the person being guarded isn't supposed to worry about walkie-talkies."

Gillian didn't like that lack of control. "But I really would like to have one. It may be too late, but—"

"Don't worry. Cora knew you'd want one, so I ended up with four. Cora and I have tested them all over the ship, and they work great. If anyone asks about them, we explain them as a nerd toy."

"Sounds good," Gillian said. "Then I shouldn't have to take someone with me wherever I go. I can use the walkie-talkie, and if I get in trouble, I can radio for backup." The walkie-talkie concept made her feel much safer. Now if the ship could only sail around the world forever and she wouldn't be required to set off on her own in Mexico, life wouldn't be so bad.

"I still think you should have someone with you," Lex said. "Although all of these precautions are probably unnecessary. Don't you think we could pick a Mafia guy out from all the nerds on board?"

Dante shook his head. "I keep trying to tell you, Mafia guys don't all look alike. You could end up with a nerdy mobster, and then where would you be?"

"Someone followed us on the freeway, probably the same guy who was parked on Cora's street," Gillian said. "But through some masterful driving, Lex got rid of him." After that last kiss, she wanted Lex to know that she'd forgiven him for scaring her to death.

"Way to go, buddy!" Dante sent Lex an admiring glance. "Way to guard the Painted Lady."

Lex shifted the *Star Wars* backpack higher on his shoulder. "Look, we really need to come up with a different code name for Gillian. Last I heard, *painted lady* meant something we might not want to associate with our client."

"Fine with me." Dante turned to Gillian. "What do you want to be called?"

She didn't even have to think about it. "Norma Jean."

"Sounds good," Dante said. "Does that work for you, Lexter?"

"It's better than Painted Lady, but this whole code name business seems silly. I agree the walkie-talkies are a good idea, but we'll all recognize each other's voices. The code name thing seems like some B-movie schtick."

"Then don't think of it as a code name." Gillian held up the nametag she'd been given at check-in. "They gave us this with our real name on it, but they said we could change it to our nickname if we wanted. Don't you think it would be a good idea for me to go by Norma Jean instead of Gillian?"

He frowned. "I suppose."

She sent him a questioning glance. Dante had some good ideas, but instead of welcoming them, Lex was acting grumpy. "Anything wrong?"

"Nope." But his jaw was clenched.

"Maybe he doesn't want to be Clark Kent," Dante said. "How about Superman, instead? I picked Clark Kent because you have to wear the glasses and the nerd outfit, but we can go with Super—"

"We can talk about it later," Lex said.

"Okey-doke. Whatever you say. Well, here we are." Dante pulled a key card out of his pocket. "Cora's going to be so glad to see you two."

As Dante inserted the key card into the slot, Gillian tugged on Lex's arm, pulling him back a couple of feet. Then she stood on tiptoe to murmur into his ear, "What's bothering you?"

His expression was grim. "This isn't a game. I don't like that he's treating it like one."

"But I know it's not a game."

He stared into her eyes. "Good. Don't forget it."

Eight

FOUR PEOPLE IN ONE OF THESE ROOMS WAS A TIGHT squeeze in Lex's book. In his current hormonal state, he didn't need to be squeezed into any space that included Gillian. When she'd murmured a question in his ear a while ago, he'd nearly pulled her into his arms for another liplock.

Now he was sitting beside her—thighs touching—on a bed, for God's sake. If they lay back and scooted sideways, they'd be in business for a little horizontal tango. Instead he had to force himself to concentrate on the list of shipboard activities Cora was reading as she sat on the other bed next to Dante.

The room was so small that all four sets of knees were bumping each other. That alone should have kept Lex from thinking about sex with Gillian, but it had no noticeable effect. The warmth of her thigh against his was the only thing that seemed to register in his fevered brain.

"We have the captain's cocktail reception tonight," Cora said. "We all need to go to that so we can survey the passengers and pick out any suspicious-looking characters."

"If they all look like us, that's gonna be tough." Dante started to laugh. "Lex, could you please take off those clip-ons instead of leaving them flipped up like that? I can't concentrate with you sitting there looking like a dweeb."

Lex took off the glasses, clip-ons and all. He wasn't about to admit that he admired the design of those clip-ons. If he wore glasses he'd be sorely tempted to go the clip-on route instead of buying prescription sunglasses, or worse yet, the ones that went dark in the sun but never quite looked right in the shade, either.

"I think clip-ons look cute turned up, like miniature awnings," Gillian said. "And when you stop to think about it, don't you agree they're ingenious?"

Lex blew out a breath. Did she have to be sexy *and* kind? What was a guy supposed to do?

"Obviously, Lex doesn't agree, which is as it should be." Dante leaned toward Gillian. "The Lexter and I will be surrounded by geeks on this cruise. We have to fit in, but there's a small danger that in the process we'll become infected with geekiness if we're not careful. It probably won't be as much of a problem for me, because I was born cool, but for Lex, it's a concern. So let's not be telling him he looks cute with his clip-ons flipped up, okay?"

Lex was about to tell Dante what he could do with his pair of clip-ons, but Gillian beat him to the punch.

She leaned forward with deliberate purpose. "I wouldn't say Lex is the only one we have to worry about getting infected. You were the person all excited about the walkie-talkies and assigning us each code names."

Lex could have kissed her. Well, he was always on the verge of wanting to kiss her, but after that comment, the urge was overpowering.

"The . . . the walkie-talkies don't count!" Red crept up from the collar of Dante's shirt. "That's part of security. I didn't say I *liked* the walkie-talkies."

Gillian smiled. "You didn't have to."

"No, you sure didn't." Lex knew he was piling on, but he didn't care. Dante was too damned sure of himself and his cool factor. "The minute we got here, you were all about the walkie-talkies, and code names and stuff."

Dante flushed. "No, really. They're a tool. I'm not into them at all. It might have seemed that way, but I'm—"

"Children!" Cora rattled the paper she held in her hand. "Enough of your hang-ups. Let me finish reading the schedule. I want plenty of time to get dressed before the cocktail party."

"Right." Dante shifted his weight on the bed. "Let's concentrate, people."

Lex glanced at Gillian and caught her smiling at him. He couldn't help smiling back. The shared moment left him feeling even more turned on than he had been before. They needed to finish this strategy session, if only to let him get out of this cozy situation with Gillian before he lost it.

"After the cocktail party we have the first seating for dinner," Cora said. "Those who are in the second seating, which would be the four of us, are invited to the lounge for karaoke."

"That rocks," Dante said. "I'm great at that."

"Which misses the point of going," Cora said. "We need to scout out every possible venue looking for problems."

"And sometime after we sail," Gillian said, "I want to make a ship-to-shore call to the LAPD."

Cora gave her a sharp glance. "You want to tip off the police?"

"Yes. I can't let Neil get away with this. And I need to make the call soon, in case . . ."

Lex's blood ran cold at her implication. "In case you forget," he said quickly. "Because nothing is going to happen to you. Nothing at all. Right, gang?"

"Absolutely not." Cora gazed at Gillian. "I appreciate your impulse to do this, but be sure and take Lex with you when you go into that room. The calls are so expensive that the place is usually deserted."

"That's good." Gillian sat up straighter, as if gathering her courage. "I wouldn't want anybody to hear me make the call. Or even suspect I was about to make it."

Lex could kick himself for suggesting the call in the first place, but it had been the only way he could think of to keep her from going to the police before they sailed. Now he searched frantically for alternatives. "What about e-mail? That might be less suspicious. Everybody likes to check their e-mail."

"No e-mail on board," Dante said.

"You're kidding!" Lex couldn't believe it. "This is a nerd cruise! How can they not provide Internet access?"

"According to the person I asked, that's exactly why," Dante said. "They want the nerds to pair up. If they gave them Internet access, they'd all be glued to the computers and wouldn't take part in any of the activities."

"Okay, then." Lex turned to Gillian. "Looks like the phone is your only option, but I wouldn't rush into it. You have plenty of time. In fact, I have a great idea. Let one of us make the call on the way back, after you're safely off the ship."

"No." She was trying to seem brave, but she began to tremble. "I should do it. And the longer I wait, the more chance Neil has to get away."

"You can let it go until tomorrow, I think," Cora said. "That gives us all time to get our sea legs and scope out the situation."

Gillian visibly relaxed. "Okay. But tomorrow, for sure."

"Right," Cora said. "Now then, I believe we were talking about karaoke! And the person from our group who should sing is Gillian."

Gillian choked. "Me? I don't do karaoke."

"Norma Jean would," Cora said. "You don't want to look like a scared mouse running from the Mob because you saw someone murdered. You want to look as if you don't have a care in the world. That way, if anyone has followed you on board—"

"The guy in the black sedan tailed them on the freeway," Dante said. "But Lex lost him in traffic."

Cora's gaze fastened on Lex. "Are you sure you lost him?"

"I lost him, all right." Lex knew that wasn't the whole story, though. "But if Adamo's guys have my car identified, which it looks as if they have, then someone else could have come along later. I didn't see anyone follow us into the parking lot, but they might have been cagier this time."

"True." Cora took a deep breath. "At this point we don't know what to expect. The secret is for one of us to stay with Gillian at all times, and Gillian, you should keep to the well-populated areas, which is another reason to go to the karaoke bar before dinner, and forget about this ship-to-shore business for now."

"She's right," Lex said. "But if you don't like to sing, then—"

"I like to sing. But I confine it to the shower."

Dante grinned. "Then pretend you're in the shower. But keep your clothes on."

Now Lex had to deal with a new image—Gillian wet and naked while she sang in the shower. He was in so much trouble it wasn't funny.

"Then it's settled," Cora said. "Gillian, you can do this. Be Norma Jean."

"I'll try."

"That's the spirit." Cora consulted her schedule. "After karaoke is dinner, and we'll be seated at a table for eight, so we can find out something about the others assigned to that table."

"And I shouldn't have to mention that we all have to be careful what we say about ourselves." Lex directed his comment mostly at Dante.

"Hey, I can be discreet. I went to PI school, you know."

"Dante won't let us down, will you, Dante?" Cora peered over at him.

"Nope."

"Good. Now, back to the schedule. After dinner is a starlight trivia contest up on deck, with guest lecturer Dr. Benjamin Lawrence, retired professor of astronomy at UCLA. Here's what the brochure says about him." Her voice softened. "A distinguished scholar, Dr. Lawrence received his bachelor's and master's degrees from Stanford and his doctorate from UCLA. Prior to his retirement, he headed up a special research unit in Chile and has published several books in his field, including—"

"Uh, Cora?" Dante tapped her on the shoulder.

"What?"

"We don't really need to know all of that stuff."

"You most certainly do! I want your opinion about him. Does he sound like a good candidate?"

Lex tried not to laugh and only managed to sound emotionally choked up. "Why would you want our opinion?"

"Aw, Lex, you're such a darling. I'm touched that you're touched. And I want your opinion because I have no family to consult, and I don't want to make a bad decision because I get carried away by hormones."

Lex didn't trust himself to speak for fear he'd blow it and start grinning at the concept of Cora getting carried away by hormones. Not that he didn't think it was possible, but it made him smile, and she might not appreciate that.

Fortunately, Gillian was on the job. "You think that might happen?" she asked, her tone properly serious.

"I most certainly do. There was a picture of him in the cruise brochure, and he's a hunk. I've been dreaming about him for weeks, and I've already worked up a serious case of lust. The man is a god, but he could also be hell on women. I'm trying to decide if all those degrees mean anything."

"They mean he went to school a lot," Dante said. "I don't think they're any guarantee of faithfulness." He put his arm around Cora. "Don't worry, babe. We've got your back. We won't let you fall for a scoundrel. I'll ask him what his intentions are."

Cora laughed. "Don't you dare! But I wouldn't mind you having a man-to-man talk with him sometime and find out if he's worth the time and trouble for me to beat off all the others who will be going after him."

"I'll do that," Dante said, nodding solemnly.

"I have no doubt I can get him," Cora said. "I just want to know my chances of keeping him."

NANCY ROTH BREEZED THROUGH CHECK-IN, BUT THEN Neil knew she would. Her passport was perfect. Pulling Nancy's Louis Vuitton rolling bag behind him and wearing the adorable shoes he'd found on sale at Nordstrom today, he located the elevator and rode the short distance to D Deck. That put him too close to the waterline for comfort, but his roommate was obviously strapped for cash and had taken the cheapest thing she could get.

With a sense of foreboding, he made his way to the cabin at the far end of the long corridor. He was heading astern, which meant the room had to be almost on top of the ship's engines. Only the crew had it worse than this. Thank God these substandard accommodations were only temporary. Nancy loathed deprivation.

As he inserted the key card in the slot, the door swung open.

A very thin girl with extremely thick glasses stood there smiling shyly. She wore khaki shorts, a plaid blouse, and her hair was long, straight, and plain brown. Her face was totally devoid of makeup.

Neil tried not to stare, but in his world, nerds were a rarity. This was a cruise, for God's sake! Where were this girl's party clothes? And letting her hair do that dopey dangle thing was criminal. Neil's fingers itched for a blow-dryer and styling gel.

"You must be Nancy," she said.

"Yes, I most certainly am!" Neil flashed Nancy's best smile outlined in Manhunter Mauve, Nancy's favorite lipstick. "And *you* must be Bernice."

"Call me Bernie." The girl held out her hand.

Neil took note of fingernails filed short and an absence of jewelry. What a hopeless case. But he needed to bond with this creature who was so completely different from Nancy's flamboyant persona. He'd never shortened Nancy's name, but now seemed like the time. "Call me Nance," he said.

"Great, Nance!" Bernie's handshake was firm. "I'm

glad you're here. It makes the cruise more affordable."
Then she blinked, as if realizing that might sound rude.
"And the company will be wonderful, too, of course."

"I know! Too much fun. It's like a slumber party!"
Careful not to roll his eyes, Neil pulled Nancy's suitcase
into the itty-bitty room.

Bernie backed up, edging her way through the narrow
space between the end of the twin beds and the dresser.
Then she sat on her bed and smiled at him.

Just his luck, he was rooming with a nice girl. It was
enough to make a person barf. She'd probably never met
a cross-dresser in her life. If he'd been lucky enough to
draw a swinger, he might have considered revealing his
secret. But Bernie looked like the kind of person who
would run screaming down the hall, which was not what
he was going for.

Neil had taken Nancy on a few cruises, but he hadn't
realized they made cabins this small. Or maybe it was the
gigantic basket of fruit, cheese, and wine sitting on the
minuscule dresser that made the room seem even tinier.
"Did this come with the room?" he asked. If so, he would
rather have a larger cabin and a smaller basket.

"It's for you. You must have a secret admirer."

Neil's professionally waxed eyebrows lifted. "For *moi*?
This is a surprise." Resting the rolling bag on end, he
opened the small envelope tied with ribbon to the basket
handle and pulled out the card inside. "Welcome to the
Sea Goddess. What do you say we enjoy some of this wine
together later, in my cabin? Best, Jared."

Shit. One little mention of spanking and Jared was
delivering giant fruit baskets and expecting a rendezvous
in his cabin ASAP. Neil tapped the card against his chin
and tried to think how he could put the brakes on this

runaway train. He wouldn't mind a small dalliance, but from the size of this basket Jared hoped for something large and decadent. Neil didn't have that kind of time.

"You don't look very happy about the basket," Bernie said.

Neil sighed dramatically. "Oh, you know how it is when someone is very enthusiastic and you're . . . not."

"Actually, I don't know too much about that." Bernie looked forlorn. "I'm usually the enthusiastic one who doesn't get the time of day."

"Oh." Neil weighed his options. He wanted to look over the ship, but he couldn't start planning anything for sure until he'd identified Gillian McCormick. That couldn't happen until passengers started to mingle at the captain's cocktail reception at five.

He had about an hour to kill, and what better way to kill it than bonding with his roomie? In order for him to keep his identity a secret and promote his plan, he needed a roommate who would forgive him long sessions in the bathroom and comings and goings at strange hours of the night. Basically, he needed a roomie who was indebted to him.

Replacing the card in the envelope, he sat on the edge of the other twin bed. "Bernie, would you be offended if I gave you a few teensy-weensy suggestions to improve your look?"

Bernie's eyes grew round with surprise. "You would do that?"

"Why not? We're roomies, aren't we? That's what roomies do."

"Not the roomies I've had! We all told each other we didn't care about superficial things like hair and makeup. Then a couple of my best friends went the lesbian route, but that's so not me. I'm twenty-six, and I want a boyfriend. But I don't have the first idea what to do with myself to get one."

"Honey, you've come to the right place."

"I can see that." Bernie's glance was admiring. "You have it together."

Yes, he did. And taped and tucked, besides. "I think we should start with your name. What's your full name?"

"Bernice June Thigpen."

Neil swallowed a laugh. No wonder this poor girl couldn't get a date. She'd been marked from the day she was born. "Would you consider going by June instead of Bernie?"

"I don't feel like a June."

"Okay, do you feel like a BJ?"

Bernie's expression brightened. "Maybe, a little bit. Except I don't look like a BJ."

"Don't worry, sweetie. By the time I get finished, you will look exactly like a BJ."

AFTER LEX AND DANTE LEFT TO SETTLE INTO THEIR cabin and get ready for the cocktail party, Gillian turned to Cora. "I don't know if I can do this karaoke thing or not. I'm basically an introvert."

"Marilyn used to be scared, too." Cora patted Gillian's arm. "In fact, I don't admit this to very many people, but when I was on Broadway, I would throw up before every performance. Lots of actors and singers do. Look at Streisand. She's petrified of going out in front of that audience."

"But that's how they made their living. They had to. You had to. I don't have to."

"I think you do." Cora met her gaze. "You have some big challenges ahead, and the only way you're going to meet them is to believe you can do anything. I know singing karaoke scares you. So much the better. Conquer that and you'll be stronger, ready for the next test that comes your way."

Gillian couldn't counter that argument. What Cora said was true enough. "Damn Neil for killing Theo and ruining my life," she muttered.

"That would fall into the water-under-the-bridge category, now wouldn't it? What do you say we get ready for the cocktail party? I brought a dynamite red dress for you to wear."

"You brought clothes for me? But I have plenty in that rolling bag. I really don't need more."

"I know you didn't think so." Cora walked to the room's only closet situated right across from the small bathroom. "So I made some decisions for you. I couldn't possibly wear everything I crammed into that giant suitcase." She opened the closet door and pulled out a red chiffon cocktail dress. "Try this on. It'll give you karaoke courage."

Gillian hesitated. Once she took that dress, she'd have committed to becoming a blond bombshell tonight, one who would walk up to that karaoke stage as if she knew what the hell she was doing. But the dress was beautiful.

"Go ahead." Cora held out the dress. "You know you want to."

"You're turning me into a wardrobe junkie."

"And I'm loving it. I never had a daughter or a granddaughter to play dress up with. Let's go out there looking like a couple of divas. If you'll do my makeup, I'll do yours."

Gillian couldn't back down from the challenge in Cora's bright eyes. "You're on."

"That's my girl. We'll do makeup first, then hair, then

put on our finery." She whipped a dress out of the closet that looked as if it were made of spun gold. "This is my ammunition for Dr. Benjamin Lawrence."

"Nice."

"I hope he thinks so. I want to conquer him first, ask questions about his moral character later. I do hope that he— What's that noise?"

"Your walkie-talkie?"

Cora grabbed it off the bed and clicked a button. "Screen Goddess, here."

"Screen Goddess, this is Italian Stallion."

"Yes, yes. I know who it is. What do you want?"

"We're standing here in bow ties and really ugly jackets. I know this is part of the assignment, but I don't know if I can appear in public like this. I'm thinking we could at least— Hey! I'm talking on this thing, Lex! Don't—"

"Cora? This is Lex. Ignore the pansy-ass. If Gillian can sing karaoke, then we can dress like dorks."

After some crackling that indicated a struggle over the walkie-talkie, Dante came back on. "I didn't say I looked like a dork. I'm just not quite as cool-looking as usual. And I wondered if we could leave off the bow ties. Over."

Cora spoke into her walkie-talkie. "I think the bow ties are a nice touch, Dante. Over."

More static indicated that Lex had resumed control. "We're wearing the bow ties, Cora. No worries. Over."

"I admire your can-do spirit, Lex. By the way, Gillian is definitely singing karaoke. Wait'll you see her in the red dress I brought for her. Over."

Lex's rich baritone seemed to fill the tiny cabin. "I can hardly wait. Over and out." The walkie-talkie was silent.

Gillian rubbed her arms, which were covered with goose bumps from listening to Lex on the walkie-talkie.

"I guess that's another reason I need to do whatever it takes," she said. "Everyone else is stepping out of their comfort zone to help me. The least I can do is prove I'm worthy of the effort."

"You don't have to prove that," Cora said. "We already know you're more than worth the effort. But stepping out of your comfort zone will serve you in the long run."

"Right." Gillian escaped into the bathroom. She was picturing herself in front of the microphone, and she had the strongest urge to throw up.

Nine

LEX HAD TO ADMIT THE WALKIE-TALKIES WERE USE-
ful. He refused to use the stupid code names that Dante
thought were so cute, but he liked the idea that he could
radio either Cora or Gillian whenever he wanted to. Yes,
they could have telephoned Cora's cabin to find out if the
women were ready to head down to the cocktail party, but
using the radio was a good habit to get into.

He'd been forewarned about Gillian's red dress and
thought he'd steeled himself against displaying any emotion when she appeared. But the minute she walked into
the corridor on impossibly high heels, he heard the sound
of his quick breath. She'd probably heard it, too. Well,
she might have expected a reaction like that, considering
the dress and the woman in it.

Or rather, the woman who was partly in it. The neckline revealed more than it concealed, and the hemline
showed a generous amount of knee. He had to work hard
to keep his gaze focused at a gentlemanly level. He could
guess that Dante was ogling, and he didn't want to look at

his partner and confirm that fact, because then he'd have to smack him. Worse yet, they were about to enter a roomful of people, and logic told him that about fifty percent of them would be male.

"Does that come with some sort of jacket?" he asked as the four of them stood in the corridor assessing each other's choice of clothing. He'd rather she put on an overcoat, but that was probably asking too much. He was so preoccupied with Gillian's dress that he'd forgotten about his ludicrous bow tie and ugly brown tweed jacket. Dante's green plaid jacket was worse, though.

"I'd be happy to give her my jacket," Dante said. "I'm willing to go with the short-sleeved shirt I have on under it. Bad as it looks, the jacket's worse."

Cora gave a little huff of disapproval. "No one is covering her up. Our Gillian is gorgeous."

"I didn't say she wasn't." Lex wouldn't have stopped with *gorgeous,* either. He'd have added *stunning,* and *breathtaking,* just for starters. She was, as they used to say in the old days, a knockout. And he was mentally down for the count. "I only thought she might be cold."

"Lexter, she is the exact opposite of cold," Dante said. "Gillian, that's a great look. I don't really want to spoil it with my jacket. I was selfishly trying to improve *my* look, but as that's a hopeless cause, we might as well proceed to this cocktail party. Considering the way we look, nobody will believe a couple of babes like you showed up with a couple of losers like us."

"I keep trying to tell you," Cora said as they walked down the hall toward the elevators. "Women are less concerned about looks these days. They want a man who has some ingenuity in the bedroom, and a nerd—"

"I hear a rumbling," Gillian said. "Do you think they're starting the engines?"

Lex glanced at his watch. "We should be shoving off soon, so I'm sure they're revving up for that."

Gillian looked up at him. "I want to do that bon voyage thing. The one where you stand at the rail and throw little streamers at the people you left behind on the dock."

He was totally charmed. "Did you leave someone behind on the dock?"

"I hope so." Her brown eyes sparkled. "I'd like to think I left all kinds of people behind on the dock."

"We should all go," Cora said. "Only I forgot to bring those streamers they gave us at check-in."

"I picked yours up." Gillian opened a little silver clutch purse. "I have enough for all of us."

"Then by all means," Dante said. "Let's do the bon voyage thing."

So instead of turning left to go to the elevators, they turned right and walked through the double doors and outside to the railing. Lex took the little bundle of colored streamers Gillian gave him and stood beside the railing as the ship moved slowly away from the dock. The ship's horn bleated in a salute.

Only a handful of people lined the dock, their faces turned up toward the departing ship. The small group was spotlighted by sunbeams that were still strong at six in the afternoon. In the movies it was usually a crowd of well-wishers, but Lex hadn't expected that sort of send-off for a four-day cruise.

As he stood beside Gillian in her flame-red dress, he realized this was probably stupid. If anyone on the dock had a high-powered rifle and knew where to aim, she'd be a perfect target. But as he scanned the people on the dock, he didn't see anybody who was armed, thank God.

He did see a man dressed in black, a man who looked for all the world like Phil Adamo. Surely he wouldn't come down here. He'd send his flunkies. If it was Phil, though, he was here because he'd put one of his employees on board this cruise ship. Lex had too much respect for the guy's network to think that was impossible.

"Throw your streamers!" Gillian tossed out a blue one that arced and curled down to the churning water below.

In his concern about potential gunmen on the dock, he'd forgotten why they were here.

"I know it's silly," she said in an undertone. "But I've never been on a cruise before, and I've always imagined what it would be like to do this."

"It's not silly." He tossed an orange streamer over the railing and watched it dance on the wind. "I've never been on a cruise, either."

She threw another streamer, a green one this time. "Don't you wish we could be going just for fun?"

"You have no idea." He tossed a yellow steamer and then a white one. The streamers looked so festive, especially when Gillian threw her purple one and they all cascaded down together. In a perfect world, he and Gillian would be sailing off on a special vacation. They would be sharing a cabin, and he wouldn't have to fight his reaction to that low-cut red dress.

But the more he looked at the man standing on the dock quietly watching the ship depart, the more he thought that man was Phil Adamo. Which meant that an assassin had booked passage on this ship.

◆ ◆ ◆

NEIL WAS PROUD OF THE JOB HE'D DONE WITH BJ, even if it had made them a tad on the late side for the cocktail party. As he walked with her toward the lounge where the captain was hosting the party, he could tell that she felt prettier and more confident.

She should. He'd used a curling iron and gel on her hair and done a masterful job on her makeup, if he did say so himself. She had no contacts, so she was stuck with her thick glasses, but he'd loaned her a short, flirty skirt and demonstrated how to pad her bra. When it came to that particular skill, Neil was an expert.

Come to think of it, he could open a business teaching plain women how to make themselves over into babes. If he could transform himself, considering all the physical obstacles he faced, he could transform anybody. So much could be accomplished with the right accessories.

BJ wore earrings with attitude tonight, big hoops that gleamed in the light. Neil had loaned her a necklace, too, a tribal sort of piece that screamed sex. But his job as Pygmalion was over. She had to take it from here, although she acted as if she wanted to cling to him for support.

"Strike out on your own," he told her as they approached the room buzzing with conversation. "Don't hang around me. You don't want me as competition, anyway."

She glanced at his killer outfit, a sequined dress in hunter green that showed off his legs. "I see what you mean. I wouldn't stand a chance next to you."

"Not yet, sweetheart," he said. "Give yourself time. Before long you'll be mowing men down with the best of them." His implication was clear. He was among the best of them, and he knew it. Men couldn't seem to resist him. That was the delicious part of this charade.

"Okay, then, Nance." With a little wave, BJ walked into the room.

Neil hung back, lingering behind a potted palm so he could survey the situation.

And what a situation it was—a parade of the fashion-challenged. It made his eyes hurt. Many in the room clearly owned no evening wear. Neil saw everything from plaid and khakis to T-shirts and sweats. But those who wore sport jackets or, in the case of the women, cocktail dresses, hadn't fared much better in their attempts to make a statement.

Neil had two goals—to avoid Jared Stevenson the Third, and to locate Cora Bledsoe. Wherever he found Cora, Gillian McCormick couldn't be far behind. Neil couldn't imagine what Cora was doing on this nerd cruise, but maybe she'd decided to play matchmaker for her little nerdy friend. From Joanie's description, Neil had a fair idea what to expect from Gillian.

Joanie was a catty woman, a quality Neil admired greatly. In this case it had proved both entertaining and useful. Joanie had given Neil a vivid picture of his target. He expected Gillian to have a lot in common with BJ, except that Gillian was supposed to be filled out in a way that kept her from wearing the latest fashions gracefully. No low-rider jeans for her.

He glanced around, trying to spot Cora. It should be easy. She might be an old lady, but she was no nerd. In the process of scanning the crowd, he noticed something that had escaped him before, probably because many of the outfits were unisex.

But as he looked closer, he noticed that just like in

junior high, the guys had drifted to one side of the room and the girls to the other. Geeks to the right, geekesses to the left. Cross-dressers down the middle? Give him two minutes and he'd get this party started. But he had other fish to fry.

His protégée, BJ Thigpen, should have easy pickings if she headed for the male side of the room. Out of curiosity he tried to find her, and there she was, surrounded by nothing but females. Honestly. After all his work, she'd reverted right back to a wallflower. There was no helping some people.

Then the crowd shifted, and he saw Cora, all in gold. Vintage Oscar de la Renta—he'd lay money on it. At least someone in this sartorial swampland knew how to dress. Oh, wait! There was another bright spot, literally. That red number was also vintage, and he'd guess . . . Versace. Yes, definitely Versace. What a surprise, a fashionista nerd.

But where was the mousy little makeup artist? Neil decided he'd have to chat up Cora and see what he could find out. At least he'd be able to admire her gown while he was at it. He left his potted palm and was partway into the room when a geek came out of the pack on the right-hand side and ambushed him.

"Nancy Roth!"

Neil paused, his gaze flicking over the doughy man holding a champagne flute. His ill-fitting navy blazer looked nautical and might even be Ralph Lauren, but it was way too small. Neil wondered how the guy had known his name, and then he remembered the tacky nametag he'd been forced to wear, a hideous thing on a red cord that totally clashed with Nancy's dark green sequins. He would have left it in the cabin, except BJ had insisted they couldn't get into the cocktail party without it.

The doughy man beamed at him like a first-time lottery winner.

Nancy got that kind of reaction all the time, and Neil never grew tired of it. Basking in the admiration, he preened a little. "And you would be?"

The man's pale blue eyes became glassy with excitement. "Jared Stevenson the Third. Welcome to the *Sea Goddess,* Nancy. It's *such* a pleasure." He held out his hand.

"Oh, *Jared.*" Shitfire. He wasn't ready to deal with this turkey yet. But he didn't want to turn him off, in case they were destined to get naked and naughty before this cruise was over. Jared might be pudgy and prematurely balding, but he came from money, and that was always a promising quality. Some fun, some games, some blackmail. It was all good.

Jared's hand was damp and soft. "How did you like my basket?"

"Simply charming." Neil squeezed Jared's hand and got almost no resistance. That worked. He'd be infinitely moldable. But not now. Neil had places to go and people to see. "Especially the banana, you devil, you."

Jared gulped. "There was a banana in there?"

"Silly man, pretending you didn't know that. I'm sure you chose that banana personally."

"Oh, right! Picked the best one I could find."

"I could tell. And I *love* bananas." Neil tickled Jared's palm with his thumb. "Especially long firm ones."

"Mmph." Jared's throat worked, but no actual words came out.

"Hold that thought," Neil said. "I have some people I need to meet." He started to pull his hand away.

"Wait!" Jared tightened his grip. "What time?"

"Time?"

Jared stepped closer and lowered his voice. "In my cabin. Tonight."

"Oh, dear. I might not make it tonight." Teasing was such a huge part of the game.

"No?"

"I'm simply exhausted from all these last-minute preparations." Neil ran his tongue over his mouth in a way that usually drove men wild. He loved flirting, loved putting men through their paces like this. "I'm sure you understand."

"But . . . but . . ." Jared looked as if he might start to cry.

"Well, I'll try," Neil said. "I truly will try. No promises, though."

"Cabin 106 on A Deck. I'll be waiting. And just so you know, I have a suite."

Neil winked at him. "I'm sure everything you have is sweet."

"Omigod." Jared groaned. "You are so damned hot."

"So they tell me." Neil made his escape and was starting toward the corner where he'd spotted Cora when first seating for dinner was announced over the intercom.

Neil was almost knocked off his Manolo Blahniks by a nerd stampede. Most of the room apparently had first seating, and woe to the person who got between them and their food. Neil got tired of trying to swim upstream and let himself be carried along by the crowd surging toward the dining room at the end of the next hall.

In the process he got stepped on several times, and once he thought somebody pinched his butt, but he couldn't be sure if it was on purpose or an accident. When the hallway widened at the middle of the ship, he worked his way free and dashed for the elevators. What barbarians! Much more of that and he'd start shedding sequins.

Time to retreat, check the cruise schedule, and freshen up for the second seating in the dining room. At least he knew Cora was on board, and he was absolutely certain she'd choose the second seating. Most civilized people would. He'd be able to spot that makeup artist during dinner. After that it was only a matter of time before he'd make her disappear.

GILLIAN SIGHED WITH RELIEF WHEN SHE DISCOVered the sparse crowd in the karaoke bar. A DJ was playing tunes, but nobody looked eager to get up and perform. And she sure as hell wouldn't be the first.

"I don't think it's important to do this tonight, after all." She followed Cora, Lex, and Dante to a table. "Hardly anyone's here."

"No big surprise," Lex said. "It's logical that nerds wouldn't be big on karaoke."

"So there's really no challenge in me getting up there. Let's forget it." Gillian relaxed into her cushioned chair. "Maybe we should discuss the people at the cocktail party. I think—"

"Gillian, even if the crowd's small, you should still try your wings," Cora said.

Gillian felt like a little kid at a piano recital. "I don't wanna."

Cora glanced at Lex. "Maybe you'd be willing to break the ice and sing first?"

Lex shifted uncomfortably in his chair. "Are you suggesting that as a friend or an employer?"

"As a friend."

"In that case, I have no desire to break any ice whatsoever. I sound like a bullfrog in a bucket. Maybe you'll have better luck with Dante."

"I'm not such a bad singer," Dante said, "but nobody likes to be the first one up there. Even me."

"See?" Gillian had found allies. "Lex and Dante don't want to do it, either."

"They're not trying to change their image," Cora said. "You are."

Gillian sent a pleading glance in Lex's direction. "Do you think I need to sing?"

"I hate to say so, but I can see Cora's point."

Gillian groaned.

"Okay, I'll go first," Cora said.

Dante grinned. "I would pay to see that."

"I'm horrible. I sound like a rusty hinge in a gale-force wind, but I'll do it if that's what it takes to get the ball rolling. I'll be lucky if I'm not hooted off the stage."

"We would never let that happen," Dante said. "We'll drown them out with whistles and stomping. Hey, check this out." He picked up a card lying on the table. "A prize for the best solo number, but there's an even bigger prize for the best duet. I might be roped into a duet with someone who can actually sing."

Cora threw up both hands. "That lets me out."

"I'll do a duet with you." Gillian was ready to do anything to avoid going up there alone.

"You can sing a duet later," Cora said. "First, the solo. Do you know 'Diamonds Are a Girl's Best Friend'?"

Gillian would love to deny it, but she was an old-movie buff and she loved that song. "Um, I guess. But I think I should start with a duet. What do you want to sing, Dante?"

" 'Endless Love'."

"Okay." Gillian pushed back her chair. " 'Endless Love' it is."

"No," Lex said.

Dante frowned. "What's wrong with 'Endless Love'?"

"Nothing, except that Cora's right. Gillian should sing the solo. A duet isn't going to do much of anything except waste time."

"Not true," Gillian said. "It'll help me get over my stage fright. Come on, Dante. And would somebody please order me a martini for when I get back? I have a feeling I'm going to need it." Before she had more time to think about what she was doing, Gillian marched up to the DJ and told him that she and her friend would be singing "Endless Love."

"We judge the results by the applause meter over here." The DJ, who looked like something of a nerd himself, pointed to a device that registered decibels. "To win a prize, you have to score higher than a five."

"But the place is almost empty," Dante said. "All eight people in here could stage a riot and we'd only get about a three reading."

The DJ shrugged. "That's what they told me. I don't make the rules."

"It's okay, Dante." Gillian wasn't interested in prizes so much as she wanted to get the whole thing over with. "Let's just do it."

"I think we should have a chance at the prize, is all."

"It's really not important, you know."

He grinned sheepishly. "Guess not." He turned to the DJ. "Maestro, on the downbeat, if you please."

The music started and they launched into the song. Gillian discovered that Dante wasn't quite the karaoke whiz he'd pretended to be. He had trouble with phrasing and he stumbled over the lyrics. As he tried to cover up his goofs, he was so funny that Gillian forgot to be scared.

The worse the singing got, the more Dante hammed it up, sweeping Gillian into a dramatic embrace and gesturing wildly with his free arm. The two of them ended up doubled up in laughter, and toward the end they had to hold on to each other to keep from falling over in hysterics.

When it was over, Gillian was too busy laughing and wiping her eyes to pay attention to the applause meter, but Dante informed her they'd only registered a two. As they staggered back to the table, Cora clapped enthusiastically and kept shouting "Bravo." She seemed completely entertained by the performance.

Lex, however, did not. For some reason he was fidgeting in his chair and scowling at Dante. He looked for all the world as if he'd love to pick a fight with his partner.

Dante clapped him on the back. "Hey, lighten up, old buddy! We weren't that bad!"

"No, you weren't bad at all." Lex stood, mumbled something about getting a bowl of peanuts, and left.

Dante stared after him. "What's his problem?"

Cora smiled. "You two were so cute and seemed to be having so much fun. I'll bet he would have liked to be up there in your place, Dante."

"But he said he didn't want to!" Dante said. "He could have done it instead of me. I was only trying to help."

"I know, darling." Cora glanced at Gillian. "And I doubt he would have been willing to sing the duet, which is part of what's bothering him. The truth is, our Alexander is jealous."

Ten

LEX STOOD BY THE BAR WHILE THE BARTENDER RUS-
tled up a bowl of peanuts that Lex didn't need and no one
else at the table had asked for. He wasn't very proud of
himself. He didn't have the guts to sing a romantic ballad
with Gillian, but he couldn't stand watching Dante do it.

The performance had been about as romantic as a
sponge toss at the county fair, but that wasn't the issue.
Even when Dante had made a mess of the whole thing,
Gillian hadn't minded at all. She'd appeared to have a terrific time.

Maybe she preferred a guy like Dante, somebody who
could let loose like that in public. Just because she'd enjoyed a couple of kisses from Lex didn't mean that he had
the kind of personality she looked for in a man. He was
probably too boring for someone so creative and beautiful.

That red dress of hers was driving him insane, and he
hated, absolutely *hated* that Dante had recently had his
hands all over it. His hands had been all over Gillian, too,
although to be fair, Dante had not groped during the song.

Lex had watched carefully. The first sign of a grope and Lex would have been out of his chair.

No, Dante had behaved himself. That made everything worse, somehow, because Dante was doing a better job of ignoring Gillian's charms than Lex was. Lex had been the one handing out instructions on this matter, and now he was so conscious of Gillian's charms that he was concerned about being an effective bodyguard.

Allowing himself to be attracted to her was unprofessional. Worrying about whether she was attracted to him was idiotic. She was heading off into Mexico sometime in the next four days. Unless Lex proposed to head off into Mexico with her, it didn't matter whether she found him attractive or not. And he wasn't planning to go with her. Of course not.

Or had he been harboring that idea in the back of his mind? His reaction to her performance with Dante might be a clue that he had thought about it on some level. Maybe he'd imagined some dramatic scene where she wished him a tearful good-bye, and he would tenderly let her know that he'd considered all the angles and was coming with her. In his fantasy, she would be ecstatic about that.

The reality might be something else entirely.

"Sir."

"Hm?" Lex turned toward the bartender.

"Your nuts."

"Isn't that the truth."

"Excuse me?"

"Nothing. Thanks so much." Picking up the bowl, Lex started back toward the table. That's when he noticed a stocky, dark-haired man sitting alone in a far corner of the bar. He had a beer in front of him and he was smoking a cigarette.

He looked enough like someone who could be Mafia that he made Lex uneasy. Had he been there before? Lex couldn't remember seeing him, and he'd taken a quick inventory of the customers when they'd arrived.

He set the nuts on the table. "Be right back." A can-do PI would walk right over there and find out what the guy had to say for himself.

"Are you upset?" Dante called after him. "Because I didn't mean to horn in on your territory."

"I'm not upset, and I don't have a territory. I just need to talk to someone." What he'd say when he got to the man's table, he had no idea. With luck something would come to him.

The man glanced up as Lex approached. He wore wire-rimmed glasses and looked Italian. His dark slacks and white shirt were nondescript enough to be considered nerdy, but there was nothing distinctive about him or his clothes.

"Is my cigarette bothering you?" the guy said in a soft voice. "I was hoping if I sat over here in the corner, it wouldn't be a problem."

"God, no, it's not bothering me," Lex said. "It smells terrific, in fact. My girlfriend made me give them up a month ago, and I'm going crazy. She wouldn't let me bring any on the cruise."

The man smiled. "So you'd like to bum a cancer stick?"

"Yeah. And if we could sit and have a little conversation while I smoke it, that would be great. I told my girlfriend that I thought I recognized you from high school, but I can say that after we talked, I figured out you weren't who I thought." He tried to get a look at the man's nametag, but it hung down below the level of the table.

"She's the blonde in the red?"

"That's her." Lex decided he might as well enjoy saying that while he could, even if it wouldn't ever be true.

Taking a pack of cigarettes out of his shirt pocket, the man shook one out in Lex's direction. "She won't believe that lame story about a high school buddy, you know."

"Maybe not, but I'll chance it." He took the cigarette and picked up the lighter lying on the table. His smoking experience consisted of about a month's worth back in college. The cigarette felt like a lollypop stick in his mouth, and he had to flick the wheel on the lighter several times before he got a flame.

"I hate to be responsible for a lover's spat."

"No problem. I'm Lex Manchester, by the way." Talking made the cigarette wiggle, so he had to stop until he got it lit.

"Yeah, I read your nametag."

So far, the guy had more information about Lex than Lex had about him. Then he took a drag on the cigarette and started to choke.

"You okay?"

"Yeah." His eyes began to water. Bumming a cigarette might not have been the best move. He used the first excuse he could think of. "I'm sort of . . . asthmatic." He took the cigarette out of his mouth before he mangled it with his coughing.

"If you're asthmatic, you shouldn't smoke," the guy said.

"I know, I know. But I crave it." As if to prove his point, he took another drag on the cigarette. The smoke affected him just as much, but this time he was determined not to launch into another coughing fit. He swallowed rapidly, trying to stave off the coughing, but the strain must have shown on his face.

"You don't look good," the guy said. "Have a drink of my beer." He pushed it toward Lex.

Lex took a gulp of the beer, which helped, but he still had to do quite a bit of coughing. Some PI he was turning out to be. One little cigarette and he was hacking up a lung.

"Your girlfriend's a good singer."

"I'll tell her you said so." Lex took a deep breath and studied the glowing end of the cigarette, the way he'd seen Bogie do in a movie.

"The other guy, not so much."

"He was just keeping her company up there. So, uh, what brings you on this cruise?"

"This and that."

Lex nodded and took a short puff on the cigarette. This time he only coughed twice. "This tastes great. I appreciate it, Mr. . . ." His implied question hung between them.

"Looks like your girlfriend is going back for more."

Lex glanced over his shoulder to see Gillian standing on the karaoke stage, alone this time. "So she is. So, are you from California? Or did you fly in for the cruise?"

"I'm from Vegas. You should turn around and watch this. I think she's going to sing 'Diamonds Are a Girl's Best Friend.' I love that number."

Lex scooted around in his chair and bumped the end of his cigarette against his jacket lapel. If he hadn't brushed the ash away he would have set himself on fire. Smoking required more practice than he remembered. He made a note not to use it as a conversational gambit unless he was prepared to improve his routine.

"Man, she looks exactly like Marilyn. Does she know that?"

"I think that's what she's going for." Lex took another

nonchalant puff on his cigarette and coughed into his closed fist. He hoped that looked a little more macho.

"She could do impressions."

"Mm." Lex didn't know how Marilyn impressions would go over in South America. They might love it, for all he knew.

Then Gillian began to sing. She was tentative at first, but as the song progressed, she gained confidence. Before Lex knew what hit him, he was drawn into the moment, hanging on every phrase, his gaze glued to her as she smoothed her hands up her thighs and wiggled in a very Marilyn-like way. She was so hot, and he was . . . getting a boner. Wonderful. Just what he needed.

As the song drew to its dramatic climax, he felt a sharp pain in his index finger and looked down to discover that the cigarette had burned down to that point. With a yelp he dropped it to the carpet, which wasn't what you'd call a brilliant solution. The carpet began to smolder, and he started stomping on the spot.

Fortunately the other people in the room, including Mr. No-name from Vegas, were clapping and stomping in tribute to Gillian's song, so Lex's stomping on the smoking carpet could be disguised if he clapped at the same time. He proceeded to do that, but all in all, he wasn't very pleased with how the episode had gone.

Standing, he held out his hand in one last attempt to get something concrete for his efforts. "Thank you for the smoke, Mr. . . ."

"Michelangelo. Hector Michelangelo." The guy shook Lex's hand. "Tell your girlfriend she should try impersonations in Vegas. I think she'd make good money there."

Lex wasn't cheered at hearing the Italian name. It could mean nothing, or it could be the information that

clinched who this was. Maybe Hector hadn't figured out
who Gillian was, though. "Her name is Norma Jean," he
said, in case that would help anything at all.

Hector laughed. "Sure it is."

"No, really."

"If she wants to be Norma Jean, then let her be Norma
Jean. Nothing wrong with that."

"Thanks for the cigarette. See you around the ship."

"I'm sure you will."

Lex left the table with a crummy taste in his mouth and
no real knowledge as to whether he'd talked to an assassin or not. If Hector was the Mafia thug who was supposed to get rid of Gillian, did he know that Norma Jean
was the person he was looking for? One thing Lex was
absolutely sure about—Hector was no nerd.

GILLIAN CAME BACK TO THE TABLE FLYING HIGH. IN
spite of the tiny crowd, she'd spiked the applause meter to
a six, so she got a prize, which turned out to be a bottle of
champagne. She'd chosen the moment when Lex had
made his strange journey over to the corner of the room to
climb back up on the karaoke stage. She had no idea if
he'd caught her act or not, but he was back by the time
she returned to the table.

To her immense gratification, Dante, Cora, and even
Lex were on their feet applauding as she found her seat.
Lex held her chair for her, and she smiled at him. "Woo-
hoo! That was fun!" She hugged her champagne bottle to
her chest. "I've never won anything before."

"Congratulations," Cora said. "You were magnificent.
Marilyn herself couldn't have done a better job."

"That's for sure," Dante said. "You must have been
channeling her, because you had all the moves."

"Very nice," Lex said.

"Thanks." She wrinkled her nose. "Who around here smells like an ashtray?"

"That would be me," Lex said. "I decided to check out the guy over there in the corner."

"He must have blown a ton of smoke in your direction." Gilllian waved a hand between her seat and Lex's. Then she glanced over at the man Lex was talking about, and her elation over her performance disappeared. "Mafia."

"Now, now," Cora said. "We don't know that."

"No, we sure don't," Dante said. "You folks are profiling again. Stocky and Italian does not automatically make him Mafia."

"No, but he could be," Lex said. "He's from Vegas, and his name is Hector Michelangelo. I asked him what brought him on the cruise, and he was evasive."

"I would expect everyone on this cruise to be evasive if you asked them that question," Cora said. "Suppose you came on this cruise to find the love of your life. Would you admit that?"

Gillian decided not to look at the Italian guy in the corner anymore. Looking at him gave her the creeps. "Does he know who I am?"

"I told him you were Norma Jean. I don't think he bought it."

"Maybe not," Cora said. "But she doesn't look like Gillian McCormick anymore, either. We'll keep an eye on him, though. I'm glad you made the contact, Lex. Good work. But you stink."

"I don't mind." Gillian recognized that Lex had questioned the man on her behalf, and she was grateful. "He picked up his stinkiness in the line of duty."

"Thanks." Lex seemed pleased by her tolerant attitude.

"You're welcome." As she polished off her martini, she thought of Cora's assessment, that Lex had been jealous when she'd performed a duet with Dante. "Do you want to try a duet with me?"

He hesitated. As he opened his mouth to respond, the intercom came to life and announced the second dinner seating. "Guess I'll have to take a rain check." He looked relieved.

As they walked down to the dining room, she fell into step beside him. "Would you have done it? If the dinner announcement hadn't come in the nick of time to save you, I mean."

"I'd like to think I would have."

She smiled, happy with that response. Singing a karaoke duet was stepping way out of Lex's comfort zone, but he'd seriously considered doing it, for her. That was better than a bottle of champagne, any day.

When they walked into the dining room, she had to laugh. The nerd theme had been carried out in the centerpieces. Yes, there were flowers, but interspersed with roses and carnations were a small calculator, a slide rule, a pair of black-framed glasses, a pocket protector, a clipboard, and a GPS.

"Keep an eye out for Dr. Benjamin Lawrence," Cora said. "I missed him at the cocktail party, and I guess he's not into karaoke, but I'm counting on the fact he'll choose second seating for dinner."

"I have no idea what the guy looks like." Dante held Cora's chair for her. "I didn't see the brochure."

"No problem." Cora took her seat at the table for eight. "He has jet-black hair and a face that brings Sir Laurence Olivier to mind. You won't be able to miss him."

"How old?" Gillian asked. The age of the person Cora had pointed out in the brochure had been hard to pinpoint.

"He's retired, and so I'm assuming he's at least in his late sixties. And let me tell you, I have no problem dating a younger man. But if any of you mention my real age, I'll stab you with a salad fork."

"You don't look eighty-two," Gillian said. 'So why should we advertise it?"

"Hush!" Cora glanced around. "Let's not mention that particular number again on this cruise, shall we?"

"Okay." Gillian handed her bottle of champagne to the waiter who appeared to take drink orders. "Four glasses," she said.

"Two glasses." Lex helped her into her chair.

She glanced up at him. "You don't want even a little sip of my prize champagne?"

His expression softened. "Sure. I don't know what I was thinking."

"You were thinking that you can't drink while you're on duty, and that's admirable, but a couple of sips of champagne shouldn't impair your judgment."

"No." He smiled as he took his seat beside her and unfolded his napkin. "Compared to that dress you're wearing, a couple of sips of champagne are chump change."

"Why, thank you." She'd never captured a man's attention so dramatically, and it was a heady feeling. It wasn't Gillian creating this effect, of course, but Norma Jean, the Marilyn look-alike. Gillian didn't kid herself that Lex would be falling all over himself if she'd met him two days ago, before the transformation.

"Well, how is everyone on this fine evening?" boomed a hearty male voice. "Ready for some stargazing after dinner?"

Gillian looked up to discover that standing right beside Cora's chair was the professor in the brochure . . . sort of. His tweed jacket with suede elbow patches and his black turtleneck sweater made him look the part of a scholar. His hair was still jet black, but there was considerably less of it. With luck Cora would find his comb-over endearing.

Assuming Cora had no problem with the hair or with the wrinkles that had been airbrushed out of the brochure picture, Gillian could only see one other relationship challenge—a vertical one. Cora was at least five seven. Dr. Lawrence might be five feet even if you counted the comb-over.

To Cora's credit, she didn't register even an eye flicker of surprise to find that her hunk was vertically challenged. "I can hardly wait for the stargazing," she said. "Are we lucky enough to be sharing your table for this cruise?"

"Actually, I'll be the lucky one if you'll all allow me to join you. I was assigned to a different table, but as you might have noticed, the second seating isn't completely filled, so adjustments can be made. I was bewitched by seeing this lovely lady in her gold dress and I asked to be moved. That is, if you're willing to have me."

Cora seemed to drop ten years in an instant. "Of *course* we're willing to have you! Sit down right here next to me, you charming man. Tell us all about what we're going to see tonight."

The professor laughed as he took his seat. "Stars," he said. "You're going to see lots and lots of stars." He glanced around the table. "My name is Benjamin Lawrence. You've all heard of Big Ben. People call me Little Ben."

"All those brains and a sense of humor, too." Cora was all smiles.

Gillian had never seen Cora so excited. Obviously she'd been pining for male companionship, and she wasn't going to let a lack of hair and height keep her from enjoying what was offered. Gillian was sentimental enough to want to find out if tonight led to something permanent, but of course she wouldn't have that luxury.

Still, she could enjoy this moment with Cora. "I think we need another champagne glass," she said.

"Or maybe another whole bottle," said a red-haired woman in green sequins who came up behind Dante. "This definitely looks like the fun table. I saw the professor make the move, so I decided to follow in his footsteps. Would you mind terribly if I joined you, as well?"

Cora waved her hand expansively. "Why not? The more, the merrier."

Eleven

NEIL HOPED HE HADN'T COME ON THIS DORKY CRUISE
for no good reason. If the mousy little makeup artist was
sitting back in L.A. thinking about whether or not to call
the cops, or worse yet had actually *called* the cops, then
he was in deep shit. In any case, she didn't appear to be
with Cora.

Maybe she was seasick and holed up in their shared
cabin. That possibility made him feel a little better. He'd
hate to think he'd surrounded himself with nerds and
crammed himself into a tiny room with Bernice June Thigpen for nothing. And speaking of BJ, here she came.
Couldn't make it on her own, apparently.

She approached the table hesitantly, but she kept looking at the Italian guy with the big brown eyes and the hor-
rendous haircut. Get that boy to a decent salon and buy
him some designer clothes and he'd be stylin'. He had a
smidgen of good taste, because he'd already given Nancy
the once-over. Neil could take him on, but if BJ wanted
him, that was okay, too.

BJ stood beside the table clutching her nametag, which still read Bernice Thigpen, unfortunately. "Nance? I saw you change tables. Is that allowed?"

The blonde in the red dress spoke up. "It seems to be fine. Would you like to sit here?"

BJ nodded. "If it's okay. Nance and I are roommates, but somehow we didn't get assigned to the same table."

"Then by all means." The tall guy sitting next to the blonde stood and held a chair for BJ.

From the way BJ kept glancing over at the Italian, she would rather have had him hold her chair, but logistics were against it. Neil was pleased with the chivalry displayed, though. The miniprof had held Nancy's chair for her. Neil had tried vamping him a little bit, just for the practice, but the old guy seemed mesmerized by Cora.

Neil could understand it. She looked damned good for her age. He calculated she had to be at least late seventies, if not early eighties. His grandfather had known her back in her prime when she'd been good friends with Marilyn. Now those were the days. The blonde must be trying to relive it all. Maybe she was an impersonator, although what a Marilyn impersonator was doing on this cruise was beyond him.

Time to find out who Cora's buddies were. "I think we should do an introduction thing around the table and tell a little bit about ourselves," he said. "I'll start. I'm Nancy Roth, and I live in L.A. I came on this cruise because I was curious. BJ, you go next."

"I'm Bernice . . . I mean, BJ Thigpen, and I live in San Jose. I'm a computer programmer, and I have a cat named Steve Jobs, and I used to play the flute, but I haven't done that in a while, so I couldn't call it my hobby, but—"

"That gives us a *really* good picture of you, BJ." Neil didn't want this to take all night, for Christ's sake.

"A cat named Steve Jobs." The Italian guy grinned. "Apple Computers. I get it. That's really cute."

"And what about you?" Neil asked. "What are you all about?"

"I'm Dante Fiorello, and I live in L.A. My partner and I—that's him over there, Lex Manchester—we run an exterminating company called Bobbie's Bug Thugs. We, uh, inherited the business from Lex's dad, Bobbie Manchester."

"That's *so* interesting," BJ said. "Do you use environmentally friendly methods? Because I've heard about all these innovations, and you just look like the kind of people who would do that."

"Oh, yeah," Dante said. "We're all about the environment. Right, Lex?"

"Right." Lex waved a hand at Cora. "Why don't you go next? Nobody needs to hear from me. Dante's already given the pertinent info. And you're way more interesting."

Cora beamed at him. "I don't know about that, but here goes. I'm Cora Bledsoe, and I—"

"I knew it!" Neil slathered on the adulation. "I knew you were Cora Bledsoe! I simply *love* your movies!"

"Cora Bledsoe!" The professor pulled back to look at her more closely. "That's why you looked so familiar to me. I've been trying to place you all night. I thought you might have been one of my students, but instead you're a movie star!"

"A minor one." Cora fluttered her eyelashes.

"Don't even suggest such a thing," Neil said. "You were right up there with the rest of them—Harlow, Grable, Monroe." He turned to the blonde. "Which brings us to you, speaking of Monroe. I suppose everyone says you look like her."

The blonde seemed uncomfortable. "Actually, that's a good thing. I'm . . . I'm training to be a Marilyn impersonator. My stage name's Norma Jean."

Neil wanted more info. "What's your real name?"

"Janice. Janice Collins."

"But we all call her Norma Jean," Cora said. "You know, like Cher. Well, except not exactly like Cher, because that's one name, one syllable, whereas Norma Jean is two names, three syllables, but you get the idea."

"She used to be Cher Bono, though," BJ said.

"Nobody thinks about that now," Cora said. "Anyway, to help her stay in character, we call her Norma Jean."

The blonde nodded. "Right."

Neil sensed something else going on, and he was going to find out what it was, eventually. But he'd drop it for now. He had some time. Until the ship docked in Mexico, nobody was going anywhere.

JUST BEFORE DESSERT WAS SERVED, THE WAITERS REmoved all the centerpieces. Cora said it was strange, but Gillian had never been on a cruise before, so she didn't think anything of it.

"It's almost as if they think we'll steal part of it," Cora said. "That's insulting."

"They wouldn't have to worry about me stealing anything from that centerpiece," Nancy said. "But I'm not too sure about the folks at that table where I started out. They were in love with the stuff in there. When I left they were using the slide rule to calculate the exact dimensions of the table and figure out if the place settings were equidistant from each other."

BJ brightened. "What a great idea! I wish I'd thought of it, and now it's too late."

"If you want to do it tomorrow night, I'll see if I can scare up a slide rule," Dante said.

Gillian glanced at him to see if he was kidding, but he seemed perfectly sincere. If she didn't know better, she'd think that Dante was trying to make points with BJ, and yet BJ was so obviously a nerd, not Dante's type at all. Maybe he was just trying to play his part really well.

If so, she felt a little sorry for BJ, who seemed like a sweet person who didn't deserve to have her heart messed with. As Gillian was making up her mind to say something about that to Dante at the first opportunity, a pudgy man in a too-small navy blazer came into the dining room holding a cordless microphone.

"I'm Jared Stevenson the Third, your cruise director," he said. "Welcome to the *Sea Goddess*!"

"Oh, joy," Cora muttered. "A word from Mr. Pomposity himself."

"We have lots of fun and games planned for you." Jared obviously loved having the limelight. "Some of you have already enjoyed the dynamite karaoke bar, and later tonight we'll have an astronomy lecture and starlight trivia quiz on the upper deck with our resident expert, Dr. Benjamin Lawrence. We'll be turning out all the lights for this one, so don't do anything I wouldn't do!" At that he paused to laugh at his own joke.

In the silence, he eventually stopped laughing and cleared his throat. "Moving right along, your waiters are coming around with pencil and paper for each of you. You may have noticed that the centerpieces have disappeared. This is a memory and observation test. Write down all the things you can remember from that centerpiece. Those who get them all will win a free couples massage!"

"Yikes," Dante said. "I wasn't paying much attention. And that sounds like a fun prize."

"I think I remember most of it," BJ said.

Dante winked at her. "Can I copy off you?"

She laughed. "No!"

"Then when you get the prize, will you share?"

"Maybe." BJ's cheeks turned a bright shade of pink.

Gillian made a decision. She'd talk to Dante and get him to stop leading poor BJ on. It wasn't fair to her.

Meanwhile, she needed to see how many items out of the centerpiece she could remember. Being a makeup artist gave her an eye for detail and she'd been impressed with the creative centerpieces. Picking up her pencil, she began to list what she could. Just in time she remembered to label her paper with the name Norma Jean.

"Time's up!" Jared said. "Picking up the papers, now!"

Gillian handed her paper to the waiter and glanced over at Lex. "How'd you do?"

"We'll see."

"Well, I'm sure I didn't win," Cora said. "I'm terrible at that stuff."

"Me, too," Little Ben said with a sigh.

"Oh, who cares?" Nancy said. "It's not that big a deal."

"It would be for me," BJ said. "I've never had a massage at all, let alone a couples massage."

Gillian found herself getting excited as Jared started reading off the names of those who had guessed ll the items. BJ's name was the first one read from their table. Gillian watched BJ blush and glance over at Dante, who smiled back at her. Uh-oh. This was developing into a genuine problem.

When Gillian heard Norma Jean called, she didn't react right away, and then she realized it was her. She was overjoyed to have won, which was sort of silly, because she wasn't on this cruise to win massages. And it was a couples massage, besides.

She could give it to Cora and Ben, of course. Except she didn't want to. Naughty girl that she was, she wanted to enjoy it with Lex.

He might not be game, though. She had a feeling that would be another thing out of his comfort zone. She leaned toward him and lowered her voice. "Will you do it with me?"

His gaze met hers. "It's probably a bad idea."

"I know. Let's do it anyway."

Heat flared in his eyes. "I'll think about it."

"You do that."

LEX COULDN'T IMAGINE ANYTHING MORE DANGEROUS to his libido than sharing a couples massage with Gillian. But if he refused, he'd look exactly like the uptight guy she might think he was. He hadn't been willing to sing a duet with her, so if he opted out of the massage, too, she'd probably give up on him. And that would be a good thing.

He debated the matter internally all through dessert, and by the time everyone had headed to the upper deck for the astronomy lecture, he still wasn't sure what to do. But he couldn't think about it anymore. His job at the moment was guarding Gillian.

But wait. Wasn't that why he had to do the couples massage? He couldn't let her go alone, could he? What if she chose someone else? No telling who she might end up with. So it was his duty to go. That decided, he surveyed the area that would be used for the lecture.

The deck ¯had been arranged with rows of lounge chairs set up in pairs, and notebooks had been placed on all the chairs. A large screen was positioned just below the ship's bridge.

Not all the passengers had shown up for the stargazing program, which made him nervous. Unaccounted-for passengers meant people could be lurking around, people who had an agenda, like getting rid of Gillian. Lex said as much to Dante while everyone was milling around the deck.

Cora had volunteered to be Ben's assistant during the lecture and she stood next to him, Natasha to his Boris. Gillian was over talking to BJ, and Nancy Roth had taken off for the ladies' room. That left Dante and Lex alone for a few minutes.

"I wouldn't worry about the lack of participation," Dante said. "I think it's par for the course when it comes to nerds."

"But they paid for this. You'd think they'd want to take advantage of everything."

"Just the ones who've found somebody they're interested in. We have only couples up here, if you notice. I'm thinking nerds are slow to couple up." Dante took off his jacket. "I don't know about you, but without the benefit of air-conditioning, my jacket is both ugly and hot."

"Good point." Lex took his off, too. "What do you think of Nancy Roth?"

"She's one hot tamale. She gave me the eye a couple of times."

"And you're not going to do anything about it, right?"

Dante looked offended. "Well, I couldn't, now, could I?"

"I'm glad you realize that."

"I mean, it wouldn't be fair. She's a juicy woman who came on this cruise because she wants to get herself hooked up with a nerd."

"She didn't say that." Something about Nancy bothered Lex, but he couldn't decide what it was. "She said she was curious."

"Like Cora said a while ago, nobody's going to admit they came on this cruise to find a soul mate, especially not somebody as together as Nancy. But why else is she here?"

Lex nodded. "That's my question."

"She wants a nerd, that's why. The ship is lousy with them, but I don't happen to be one. She probably thinks I have this great nerdy business going on, Bobbie's Bug Thugs. She'd be crushed to find out I'm a dashing PI without a nerd bone in my body."

"Yeah, I'm sure she'd be devastated."

"Besides, Nancy doesn't do it for me. She's hot, and I can imagine taking her to bed for one night of sweaty sex, but that would be the end of it. Nothing long-range going on there. So, um . . . what do you think of BJ?"

Something in Dante's tone put Lex on alert. "Why?"

"Well, Gillian's already landed into me because she thinks I'm leading BJ on. I'm sure Gillian's over there this very minute warning BJ about me."

"Now that you mention it, you have been leading BJ on, and I'm glad Gillian said something. BJ seems like a really nice person, and she's not your type."

"Are you saying nice people aren't my type? Thanks a whole hell of a lot. Remind me to put crackers in your bed tonight."

Lex rolled his eyes. "A nice person could be your type, but not a nerdy nice person. You've never dated anyone like that in your life."

"Could have been a mistake on my part."

"But Dante, you just said that women come on this

cruise looking for a nerd. That's BJ, too, right? Wouldn't she also be disappointed to discover you're a dashing PI?"

"I don't think BJ came on the cruise looking for a nerd. I think she's looking for a guy, period. I don't think she's had a lot of experience, and that turns me on."

Lex cleared his throat. "There's another issue. I don't know how to put this delicately, but in the past you've been all about hooters."

"Yeah, I know." Dante gazed dreamily off into the distance where there was nothing but black ocean and the frothy wake of the ship illuminated by the cabin lights. "Weird, huh? I don't think I've ever gone for a flat-chested woman before, but there's something about BJ. I mean, she named her cat after the guy who founded Apple. How cute is that?"

"I didn't know you knew who founded Apple."

"You told me. You said it was your job to educate me. Trust me, all my nerdy knowledge I owe to you. And that reminds me, why didn't you win that couples massage thing? I know you had the centerpiece list nailed. I expected you to win and even get bonus points."

Lex lowered his voice. "I cheated."

"In reverse?"

"Exactly. I was hoping Gillian wouldn't try for it, but as luck would have it, she did, and she won."

Dante grinned. "And you'll have to sacrifice yourself and do the couples massage with her. Am I right?"

"I don't know how else to handle it. I can't let her go in there alone, and I definitely can't let her go in there with another guy."

"Of course not. It's a tough job, but somebody has to do it. I'm impressed with your dedication, buddy. I really am."

"Go to hell, Dante."

"I always thought that would be my ultimate destination, but looking at BJ over there, I'm not so sure anymore. I might be salvageable."

"What are you saying?"

Dante scratched the back of his head. "Have you ever heard guys say that they met somebody, and bam, that was it?"

"Yeah, and I always thought it was a load of bull." If he'd had any slight reaction like that to Gillian, he'd crushed it. They had no future.

"I thought it was bull, too." Dante turned to look at BJ. "But now I'm not so sure."

"I take it you're pairing up with her for this lecture?"

"I am. And I think it could turn out to be a romantic evening, unless . . ."

"Unless what?"

"Unless this old guy doesn't know how to pronounce Uranus."

TECHNICALLY, NEIL HAD BEEN SHIELDED FROM THE family business while he was growing up. His mother hadn't wanted him to understand the work his father was involved in, or, later on, the work his stepfather was doing. But what his mother didn't know wouldn't hurt her.

As a teenager Neil had acquired all sorts of specialized knowledge from people indebted to his father. For example, he knew how to get into any locked room, including the key-card type. By paying close attention during dinner, he'd overheard Cora telling the professor her room number.

He still wasn't sure whether he'd find Gillian McCormick in Cora's stateroom. The blonde who called herself Norma Jean might, in fact, be Gillian in disguise. She hadn't answered right away when her name had been called for the centerpiece quiz contest. Norma Jean was obviously an alias, but whether her real name turned out to be Gillian remained to be seen.

The hallway on C Deck was deserted, but Neil wasn't worried even if it hadn't been. He was a passenger with a nametag. On this first night of the cruise, anyone could be forgiven for getting confused and going to the wrong room. And passengers weren't familiar with who was on their deck at this point. Nobody would question him.

His heart raced as he neared Cora's room. If Gillian was in there, it would be the end of her. He had a small vial of ether and a hanky in his evening bag, and he would use that to knock her out. After that, he'd simply strangle her.

Cora's room was located right next to a double door leading out to a promenade. With a little luck, Neil could get her out those doors and over the side into the water. She would simply disappear.

Getting the door open took a little more effort than he would have liked. He was out of practice. But finally it yielded, and he held his breath, listening for any signs of occupancy. He wanted to hear those sounds, because it would mean he could finish this and get on with his life. Quietly he pulled on a pair of surgical gloves he'd tucked in Nancy's sequined evening bag.

But the room was silent. Closing the door behind him, he stepped inside a room slightly bigger than his, but arranged in a similar way. From the evidence of clothes in the closet and makeup in the bathroom, two women lived here, not one.

He began going through drawers, looking for something, anything that would help him identify that second woman. And there, at the bottom of one dresser drawer, was a passport. He opened it and saw a picture of the person he'd expected to find on this cruise. True, passport photos never showed anyone to advantage. Nancy's was hideous, and Nancy was so gorgeous that she could stop construction if she walked past a building site.

In any case, this washed-out photograph of a long-haired brunette, flattering or not, answered the question. Gillian McCormick was staying in this room. That meant she was somewhere on this ship, and she wasn't cowering in the stateroom because of seasickness, either. She was out there somewhere, and he was going to find her.

As he rummaged through the drawers and closets, he found no clothes that would match up with the woman in the passport photo. Even the underwear was classy— some of Victoria's Secret's best. He should know. Nancy shopped there all the time.

That left him with one obvious conclusion. He was dealing with someone who had decided that she needed a makeover to confuse the issue. Cora Bledsoe was part of the Marilyn era. Rumors had it that she'd been a close friend and confidante of Monroe. If she'd helped Gillian with a plan, chances were she would have leaned toward a Marilyn disguise.

Neil checked the sizes on the dresses hanging in the closet. Those that had tags were a ten. Nancy wore a respectable size six, unless she bought something at Chico's, in which case she was a zero. But Neil had heard that Marilyn had known how to pig out. That hourglass figure was legendary, but rumor had it that the legend had sometimes gone up to a size twelve.

Apparently Gillian McCormick had decided that it would be convenient to morph into La Monroe for the duration of the cruise. Neil didn't mind so much. He was just glad to know who he was after—the blonde in the red dress, the one who had called herself Janice Collins, probably on the spur of the moment. She didn't know he was right behind her, though, and that clashed with his flair for drama.

He liked the idea that she might get a little bit scared if she knew that she was being stalked. She was screwing up his life, so it was only right that he should screw up hers, or what was left of it. So he left the drawers in disarray and swiped her passport. Let her worry about that for a little while. She wouldn't be needing it where she was going, anyway.

Letting himself back out of the room, he congratulated himself on a good night's work. He deserved a reward, and he knew exactly where he could get one. In a suite up on A Deck, Jared Stevenson the Third was waiting. First Neil would stop by his room and freshen up.

While he was there, he'd pluck a few things from that giant basket Jared had provided. Apparently the man hadn't realized how erotic his gift had been, but Neil would teach him. Jared had no idea what treats were in store for him tonight.

Twelve

GILLIAN KNEW THIS WASN'T A PLEASURE CRUISE FOR her, but when the ship's crew turned out the lights and she found herself lying on a lounge chair right beside Lex, with a canopy of stars above her, she felt pleasure.

"Nobody looks at the stars anymore," she said.

"You can't see them in L.A.," Lex murmured.

"That's sort of funny, when you think about it. L.A. is full of stars, and they're all human ones. You can't see the stars in the sky. At least not anything like this."

"I don't think I've ever seen the stars this bright," Lex said.

"Me, either." She slipped her glasses out of her evening purse and put them on. "That's better. Now it doesn't look so much like powdered sugar on a brownie."

He glanced over at her. "I hope you keep those glasses handy. There might be times it would be useful to see what the hell's going on. Oh, and nice save at the dinner table, Janice."

"Janice Collins was one of my best friends in grade

school. I figured I had to come up with something quick if I didn't want to bandy the name Gillian McCormick around."

"Which you don't. But I'll bet you can stick with Norma Jean for the rest of the cruise."

"I hope so. I'm already having an identity crisis." And she didn't feel like talking about her perilous circumstances anymore. "Do you know anything about astronomy?"

"A little bit."

Gillian recognized humility when she heard it. She'd used it herself enough times so she wouldn't seem to be a brainiac. "I'll bet you know more than a little bit. I took it in college. Got an A, in fact."

"Me, too," he said in a low voice. "But don't let that get around. I'm trying to keep Dante from labeling me a nerd."

"I wouldn't care." She thought about telling him that she was basically a nerd, herself, that before Cora had transformed her into Norma Jean, she'd thought of herself as being on the frumpy side. But she couldn't bring herself to say any of that. Putting on her glasses was as far as she was willing to go in spoiling her image.

After all, she was lying on this lounge chair in a vintage red gown that made her look like a sex goddess. Lex had already told her that the dress drove him crazy. She'd be dumb to sabotage the effect of the dress by thoroughly describing the nerd who was wearing it. Better to keep herself something of a mystery.

The professor's voice sounded over the intercom. "Lift your eyes to the heavens, my fellow voyagers. Prepare to take a journey to the stars. On the way to the stars, we'll pass the planets in our tiny galaxy. We'll talk about the beauty of Venus, the wonders of Mars, the rings of Saturn, the mysteries of Uranus."

"Whoops, he said that wrong," she whispered.

Nearby, she heard Dante's muffled laughter.

"It's not exactly wrong," Lex said. "There are two versions."

"But one makes people laugh and one doesn't."

"Correction. One makes Dante laugh. I swear his mental age is fourteen."

"Let's begin with the North Star," the professor said. "Can anyone tell me where to look for it?"

"In the north?" Dante's comment was followed by a slapping sound, as if someone had whacked him on the arm.

"Off the lip of the Big Dipper," BJ said.

"Try saying that ten times." Then Dante yelped. "Hey, she pinched me. And not in a loving way, either."

"Dante, behave yourself." Cora turned in Dante's direction. "Don't make me come over there."

"It's okay, Cora," BJ said. "I'll take care of him."

"Oh, I hope so," Dante crooned.

Gillian couldn't see what was going on, but she was worried about BJ getting her heart broken. She turned on her side, so she could talk softly to Lex. "You know he's flirting with her like crazy. That's not fair if he's not serious."

Lex turned on his side, too, which put them inches from each other. "Believe it or not, he told me he really thinks she might be the one."

His warm breath tickled her mouth. "Really?" She lost interest in the astronomy lecture as she realized how easy it would be to move her head a little closer to his and kiss those tempting lips.

"Yeah. But now is not the time. I don't want him distracted by sex."

"I suppose not." Gillian understood the implication.

Dante wasn't supposed to be distracted by the pleasures of the flesh, and neither was Lex. She turned onto her back again and gazed up at the diamond-bright sky.

It would be fantastic to make love up here on deck under a sky like this. Well, that would only be true if you were the one on the bottom and could look up and see it. The one on top would miss the view. Or maybe, to keep things fair, you could alternate.

If she were choosing, she'd take the top first and save the bottom and the view of the stars for last. Being on top was fun, but she'd always liked the bottom position a little better. That way, when she came, she didn't have to keep herself balanced. She wondered if Lex had any preferred positions or if he liked it all.

She thought about asking him, but that would bring up the subject of sex, the subject he and Dante weren't supposed to be distracted by. Gillian thought that might be impossible, considering they were on a tropical cruise and the nights were so warm she felt like taking off all her clothes. Lex might object, at least at first.

Gillian tried to concentrate on the astronomy lecture, but as the professor described the constellations of Ursa Major and Ursa Minor, she began picking up other sounds. From the various lounge chairs on the top deck she heard the soft scratching of pens as a few took notes. She'd expected that from a ship full of nerds.

But there were other noises that captured her attention. The sound of the ship moving through the water was a constant whooshing, of course, but there was something else. Either people all over the deck were eating finger food, or a make-out session was in full bloom.

Gillian listened closely. Definitely a make-out session. Because she'd been recently kissed herself, she couldn't mistake the slurp of lips against lips, the soft chirp of suction as the kiss deepened, followed by moans and quickened breathing. The salt air coming off the water smelled like sex. Gillian wondered if this was about to become an orgy.

The professor seemed oblivious as he launched into an explanation of the stars that made up Orion's belt. Speaking of belts, was that the rasp of a zipper? She would swear it was. Some people were wasting no time.

She turned on her side and kept her voice low. "Lex."

"Mm?" He swiveled his head in her direction.

"The nerds are getting it on."

He moved to his side so he was facing her again. "Uh-huh."

"So you heard it, too?"

"Can't help it."

"But what about the professor and Cora? Can't they hear all that smooching going on?"

Lex smiled. "Maybe not, if they're both hard of hearing."

"You know, I've wondered that about Cora."

"She covers it well by reading lips. I'll bet he's a little deaf, too. And if she's hanging on his every word . . ."

"Makes perfect sense." She gazed at him. "Well, I'm not hard of hearing, and I distinctly heard zippers."

He swallowed. "I don't really want to talk about that."

"Me, either." The way she looked at it, she could lie here and be a good girl, and have no hot memories to take with her when she disappeared into some humble village to pluck chickens while her roots grew out.

Or, she could take advantage of her current blondness and possession of a dynamite red dress that excited the man beside her so much that he was forever ogling her in it. He was ogling her now, as a matter of fact.

Good girl and no memories versus bad girl and hot memories. Sounded like a no-brainer to her. The top deck was awash in hormones, which made the decision even easier. Slowly she pulled her glasses off and slipped the earpiece into the neckline of her dress.

He followed her action, his gaze lingering on her cleavage. "What are you doing?"

"Enjoying the lecture, just like everybody else." She reached for his glasses.

"Gillian . . ." His protest was weak, and he didn't stop her from taking them off.

"That's Norma Jean to you." She folded his glasses and tucked them in the pocket of his shirt. "Move over. I'm joining you."

"That's a really bad idea."

"No, it's a really good idea." She slipped quietly off her lounge chair. The silky material of her red dress made that easy. When she eased herself down on Lex's chair, he had no choice but to move to accommodate her.

It was a snug fit, so snug that as she settled against him, she found out something extremely validating. Lex was hard. "I thought you didn't like this idea," she said.

He wrapped his arms around her. "I didn't say that. I said it was a bad idea."

She pressed her advantage right up against his rebellious body part. "Some of you disagrees."

"There's a lecture going on. You're supposed to be quiet."

"Make me."

"I feel like a teenager at a drive-in."

"I know." She rubbed against him. "Isn't it great?"

"Yeah." With a little groan of surrender, he kissed her.

By now she should be used to the impact of that kiss, but instead it seemed more potent each time. These kisses they'd shared were working up to something important, and from the way Lex's penis pushed against her thigh, she had a good idea what that important event would be.

Probably not here and now. Little Ben and Cora might be partly deaf, but there were limits as to what Gillian would do in public. She and Lex wouldn't always be in public, though, at least not if she could help it.

At least they were finally horizontal, and that made for some interesting developments. After thoroughly exploring the options in mouth-to-mouth contact, Lex began journeying elsewhere. As his warm lips moved down her throat, she had the presence of mind to reach between them and pull her glasses out of her cleavage.

"I shouldn't be doing this," he muttered as he kissed the tops of her breasts. "Tell me to stop."

"There's a zipper in back. And you should know how the bra unhooks. You bought it."

"You're shameless." He nipped at her skin, but he found the zipper and inched it down. Then he unhooked the bra with a snap of his wrist.

Her dress gaped open a little, but not enough for what she had in mind. "More zipper."

The professor's voice droned on. "And now, let's consider the dazzling sight of the Milky Way. Milk has always been a powerful symbol to mankind, signifying his awe of the nurturing qualities of a woman's breast."

With perfect timing, Gillian's dress came free.

"Nurture me," Lex whispered against her skin.

The man had technique. An amazingly quiet technique, too. Without making any of the usual sounds that would reveal what he was doing, he soon had her writhing in his arms and clamping her mouth closed to keep from moaning out loud.

So that he had access to both breasts, Lex had changed their positions so that she was under him, which gave her the cherished view of the stars. Without her glasses the stars were blurry, but she didn't care. She buried her fingers in Lex's hair and noticed that starlight reflected in the silky strands. If this wasn't heaven, she didn't want to go.

All around her she could hear others enjoying each other in the warmth of the night. The sounds of rustling clothes, smothered groans, and half-swallowed whimpers were carried off on a sea breeze. Whether it was from group pressure or Lex's technique, she was venturing closer and closer to an orgasm.

She wanted that desperately, but there were considerations. Reluctantly, she cupped Lex's head in both hands and tugged him free. "Up here," she whispered.

He leaned his forehead against hers and gulped for air. "Am I doing it wrong?"

"You're doing it so right that I'm going to come in a minute."

His soft laugh was pure male. "Go for it."

"Not in this dress. Not in these fancy panties you bought me."

"Damn." He muffled his labored breathing against her shoulder. "Okay, we can do this." He reached up to the back of the lounge chair where his jacket lay folded and pulled it down. Then he put his mouth close to her ear and explained how she could have her orgasm and save her dress.

"But what about your jacket?"

"As if I care. Come on."

It took some subtle maneuvering, but soon he had her panties in his hand. He stroked them over his cheek. "Already damp." He sounded pleased.

"I told you."

"The red ones?"

"Serendipity. The bra and panties went with the dress."

"And now the panties belong to me." He shoved them in the pocket of his slacks.

"Lex." She was both scandalized and thrilled. He had the makings of a rogue.

"Even nerds should enjoy a thrill now and then." Using his jacket as cover, he pulled up her skirt. With the jacket under her and the lapels open enough to give him access, he slid his hand between her thighs. "Are you loud?" he murmured. "I'll bet you're loud." He teased her lightly with his fingers.

"I'll be quiet." She quivered with longing. "I promise."

"I'm taking no chances." He covered her mouth with his as he sank his fingers deep inside her.

His head blocked her view of the stars, but considering what he was doing with his fingers, she didn't mind. Between his kiss and his relentless stroking, she was seeing stars soon enough—the shooting kind that rocketed past as her body clenched in a glorious climax. When cries rose up in her throat, he deepened his kiss.

But she was very much afraid she'd made the lounge chair creak. Considering the force of her orgasm, it was a wonder she hadn't fallen off the darned thing. Wow. She didn't know whether to attribute the glory of it to Lex, her, the sexually drenched surroundings, or a combination of the above. But she was one happy chickadee.

Gradually Lex eased up on his kiss. When he finally lifted his head, he wasn't breathing too steadily, either. Slowly he withdrew his hand and wrapped the jacket lapels around her thighs. "I almost joined you on that one."

"And then what would we have done?"

"I would have carried my multipurpose jacket in front of me all the way back to the cabin."

"Don't you love that jacket?"

"It's quickly becoming my favorite accessory. But we probably should put you back together before Little Ben winds up the lecture and starts with the quiz."

She reached up to touch his face. "Thank you." She wished she could see his eyes better, so she could tell how he'd reacted to this latest event.

He heaved a sigh. "You know I loved every minute. But we really have to stop this craziness." He hooked her bra and zipped her dress. "What if someone had tried something while we were involved?"

"With all these people around? Besides, the Italian guy from the karaoke bar wasn't here. I checked."

"I checked, too, but that doesn't mean he couldn't be lurking in the shadows."

"I still say I'm safe in a crowd."

Lex blew out a breath. "Safe from everyone but me."

CORA DIDN'T SPY ON LEX AND GILLIAN, BUT SHE WAS well aware that they'd become involved in some serious canoodling during the lecture. Excellent. All along she'd hoped that they would become interested in each other.

The Marilyn disguise was part of her plan in that regard, besides being a good subterfuge. Gillian had needed more self-confidence to attract a man like Lex. He wouldn't care what color her hair was or whether she wore sexy clothes. But he was attracted to confidence. Gillian was developing more every minute.

Dante, on the other hand, needed someone who needed *him*. Cora had known he wouldn't fall hard for the hootchie-mama types he usually dated. They were a little *too* confident to awaken Dante's protective instincts. Cora hadn't counted on someone as perfect as BJ showing up, but here she was, and Dante was soon going to be her slave.

So far, Cora was pleased with the way things were working out. Dante needed a steadying influence in his life, especially if he couldn't lean on Lex anymore. Lex could very well end up leaving the country at the end of this cruise, which would make BJ's presence in Dante's life vital.

Assuming Gillian had to make a run for it, Cora felt sure Lex would decide to go with her. After all, they could have great sex in Brazil or Chile as easily as they could have great sex in L.A. With the sparks flying between the two of them, Cora had no doubt they would have great sex. They'd made a reasonable start tonight.

"And that concludes the lecture portion of the program," Benjamin said. "Put your thinking caps on, because now we'll have the trivia quiz, and after that, we'll take a peek into astrology!"

Cora smiled. *Put your thinking caps on.* Benjamin was too cute.

He turned to her. "Ready to help me with the transparencies for the quiz?"

"Of course."

"I think the lecture went well. Do you think they enjoyed it?"

"Oh, I'm sure of it. You were a smash hit." Someone could shove splinters under her fingernails before she'd ever tell him that his audience had been making out like mad during his lecture. "I keep forgetting to ask you. Did the cruise line give you a roommate?"

"Uh, no, they did not. I have a single." He turned on the projector and glanced over at her. "I hope that's a leading question instead of idle curiosity."

"My dear man, I never ask questions out of idle curiosity."

"A woman after my own heart."

"I couldn't have said it better myself." Benjamin might be vertically challenged, but at her stage of life, Cora didn't consider that a problem. She didn't give a damn what people thought of her choice of a beau, and once they were horizontal, all sorts of adjustments could be made.

Besides that, she'd noticed that Benjamin had a very prominent nose. In her experience, that meant that his height had nothing to do with the price of beans. When it counted, he'd be there for her.

Thirteen

NEIL NOTICED THAT THE LIGHTS WERE STILL OUT ON Deck A where the astronomy lecture was being held. Briefly he considered whether he could make use of the cover of darkness to take care of his little problem. Gillian would be out there, no doubt, with her nerdy boyfriend, Lex.

But so would a bunch of other people, not to mention the professor and Cora. Neil didn't have a plan in place, so acting on impulse might be a huge mistake. When he made his move, he wanted the result to be final. Score: Neil Rucker, 1; Gillian McCormick, 0. As in, dead.

He couldn't guarantee that would happen if he went off half-cocked. Just because he could identify her now didn't mean he should act immediately. He'd had a little problem with impulsive behavior in the past, but that wasn't going to screw him up now. This time he'd do exactly what needed to be done, but no death would take place before its time.

Smiling at his own wit, he searched for number 106. If Jared Stevenson the Third wasn't waiting in there, hyperventilating at the thought of a visit from Nancy Roth, then Neil would give up his entire collection of sex toys. And he wasn't about to do that.

There was an actual doorbell next to the door, but Neil thought that was pretentious. A meeting such as this required a soft rap on the door, so that's what he did.

The door opened almost immediately, and Jared stood there, literally panting. He'd ditched the navy blazer and stood there in—Neil had to bite the inside of his cheek to keep from laughing—a burgundy silk smoking jacket. "Nancy! You came!"

"May it be the first of many times." Neil looked to see if Jared got the double entendre, but it had obviously been lost on him.

"Indeed!" Jared smiled, revealing teeth that only an orthodontist could love. What an oversized set of choppers. "I hope this is the first of many rendezvouses."

Neil managed not to shudder. Jared knew just enough French to be dangerous. "That's my hope, too." He batted his fake eyelashes. "I brought us a few things to enjoy." He held up the bottle of wine, a banana, and an apple. The apple was a joke that only he would be able to appreciate in the course of the evening, but then, this was mostly about him, wasn't it?

"Welcome to my little part of the ship." Jared swept an arm to encompass a place that was easily twice as big as the dinky little cabin Neil shared with BJ. The bed looked king-sized, not that they'd be needing that for what Neil had in mind. There was also a sitting room and a sizable bathroom, from what he could see.

"It must be nice to be you," Neil said.

"I'm not so sure. Do you know what it's like to be the only one around who gets it?"

Neil nodded. "Trust me, I know exactly what it's like."

"I'm a member of Mensa, and yet nobody wants to give me any control. Does that make sense? I have more brains than all of them put together!"

"It must be frustrating." Neil could imagine the Stevenson family in a panic over how to manage this clueless guy who thought he knew everything.

"You have no idea. But enough of that. Shall we open that wine you brought?"

"My thoughts, exactly."

Jared's eyes gleamed. "I knew from the minute we talked on the phone that you and I were in sync. We understand each other."

"I believe that's true." Neil waited while Jared uncorked the wine, poured them each a glass, and drained his. It was good wine, which made the gulping even more of a travesty. But getting Jared a little tipsy served Neil's purposes. "Another glass?"

"Why not?" Jared splashed more of the wine into his goblet and drained that one, too. He was either eager or nervous. Maybe both. "You're not drinking much," he said.

"I had champagne at dinner. I'm still feeling it." A total lie.

"You moved to Cora's table, didn't you?" Jared poured himself more wine. "An old friend of the family, Cora is. I helped her out with some room arrangements."

"Really?" This might be news he could use.

"She wanted a couple of her friends, two nerds with no social skills, to be in the stateroom next to hers. I saw no harm in it, so I made the arrangements."

"That would be Lex and Dante?" Neil didn't see either one of them as true nerds. Lex might be more so than Dante, but outfits did not a nerd make.

"That's right!" Jared's pointy finger wobbled a little as he jabbed it in Neil's direction. "Give that man a prize."

"I know what my prize would be, if I could have anything I wanted."

"Well, you *can* have anything you want, Nancy!" Jared leered at Neil. "You are so hot."

Neil sauntered closer, swinging his hips as he went. Then he leaned in for a kiss, which totally reduced Jared to a puddle. "I want you naked," he murmured.

"Oh, God." Jared couldn't get his clothes off fast enough. Soon he stood in the middle of the room like a giant pink baby with an erection. The man had zero muscle definition except for the prominent display between his legs. "Now what? Will you get naked, too?"

"Not this time, Jared, honey." Neil had decided to wait to reveal his little secret. First he wanted Jared to be completely under his spell. After tonight, he would be. "First Nancy's going to give you a spanking. You know you need one."

Jared's eyes bulged. "Uh, well, I—"

Neil positioned himself on the sitting room couch and patted his knee. "Come here. Nancy's going to turn you over her knee. It's what you deserve, you bad boy."

With a bleating sort of moan, Jared did as he was told. His rigid penis fit between Neil's thighs, his pink butt shone rosy in the lamplight, and his head and arms hung toward the floor. Combined with the wine he'd drunk so fast, he must be dizzy as a daisy in the wind. So much the better.

Neil wasn't hugely into S and M, but there was a certain amount of excitement in slapping his open palm against that quivering butt until the skin turned red. Judging from Jared's moans, the cruise director was into it. When Neil decided the time was right, he jammed the banana up Jared's ass. Jared came immediately, bellowing out his gratitude. That was the moment when Neil stuck the apple in Jared's open mouth.

The crunch of those teeth on the apple nearly brought Neil off, but he controlled the urge. A person didn't want to give in to a climactic urge while fully taped. When he stood, Jared thumped to the floor and lay there, an apple in one end and a banana in the other. Fruit cocktail.

Neil took his leave. He was reasonably certain that Jared had never had an evening quite like this one. He would want more, and Neil assumed he wouldn't much care whether Neil was a cross-dresser or an orangutan, so long as Neil could deliver the goodies.

And the more goodies Jared wanted, the more black-mailable he became. Neil hadn't counted on a situation such as Jared presented, but he wasn't about to pass up the opportunity now that it had presented itself.

The lights were back on for the quiz part of the astronomy lecture. Eventually BJ would return to the room, probably wanting a gab fest. Neil planned to change into his designer nightwear before she arrived, and then he'd gab as far into the night as she wanted. She was his cover, and he wasn't about to mess with that.

BY THE TIME THE LIGHTS CAME UP, LEX HAD HELPED Gillian straighten her clothes and she was once again lying on her own lounge chair. She'd even located her glasses, which had dropped to the deck sometime during the action. When she put them on and glanced at him with a secret smile, he fought the urge to suggest they go below and hang a DO NOT DISTURB sign on his cabin door.

If he did that, he knew he'd never be able to explain it to Dante, not after the lecture he'd given Dante about getting mixed up with a client. Lex had to talk with Dante and admit his failings, and soon, because Dante was no dope. He'd figure things out.

Lex glanced over to where Dante and BJ were snuggled on the same lounge chair. Dante caught Lex's eye and gave him a thumbs-up. Lex wasn't sure whether to return the signal or not. Returning it could mean that he'd spent the lecture period making out, too. Although he had, he wasn't ready to advertise it. So he gave Dante a noncommittal wave.

"Who're you waving at?" Gillian asked.

"Dante."

Gillian craned her neck to look and then settled back with a smile. "They look cozy. Are you sure we need to stay in our own chairs?"

"I think it's a good idea for several reasons."

"So there's reason number one and reason number two?"

"At least."

"Are you going to tell me what they are?"

"Nope." His main reason was her current lack of panties. No way could he cuddle without reacting to that private knowledge.

Secondly, he wasn't ready to advertise their new status to Dante. Fortunately, Dante was too involved with BJ to notice anything unusual about Gillian. She looked a little rumpled and flushed, but her makeup was still perfect. He couldn't get over that mystery. Except for the wet spot on his jacket, which he'd folded inside so it wouldn't show, and her panties in his pocket, there was no real evidence of what had happened.

That didn't change the fact that Lex had succumbed to temptation. He could tell himself that it wouldn't happen again, but he wouldn't believe it. Knowing someone as beautiful as Gillian was hot for him had seriously compromised his moral stance. Considering what had just taken place, he thought she might actually welcome a suggestion that he go with her to South America.

Consequently, at this point he was making bargains with himself. The argument went something like this— his job was to keep Gillian from harm. In order to do that, he had to stay physically close to her. Because of their sexual chemistry, that closeness naturally led to activities such as they'd recently enjoyed. Such activities could be allowed if, and only if, there was no immediate danger.

He pictured himself making that argument to Dante. Then he pictured Dante falling on the floor in a fit of hysterics. Okay, so Lex's recently minted argument made mincemeat of the *Don't get involved with clients* rule.

Too bad he'd ever said such a dumb thing, but it had sounded reasonable at the time. Now he'd have to put up with Dante's ridicule. Given a choice between Dante's ridicule and never touching Gillian's breasts again, Lex would take the ridicule.

Maybe he'd tell Dante his eventual plan of going with Gillian when she jumped ship. No, he'd better not say anything about that yet. Dante might not take well to losing his partner so early in their PI career. Lex would have to think of how to make that up to him. For one thing, he could have all of Cora's fee.

Gillian nudged his lounge chair. "The first question to the starlight trivia quiz is up on the screen. Partners are allowed to share answers. What's the name of Pluto's moon?"

Because he'd missed most of Little Ben's lecture, Lex had to dig into his memory. "Charon."

"Thanks!" Gillian scribbled in her notebook. "I'll turn in the answers for both of us."

"You're trying to win another prize?"

"Sure, why not?"

"Because we didn't listen to the lecture, in case you've forgotten."

Her smile told him she'd forgotten nothing. "How do you know I wasn't multitasking?"

"If you heard that lecture . . ." He paused and leaned closer. "Then I deserve a failing grade in sexual stimulation."

"Actually, I'd give you an A, even a weighted A. I totally missed the lecture, but we both aced our astronomy classes, so I'll bet if we pool our resources, we can win."

If that meant he'd get to lean close to her and look into those big brown eyes, he was in. "Okay."

"Good. I've got the next one covered. The giant volcano on Mars is Mount Olympus."

"Good thing you knew that. My brain's still fried. By the way, what's the prize?"

"I don't even know." She filled in their answer. "I just love any kind of trivia. Don't you?"

"Yeah. Yeah, I do." And in that moment, he knew exactly what Dante had been trying to explain when he'd said that, bam, he knew he'd found the one. On the face of it, that kind of certainty made no sense. So far all Lex knew was that both he and Gillian loved sex and trivia. Logically that wasn't enough to base a lifetime on. And yet, here under a summer night of stars, it seemed like more than enough.

"I CAN'T BELIEVE LEX TURNED OUT TO BE AN ARIES! I knew Aries men and Cancer women weren't a good match, but I had no idea it was so bad. Maybe I've been kidding myself that we're compatible." Gillian followed Cora into their shared cabin.

"Don't let astrology ruin a good thing." She picked up a piece of a paper lying on her pillow. "Here's our schedule for tomorrow."

Gillian wasn't interested in the schedule. "But do Lex and I really have a good thing? You heard him just now when we were arguing in the hall. He thinks astrology is bogus. He's completely closed his mind to the—"

"Of course he has. Astrology is telling him you two aren't meant for each other, and he doesn't want to hear it. That's a compliment, if you ask me. He wants that connection." She glanced at the schedule. "Oh, look! A limbo contest."

"All he really wants is sex."

Cora laughed. "That's the case with ninety-nine percent of the male population. First comes sex, then comes marriage, then comes the bambino in the baby carriage."

"When you put it that way, I suppose it was stupid for us to argue about it. Whatever we have isn't going to amount to marriage and bambinos, considering my future plans, but still, I was enjoying the moment."

"So keep enjoying it."

Gillian sighed. "I suppose, but now I'll be looking for things like his lack of a romantic attitude, whereas I'm all about romance. How can I be involved with a man who doesn't have a romantic bone in his body?"

"Get interested in a different bone." Cora took out her diamond earrings and dropped them into the jewelry box on the dresser.

"Cora!"

"Hey, sweetheart, I'm old, but I'm not dead. In fact,

I'm wondering if I would throw my back out if I tried the limbo. I used to love that."

"I need romance."

"I'll bet Lex could do romance if you let him know that's what you need."

"You think?" Gillian sat on her bed. "Name one romantic thing he's ever done."

"That would be difficult considering he's never tried to woo me."

"He hasn't tried to woo me, either. It's just been . . . convenient." And she was the one who'd suggested what happened tonight. She'd been the one bewitched by the stars and the warm night. "Look at Dante and BJ. They're probably still strolling around the deck together. His Libra goes great with her Gemini. And your Leo goes even better with Little Ben's Gemini. You two are the perfect match."

"I do think it might work out. Ballroom dancing might be a little awkward, but I suppose he could stand on my feet, like one of those dancing dolls."

"Cora, he's not that short."

"He's pretty short. But dancing isn't everything. Hey, I wonder if he can limbo?"

"I don't even know if Lex dances." Gillian stood and walked over to the dresser to get out one of the nightgowns Cora had loaned her. Might as well go to bed. "If he does dance, he probably doesn't think there's a single romantic thing about it."

"There was another event for tomorrow that sounded like fun. Couples get in the pool together and go underwater. Then you have to guess the word your partner is saying."

"Oh, God. Bathing suit time. I'd forgotten about that."

"You'll look great. And Lex's tongue will be hanging out."

"Well, sure. Because he's all about the sex, and bathing suits are sexy." Gillian sighed. Until the professor had introduced Couples Astrology, the evening had been going along so well. They hadn't won the trivia contest but they'd come close, and Gillian had thoroughly enjoyed the flirting that had been involved in collaborating on the answers.

Then, supposedly just for fun, the professor had thrown in the astrology info. That's when she'd discovered the Aries and Cancer situation, and the professor had provided an overview of that combination. None of the news had been good.

Afterward, Dante and BJ had wandered off for a stroll around the deck, but Gillian hadn't felt like it, especially after Lex had said he thought astrology was stupid. So when Little Ben had said he'd walk Cora to her stateroom, Gillian had decided to go back with them and turn in. Lex had followed, and they'd argued all the way down the hall.

All the good feelings from the day and evening they'd spent together had vanished. Now she wanted her panties back. But she could hardly have asked for them with Cora and Little Ben right there.

The older couple had tried to mediate the argument, but it had been no use. Finally Little Ben had given Cora a sweet good-night kiss on the cheek and left. With a glare, Gillian and Lex had parted, each going into their separate rooms.

What a crummy ending to the evening. Disgusted with the outcome, Gillian wrenched open the drawer to get her nightgown. Then she paused in confusion. Everything in the drawer was a jumbled mess. Bathing suits, shorts, and T-shirts were all tumbled together as if they'd been whirling in a dryer.

Surely she hadn't left it that way. "Cora?"

"What, darling?"

"Did you go into this drawer looking for something?"

"Sweetheart, that's your drawer. I wouldn't go rummaging through it without asking you first. You know, I think I'm going to try that limbo contest. What's the worst that could happen? I could end up in traction. Then Benjamin would have to visit and bring me flowers."

"You're absolutely sure you didn't look for something in the drawers I'm using?"

"Yes, dear, I'm sure. I may be a little absentminded, but I would remember going through your things, which I definitely didn't do." She paused and looked at Gillian. "Is something wrong?"

"I hope not." She opened the other drawer where she'd put her underwear. Complete chaos. Her stomach started to hurt. But everything seemed to be there. Everything except . . . with growing panic she pawed through the silky Victoria's Secret items that Lex had bought her.

"Gillian, what is it?" Cora came over to stand beside her. "Is something missing?"

"I put my passport in this drawer." She started throwing the underwear out on the floor. "I know I did."

"Maybe it's in the other drawer. Sometimes I'm sure I've put something somewhere, and it turns up somewhere else."

"God, I hope you're right." She emptied the drawer and opened the other one. When she'd emptied that one, too, and she was surrounded by piles of her clothes, she tried to think. Had she moved it somewhere else?

But even if she had, that didn't explain the state of the drawers, which had been ransacked.

Her throat dry, she stood on shaky legs. "Cora, I hate to say this, but somebody's been in here. And I . . ." She swallowed. "I think they took my passport."

Fourteen

STEWING IN HIS FRUSTRATION, LEX HAD TROUBLE realizing that the noise he was hearing was his walkie-talkie. He grabbed it from the dresser where he'd tossed it when he'd stalked into the room.

If it was Gillian wanting to make up, he shouldn't do it. What he'd told Dante was absolutely right. Getting involved with a client was a mistake, and he should have that tattooed on his butt. Better yet, he should have it tattooed on a body part that he was more likely to see every day. Like the body part that had gotten him into this fix in the first place.

He clicked the button on the walkie-talkie. "This is Lex."

Gillian didn't sound like she wanted to make up. Instead she sounded petrified. "Someone's been in the room. I think they stole my passport. Uh . . . over."

"I'll be right there. Over." Lex clicked off the walkie-talkie. Then he switched to Dante's frequency and headed for the door as he waited for Dante to answer. Lex was in the hall by the time Dante responded. "Someone's been in Gillian's room," he said. "Get down here. Over."

"I'll be right there. Over."

The metallic taste of fear sat bitterly on Lex's tongue. Someone had penetrated the Marilyn disguise. *Damn it, damn it, damn it.*

Embarrassing as it was to admit, he'd been trying to convince himself that nobody on board this ship was a threat to Gillian. He'd wanted her to make a clean get-away via this cruise ship, but that had been unrealistic. Phil Adamo had a reputation for a reason. Obviously he didn't want his stepson to go to prison, and the only way to guarantee that was to eliminate the witness.

Lex knocked on Gillian's door once, and she flung it open immediately. Dante came running down the hall, and they both crowded into the room and locked the door behind them.

"Locks don't mean anything." Gillian was breathing hard. "They were in here. We noticed some other things— makeup moved, shoes out of place in the closet, clothes on hangers shoved to one side. I've messed up my two drawers, but Cora hasn't touched hers and they're in the same condition."

Lex took a look in the closet and opened a couple of dresser drawers. There was no doubt someone had been going through Gillian and Cora's stuff.

"Not very subtle, were they?" Dante said.

"That's what worries me," Lex said. "If they got in that easily, they could have looked for what they wanted without disturbing anything. It's as if they want us to know they were here."

"Why?" Gillian was wide-eyed, obviously fighting terror.

"I don't know." Lex couldn't make any sense of it. If Adamo had a man on the cruise who was assigned to get rid of Gillian, maybe even Hector Michelangelo, he'd have no emotional investment in the job. He'd be efficient, careful. He wouldn't ransack someone's room and steal things.

"This is sort of creepy," Dante said.

Lex agreed, but saying so wasn't going to help Gillian any. He turned to her, and all he wanted to do was take her in his arms, but that wouldn't accomplish much at the moment. "Are you sure the passport is missing?"

"I don't know where it could be if it's not in one of those drawers. You're welcome to double-check. I dumped everything back in the drawers, and I didn't find it, but maybe I'm too upset to see what's in front of my eyes."

"I'll look," Dante said.

Lex shouldered him aside. "I'll do it." He had the same aversion to Dante's going through Gillian's underwear that he'd had earlier today. Was it only this morning that he'd gone shopping at Victoria's Secret?

"I'll check my suitcase and my purse." Gillian hauled her rolling bag out from under the bed while Lex went down on his knees in front of the dresser.

He checked the bottom drawer first, and there was no passport lurking in the midst of her nightgowns, bathing suits, shorts, and T-shirts. Then he tackled the next drawer. Ah, that underwear. He'd agonized over what to buy, and here it was, ready to cradle her voluptuous body.

He had much more knowledge of that body, now, and touching her bras and panties brought back the pleasure of making love to her up on deck under cover of darkness and a very boring astronomy lecture. None of that mattered now. Everyone would be much happier if he could find her passport tucked somewhere in the midst of all this colorful silk and lace. He needed to concentrate on that.

But there was no passport. He closed the underwear drawer. "Sorry. It's not in there."

"It's not in the suitcase or my purse, either." Her color wasn't good.

"We need to check the floor," Cora said.

"Right." Lex started with his quadrant. "Cora, you don't have to do this."

"Thank you for the special consideration, Alexander, but I can still get on my hands and knees."

"Okay, then let's each take a quarter of the room. Look under both beds."

For a couple of minutes, there was no sound in the room other than the scuff of knees and hands over the carpet. They kept bumping heads and fannies in the process.

"I would hate for this to end up on *America's Funniest Home Videos*," Dante said. "Four people crawling around on the floor of a place this size is not cool."

Gillian sat back on her heels, and her voice quivered. "We're not going to find anything."

"I don't think we are, either," Cora said. "And I'm happy to report that my back didn't go out."

"Glad to hear that, at least," Lex said. "Dante?"

He got to his feet. "I think we have to face the fact that the passport's gone."

"So do I," Lex said. "We've scoured the place. Assuming someone was in the room, it seems likely they took the passport."

"They could have had anything in here." Gillian twisted her hands in front of her. "Why that?"

Lex grasped at anything that might calm her. "I suppose it could be a crew member who is into identity theft."

"That wouldn't explain the stuff tossed around," Dante said. "Someone who wants to steal her identity wouldn't want her to discover that the passport was missing right away. They might even plan to return it after they'd scanned in all the info. So they'd want to be very careful and not leave a mess like this."

Cora stood and smoothed her dress. "So they intended for us to know they were here. What now?"

"Ordinarily we would notify ship security," Lex said. "But if we draw extra attention to the situation, the crew will be watching Gillian like a hawk and it'll be harder for her to disappear once we dock in Mexico."

Gillian swallowed hard, loud enough so that everyone could hear her. "Or m-maybe I'll disappear s-sooner than that. Maybe soon I'll be swimming with the f-fishes."

Lex glanced at her and could tell she was about to lose it. She was blinking fast, but the tears gathering in her eyes would start falling any second. "Here, take my handkerchief." He reached into his pocket and pulled out . . . her panties.

For one awful moment, everyone stood staring at the red Victoria's Secret item dangling from Lex's hand. There was no retracting what he'd done. Each person in the room knew exactly what he'd pulled out of his pocket.

"Wow," he said. "This is awkward."

Dante coughed. "What I have to know is whether you had them in your pocket *before* you came in the room just now, or whether you filched them from Gillian's underwear drawer while you were looking for her passport."

"Um, well, I—" Lex snuck a peek at Gillian. She looked on the verge of something. She was sort of red in the face, but he couldn't tell if she was about to laugh or cry.

"Take your time, buddy," Dante said. "If it's answer A, then okay. You're a stud and I have to give you credit. If it's answer B, then there are some things you and I need to talk about, you being my partner and all. I mean, you did insist on shopping for that stuff, and I didn't think too much about it at the time, but—"

"Before," Gillian said. "He had them in his pocket before." Then she burst out laughing and snatched the panties from Lex's hand.

At least Lex hoped she was laughing. It sounded like it, but tears were streaming down her face at the same time. He dug deeper in his pocket, and this time he came out with an actual handkerchief. "Here," he said. "And I'm sorry."

"Personally, I'm relieved," Dante said. "I'm all for alternate lifestyles, so long as somebody else is leading them. I might have been able to work through discovering that my best friend was into women's underwear, but I'm not saying it would have been an easy transition for me. We go back a long way, and I—"

"Dante," Cora said. "Shut up."

"Yes, ma'am." Dante sat down on Cora's bed.

Gillian used Lex's handkerchief to mop her eyes and blow her nose. "Thanks." She held the handkerchief in one hand and her panties in the other. "I've never known the etiquette of this."

Cora cleared her throat. "I don't believe Emily Post ever envisioned something along these lines, darling. If you gave the panties to Lex and you want him to keep them as a souvenir, then I suggest you return them now. We'll all pretend this never happened."

"You can pretend if you want," Dante said. "But I'm here to say I'll never forget it. The look on the Lexter's

face when he pulled those undies out of his pocket . . .
now there's a moment for *America's Funniest Home
Videos!*"

"Dante . . ." Cora sent him a warning glance.

Gillian hiccupped. "I wasn't talking about the panties.
I meant Lex's handkerchief. Do I give it back to him now,
or what?"

"Full of snot?" Dante made a face. "I should hope you
wouldn't. See, this is why tissues were invented, although
if Lex had been a tissue kind of guy, we wouldn't be sharing this special moment."

"You can give me the handkerchief," Lex said.

"Well, now." Cora glanced at Gillian. "I would say
that's a very romantic gesture."

Dante wrinkled his nose. "You would? Then let me
pass that on to Little Ben. We'll see if he has any used
hankies around. Maybe he could make a little bouquet of
them."

"Honestly." Cora put her hands on her hips. "That's
not what I meant and you know it."

"I know. I'm the comic relief around here, although the
Lexter's giving me a run for my money with his panties-
in-the-pocket routine. Hey, there's an idea. How about
Gillian keeps the hankie and Lex keeps the panties?"

"I'll keep both things," Gillian said. She smiled at Lex.
"And thanks for making me laugh so hard. I feel much
better, now."

"That's a plus," Cora said. "But we still don't have a
course of action."

Lex had been thinking about that, once Gillian had let
him off the hook about the panties. Until she'd been ready
to admit how he'd come by those panties, he'd been prepared to look like a deviant to save her reputation. It

warmed his heart to know that she'd sacrifice that reputation for his sake, even though they'd had that dumb argument about astrology.

Considering that recent argument, he wasn't sure if she'd go for his plan, but it was the only one he could think of. "With all due respect, Cora, I don't feel good about leaving Gillian alone in this room with only you as protection."

Cora sighed. "I knew I should have taken that tae kwon do class when I had the chance."

Gillian studied Lex with interest. "So what do you have in mind?"

"We need to switch roommates."

NEIL HAD ACCEPTED THE FACT HE'D HAVE TO SLEEP in his wig, but fortunately it fit him perfectly. He'd become good at giving himself a buzz cut that acted like Velcro to hold it on. Someone could yank it off, but he wasn't about to let that happen.

He wasn't crazy about sleeping with his privates taped, though, especially after he'd made himself feel so good in the shower. And he loved the way his jade silk pajamas felt against his quite happy dick. Wearing a padded bra was necessary to make the top look right, but the bottoms were roomy and should cover the situation adequately, especially if he stayed in bed while BJ roamed around the room.

By the time BJ's key clicked in the lock, Neil was freshly shaved with a light dusting of makeup on. He'd propped himself up in bed with the covers drawn to his waist as he read the issue of *People* he'd thrown in his suitcase at the last minute.

Instead of coming right in, BJ called through the door. "Nance? You decent?"

Almost never, sweetie. "Sure!" He wondered if she was really that modest that she didn't want to chance walking in on him when he was undressing. That could be a good thing.

"Can I bring someone in?"

Hm. This was unexpected. "Male or female?"

"Female, of *course*. I wouldn't dream of having a *guy* in our room at this time of night."

What she didn't know. He put down the magazine, arranging it over his lap for good measure. "Then come on in!"

"Great." BJ appeared looking a little mussed, followed by a young woman with wire-rimmed glasses and her blond hair in . . .

Braids? Neil didn't think anybody over the age of ten wore braids these days. Between the braids and being on the skinny side, this girl looked about as alluring as a lamppost.

"Nance, this is Dorothy Sexton," BJ said. "This afternoon we shared a cab ride to the dock and then sort of lost track of each other. She saw me tonight with Dante, and—"

"That's working out, then?" Neil figured the mussed look was a good indication.

BJ's face turned pink. "Yeah, it is. Thanks to you."

Damn straight. But he didn't want to seem arrogant. "It might be the makeover that caught his eye, but after that, it was all up to you."

"It doesn't hurt that I'm a Gemini and he's a Libra. We found that out tonight at the lecture. You didn't come to that, did you?"

"No, no. I felt like a bubble bath and a good book."

"But we only have a shower."

Neil laughed. "A bubble *shower* then. I just know there were bubbles involved." And some jollies. He had to be the world's best masturbator, hands down. Or hands up and down, more like it.

"Fragrant bubbles," BJ said. "The room smells terrific."

"Why, thank you." Nancy did love her sweet-smelling lotions and potions.

"I see you're all ready for bed, and everything," Dorothy said. "We shouldn't be bothering you."

Neil stretched and yawned. "Well, I am a little bit tired." He had a good idea what this was all about, and it would require him getting out of bed and taking a chance his main man would create an unexplainable bulge in his silk pajamas.

"Then never mind." Dorothy started for the door.

"No, wait," BJ said. "Let Nance at least give you a few pointers before you go. You want to be ready for Hector in the morning, right?"

"Who's Hector?" Neil asked.

"This guy Dorothy met at dinner. Hector Michelangelo. Dorothy thinks he's really cute, but he's not paying attention to any of the women, out of shyness, probably."

"Probably." Dorothy nodded, which made her braids bob up and down. "And I'm shy, too, which makes things difficult."

"See, I told Dorothy that getting some pointers on my appearance made it easier for me to talk to Dante. And now look what's happened. We spent the whole lecture together and went for a walk afterward." BJ sent Neil a pleading look. "Could you give Dorothy a little bit of time? Maybe five minutes?"

Neil wanted to seem like a good egg. The more BJ liked him, the better this roommate situation would go.

A good egg would help Dorothy down the Yellow Brick Road of feminine attractiveness.

"Take down your braids." He eased back the covers and climbed carefully out of bed. So Pygmalion would ride again. Neil thought a haircut was in order, and he might have to loan out his spare tube of hair gel. His wig didn't require much styling, fortunately.

"What gorgeous pajamas! Is that silk?" BJ reached out, looking for all the world as if she intended to grab a handful of Neil's pajama bottoms.

"Yep." He dodged away and lost his balance. Somehow he managed to fall facedown across BJ's bed instead of faceup. No telling how the silk would have arranged itself.

"Nance, I didn't mean to scare you."

"It's okay." Neil eased himself off the bed and made sure his pajama bottoms were draped to effectively hide his pride and joy. "I'm just very, very ticklish."

"Oh! I'll have to remember that," BJ said. "Everywhere?"

"Absolutely everywhere. Even my ears are ticklish." Neil couldn't be sure, but he thought Dorothy was eyeing him with some suspicion.

If he did indeed give her a haircut, he'd have to be damned careful not to accidentally nudge her with his crotch. Behind those wire-rimmed glasses were the eyes of an intelligent lass. Neil didn't want to push his luck.

Fifteen

GILLIAN WASN'T PARTICULARLY SURPRISED BY LEX'S
announcement that they needed to switch roommates.
She didn't feel all that safe with only Cora in the room,
either. She had a good idea how Lex intended this switch
to go, too.

Now that she knew he was an Aries, she could see right
through him. He had her safety in mind, no doubt, but he
had a few other things in mind, too. If he slept in the same
room with her, that would relieve him of the need to be romantic to get what he wanted. Or so he might reason out.

She had other ideas on the matter. She would start with
pretending to misunderstand. "You want Dante to move
in with me?"

"Well, no. I thought—"

"Hey," Dante said. "If that's the way it has to go, I'll
live with it. I realize my personal life shouldn't play any
part in this. But I don't know how I'll explain it to BJ."

"Nonsense," Cora said. "You're not going to have to
explain anything to BJ. Having you move in with Gillian

would be ridiculous. Everyone has seen that Lex and Gillian are pairing up. If you and I arrange it so they can share a cabin, BJ will think you're a hero. She's not going to be worried about you sleeping with an eighty-two-year-old woman."

Dante grinned at her. "I don't know about that. You put on a convincing show for the guy in the black sedan this morning. Anybody who still knows exactly how to pinch a guy's butt can't be counted out."

"Why, thank you." Cora looked pleased with that assessment. "And if necessary, I'll talk to BJ. You're a sweet boy, Dante, but my tastes run more toward short professors of astronomy."

"Then it's settled," Lex said.

"Not quite." Gillian gazed at him. "Unless I missed something, you didn't ask me if I wanted you to move in here."

He met her gaze. "It's the only logical thing to do. Dante could serve the same function, but that causes more complications, and the other passengers, like BJ, for example, probably wouldn't accept that as easily."

"Gillian, darling." Cora walked over to her and put an arm around her waist. "I know this isn't quite what you envisioned. I wish it could be different, but we have someone on board with breaking-and-entering skills I hadn't imagined before this. I'll sleep much better knowing Lex is here to protect you."

Gillian didn't think she was going to sleep at all. Between sharing the room with Lex and having a killer stalking her, she might have to stay awake until they docked in Mexico. But this arrangement did make the most sense, and she didn't want Cora to worry. The woman had already put considerable effort into keeping her friend safe, and Gillian appreciated that more than she could say.

"Okay." She glanced at Lex. "We'll try it and see how it goes."

"Good." He didn't smile or show any emotion whatsoever. From his blank expression, anyone would think he'd just arranged to have his car taken in for repairs.

Maybe car repair would have brought more animation to his face, Gillian thought. He seemed to like his car a lot. She wouldn't have wanted him to gloat at his success in setting up this cohabitation, but she wouldn't have minded a little show of feeling. He'd certainly enjoyed their make-out session up on deck, and now he was proposing to spend entire nights with her. Surely that presented some possibilities to him.

If it did, he gave no indication as he left to pack up his belongings. Once he was gone, Gillian ducked into the bathroom and put her panties back on. Then she tucked Lex's handkerchief in a laundry bag provided by the cruise staff. Later on, she'd decide whether to send it to be cleaned. Right now she had more pressing concerns, like the issue of spending an entire night with the owner of the handkerchief.

As Gillian helped Cora get her things together, she discovered she wouldn't gain as much closet space as she'd expected. It turned out that Cora had brought the huge suitcase loaded mostly with outfits for Gillian.

"I knew you wouldn't bring them if I left it up to you." Cora stepped over the little sill into the bathroom and started packing her toiletries. "And I wanted you to have a dynamite wardrobe with plenty of choices for these few days, considering . . . well, under the circumstances."

Gillian leaned in the door of the bathroom and wondered

how in the world she'd feel comfortable sharing this tiny space, including a small shower, with Lex. "The circumstances being that I'll have to leave with only the clothes on my back," Gillian said.

"I didn't want to put that fine a point on it."

"It's okay. You can put a fine point on it. I need to face reality. For one thing, I don't have my passport. That could cause me problems." It occurred to her that the person who took it was sending a subtle message that she wouldn't be needing that passport anymore. What an awful thought.

"Don't you have a copy of it somewhere?" Cora asked.

"In my apartment, but how does that help?"

"Once you get settled, you can send me your address. I'll mail you your passport copy, plus anything else you need."

Cora's calm belief that Gillian would make it to safety and establish a mailing address was comforting, but Gillian couldn't ignore the dangers of that. "What if the Mob traces me through you?"

"I'll research the best way to keep that from happening. We can work through my lawyer, for one thing. Don't worry. I'll be very careful."

Gillian was cheered by the thought of contact with Cora. Jumping off into the middle of nowhere was frightening, but knowing there would be contact from home now and then helped a lot.

"It'll be fine," Cora said.

Gillian took a deep breath. "It will. I was getting really scared a little while ago, but the whole panty thing wiped out that hysterical reaction."

Cora kept packing her makeup case, but a little smile dimpled her cheek. "I thought something exciting was going on between you two during the lecture, but I couldn't see very well, and besides, I didn't want to spy on you."

"It was exciting," Gillian said. "And sexy. But I wouldn't say it was romantic."

Cora zipped her flowered case and turned to Gillian. "Did you happen to notice that Lex wasn't going to mention how he got those panties? He was waiting for you to say something. If you'd stayed quiet, I think he would have let Dante and me think he stole them out of your underwear drawer."

"I wouldn't have let you think that. It wouldn't have been fair to him."

"I know you wouldn't, but I'm only pointing out that until you told us, he was going to protect your honor. Revealing the circumstances was totally up to you."

Gillian hadn't thought of that. It was noble, in a way, now that she replayed the interaction. Dante had asked Lex, point-blank, and he hadn't answered.

"I think that's sort of romantic," Cora said.

"Sort of. I guess." Gillian wasn't going to suddenly agree that Lex was a romantic guy, because she had a hunch that he wasn't that way often, certainly not often enough for a person like her.

But once again, she was debating something pointless. The person who excited Lex looked like Marilyn Monroe. Gillian McCormick might not excite him at all.

A knock sounded at the door.

"Check the peephole," Cora said. "You have to remember to do that from now on."

"Right." She peered out and there was Lex, his image distorted by the fish-eye lens of the peephole. He had his backpack slung over one shoulder, but he was carrying his jacket, which was still folded the way it had been when they'd left the top deck.

Maybe using his jacket to save her dress had been sort of romantic, too. But she didn't want to go looking for romantic gestures and fool herself into thinking he was somebody he was not. It didn't matter anyway. In two days she'd never see him again.

CORA WASN'T HAPPY THAT SOMEONE HAD BROKEN into Gillian's room and stolen her passport, but she was overjoyed that Lex had decided to move in and protect Gillian from whatever lurked out there. Still smiling over that, she allowed Dante to help her pull her suitcase inside.

"You look like the Cheshire cat," he said. "Are you playing matchmaker with those two?"

"That would be foolish, wouldn't it? Lex has to go back to L.A. and work with you, and Gillian has to take off for South America."

Dante maneuvered the suitcase into the room. "I'm glad to hear you say that. I'd hate to think you were trying to get my partner to go to South America with Gillian."

"Did he say anything about that?" Cora's heart beat faster at the thought that her plan might have already taken root. To hide her excitement, she unzipped her suit-case and started hanging up her clothes.

"You know Lex." Dante plopped on his bed and lay back, his hands behind his head. "Plays his cards close to his vest. But he wouldn't want to leave me in the lurch. I trust him not to do that."

Cora loved Dante like a grandson, and she didn't want him to suffer. "Let's say Lex made the decision to go with Gillian—"

"Aha!" Dante bounced upright. "You are plotting for that to happen!"

"Dante, calm yourself. Lex isn't the only PI in the world. I'm sure you could find someone else who would make a good partner."

"Omigod. You do see him leaving. And no, I couldn't find someone else who would make a good partner. Lex is the steady one, the person who remembers to pay the rent, the person who convinces clients that we're legit. We all know I'm a loose cannon."

Cora paused, a purple dress over her arm. "That's your choice. You don't have to be a loose cannon."

"Cora, I've been loose ever since I knew the meaning of the word. It's what I am, what defines me. It's my essence."

"Oh, cut the psychobabble. Have you been seeing that shrink again?"

"Yeah, but only because she's hot. She likes my loose-cannonness."

Cora sighed and hung her purple dress in the closet. She'd never raised children of her own, but dealing with Lex, Dante, and Gillian gave her a good idea of the frustrations involved. "Dante, is BJ somebody who could be important to you?"

He looked away. "Uh, maybe."

"She doesn't strike me as the kind of girl who goes running after loose cannons."

"Look, we're veering off the subject here. BJ is a whole different thing. And if I expect to get her, I need to be a respectable PI. And to be a respectable PI, I need to be in business with Lex Manchester. End of story."

Cora decided nothing was going to be settled tonight. "We could be talking about something that could never happen."

"Yes, but I have the distinct impression that you're *promoting* this thing that might never happen. You're tickled pink that they're tucked into that room together, aren't you?"

"Yes, because it will help ensure that Gillian stays safe."

"That's not all that will take place in there, and you know it." Dante's dark eyes bored into hers.

"Don't be so certain. She's a Cancer and he's an Aries. That could ruin everything."

"You don't buy in to that any more than you buy in to whatever my shrink tells me." Dante flopped back on his pillow, his tone resigned. "Those two have chemistry, and once they're locked in the same room together, the inevitable will happen. I'm just praying it won't go to my buddy's head and make him decide to jump ship with her."

"You have no control over that."

Dante sat up again and snapped his fingers. "Maybe I do! I could use the walkie-talkie to call their room every ten minutes. That would interrupt the flow."

"You do that and I'll smother you with my pillow."

"It was only a thought."

"Sometimes the way your brain works frightens me, Dante. Do you want the bathroom first, or shall I take it?"

"You can have it first."

"Fine. I'll be out in a few minutes." She paused in the doorway. "Do I need to use my ear plugs tonight?"

"Meaning?"

"Do you snore?"

He looked offended. "No! Do you?"

"Probably." She laughed. "But don't worry about it. It's quite possible that by tomorrow night I'll be sharing Benjamin's room."

"Really?" Dante looked happier than he had since the discovery that Gillian's passport had been stolen. "You might not be spending the nights here?"

"Maybe not."

"Excellent." Dante gazed up at the ceiling, a broad smile on his face.

"I can guess where you're going with this thought."

"Yeah, you probably can. You were quite a swinger in your day, weren't you, Cora?"

"I had my moments. And speaking from that vast well of experience, may I offer one suggestion?"

"If it has to do with technique, I don't want to hear it. You're practically like my grandmother. That would be too weird."

"This isn't about technique. It's about babies. Use condoms."

"Oh, geez. I know that, for crying out loud. Geez."

"Protest all you want, but you keep saying you're a loose cannon. I want an assurance that your cannon will be wearing a rubber."

GILLIAN FELT THE TENSION GROWING AS LEX MOVED around the room putting away his stuff. He didn't have much stuff, not like Cora, but he was so much bigger. Every time he moved, she was aware of how much space he took up, just by breathing.

Eventually he turned to her. "I need to check something before we go any further. I should have done it before."

"What's that?"

"I need to see if they planted any bugs. I can go over the bathroom last, if you want to go on in there and start getting ready for bed."

Bed. Oh, God. This was going to be quite a night.

"Okay." She made a dash for it. She'd stripped to her underwear before realizing the nightgown she'd intended to put on was still in the drawer. She could either get dressed again and go back out, which would look dorky, or she could ask him to bring it to the door. Neither option was worth a damn.

She brushed and flossed her teeth while she thought about it. Then she took off all her makeup. Why hadn't she remembered to grab the nightgown? And for that matter, why hadn't she left a bathrobe hanging on the back of the door? She knew the answer to that one. She didn't have a bathrobe.

Finally she opened the door a crack. "Lex, could you please go in the bottom drawer and get my nightgown? I forgot to bring it in here." God, she felt like such an idiot.

"Sure thing." A drawer opened. "Which one? There's a black one and a white one in here."

She tried to remember exactly what they looked like. The black one was knee length, lace on top and satin for the skirt. The white one was shorter and had little spaghetti straps. "The black one," she said.

"Coming up." His footsteps approached the door.

She stuck her hand out through the opening and he placed the nightgown in it. Of course she dropped it. "Sorry."

"No problem. I didn't find any bugs, by the way." His bones cracked as he crouched down to pick it up again.

Something about that vulnerable little sound of bones popping got through her defenses. "Lex, I'm sorry if I've been a bitch."

He put the nightgown in her hand again. "I'm sorry if I've been a bastard."

"You haven't." Pulling the nightgown successfully through the opening this time, she closed the door and leaned against it, breathing hard. Had they made up? And if they had, what would happen now?

She left her underwear on and pulled the nightgown over her head. Of course it was one of Cora's, and Cora had never owned anything remotely sexless. Gillian had hoped the knee-length skirt would make this one seem modest. On a woman with a smaller chest, it might have been, but the bodice was constructed of black stretch lace that managed to schmoosh Gillian's breasts together so she had even more cleavage than usual.

Standing in front of the bathroom mirror, she pulled the lace this way and that, trying to make herself look less provocative. The red bra peeked through the lace, which made her think of a streetwalker with hang-ups. But if she took off the bra, the red would be replaced by bare skin.

With a soft curse she pulled the bodice down and took off the bra. Then she tugged the lace back up over her breasts. Now she looked like a porn queen. A black lace rose covered each nipple, but they were no better than pasties. She'd had no worries about either nightgown when she'd been rooming with Cora.

Should she have chosen the white one? She tried to picture herself asking Lex to bring her the other nightgown. No, that would make everything worse, and the white one wasn't going to turn out any better.

She gazed at herself in the mirror. Before she went out there, she had to make a decision whether she intended to have sex or not. One look at her and Lex would be ready. She couldn't blame him. The nightgown was an open invitation.

But they couldn't have sex. There were no condoms in the room. She should have thought of that earlier. Lex wouldn't have any. He'd come on this cruise to preserve and protect, not do the wild thing with his client. Okay, no condoms. She would go out there, and no matter how he reacted, she'd remind him of the facts of life.

Bracing herself, she picked up her clothes and opened the bathroom door. Stepping over the sill, she walked across the entryway to the closet opposite the bathroom. From the corner of her eye she could see him sitting on the edge of the far bed, watching her. She would hang up her dress and pretend that her heart wasn't trying to hammer its way out of her chest.

"All done?" he asked quietly.

"It's all yours." Then she heard what she'd said. Eyes wide, she turned. "I didn't mean that the way it sounded."

"Are you sure?" He stood and walked toward her. His gaze traveled over her nightgown, and his nostrils flared.

"Absolutely sure. Even if we wanted to have sex, we—"

"*If?* Any straight man in the universe would look at you in that black number and want to have sex." His eyes glowed with a definite heterosexual light. "Gillian, are you playing games with me?"

"No. No games. Cora loaned me two nightgowns, and both are . . ."

"Suggestive?"

"Uh-huh." She had trouble breathing, and damned if she didn't want to have sex, too. And he hadn't said anything particularly romantic, either. She was too easy.

"So it's not your fault that you look like a wet dream?"

"No. And besides, we don't have condoms." She spoke quickly, in order to get the information out before they lunged at each other. "So we can't have sex."

"Then I take it you weren't the one who put these under my pillow?" He stretched out his hand. There, lying in his palm, were two foil packets.

She looked up at him and tried to catch her breath. "No."

"Then it must have been the condom fairy." He smiled at her. "But don't worry. We won't have sex unless you want to." Closing his hand over the packets, he stepped into the bathroom and closed the door.

Sixteen

IN THE BATHROOM, LEX LEANED AGAINST THE SINK and gulped for air. How he'd restrained himself when confronted with Gillian in that nightgown, he'd never know. If they gave a medal for controlling your sexual urges, then he should be presented with a big fat one. With the way she was rapidly killing him, it might have to be awarded posthumously.

Going through the ritual of brushing his teeth steadied him some. So Cora had been the one who'd left the condoms. That clinched something that Lex had suspected all along—Cora wanted Lex to get involved with Gillian. Hiring him as a bodyguard had been the first step in roping him into her life for good.

If Cora had been setting a sexual trap, she'd done one hell of a job. Lex was in danger of walking around with a permanent hard-on, and he couldn't imagine how he'd make it through the night without crawling into bed with the bodacious Ms. McCormick. Wowza.

Cora had hired Dante, too, though. Had she been willing to hook Gillian up with either of them? That idea didn't sit well with him. He and Dante were best friends, but they weren't interchangeable parts in some grand scheme that Cora had dreamed up.

Gillian hadn't been given much chance to choose Dante, though. Circumstances had thrown Lex into the role, but maybe that was only the luck of the draw. She was in a vulnerable spot right now, so if Dante had stayed behind in order to drive her to the dock, he might have been the one who would have ended up next to her on a lounge chair, the one who would have volunteered to share a stateroom with her for the duration of the cruise to Mexico.

Okay, there was a train of thought capable of cooling his cannoli. He didn't relish being the convenient sex object. If Dante would have filled that position as easily, then that didn't make what he and Gillian had experienced special.

Maybe she was wishing Dante had been the one after the argument they'd had. Maybe a Libra man worked with a Cancer woman. What did he know about that hogwash, anyway?

By the time he'd left the bathroom and turned out the light, he was in a state of righteous indignation, which was preferable to a state of blue-balled arousal. He left the condoms in the bathroom. Maybe he should have thrown them away, but that might have been taking his current attitude a little too far. He didn't want to completely destroy his options.

He'd planned to sleep in his T-shirt and boxers during this trip, so that's the way he walked out into the room. Gillian was under the covers in the bed nearest the bathroom. With the sheet up to her neck and her eyes closed, she looked less like a sex goddess.

The hell she did. He knew exactly what she looked like under that sheet, and her coy pretense of being asleep only fired him up again. So much for righteous indignation. It evaporated in the heat generated by Gillian's presence in this small, very small, room.

"Suppose Dante had driven you to the dock?" he asked. "What do you think would have happened then?"

Her eyes popped open and she sat straight up, which meant the sheet fell down and her incredible breasts were once again on display as they threatened to break free of the stretchy black lace. "Exactly *what* are you implying?" Her dark eyes flashed fire and brimstone.

He was a little taken aback by the fury in her expression. "You're under a strain. You need someone to be there for you. I happen to be the one who—"

"That is quite enough!" Throwing back the covers, she jumped out of bed and grabbed the walkie-talkie. "Maybe I'll just call Dante right now and get him over here, because I'm damned sure not going to spend the night in the same room with *you*."

"Hold on." He didn't want this argument spilling over into the next room. He tried to grab the walkie-talkie, but she jerked it out of reach.

"You think that everything that's happened between us is only because you're handy? Is that what you think?" She tried to punch buttons on the walkie-talkie, but she was obviously too upset to make it work. "Damn it, how does this thing turn on?"

"Don't turn it on." He grabbed her. God, her skin was so soft.

She struggled against his grip. "Let me go."

He couldn't bear to. "Listen to me. You're in a bind, grasping at straws. It would only be logical that—"

"Logical? What about us is the least bit logical?" She wrenched away from him, and he had to let her go or risk bruising those soft arms.

"Gillian."

"Damn this thing!" She gave up on the walkie-talkie and threw it on her bed. "You talk about logic? I'm running away to South America! I have no business letting myself fall for anybody, let alone some PI who is trying to build a business in L.A., only likes me because I look like Marilyn, and is an *Aries*, for God's sake." She stood there breathing hard and glaring at him.

The glaring was one thing. He didn't like being glared at, but he could handle it. The hard breathing was the part that could break through his control. This was a woman who had made the mere act of breathing a piece of performance art.

Watching her breathing like that made it tougher to concentrate on what she was saying, but he had the feeling that what she'd just told him was very important. He fastened on the one statement that he knew was wrong. "You think I like you because you look like Marilyn?"

"Sure. She was a sex symbol. Everybody wanted to go to bed with her. Now Cora has made me over to look like her, complete with the dresses, the hair, and the makeup, so it's natural that you would see me and think Marilyn, which translates into bedroom thoughts."

Lex groaned. "That is so not true. I do look at you and think about a bedroom, but it's not because you look like some long-dead movie star."

She put her hands on her hips. "Well, I think it is. The real me has long brown hair, not short and blond. And I don't like wearing much makeup, and I don't dress in slinky outfits, and—"

"You're not wearing any makeup now, and you're still hot enough to bring me to my knees."

She blinked, as if she'd forgotten that she'd taken off all the war paint. "Oh." She put her hands up to her hair. "But I'm still blond, and I'm wearing this sexy night-gown."

"Is that your real body under the nightgown? Or are you about to reveal that you're wearing some sort of vinyl suit that gives you those curves? I know you didn't have time for implants, and everything looks real, so naturally I assumed that what I see is what you've got."

"Uh . . . it's all me." A smile struggled to break through and spoil the hissy fit she had going on. "My charms have always been . . . ample."

"Yeah." Saliva pooled in his mouth. He wanted her so much. "And that's a very good thing."

"But what about the brown hair? I'll bet you're partial to blondes and I currently fit the bill. But once this grows out, I'm done. I'm not into dyeing my hair."

She might not believe him if he told her brown sounded nice, so he tried a different approach. "I don't have a favorite hair color. I'm more interested in what's going on inside your head than what's growing on the outside. I like that you got an A in astronomy."

Her expression said she was only partly convinced. "But you think I would have been just as happy to share that astronomy lecture on deck with Dante? Is that what you were hinting at earlier?"

He was afraid to confirm or deny. She'd settled down and stopped trying to communicate with Dante on the walkie-talkie, so he hesitated to say anything more on the subject and get her riled up again. He wanted to contain this discussion within these four walls.

"Because if that's what you think, then you've insulted me and you've insulted yourself." She gazed at him for several seconds. "I've been attracted to you from the first minute I saw you." She pointed a finger at him. "*You,* not Dante. I like your blue eyes, your easy smile, your lean body, and the fact that you got an A in your astronomy class."

He was completely confused. "Then why don't you want to have sex with me?"

"I do want to have sex with you."

"All right!" He reached for her.

She stepped just out of reach. "But now that I've had some time to think about it, I sincerely believe it would be a bad idea."

"Is this about that Cancer, Aries thing?" If so, he was ready to strangle Little Ben.

"Partly."

"You know what I think about that."

"Yes, and you don't have to go into it again. I can see some basis for the evaluation, but if you can't, then—"

"What basis?" He really was going to have a word with that little Ph.D.

"I'm the candlelight, wine, and flowers type, and you, obviously, are not."

He blew out a breath and prayed for patience. "We're not exactly in a candlelight, wine, and flowers situation."

"No, but a guy with some romance in his soul could have improvised."

"Like how?" He'd love to hear how she thought he should have handled the past twenty-four hours differently.

"While I was in the bathroom just now, you were out here waiting, thinking we'd have sex. Am I right?"

"My mistake. I found the condoms under my pillow and thought you'd put them there. Now I know it was Cora."

"Even if I had put them there, you could have set the scene to make it more romantic."

He glanced around the room in complete bafflement. "Like how? I don't have candles, wine, or flowers."

"You could have folded back the covers on my bed. You could have used one of your shirts to cover the light and make it softer. You could have written me a sweet poem and propped it on my pillow."

"A *poem*? Are you sure you don't want Dante? He even has the right name to be a poet."

She sighed. "No, I don't want Dante. But you're making my point for me. I can tell from your reaction that you think all that would have been stupid. Whereas I would have been touched."

He studied her for several long seconds as he wrestled with the challenge she was throwing out. "You're right that I didn't think of any of that. Not once. Let me tell you what I was thinking about."

"That you only had two condoms?"

"Very funny." Actually he had thought about that. Knowing how she affected him, he hadn't thought that would be enough. But he wasn't about to admit that. "I was thinking that someone has the ability to get in the room, and I didn't want us to be involved in sex and have someone creep in here."

"Eeuuww." She shivered. "That's another really good reason not to have sex. Or fall asleep, for that matter.

Maybe we should all spend the night in the other room. That would fake them out."

"I came up with an idea that would solve the door problem and the sex problem. That's what I was thinking about when you were in the bathroom." And he was proud of his solution, too. She might not think he was romantic, but he had come up with an answer to the sex question.

She seemed intrigued. "And what is that?"

"Simple. We take the mattress off the bed. Because it's a twin, it will fit exactly into that space between the bathroom and the closet."

"You're sure?"

"I measured. With the mattress in place, and especially if I'm sleeping on it . . . or, better yet, we're having sex on it, no one will be able to get in the door."

She glanced over at the entryway that had the bathroom on one side and the closet on the other. Then she looked at his bed. "That's pretty clever."

"I thought so."

"It's not romantic, but it's very clever. We should definitely wedge the mattress up against the door. I'm feeling safer already."

He was encouraged that she thought so much of his plan. She hadn't mentioned whether she'd go along with the sex part, but the mattress move was definitely a go. "We can do it now, if you want. I wanted to wait until we were both out of the bathroom. We could end up blocking that door, too. I think the mattress will come up over the sill. And I'm not sure if we'll be able to get in the closet. Maybe not."

"I don't care about that. Blockading the door is more important than anything. Good thinking, Lex. Let's do it."

"I can handle it." He was more than willing to show off

his he-man qualities. Maybe she'd be swayed by that. Maybe it would substitute for flowers.

"No, I want to help. Besides, in a room this small, I need to help or risk being knocked over in the process."

Because he could see the logic in that, he agreed. "Okay, but let me do the heavy lifting."

"We should strip off everything first."

For one wild moment he thought she was talking about their clothes, but when she pulled off the bedspread, he let go of that fantasy. She wasn't ready to move the mattress and then jump on it. Or if she was, she wasn't saying.

She had the sheets off in no time and had tossed them, along with the pillow, on her bed.

"I'll get the foot and walk backward toward the door," he said. "You can guide it from the top."

She walked up to the head of the bed. "Ready."

"Here goes." He lifted the mattress, grabbing it as best he could, and pulled it sideways toward the doorway. Gillian was able to get a corner, but she was standing between the two beds and didn't have much room to maneuver.

In his mind, moving the mattress had been easier. It wasn't heavy, but it was awkward. Then too he had to look at Gillian leaning over. Oh, Lordy. When she did that, he could see—

"Watch out!"

He turned, but too late to keep the lamp on the dresser from crashing to the floor. "Whoops."

"Just keep going," Gillian said. "We'll worry about the lamp later."

But at that moment someone started pounding on their door. Dante was shouting their names. "Lex! Gillian! If you don't open up, I'm calling security!"

Lex sighed. The crashing lamp had brought Dante. "We're okay!"

"I'm not believing that until I see the whites of your eyes, buddy. Somebody could be holding a gun to your head or a knife to your throat."

Lex eased his end of the mattress to the floor. "Keep it steady." Then he walked over, unlocked the door and opened it. Dante stood there in his Big Dog boxers. "Here they are, the whites of my eyes," Lex said. "Thanks for responding, though. I do appreciate it."

Dante peered past him. "We heard a crash."

"I knocked over a lamp."

Dante's jaw dropped. "You're the man! I've never knocked over a lamp while I was having sex. That's awesome."

Lex glanced up and down the hall. Then he lowered his voice. "Keep it down, okay? And for your information, we weren't having sex. We're moving a mattress."

"Moving a mattress?" Dante scratched the back of his head. "I don't know what good that will do. I know twin beds suck, but those frames are bolted to the floor. There's no way you're going to turn those twins into a king. I suggest using it to your advantage. More excuse for close contact. It could be cozy."

Lex didn't want to discuss it. "Dante, just go back to bed. But thanks for checking on us."

"If you're sure you're okay."

"We're fine over here."

"I'm sure you're fine. Please don't feel guilty because I'm over there with a Snorasorus. I'll be lucky if I get any sleep at all, but that's okay! I'm here to serve."

"I'm grateful for your sacrifice."

Dante grinned. "Yeah, well, what goes around comes

around. I'm expecting my reward any time now. See ya." He turned and sauntered back to his room.

Lex closed and locked the door. Then he turned around to find Gillian dragging the mattress toward the door.

He moved to take it from her. "Here. I've got that." She smelled like a million bucks. The effort to get the mattress in place must have activated her perfume. He'd heard that heat could do that.

She didn't give up her corner. "Grab the other corner. It's almost there."

Dragging it into the entryway with her meant a lot of bumping of bodies, and he was getting into that. If the entryway could have been about forty feet long, he would have happily dragged that mattress all the way, happy to be nudging her hips and even, once, her left breast.

When they were both mashed up against the door, they had to drop the mattress.

"Tight quarters." She was panting a little, and she didn't look at him.

"Yeah." He didn't look at her, either, but he was getting aroused. Any minute now he'd be erecting a tent in boxerland. "One of us has to walk back there first. We can't both fit at the same time. You go."

"Okay." Steadying herself against the wall, and then the closed bathroom door, she walked barefoot over the mattress. Pranced, was more like it. The spongy surface wouldn't allow a straight walk.

He shouldn't have watched her move across that bouncy mattress, but he did. Her breasts jiggled and her hips swayed, and now his condition was worse. He made the mattress trip quickly, before his erection became more obvious.

"Now I guess we just shove it in," she said.

She would never know how that innocent statement got to him. "Right." Somehow he leaned over, painful though it was, and helped her push the mattress up tight against the door.

"There you have it," she said.

"Yep." He gazed at the expanse of mattress and imagined all the things that could take place there. But she wanted candlelight, wine, and flowers. Poetry, even. He was a little scarce on those things.

"I suppose we should get a sheet."

"Uh-huh." He couldn't seem to move from this spot at the end of the mattress. That cushy surface had such potential.

"Want me to get a sheet?"

He decided to go for broke. Gathering his courage, he looked at her. Then he took her hand. She was trembling. "Gillian, I don't need a sheet. I don't need anything but that mattress . . . and you. Please . . . join me."

Her lips parted as she sighed. "That was beautiful."

Victory!

"Then you will?"

"I would love to, but . . ."

"But what? What's wrong now?"

"The mattress blocks the bathroom door."

"So what?" He was a desperate man. "We can worry about that later!"

"I don't think so. You took the condoms in there. I didn't see you bring them back out."

Seventeen

GILLIAN HAD NEVER SEEN ANYTHING LIKE IT. AS IF
he were a man possessed, Lex grabbed the end of the
mattress and hoisted it straight up. He scraped the over-
head light in the ceiling of the entryway in the process of
shoving it flush against the door, but he didn't seem to notice. The effort reminded her of footage she'd seen of
people lifting cars in a rush of adrenaline.

Breathing hard and holding the mattress steady with
both hands, he glanced over his shoulder at her. "Can you
open the door, now?"

"I would think so." She managed not to laugh. He'd
been so quick to remedy the problem, but he probably
wouldn't appreciate having her laugh at his effort. "Yes.
Yes, I can."

"I left the condoms on the counter. I'll hold the mattress while you get them."

"Right." She hopped over the sill. "So you want me to
bring both of them?" She knew the answer, but she wanted
to hear it from him.

"God, yes."

His response thrilled her to her toes. Eagerness was so good for the ego. And maybe his comment about not needing anything but a mattress and her wasn't quite in the same league with "a loaf of bread, a jug of wine, and thou," but it was close enough to suit her.

He'd tried to be romantic, as romantic as an Aries like Lex could be, and she would give him points for that. Truth be told, if she didn't get to make love with Lex tonight, she might combust. No matter how many times she'd told herself that it was a mistake, when confronted with the actual man and a convenient mattress, she couldn't help herself.

It wasn't a perfect union. She still thought her Marilyn look was a significant element in their relationship. But if she considered the fact that they'd be saying good-bye in two days, did it matter?

Whether he was romantic enough, or stuck on blondes, or right for her in every respect—so what? She would never ask him to ride off into the South American sunset with her. No one should be asked to cast their life aside like that, especially someone as terrific as Lex. Besides, Dante needed him in their PI partnership.

And the other thing, the concept she didn't want to examine too closely, was the possibility that she wouldn't ride off into the South American sunset, after all. Mafia hit men were usually effective. If her days were numbered, then she deserved to have some fun before she bit it.

"Hey, did you find them?" He sounded a little weary, as if he might be getting tired.

Whoops. She'd been standing in the bathroom thinking while he was supporting the mattress and waiting for her to reappear with condoms. "They're right here." She scooped them up, stepped over the sill, and closed the bathroom door. Then she moved back so he could lower the mattress.

With a sigh of relief, he let the mattress slide to the floor. In no time they were standing side by side at the end of their little strip of paradise.

She turned and handed him the packets she'd picked up on the counter. "Your condoms, sir."

"Gillian, I just want to say—"

"Don't say anything." She crouched down and crawled onto the mattress. Once there, she lay back and held out her arms. "Just come here and make us both happy."

LEX FIGURED HE MUST HAVE DONE SOMETHING right to deserve this. He was very unclear on what constituted a romantic gesture, but by accident he must have made one. Maybe heaving the mattress on end so that they had condom access had done the trick.

In any event, he was gazing at a vision in black satin and lace, and she wanted *him*. She did look a lot like Marilyn in that pose, but he wasn't about to tell her that. She'd made it very obvious that he wasn't supposed to be attracted by all the Marilyn stuff. And he wasn't, not really.

But a body like Gillian's didn't come along every day, and although he loved the way her mind worked, right now it wasn't her mind that had him tossing aside the condom packages so he could pull off his T-shirt and shuck his boxers.

"Oh." Her eyes widened as she stared at his equipment.

"Is something wrong?"

"No, not at all." She swallowed. "I've just . . . led a sheltered life."

He froze. "Tell me you're not a virgin." Fate wouldn't be so unkind. He'd been to bed with one virgin in his life, and he didn't recommend it. Some rudimentary experience with male anatomy was a huge help when embarking on this course of action.

"I'm not a virgin." Her smile turned into a sexy little chuckle. "But I've never been with a man who had such an embarrassment of riches. You're very well hung, Lex. And that's kind of cool. I didn't know I'd be so blessed."

Lex blushed, and of course looked down at his cock. Then he glanced up again, quickly, not wanting to be caught studying his own penis. "I think I'm in the normal range."

"If that's the normal range, I've been seriously deprived."

"Seriously, I'm not that special." He'd never been into comparisons, which seemed stupid to him. You had what you had, and so what? Yeah, a couple of women had remarked on his size, but he'd put that down to pillow talk, the kind of thing that women said to make a guy feel studly.

"You look special from here. And I'm even taking the angle into consideration."

"You're flattering me." And he had to admit he loved it.

"No, I'm not. That's one gorgeous package."

How could a guy not feel special with comments like that? "Guess it's time to wrap it, then." Feeling very manly, indeed, he picked up one of the condoms.

"Not yet." Her color high, she beckoned to him with both hands. "C'mere."

"You mean . . . wait on the condom?"

"Yes, please." She laughed softly. "I can't believe I'm being so assertive. I'm never assertive in bed. But I want . . . I want to touch you."

"Okay." He sounded so calm, when inside he was going

crazy. She wanted to touch him, fondle him, maybe do some other things, things that he certainly hadn't expected on this first night together. But he wasn't going to argue.

As he crawled onto the mattress, his heart beat like an engine about to throw a rod. "Where do you want me?"

"I think . . . sitting with your back against the door. That will give me the most room."

She needs lots of room. He wondered if he'd pass out from anticipation. All he'd expected was regular sex and the chance to bury his face in her glorious breasts. But no matter what she did with all that room she wanted, he wouldn't come. Coming first was not a good thing, especially after a woman had been so complimentary about a guy's package.

Following her directions, he sat at the head of the mattress and leaned against the cold metal door. He hadn't realized how hot his skin was until it touched that door, which felt like ice. But he didn't say a word about the cold door. A cold door was nothing when a woman was looking at your cock as if she'd just been served a banana split.

"Impressive," she said. Propped on one elbow beside him, she let her hand hover over his erect penis. "May I?"

"Uh-huh." *Most definitely. Dive right in.* He was shaking, which made his cock quiver the tiniest bit. But then she wrapped her fingers around it, and the quivering didn't matter anymore. What mattered was that he had the urge to come *now,* and she had barely started.

"So silky." She stroked her hand up and down.

"Mm." He clenched his jaw and closed his eyes. Watching her massage him, her lace-covered breasts brushing his thigh as she stroked, added another challenging dimension. So until he got himself under control, he wouldn't look at what she was doing.

Her voice dropped to a sexy murmur. "I can see why men like to masturbate. This feels good to me, and I'm not even the owner."

Oh, God. He hadn't counted on her saying that kind of thing to turn up the heat. He could stick his fingers in his ears, but that didn't fit his image of a sexually evolved guy.

Somehow he had to get her to shut up, at least for a little while. "Don't . . ."

"You don't masturbate?" She used her thumb to rub the underside of his penis, right near the top, where it counted. "Of course you do. With this beauty between your legs, you'd be a fool not to."

"Please . . . don't . . . talk." He gasped for breath.

"Ah. I get it. You're trying not to come, and talking about masturbating makes you want to."

He gulped. "Brilliant deduction."

She slowed her strokes. "I'll take it easy. I've never given myself permission to openly play with a man's sexual equipment before, but if not now, then, when? And it's turning me on like you wouldn't believe."

"Um, you're . . . talking."

"I am talking. Sorry." With that she rolled between his legs and scooted up so that her breasts nestled against his thighs and cradled his twins. "This should keep my mouth shut." And she began to lick.

He reached out and gripped the edges of the mattress. He wouldn't come, he wouldn't come, he wouldn't come.

She paused. "But just let me say that you taste great. Salty. Like a big pretzel, only hard. Yum."

He moaned softly. Heaven help him, every move she made, every comment that came out of her mouth, ratcheted up the stakes. He'd never had sex with a woman who was so verbal, so curious . . .

And then it hit him. He might be turned on by Gillian's body, but she was driving him insane with her mind. Only someone with a brain like hers would think to say the things she was saying.

He'd thought having sex with her would be physically incredible, but he hadn't realized that mental sex would be involved. She was caressing him lightly with her tongue, which made him quiver and struggle to hold on, but he'd bet she could talk him into a climax without touching him at all.

Then again, two could play at that game. The only problem was finding enough breath to manage it.

He drew in some air. "That feels good," he murmured.

"I hope so. I'm loving this." She closed her lips over the tip of his penis.

Although he had a follow-up line, he had to take a rain check until he'd regrouped. That mouth of hers could be his undoing. Finally he was able to breathe again. Sort of. "I'll bet you . . . taste good, too."

She paused in mid-suck.

"Women are so . . . interesting. I love exploring . . ." He took another lungful of air. "With my tongue. Licking those soft, moist . . . folds, and then . . ." This routine could work against him, too. While getting her excited, he was veering closer to his grand finale.

Slowly she lifted her head. Her voice was a feathery whisper. "Then what?"

"Then . . . concentrating on that sweet . . . little center point . . . licking, sucking, until—"

"Condom time!" She wiggled free.

If he hadn't been so short on air, he would have laughed. Instead he used what little oxygen remained for one word. "Hurry."

"You betcha." She found the foil packet and tossed it to him. "Put this on while I take off my nightgown and panties."

He ripped open the packet. *"Panties?"* Hadn't they already done that part earlier? Oh, well. He rolled the condom over his throbbing penis.

"I put them back on." She tossed those at him, too. "This time you can have them for real."

Lex stared at his lap in disbelief. If they'd been playing ring toss, she would have scored with the panties.

"There's a visual for you," she said.

He glanced up and for the first time was treated to a view of Gillian, undressed. Her lush body made him dizzy with lust. "There's a better one. You're—" He cleared the emotion clogging his throat. "You're sensational."

Dark eyes flashing fire, she crawled toward him, her breasts swaying gently, her voice husky. "Lex, it seems you're wearing my panties."

Dazzled by her naked beauty, he'd forgotten all about the red satin ringing his cock. He met her hot stare. "It's your fault."

"They look good on you. Tell me, do you like how they feel?" She reached out and took hold of the panties, rubbing them up and down his shaft.

"Mm. Nice."

"So you like them?"

"I like anything that's been close to you."

She twisted the panties so they tightened around the base of his penis. "I want you so much I could scream."

"Then it's time." He took hold of the panties and wrenched them out of her grasp. They ripped as he pulled them away and threw them across the room. In one quick motion he rolled her onto her back.

Panting, she gazed up at him. "How did you know?"

"Know what?" His heart beat fast and furiously as he moved between her thighs.

"That I like this way best of all?"

"Lucky guess." His forearms trembled as he braced himself. "Are you really ready to scream?"

"Yes. Really."

"If you do, Dante will show up."

"Then I won't."

"I don't believe you." Leaning down, he kissed her as he shoved his penis deep into the warmest, slickest vagina he'd ever had the pleasure to enter. Her muffled groan melded with his as he pumped once, twice. On the third stroke they both came in indescribable splendor.

The glory of it was so complete that Lex forgot about muting his reaction, forgot that he was lying on a twin bed shoved against the door to keep out a potential killer, forgot that Gillian thought their stars were out of alignment. This was the most perfect moment of his life. The smart thing would be to give up sex right now, at the pinnacle of sexual achievement. Nothing could ever be this good again. Nothing.

OUTSIDE GILLIAN'S DOOR, NEIL STOOD LISTENING IN absolute fascination to the interchange. It played hell with his plans to know Gillian was in there with Lex Manchester, but discovering that Lex enjoyed wearing women's undies was almost worth the setback. People constantly surprised him.

Here he'd thought his target was a mousy little makeup artist, and she'd turned out to be a blond bombshell who wore designer dresses. And now she had an honest-to-God boyfriend, which complicated matters quite a bit.

The boyfriend wouldn't be as easy to work around as an eighty-two-year-old woman.

And what a boyfriend Gillian had! Neil had pegged Lex Manchester for a semigeek who wasn't nearly flashy enough for the likes of Gillian. Neil still wasn't sure about the flashy part, but Lex had the kinky scene covered.

Even more interesting, Gillian seemed excited that Lex wanted to model her underwear. Neil would never have guessed that she would like that. Some women were horrified by such a discovery, but Gillian had been so turned on that they'd done it right there on the floor by the closet. Just his luck, Neil was taped up again and couldn't fully enjoy the vicarious thrill of that.

He'd left BJ and Dorothy back in the room playing with makeup and clothes. He'd had to change the dynamics that had been going on in that room, because being unfettered under his silk pajamas had made him increasingly nervous. He'd accomplished the haircut, but there had been a few close calls when he could have sworn Dorothy suspected he wasn't one hundred percent female.

Finally, when the party had shown no sign of winding down, he'd suggested going to the bar and rummaging up some drinks for them. They were more than happy to let him do that and avoid a room service charge. So he'd gone back into the bathroom, taped himself again and dressed in sweats.

He hadn't minded the way things had developed, because while cutting Dorothy's hair, he'd come up with what had seemed like a fabulous idea. Without Lex Manchester to deal with, it would have been.

Neil's manicure scissors hadn't been the best thing to use for a haircut, but struggling with them had made him realize that they could be a weapon, a weapon that was easily discarded over the side when he was finished. Everyone had manicure scissors. If he used surgical gloves, no one would be able to trace anything to him.

Bruise marks were more distinctive, so it was a good thing he hadn't gone through with his earlier strangling plan. Tucking his small bottle of ether and a hankie in one pocket, the scissors and the gloves in the other, he'd left the room ostensibly bound for the bar. No one would ever have to know about his detour past Gillian's room.

He'd expected to find her in there with Cora. Rumor had it Cora was going slightly deaf, so he might not have to knock her out with the ether. He could start with Gillian, and once she was unconscious, go to work with the manicure scissors. She'd bleed to death by morning.

But now Gillian had a new roommate, one who liked to wear satin panties. That put a whole new light on things. Although his plan was foiled, Neil had to admit it made the game more interesting.

Eighteen

JARED STEVENSON THE THIRD'S VOICE CRASHED INTO Gillian's dreams. *"Breakfast, featuring our special French toast with blueberry sauce, is now being served in the dining room."*

Gillian pulled the covers over her head and tried to block out the irritating announcement, but it wouldn't go away.

"A fine array of pastries and fruit is also available on the terrace on A Deck. Don't forget to join us for the calypso party and limbo contest this morning at eleven on A Deck."

Limbo contest. Cora. *Lex.* She'd spent the night with Lex. Cautiously she peered out from the covers, but he was no longer in bed with her.

"And for more fun than you can stand, don't miss our special Underwater Charades at two this afternoon. In case you can't guess, it takes place in the pool! If you don't have a partner, see Dr. Lawrence and find out who on board is your star-crossed lover. It's a gorgeous day at sea!"

"Good morning."

At the sound of Lex's deep baritone, Gillian rolled over, which wrapped her like a mummy in the bedspread. There had been no bedspread when she'd zonked out, exhausted from stress and sex. The man standing at the end of the mattress, the fully dressed man, must have fetched the bedspread during the night.

Despite a growth of beard, he still looked good, damn him. It wasn't fair that men could get up in the morning, run their fingers through their hair, throw on their clothes, and be presentable. She was afraid to see what her hair looked like. When it had been long and straight, she'd had some control, but this short blond arrangement could turn into a fright wig overnight.

She didn't want Lex to see that and have all his illusions destroyed. She and Lex had enjoyed quite the time last night, but this morning, with him completely clothed and her still naked inside the bedspread, she felt at a disadvantage.

"You got dressed," she said. It came out sounding like an accusation.

He grinned. "So sue me."

Well, that was an Aries for you. A romantic would have stayed in bed with her and kissed her awake, instead of waiting until Jared Stevenson the Third blasted her with cheerful announcements of activities she didn't want to do in the first place. A romantic would have cuddled with her and told her what a magic night they'd had together. Then he would have suggested room service for breakfast.

An Aries would get up, get dressed, and—when confronted with the fact—say *so sue me*.

"You don't look happy," he said.

"Never mind. You wouldn't understand." She desperately wanted to tell him to go get himself a cup of coffee, or find a way to make her own graceful exit. That's when she realized the pickle she was in. They were officially sharing the same room.

Worse than that, no one could leave, or even get into the bathroom, until someone moved this mattress. There was no way in hell she was moving this mattress naked. She was already feeling awkward about everything that had happened while she was in this condition.

That awkwardness could have been prevented if he'd stayed naked and in bed with her. Then they would have had a level playing field. But that wasn't how things had turned out, and now she had to figure out her next move. She didn't want to end up looking dorky.

She had a bad feeling she'd behaved like a wild woman last night. Her hormones must have been in full flood. He'd taken off his clothes, and she'd gone ballistic over his sexual accoutrements. Why would a guy think he had to be romantic when a woman had spent the whole night worshiping his guy stuff?

"Hey, Gillian," he said softly. Crouching down, he crawled toward her. "I don't know what's bothering you, but I'll help if I can. Maybe you'd like to unwind yourself from that bedspread. Pretend you're Cleopatra, rolling out of that rug in front of Caesar."

That made her smile. It wasn't every man who would come up with an image like that. "How'd you do in Roman history?"

"Aced it."

"Me, too."

He pulled the bedspread aside so he could give her a

soft kiss on the mouth. "You know the amazing thing about the Romans?"

"They could really throw a party?"

"That, too. But they had bathrooms that actually worked. It was very civilized." He paused. "Unlike this stateroom at the moment."

"I see your point. If you'll go stand over by the window, I'll move off the mattress so we can get the room back in order."

He laughed. "Gillian, it's not like I haven't seen you naked."

"But not in daylight." Because he was a guy, and an Aries besides, she wondered if he'd understand the difference. Probably not. "Please go stand over by the window."

"You're going to deny me the pleasure of watching you walk around with no clothes on?"

"Um . . . well." That was a little better. A compliment like that tended to put more sparkle in the day.

He smoothed his hand down the bedspread that was rolled so tightly around her that she was beginning to feel a little claustrophobic. "You'll be like a butterfly coming out of a cocoon," he said.

"I'll be like a gopher crawling out of a hole." But she was cheered by the butterfly comment. That was definitely on the romantic side.

"Come on." He started unwrapping the bedspread. "Give me a little eye candy to start the day."

"Now you're being silly." But she let him peel the bedspread away. His approach had improved greatly from his first comment of the morning. Of course, he was a smart guy. And no doubt he expected that what they'd had last night would recur if he could keep her happy.

"Ah, Gillian." He gazed down at her. "Now that's what I call sunny-side up." Leaning down, he nuzzled her breast and took her nipple into his mouth.

She tried to stay uninvolved, but soon she was moaning and combing her fingers through his hair. He knew exactly how to roll her nipple with his tongue to get maximum effect. The rough scratch of his beard against her skin made the contact that much more excellent.

Slowly he raised his head. "If I didn't have to pee so bad, I would talk you into using that second condom."

She looked into his eyes and saw the laughter there. She couldn't help smiling. "That's about the most romantic thing anyone's ever said to me."

"I knew you'd be impressed." Grinning, he levered himself off the mattress, caught her hands and pulled her up with him. Then he stood back to look at her. "Then again, maybe I can hold it."

"No, no. We need to move this thing. It's a great security measure, but it severely—"

A walkie-talkie buzzed.

"That's mine." Lex walked over to the dresser and picked it up. "Lex." He listened intently for a few seconds. "We'll be right there. I'm sure she's in the professor's room. Right. See you soon. Over."

"What?" Gillian fought rising panic. It was becoming far too familiar a feeling.

"Dante woke up to find Cora gone. No note, no nothing. He tried to reach her on her walkie-talkie, but no answer."

Gillian's mind raced through a dozen horrible possibilities. "She's probably fine." But she turned immediately to the mattress and tried to pull it out of the entryway.

"Here. Let me."

"We'll both pull. I'm sure Cora's fine."

"I'm sure she is."

"But she's eighty-two." Gillian pulled hard on the mattress. They'd wedged it in tight with all their shenanigans.

"Yeah." Lex gave a mighty heave and the mattress came free. They both almost lost their balance. "But she's been taking care of herself for a long time," he said.

"Nobody would be after her, would they?"

"I can't think why." He put down his corner of the mattress. "Let it go. I'll get behind it and lift it from that end."

"Lex." Gillian tried to shut out the ghastly thought, but it wouldn't go away. "What if someone kidnapped her and plans to use her to get to me?"

"I think that's highly unlikely."

"Do you?"

He looked at her. "I hope to God it is. Let's leave this mattress in the middle of the floor and just get going."

MOMENTS LATER, LEX HURRIED OUT THE DOOR OF the stateroom, Gillian by his side. He hadn't shaved, and neither of them had showered. They'd thrown on clothes, not caring how they looked. It wasn't important. He'd barely remembered to grab his nerd glasses, but at the last minute he'd remembered to put them on. He clicked on his walkie-talkie. "Dante, where are you?"

The walkie-talkie crackled. "I've checked the dining room and the terrace where they're serving the continental breakfast. She's not there. I tried to find out where the professor's room is, but they won't give out that information. Listen, what do we know about him, anyway? Over."

"Only what's in the brochure," Lex said. He didn't say that the professor could be a serial killer, but it was what his out-of-control brain was suggesting. The good professor could be a person who preyed on sweet old ladies. "Did you try calling his room? Over."

"Shit! That's so obvious! I panicked when she wasn't there and started chasing around the ship. There's a house phone right here where I am. Let me try that and get back to you. Over and out."

Gillian tugged on Lex's arm. "I have an idea."

"Let's hear it."

"These two people are old, right? They get up early. What if they went for a walk on deck, and—"

"Fell over? Oh, my God."

"I hadn't thought of that!" She clutched his arm. "Maybe we should tell them to stop the ship."

"Wait. What were you about to say?"

"But if they could have fallen overboard, then—"

"I shouldn't have jumped to that conclusion." He caught her by the shoulders. "You had an idea. What was it?"

"That they might have found a secluded spot to watch the sunrise."

"Then why didn't Cora answer her walkie-talkie?"

"Between the sound of the engines and the water churning past, and taking into account her hearing, she might have missed the signal."

Lex nodded. "Sounds logical. I hope you're right." His walkie-talkie buzzed again and he answered it. He listened for a moment. "Hey, Dante, thanks for checking it out. Gillian thinks they might have found a private spot on deck to watch the sunrise. You take A and B, and we'll take C and D. Keep in touch. Over and out."

"They didn't answer the room phone?"

Lex clipped the walkie-talkie to his belt. "No. So keep your fingers crossed they're relaxing on a deck chair somewhere on this ship." He grabbed her hand and headed inside to the elevators.

Three guys and two women waited by the elevator, each of them watching the flashing numbers. None of them were paired up, and Gillian had to admit they all fit the geek stereotype—smudged glasses, mismatched clothes, and bed-head. Judging from their relaxed stance, they were totally unconcerned about how they looked.

"Like, beam me up, Scotty," said one guy who held up his hand, middle two fingers spread in the *Star Trek* Dr. Spock greeting. "Somebody needs to reprogram the system that runs these elevators."

"Or put booster rockets on them," said his friend.

"I knew a guy who did that," said a girl who was wearing glasses with the earpiece taped on. "Sent the elevator through the roof."

"Really?" The *Star Trek* fan moved in her direction. "Cool! Uh, what's your name?"

Gillian didn't hear any of the rest of the conversation, because the elevator arrived heading down, which was the direction she and Lex wanted to go. All five nerds groaned. They obviously were headed up to the continental breakfast on A Deck. As Gillian stepped into the empty elevator with Lex, she hoped the *Star Trek* guy and the taped-earpiece girl got together.

Just as the elevator door started to close, she saw a man in a luau shirt hurry toward it. Her first reaction was to reach for the button to hold the door.

"Don't," Lex said.

Then she recognized the man who'd just missed the elevator, and her blood chilled. "It was him. The guy from the karaoke bar."

"Yeah. I didn't want to scare you, but he's been shadowing us for a while."

She turned to him, her heart thumping. "And he tried to get on the elevator with us. Do you . . . do you think he's armed?"

"I don't know how someone would smuggle a gun on board."

"In pieces, that's how! They disassemble it so on the X-ray it doesn't look like a gun."

Lex shook his head. "With the kind of security we have these days, I'd be amazed if even that worked. I'm not saying it's impossible, but it would be chancy, and if he's who we think, he wouldn't want to risk getting picked up."

"So how's he going to do it?"

Lex gazed at her. "Look, we don't know that he's Mafia. He might be a nerd with an Italian name who's looking for the love of his life."

"But you think he might have been following us."

"It's possible." The elevator clunked to a stop at D Deck and Lex took her hand again. "Come on. Let's go look for Cora."

"But if he doesn't have a gun, how's he going to do it? I mean, suppose he trapped us in the elevator, or trapped us anywhere, for that matter. He still has to deal with both of us."

"Exactly. He could be hoping for a time when you're by yourself. That's why you need to stay right by me." He pushed through the double doors onto the open deck.

As a blast of warm, salty air engulfed them, she thought of how great this would be if she weren't thinking she'd be murdered any minute. She clutched Lex's hand tighter. "You really think he's the hit man, don't you?"

"I don't know. But we're not going to give him a chance to prove it, one way or the other."

"I appreciate that." She took a deep breath. The ocean and salt air were supposed to have a calming effect, but she wasn't feeling the bliss. "Man, I hope we find Cora soon. Between the Mafia guy and Cora going missing, my insides are churning like a washing machine on spin cycle."

"Yeah, I'm not all that cool, myself." Lex paused to glance up and down the covered deck area. The chairs lined up there were all empty. "Damn."

"When we find her, I'm going to give her such a talking-to."

"You and me both." He gazed upward at the row of lifeboats hanging there, each covered in a bright orange tarp. "Omigod. You don't suppose she and Little Ben are having a *Titanic* moment."

"Lex! The guy in the *Titanic* stood on the prow of the ship! Please tell me that isn't what you meant."

"No. Look at that lifeboat."

"Which lifeboat?" She saw a bunch of them hanging there above their heads, right over the railing and ready to be launched if necessary. In general, Gillian didn't like to spend too much time looking at lifeboats, especially in a discussion that had recently included *Titanic*.

"See the one that's rocking?"

She looked more closely, and sure enough, one of the lifeboats in the middle of the row was swaying slightly. "It could be the motion of the ship doing that." She didn't really want to think about any other possibility.

"Then they'd all be swaying. They're not. Just that one. Let's go closer." Before he started toward it, though, he glanced over his shoulder. "Shit."

"The man in the luau shirt?"

"Yeah. He's sitting in a deck chair pretending to read a newspaper."

"Maybe he's not pretending." Gillian wanted desperately to believe that. "Maybe he's really reading it."

"You keep an eye on him while we walk down and investigate that lifeboat. See if he changes his position."

As they walked, Gillian kept glancing back. The man didn't move except to turn the pages of his newspaper. "He's just reading it. That's all."

"I just thought of why that's so strange."

"Lex, there's nothing strange about it. People do it all the time."

"Not on board a cruise ship. They don't sell a metropolitan daily here. Think about it. Is a helicopter going to fly over and drop a load of newspapers on deck?"

"So he brought it with him to read."

"Or he brought it as a prop, but he's not up on cruises and didn't realize it would stand out like a sore thumb."

Gillian moaned. "You are scaring me to death."

"Sorry." He gave her hand a squeeze. "Don't worry. I'm right here." Then he lowered his voice. "See where the orange tarp has been unlaced?"

Gillian looked, and sure enough, the cover had been loosened. "How would someone do that?"

"Stand on a deck chair, maybe. Or I suppose a person could climb on the railing and manage it. Sheesh, talk about crazy."

"Cora wouldn't have done that."

"I don't know. She keeps in shape."

"Yes, but I can't picture her swinging up from the railing in order to get in there." Gillian really didn't want Cora to be in that lifeboat.

"Maybe she didn't, but someone did. Be very quiet and listen. Tell me what you hear coming from that lifeboat."

Gillian was still thinking about the guy with the newspaper, so she found it tough to listen carefully while her heart was pounding so loud. But eventually she made out a rhythmic slapping noise, combined with what could very well be heavy breathing. The whimpers and groans only added to the obvious conclusion. She looked at Lex.

He raised both eyebrows. "Sound familiar?" he murmured.

In circumstances such as these, she had no business getting turned on. But after all, she was holding the hand of the person who had recently shared that very activity with her. "Um, yeah."

"We have to do something about it. That's very dangerous."

A terrible thought came to her, one that completely drowned any flickering flame of passion. "What if it *is* Cora and Little Ben?" She wanted to cover her ears and run away.

"All the more reason. Those two old people could kill themselves, not to mention getting thrown off the ship."

"Literally?" Gillian pictured Cora and Little Ben walking the plank, blindfolded, with sharks below, jaws open.

"No, of course not. They'd be put off when we dock and have to fly back to L.A. at their own expense."

"What are you going to do?"

"Rap on the side of the lifeboat."

"Can I leave now?"

"No." He glanced down toward the man reading his newspaper. "Not with Hector Michelangelo right there, watching your every move."

"But this is so embarrassing."

He smiled. "Nobody's ever died of embarrassment before."

She swallowed and gazed up at the swaying lifeboat. "That's what you say." Closing her eyes, she prayed that Cora and Little Ben weren't the people making that boat move.

Nineteen

LEX WASN'T LOOKING FORWARD TO ROUSTING OUT the lifeboat lovers, either. If it turned out to be Cora in there, he'd be pissed. Blaming it on Little Ben would help the situation, but if Lex knew Cora at all, it could have been her idea.

Still, the woman was eighty-two, for God's sake. She didn't need to be doing the horizontal Macarena in a lifeboat. Taking a deep breath, he reached up and rapped sharply on the side of the fiberglass hull.

If he'd expected an instant response, he wasn't getting one. Instead the slapping rhythm became faster and the moans more frantic.

Gillian leaned close to him. "Maybe you should let them finish."

He stared at her. *"Finish?"*

"You know." She raised her glance to the lifeboat, which was swinging more vigorously. "Finish."

"I know perfectly well what you mean. What if all that movement tears something loose?"

"Oh, I don't think so. I realize they're both pretty old, but even at their age, their body parts should hold together during sex."

Lex was losing patience. His nerves were on edge, anyway, and thinking of someone he cared about taking chances like this didn't help at all. "I meant what if something comes loose on the *lifeboat*."

"Oh."

"What if the rigging gives way and the whole thing comes crashing down? It could fall all the way to the water. They could kill themselves. This isn't about orgasms, it's about safety!"

"All right, then."

As Lex raised his hand to bang on the lifeboat again, a little shriek was followed closely by a long, drawn-out groan. Then the lifeboat was still.

Lex sighed and glanced at Gillian. "Now can I get them the hell out of there?"

"Yes, but don't be too rough on them. You know how it is."

"No, I don't know how it is. I have never contemplated climbing into a lifeboat hanging three stories above the waterline so that I could do the wild thing. That's insanity. As it is, they're getting a huge break because I'm the one catching them instead of a crew member."

"True. Cross your fingers it isn't anyone we recognize."

"Trust me, I'm doing exactly that. Although at least then we'd know where Cora is." He rapped loudly on the boat. "Party's over!"

Scurrying sounds came from inside and the boat trembled. Eventually a head poked out from under the orange tarp. Lex sighed with relief. It wasn't anyone he knew.

A young guy with hair sticking out at all angles peered down at them. "Are you, like, with the cruise line?"

Lex gestured toward his khaki pants and plaid shirt. "Do I look like I am?"

"I don't know. I can't see very well without my glasses." Just then a hand snaked out from under the tarp and held up a pair of glasses. "Oh, thanks, Emily."

"Irwin!" squealed the woman in the lifeboat. "Did you have to say my *name*?"

"Sorry, Emily."

"You said it *again*!"

"Oh. Yeah, I did." Irwin put on his glasses and peered down. "Whoa. This looks a lot scarier in the daylight."

"You need to get down before someone comes along and catches you," Lex said.

"Yeah, I know." Irwin grinned. "We heard you rap the first time, but Emily was so . . . you know . . . close."

"*Irwin*. You're mortifying me."

Irwin peered into the boat. "It's okay. People don't talk about sex enough. It's a natural bodily function. It wasn't your fault that you couldn't climax the first couple of times."

Emily moaned. "I'm never coming out. I'll live the rest of my life in this boat. Which is appropriate because it's a lifeboat. Ha, ha."

"Come on out, Emily," Gillian said. "I've been in embarrassing situations myself. You live through it. And Lex is right. If the crew catches you in there, you're in big trouble."

"Okay," Irwin said. "We've almost put ourselves back together."

"How did you get up there?" Lex asked.

"Used the railing." Irwin surveyed the situation. "But I didn't realize it was so far down to the water from here. And we'd had a few drinks. I don't know what they were called, but they were blue. And tasty."

"Tell you what," Lex said. "I'll stand under you, and you can step on my shoulders. You come first, and then we'll get Emily out."

"I appreciate that, man. Just let me get my pants on." A zipper rasped. "All set. Emily, are you good to go?"

"Only if somebody has a bag I can put over my head."

Lex felt sorry for her, but now that he knew Cora wasn't up there, he'd started worrying again. Where could she be? So far he'd heard nothing from Dante. But he had to finish this rescue operation before he and Gillian could keep looking.

Irwin climbed out first. He didn't weigh much, so Lex had no trouble supporting him on his shoulders. Once Irwin was on the deck, Lex turned back for Emily.

She poked her head out, her red hair looking like it had been styled in a wind tunnel, her freckles almost obliterated by her deep blush. She looked down, and the blood drained from her face. "Yikes," she said softly. "I'm afraid of heights."

"You weren't afraid at five this morning," Irwin said. "Remember? *You, Tarzan. Me, Jane.*"

"*You, drunk. Me, drunker,* is more like it, Irwin. Nobody's afraid when they're blitzed."

Lex held up his arms. "Take hold of my hands and stand on my shoulders."

"He's very strong," Gillian said. "He can lift a mattress over his head. You'll be safe."

Lex snorted. Trust Gillian to bring up the mattress thing. She was probably subtly reminding him not to lecture these horny little nerds. Well, he wouldn't lecture them. They'd scared themselves so much he didn't think they'd try this stunt again.

Emily came down, trembling and gasping, but she came down. She was heavier on his shoulders than Irwin. From the way Irwin hugged her when she made it to the deck, the guy didn't mind if she was on the plump side.

"Thanks." Irwin stuck out his hand. "Let me know if there's ever anything I can do for you."

Gillian stepped forward. "If you were out here at five, you didn't happen to see an older couple go by, did you? She's about my height and he's shorter."

Irwin snapped his fingers. "I did see a couple like that! Right after we climbed into the lifeboat, I heard voices and looked out. They were walking that way." He pointed toward the bow.

"Nobody's sitting there," Gillian said.

"There's a little cubby down at the end," Emily said. "That's where Irwin and I started making out, because we both have roommates and couldn't go back to either of our rooms. Then Irwin got the brilliant lifeboat idea."

"Thanks for the tip," Lex said. "Come on, Gillian."

"Gillian?" Emily looked at Gillian's nametag. "It says 'Norma Jean' on your tag."

"Uh, yeah." Lex shot Gillian an apologetic glance. It might not matter, now that someone had her passport, but he still needed to remember to use "Norma Jean." "She's Norma Jean. I just sometimes use a pet name."

"We should have pet names for each other," Irwin said. "Let's go get breakfast and think of some. See you both later."

"Right." Lex was already tugging Gillian toward the

bow. Belatedly he remembered to look back and check on Hector.

"He's gone," Gillian said.

"Really? When did he leave?"

"About the time you were getting Irwin down. I glanced over to check, and just then a thin woman with short blond hair came up to him and started talking. Eventually he left with her."

"Interesting."

"A Mafia hit guy wouldn't get involved with one of the other passengers, would he?"

"Depends on whether it would be useful to him, I guess. God, I hope Cora and Little Ben are around this corner. I'm sick of this wild-goose chase we've been on."

They rounded a slight curve, and Gillian chuckled. "Wild geese located."

In the shelter of a nook just big enough for two deck chairs, Cora and Little Ben were tucked in together, holding hands . . . and snoring.

"I AM SO, SO SORRY," CORA SAID FOR THE HUNDREDTH time as Lex, Gillian, Dante, and Little Ben all sat eating pastries and fruit on A Deck.

Gillian marveled that Cora looked so fresh, while Gillian, who had raced out of the room without putting on makeup or even running a comb through her hair, felt like a total wreck. She needed to find out more of Cora's beauty secrets.

"I want to know how in hell you left the room without me hearing you," Dante said. "I swear I didn't close my eyes all night. Then suddenly, it's light outside, and you're AWOL."

Cora reached over and patted his hand. "Dante, sweetheart, you sleep like the dead. A chorus of dancing girls could have come through the room and you wouldn't have heard a thing."

"Not so!" Dante puffed up with indignation. "A chorus of dancing boys, maybe. A chorus of dancing girls, and I would have been wide awake."

"In any case, I should have left you a note, but I wasn't sure what to say. I was going to Benjamin's room, but I didn't know if we'd stay there, or go for a stroll, or what. So I took my walkie-talkie, thinking you could call me when you woke up."

"Which I did. And you didn't answer."

"Because Benjamin and I had dozed off in our lounge chairs. My mistake."

"It's all my fault," Little Ben said.

"How can it be your fault, Benjamin? I started the whole debacle. I'm the one who came and knocked on your door at four-thirty in the morning."

Little Ben's cheeks turned a light pink as he shot Cora a fond glance. "I could have said no."

"I doubt that. Early morning is a prime time for senior citizen nooky." Cora patted her hair and smiled. "So I made you an offer you couldn't refuse." Then her eyes widened as she looked at Gillian. "Sorry. I wasn't thinking."

"It's okay." Gillian had felt sick to her stomach at hearing the *Godfather* line, but she couldn't expect everyone else to be sensitive on the subject. Still, the croissant she'd been munching now tasted like cardboard. A few tables away, Hector Michelangelo was having breakfast with the thin blonde who wore wire-rimmed glasses. Even though he'd found himself a girl, he still made her nervous.

Little Ben laughed. "I take it Norma Jean isn't a fan of *The Godfather* movies?"

"Actually, I am." Gillian decided to ignore Hector. He wouldn't make a move out here in the open, anyway. "Watched them all."

"It's great entertainment." Little Ben stirred cream into his coffee. "But those things don't happen anymore, thank God."

An uncomfortable silence settled over the table.

Little Ben glanced around. "That was a conversation stopper! Does someone have information about the Mafia that I don't?"

"Not really." Lex reached under the table and squeezed Gillian's knee. "So, what's everyone going to do today?"

"Limbo contest!" Cora said immediately, as if grateful for the change of topic. "I want to see if I can still shake my booty. Benjamin, will you take the limbo challenge? You get extra points if you go under the bar as a couple."

"Let me think about it."

Cora smiled at everyone. "He'll do it."

"BJ and I are doing it," Dante said. "I called her room and asked her to meet me up here, but I guess she's primping."

"I'm right here." BJ walked up to the table in lime-green shorts and a matching halter top. "Nance and I are both doing the limbo, right, Nance?" She turned to her roommate, who strolled over in a black and white striped miniskirt and a white sports bra. She'd accessorized with gold bangle bracelets and gold hoop earrings.

Nancy smiled. "Don't you know it, girlfriend. I've talked Jared Stevenson into being my limbo partner." She shimmied her hips.

"Jared?" Cora's perfect eyebrows rose. "Doing the limbo? That will be worth the price of admission."

"Don't look now," Dante said, "but you already paid it. So you might as well enjoy the show." Then he glanced at Lex. "What do you say, buddy? Are you limboworthy?"

"That's not my thing," Lex said.

"Well, it needs to be your thing," Cora said. "I'll bet Norma Jean wants to compete, don't you?"

"Uh, I don't really—"

"She does," Cora said. "I can see it in her eyes." Then she gave Gillian a warning glance. "You want to be part of the action, don't you? Lots of people will be on A Deck, ready to try this. You don't want to miss out."

Gillian got the message. The more she stayed with crowds of people for the next forty-eight hours, the better. She hadn't tried the limbo since college, but staying out in the open during the day made a lot of sense. And Norma Jean would definitely limbo. Gillian needed to stay in character.

"Okay," she said. "I'm in. Lex?"

"Uh . . ."

"Hey," Dante said. "If you don't want to, Lex, I can see if they'll bend the rules and let me limbo with two different partners. I don't mind. It'll be fun."

As Lex stared at Dante, a mutinous light flared in his eyes. "Nope. I'll do it."

"You don't have to," Dante said. "I'm sure they'd let me go through twice. I just couldn't win twice."

"I'll do it," Lex said again, although he didn't look particularly happy about the prospect.

Gillian felt a little bit sorry for him, but on the other hand, she'd love to find out if he could pull it off. Watching him attempt the limbo would be a great way to take her mind off the possibility of getting whacked.

"Thanks, Lex," she said.

"It won't be the first time I've made a fool of myself." He pushed back his chair, and his expression became more cheerful. "Guess we'd better head back to the room and get ready, huh?"

That's when she realized that the limbo contest didn't start for another hour and a half. A lot could happen between now and then.

NEIL HAD FOUND OUT WHAT HE NEEDED TO KNOW. Little Miss Norma Jean would limbo. Excellent. A large metal drum filled with emergency equipment was tethered to a catwalk conveniently located above the area where the contest would take place. Neil had noticed it earlier and thought it might work to his advantage.

After Dante excused himself and left for his cabin to get ready for the contest, BJ turned to Neil. "I saw Dorothy already this morning. I talked to her while you went up to see Jared and ask him about the limbo contest."

Neil smiled. Before he'd proposed being partners in the limbo contest, he'd given Jared the blow job of his life. The poor man would have agreed to swing naked from the flagpole by the time Neil had finished with him. But all Neil had really wanted was a limbo partner, which would give him a reason to be there, and a cover if he should suddenly have to take a leak . . . aka, a quick trip to the catwalk.

"So how did Dorothy look?" Neil asked.

"Really good. She's so grateful for the time you took with her, plus treating us to drinks and stuff."

"She's more than welcome." The *stuff* had been a frank talk about sexual techniques. Neil had discovered that BJ and Dorothy needed a few pointers, and after the three of them had shared two bottles of champagne, they'd all been in the mood to get down and dirty. Neil felt confident that both women were now ready to make slaves of the men they took to bed.

"Dorothy went up to Hector this morning and started a conversation. They had breakfast together. He may even do the limbo contest with her this morning."

"That sounds like progress." Neil was taking a certain amount of pleasure in spreading sexual freedom throughout the ship. He'd definitely liberated Jared Stevenson the Third, and it sounded as if Dorothy and BJ were on their way to some good times.

Neil, however, hadn't indulged in anything more than vicarious thrills so far. He thought that might change soon. Jared was having too much fun to be put off by discovering that his current love interest was slightly different than he'd imagined. Tonight Neil might reveal himself and see what interesting trouble the two of them could get into in that plush suite Jared occupied.

But in the meantime, Norma Jean was the main person on his mind.

Twenty

AS LEX STARTED WALKING BACK TO THE STATEROOM with Gillian, he thought about the leftover condom. He might have to humiliate himself up on A Deck in another hour and a half, but before that happened, he had a chance to give Gillian another couple of orgasms. Maybe then she would think more kindly of him when he fell on his ass going under that damned pole.

"Now would be a good time to try my ship-to-shore call," she said.

"I think you should wait." It might have been his idea originally, but he didn't want her to try it now, or ever. He didn't want her to even think about it or walk past the room where they had the ship-to-shore telephones.

"I don't want to wait. Everybody agreed I could do it today. Neil could be on a plane headed for Tahiti by now. The longer I wait, the harder he'll be to hunt down."

"By going into that room and making a call, you label yourself as a witness ready to cooperate. If someone on the ship is watching you, and I'm not saying they are, but if they are, then once you go in that room, they'll know you're a threat."

They'd reached the bank of elevators, and Gillian paused. "I don't even know where the place is. I need a map of the ship."

"I'll bet there's one in our room."

She glanced up at him. "That was a fast suggestion."

"It's the easiest way to find a map." As he punched the down button on the elevator, he wondered if there was any chance she'd buy his logic. Probably not. "Otherwise you have to go all the way to D Deck and ask at the purser's office."

"I think going to our room is part of your devious plan to distract me from making that ship-to-shore call."

"Look, it's no secret that I don't want you making that call. I think trying to do it puts you in more danger. Let's say you walked down there and someone else was in the room."

"I'd have to try again later." The elevator door opened and she stepped inside.

He followed her in and punched the button for C Deck. Fortunately they were all alone in the elevator. "And suppose someone saw you go in there and come out again? They'd know you intended to make a call, a call you didn't want anyone else to overhear. Wouldn't that motivate them to get more serious about taking you out?"

"I guess so." She played nervously with the hem of the T-shirt she'd thrown on when they'd left the room in such a hurry. "But I don't know if it makes much difference. If they're watching me, they're looking for an opportunity to take me out, anyway."

"Not necessarily." Lex wasn't sure of his argument, but he'd make it for all he was worth if it would keep her out of that ship-to-shore phone room. "I have a new theory."

"I'm listening."

"Let's assume Neil's stepfather knows that you saw Neil kill Theo."

She ran her hands through her hair and blew out a breath, as if releasing tension. "I think we can safely assume that."

He made himself forget about how tempting her breasts looked under that thin T-shirt. "Then he finds out that you jumped on this cruise instead of going back to work. Didn't give any notice at work, just left for Mexico. What's he going to think?"

"That I'm running away?"

"Yep. And maybe he's willing to leave it at that. If you're running because you don't want to get involved in this nasty murder case, that could suit him just fine. He just wants to make sure that's what you're doing, so he sends someone to watch you."

"Hector Michelangelo."

"Maybe." Lex still wasn't sure about that, especially if Hector had found himself a girlfriend, but nobody else had popped up who looked like a Mafia type.

"So you're saying as long as I act like I'm on this cruise to have a good time, they might just let me go?"

"Could be."

"What about them stealing my passport?"

"Maybe it was simply to let you know you're being watched. Maybe if you don't make any false moves, they'll return it." The elevator stopped at C Deck and Lex gestured for her to go out ahead of him.

"This is C Deck," she said.

He pushed the button to hold the door open. "I thought you wanted to go back to the room to get the map. Would you rather head down to the purser's office and ask for one there?"

She stood in the elevator doorway, her eyes filled with indecision. "Lex, I don't want Neil to get away with this."

"Let me make the call on the way back." He wasn't planning to come back, but now wasn't the time to discuss it. He didn't want Neil getting away with murder, either, but Gillian was more important to him than bringing Neil to justice.

If that made him a washout as a PI, then so be it. His career as a PI was over, anyway. Until he learned to speak better Spanish, his job options in South America might be severely limited. Fortunately he was still strong enough to dig ditches.

"I'm afraid if you call on the way back, it'll be too late," she said.

The elevator buzzed in protest at the length of time Lex had kept his finger on the button holding the door open. "Let's talk about this in the room, okay? You can look at the map and decide what you want to do."

"Okay." She stepped into the hall.

It was a small victory, but he'd take it. Once he got her into the room, he planned to convince her that there were far better things to do with the next hour than make phone calls.

GILLIAN STILL HADN'T MADE UP HER MIND WHAT TO do by the time Lex unlocked their room. They'd had the foresight to hang a DO NOT DISTURB sign on the door before they'd left, and Lex replaced it on the outside before closing the door. The twin mattress was where they'd left it leaning against the built-in bed frame on the far side of the room.

The blinds were closed, but the sound of foot traffic outside on the deck filtered through the window. Gillian was very aware of Lex watching her as she stepped around the mattress so she could reach the small built-in desk next to the dresser. On top lay the leather-bound book that contained all the important facts about the ship.

She flipped it open and adjusted her glasses against the bridge of her nose. Eventually she found the section on ship-to-shore calls. The phones were located in a lounge on D Deck across from the purser's office, and right in the flow of heavy passenger traffic. Going in there unnoticed would be almost impossible.

Earlier she'd convinced herself that she had the guts to make the call, but Lex had scared her enough that she wasn't quite so eager to be a hero. His logic made sense, or at least she wanted it to make sense. If the Mob had wanted her dead, wouldn't she be dead by now? Hit men didn't mess around.

But playing along would let Neil off the hook, the very thing Neil's stepfather probably wanted. Gillian didn't want that. She and Phil Adamo had a difference of opinion, but it wasn't likely to be settled in a civilized fashion.

She glanced up at Lex, who was leaning casually against the door. She didn't think his position was casual in the least. He was blocking her exit.

She faced him. "Lex, I have to do this thing. I picture Neil jetting off somewhere, covering his tracks with the help of his connections. I've already let the information sit too long."

"I can't believe twenty-four hours will make that much difference. We dock in Vista Verde tomorrow morning. Once you're safely off the ship and on your way, I can make the call. Or Dante can."

She shook her head. "Twenty-four hours will make a lot

of difference. The investigators will have a tough time, especially if there's no corpse. They need to get started now."

"That's a matter of opinion." He crossed his arms over his chest and braced his legs a little farther apart.

"How can you say that?" She wondered if he knew how much his body language revealed. He was widening his stance to appear more formidable, but it also made him more sexual. She thought he intended to use everything at his command to keep her there.

"I'm the professional, remember? And it's my professional opinion that this call can wait twenty-four hours."

She stepped around the mattress and walked toward him. "Is that your unbiased professional opinion?"

"Absolutely."

"Bullshit." She got right in his face. It was a very attractive face, with the most gorgeous blue eyes, but at the moment the man and his attractive face were obstructing what was right. "You're letting your feelings for me cloud your professional judgment, and you know it."

"No, I don't know that." He met her gaze with maddening calmness. "My professional judgment is clear as a bell. It tells me that you'll put yourself in greater jeopardy by attempting to make this call."

"But it's the only way to catch Neil!"

"That could well be, but I've considered the cost/benefit ratio very carefully, and—"

"The *what*?" She clenched her hands, torn between the urge to grab him and pull him away from the door, and the urge to grab him and tear his clothes off. He was being impossibly male, and she was frustrated on many levels, including sexually.

He continued to lean against the door, but he uncrossed his arms and took off his glasses. "The cost/benefit ratio indicates that the cost is way too high for the potential benefit, a benefit I didn't hire on to guarantee, by the way. It's not my job to help the cops catch Neil. It's my job to keep you safe."

"Move your body, Lex." She could feel the heat coming from him, heat that collided with her own. "I'm going down to that phone room. If you want to come, that's fine."

He didn't move, but his breathing had changed, becoming heavier. The plaid material of his nerdy shirt quivered with each expansion of his chest. "I advise you to reconsider that plan of action."

"No. I'm going."

Determination turned his eyes to steel. "I don't think so."

She grabbed handfuls of his plaid shirt. "Let me go, damn it!"

He shook his head.

"You have to!" Then she gave in to the urge that had been taunting her and ripped the shirt, tearing it away to reveal his chest glistening with sweat. The material drifted from her hands as she reached up and smoothed her palms over his hot, damp skin. Slowly she raised her head and looked into his eyes.

With a groan he crushed her to him. Taking off her glasses, he tossed them over her head. They landed with a clatter somewhere behind her. Then his mouth was everywhere, scorching her face, her neck, the shoulder he laid bare when he ripped her thin T-shirt aside. She felt his teeth against her skin as she fumbled with his belt and zipper.

Pulling at each other's clothes, they staggered toward her bed. He pushed her down to the mattress as he wrenched away any obstacle to his questing mouth. Buttons popped and seams gave way, until at last he lifted her hips and buried his face between her quivering thighs.

It was a take-no-prisoners assault, an invasion that allowed her no place to hide. He took complete possession of that very private terrain and made it his playground. She lay helplessly gasping for air, awash in the pleasures of his demanding mouth and relentless tongue. She came twice before he slowed the pace.

Scooting her higher up on the bed, he kissed his way to her mouth. He tasted of sex. "I'm going for the other condom."

She closed her eyes. "Yes." It was the only word she knew. He could have anything he wanted, anything at all.

"Oh, and by the way, I love your natural hair color."

It took her a full three seconds before the meaning of that became clear. When it did, her eyes flew open. She'd never dyed her hair before, so she'd never had to think of the possibility that she wouldn't match.

Squeezing her eyes shut again, she gave thanks that she'd found a man who cherished every part of her, the dyed hair and the not-dyed hair. He'd even given her hope that he wouldn't mind so much if she got rid of the blond. Then she remembered that none of that mattered, because in the time they'd be together, her hair wouldn't have a chance to grow out.

That was the kind of depressing thought she could live without, and she vowed to put it out of her mind. If she didn't experience these moments fully she'd never forgive herself. Lex was searching out the second condom. Nothing mattered but that.

Soon she felt his weight on the bed, the warmth of his body drawing near, the brush of his thighs against hers, his mouth feathering her chin, her cheeks, her closed eyelids.

Then came the firm thrust and the glorious sensation of his cock buried deep inside her.

Eyes still closed so that she could concentrate on her sense of touch, she cupped his tight butt and wiggled closer, wanting to take in every last inch. "I love doing this," she murmured.

His voice was tight with strain as he began to move. "Funny thing, so do I."

Slowly she opened her eyes, wanting to see the ecstasy she felt reflected on his face. She wasn't disappointed. "You look happy."

He pumped slowly, deliberately. "Even my toes are smiling."

"Mine, too." She moved in rhythm with him, feeling lazy, sexy, not climactic yet, but the promise was there. And underneath, the gentle vibration of the mattress echoed the steady thrumming of the ship's engines. "Can you feel that?"

"I can feel everything. Your thighs rubbing mine, your vaginal muscles massaging my cock, your nipples tickling my chest if I lean down like this."

"I meant the ship's engines. The vibration in the mattress."

"A little. Through my knees and my elbows."

"I like it. Sort of kinky. I guess I can feel it more, because I'm on my back."

"I'm well aware that you're on your back." His strokes came a little faster, now. He lifted his body and gazed down at her breasts. "One of my favorite views. I love watching them take the impact."

Feeling wanton, she arched upward and cupped her breasts, bringing them within reach of his mouth. "Do take a bite."

With a soft groan, he leaned down and nipped gently at each nipple. "This is going to make me come," he murmured, right before he started sucking. The effect on her was sudden. She went from a medium setting to high heat in about two seconds. The clenching sensation of an impending climax made her gasp. "That's . . . that's good."

He sucked her breast deeper into his hot mouth as he pumped faster. She'd had two orgasms already, but she could already tell that this one . . . this one was the Mother Lode. As the pressure built, she began to pant. Her fingers dug into his butt and then . . . oh . . . my . . . God. Breathless cries spilled out as the spasms gripped her so hard she thought her body might fly apart.

Dimly she realized that he was coming, too, his body shuddering and pushing against hers, and at the very end he released her breast and groaned with such obvious satisfaction that she began to giggle in pure delight.

She hugged him tight, cradling his sweaty body against her slick skin. "Isn't this just the best sex ever?"

"Yeah." His breath was warm against her ear. "The best ever."

As she lay there getting her bearings, she once again became aware of the passenger foot traffic outside their window. "We, um, might have let a few others in on the secret."

He nuzzled her neck. "Do you care?"

She thought about that. "Not much. When I consider the cost/benefit ratio, I'm willing to give up a little privacy for the chance to have some amazing sex."

He chuckled. "Good girl."

"Lex?"

"Hm?"

"Don't think the issue of that phone call is dead."

He lay there quietly for a moment. "Don't think I won't try to seduce you every time you get the urge to call."

A little of the shine came off her bubble of happiness. "Is that all you were doing? Keeping me from calling?"

Immediately he levered himself up and gazed down at her. His blue eyes flashed with intensity. "Don't you dare think that. Not for a minute. If you'd absolutely insisted on going down there, I would have gone with you. But I— I was getting mixed messages, and I thought maybe you might want something else . . . something like this."

"Obviously, I did."

"So did I. More than you can guess. If it kept you from calling right this minute, that was a side benefit. But this time together was for me." He smiled at her. "I wanted to give you something good to remember, because I'm probably going to embarrass myself doing the limbo."

She cradled his face in both hands. "I don't care. It was sort of romantic that you decided to do it."

"Really? I thought it was sort of dumb. I should have let Dante have the honors."

"Why didn't you?" She was enjoying this conversation.

"Because I'm jealous of him. There. Happy, now?"

"Yes." She pinched his cheeks. "You have no reason to be jealous of Dante, but I don't mind if you are. It strokes my ego."

"I'd rather stroke other parts of you." He ran his hand along her hip. "I crave you, Gillian. So much sometimes that it scares me."

She felt a sharp pain in the vicinity of her heart. "Don't get too attached, okay? This is one of those ships-passing-in-the-night deals."

"We've done a hell of a lot more than pass. We've come alongside, boarded each, other and climbed the rigging."

"Lex! That was almost poetic." She wondered if discovering a romantic streak in Lex was such a good idea. If she could relegate him to the category of hot, sweaty sex, while keeping her heart free for somebody more romantic, maybe even someone who would woo her in Spanish, life would be much less complicated.

"Not bad for an Aries, huh?"

Uh-oh. Now she had a lump in her throat. Lumps weren't good when you planned to make a clean getaway in twenty-four hours. She swallowed that lump and hoped he hadn't picked up on the emotion in her voice. "Not bad. Not bad at all."

Twenty-one

THE LIMBO CONTEST WAS TURNING OUT TO BE ABOUT as bad as Lex had anticipated. Steel band music blared from the ship's sound system as nerdy passengers stood around and clapped—rhythmically or not so rhythmically—to urge on the coordinated and flexible ones. That wouldn't be Lex.

If he hadn't been shored up by that incredible hour in the room with Gillian, his lack of limboability would have bugged the hell out of him. Gillian didn't seem to mind that they were booted by the third round. But he wanted to be her champion, and he was outgunned.

Even Hector, their Mafia suspect, had lasted into the fourth round with his partner, a blonde named Dorothy. Nancy Roth had managed to get Jared Stevenson the Third through the fourth round, but they'd lost out in the fifth. Nancy looked POed by that.

But the crushing blow was that by the sixth round, Cora and Little Ben were still in the running. Or the dancing, to be more accurate. "I can't believe I've been beat out by the geriatric set." Lex watched Cora and Little Ben lean back and shimmy right under the pole like a couple of teenagers.

"It's easier for Little Ben," Gillian said. "He's short."

"Yeah, but he's old. And Cora! Look at that woman go!"

"She's so cute." Gillian beamed. "I love seeing her have such a good time. She's looked forward to this cruise for months."

"You could do better with a different partner." Lex never liked to compete in an area where he wasn't the best, so the limbo contest was torture. Worse yet, he was holding back a teammate, in this case, Gillian.

"Honestly, I don't care."

"You should have paired up with Dante." Amazingly, Dante and BJ were still up there. "I've always thought he was uncoordinated, but look at him. He must be double-jointed." Lex watched Dante practically doing a back bend as he shimmied under the pole with BJ.

"Lex, I thought it was wonderful that you tried. Don't be upset that you fell on your—"

"Ass. I fell on my ass. I'm not too proud to say it."

Gillian reached back and quietly pinched his butt. "It's a very fine ass, too."

That soothed him. "Thank you."

"Some people have . . . other talents. Less public talents."

"Now I'm feeling *much* better."

"Good." She rubbed her thigh against his. "Because I wouldn't trade what happened in our room for all the limbo prizes in the world. By the way, we still have to schedule our couples massage."

"You still want to do that?" He could think of a more private place where they could massage each other, undisturbed.

"We'll see. But it could be fun. Let's see how long this takes to finish up."

"Okay." Lex couldn't help noticing how she was wiggling her hips to the music. She wanted to be back out there, strutting her stuff. "Listen, I'm sure it's not too late for you to try again. See if they'll let you go under with Dante as a separate team from him and BJ."

Nancy Roth sashayed up beside them. "I have an even better idea. Once the teams are finished, how about a solo competition for anybody who wants to compete on his or her own? I mentioned it to Jared, and he said that sounded fine to him. I guess he thought I should get another chance at a prize."

"So should Gillian." Lex wasn't crazy about Nancy, but in this particular case she was proposing something that would make him feel less guilty about holding Gillian back. Maybe Gillian wouldn't win, but at least she wouldn't be dealing with a handicap.

"I don't really need a singles contest," Gillian said.

"Hey, go for it." Lex decided to be a cheerleader for the idea. "I want to see what you can do. While we were going under together, I was too busy trying to stay upright to appreciate your technique."

"There you go, girlfriend." Nancy winked at Gillian. "Give yourself a chance to turn the guy on. Personally, I think Jared wants to watch me do it for the same reason. It'll get him hot. Lex, talk her into it. I'll go round up some more contestants."

Once Nancy was gone, Lex put an arm around Gillian and leaned down to murmur in her ear. "Do it. Nancy's right. I want to see you go under that pole because it's a turn-on. Limbo for me and get me hot."

She looked at him with narrowed eyes. "You need a limbo to get you hot?"

"Maybe not, but there's nothing wrong with stoking the fire a little, is there?"

"If you say so." She nudged his hip with hers. "Unless you consider the supply of condoms."

"You enter the singles limbo contest, and I'll take care of the supply of condoms." He was getting hard just thinking of that. The gift shop had to be stocked to the rafters, considering this was supposed to be a matchmaking cruise. He'd probably discover they had colored ones.

"Okay," Gillian said. "I'll do the singles contest." She turned, glanced up at him, and smiled. "Try to control yourself."

She had no idea how difficult he was finding that task. But during a public limbo contest, he should be able to manage. Once they were alone again in the room, he'd make no promises.

He'd debated when to broach the idea of going with her to South America. His instincts told him to hold off. She might have some idea that he couldn't leave his home and job to go running off into the unknown with her. But the more time they spent together, especially in bed, the better chance he had of convincing her that was the only course of action that made sense.

The couples limbo contest came to a rousing conclusion, and contrary to Lex's opinion of Dante's coordination, his partner and BJ walked off with the prize of a bottle of champagne and assorted cheeses. He wished Dante hadn't done a spastic end-zone dance after accepting his prize, but that was Dante.

Cora and Little Ben lost out, but Lex enjoyed watching Irwin and Emily, the couple from the lifeboat, take second place. They looked thrilled as they accepted their prize picnic basket. Lex realized it made sense. Anybody with the agility to climb into a lifeboat and have sex in there without crippling themselves should be able to manage a decent limbo.

"Attention, everyone." Jared wielded the cordless microphone like a rock star. "I've had a request for an additional event here this morning."

"You go, Jared, baby!" Nancy wiggled her hips and pointed a finger in his direction.

Jared temporarily lost his focus. His eyes glazed over as he looked at Nancy and for a long moment he just stared at her and licked his lips.

"Jared!" Nancy squealed and covered her face. "You're embarrassing me!"

Blinking rapidly, Jared shook his head as if to clear it. "Uh, right. Where was I?"

"An additional event," Nancy said.

"Yes. Precisely." Jared straightened his tie and brought the microphone up to his mouth. "We're going to do a special singles event for those of you who were, shall we say, hampered by your partner."

"Like me," Lex said.

"Oh, stop it." Gillian squeezed his hand.

"We'll divide it by gender," Jared said. "Ladies first. The prize is a manicure and pedicure in the spa. Then we'll let the men try it. We'll give the winning man a complimentary haircut and style."

Gillian leaned close to Lex. "I don't want to take time for a manicure and pedicure. We could skip this if you want to."

Her implication was clear. They could duck out of the singles limbo contest and go back to their cabin. The DO NOT DISTURB sign was still on the door, and it could stay there for the duration of the cruise so far as Lex was concerned. They'd been too involved with each other to straighten the room in preparation for the maid. They'd barely made it to the limbo contest on time.

God, he was tempted to take her up on her offer. They could make a quick detour past the gift shop to get a package of condoms. But that was his selfish side talking.

No telling what would be in store for her beginning tomorrow. He should give her a chance to shine, even if she didn't care about the prize. And yet . . . an image of Gillian stretched out naked on one of the twin mattresses was very appealing.

Right when he was ready to suggest they leave, Cora walked up beside Gillian. "A solo limbo contest! I am so there. Come on, Norma Jean. Let's go for it."

"You know, Cora, I think I'll pass. I don't want the prize, and—"

"If you win, you can give it to me. I'd love a manicure and pedicure. Lex, don't you think Norma Jean should be out there?"

He thought about his new theory, that the Mafia guy was only watching to make sure Gillian had no intention of turning state's evidence. Getting into a limbo contest was better than disappearing into the room for long periods of time, much as he loved that idea. "I definitely do," he said.

She gave him a long look. "Okay, you've got it. Hold my glasses." And off she went to join the other contestants, about twenty in all.

He had it, all right. He had it bad. As he surveyed the group, which included Nancy, BJ, Dorothy of the short blond hair, and Emily from the lifeboat, he couldn't stop looking at Gillian. She was by far the most beautiful woman there.

Dante sauntered over to stand beside him. "You might want to wipe the drool off your chin."

"Can I help it if she's gorgeous?"

"I'm assuming you're referring to Gillian."

"Who else? Nobody holds a candle to her."

"I beg to differ, buddy. BJ has them all beat."

Lex shook his head. "You're no judge, Dante. You're prejudiced."

"Oh, and you're not?"

"It's perfectly obvious who's the most beautiful woman standing on this deck. Yeah, BJ is attractive, in a waifish sort of way."

Dante turned to him. "Are you calling my girlfriend skinny?"

"Your *girlfriend*?" Lex eyed his partner. No matter what Dante had said about his feelings for BJ, he was famous for hit-and-run romances. "Is that a shipboard term, or something that might last beyond Sunday morning?"

Dante didn't answer right away. "Want to know something weird?" he said at last.

"I'm not sure if I do or not. You're the grand master of TMI."

"We've decided to put off having sex until we leave the ship. We both want to, but we're holding off, getting to know each other first. That's a little tough because I can't level with her about what I do. She still thinks I'm an exterminator."

"Then let's hope that's not what's turning her on about you, Mr. Bug Thug."

"Trust me, we don't talk about bugs."

Lex was intrigued. "What do you talk about?"

"The meaning of life."

"You're kidding, right?" He'd never known Dante to have philosophical discussions with anyone, let alone a woman he was attracted to.

"Nope, not kidding. BJ's deep. It's fun listening to her, and I'm learning all kinds of things. I mean, we've made out and stuff, but when it gets too intense, we stop and take a walk."

"Huh." Lex couldn't help but compare that to how he'd behaved with Gillian. "I suppose that's easier if you aren't stuck alone together in a bedroom for any length of time."

"Well, yeah. I can see why you caved."

Dante had no clue the extent to which Lex had caved. "I'll bet you could have your and Cora's room tonight for the asking. For sure she'll be with Little Ben."

"She's already told me that. But I think BJ and I won't test the system and stay together all night. We'd never make it, and it's kind of cool, holding off."

"I guess." Lex wouldn't know. He hadn't intended to get sexually involved with Gillian, but he hadn't been strong enough not to.

"I'm not passing any judgments, buddy, just so you know. You have an entirely different situation. Gillian will be gone by tomorrow. In your shoes, I'd take advantage of every opportunity, too. But for the first time in my life, I'm looking long-range."

"That's good." Lex clapped him on the shoulder. "That's excellent." He wasn't going to say that he was thinking long-range, too, which would upset Dante no end. But if Dante had BJ, that would help him deal with Lex's taking off.

"Looks like they're ready to start. Want to put some money on the line?"

Lex was horrified. "You want to bet on how our girl-friends finish up?"

"Sure. Why not?"

"Oh, I don't know. Because it's unbelievably tacky?"

"Hey, I bet on my favorite football team, don't I? What's the big deal?"

"That's sports. This is . . ." Lex wasn't sure what to call it, except that he thought betting on the outcome wasn't cool.

"This is about supporting your favorite limbo dancer. If I put a ten spot on BJ, that shows I have confidence in her. Don't you have confidence in Gillian?"

"All the confidence in the world." He knew firsthand what kind of guts and determination that woman had. If he hadn't stopped her with a few well-placed kisses, she would have called the cops by now.

Dante waved a ten-dollar bill in Lex's face. "Then don't be a wimp. Put your money where your mouth is."

"Is somebody taking bets?" Little Ben hurried over. "Because my money's on Cora." He pulled out his wallet.

"Emily can beat all of them." Irwin dug into his pocket and pulled out several crumpled bills. "What do I need to get into the pot?"

"Ten." Dante collected money from Little Ben and Irwin. "Lex? You in?"

"I'm in." Hector Michelangelo walked over holding a crisp bill. "Are we betting win, place, and show, the quinella, or what?"

Dante coughed. "Just betting to win."

"Okay, then. Put my ten on Dorothy."

"I'm not actually keeping a list," Dante said. "I can remember who goes with who."

"Fine." Hector waved a hand and walked away. "I trust you."

"He trusts me," Dante muttered under his breath to Lex. "Did you catch all that bookie talk?"

"Uh-huh."

"Keep an eye on him. I agree with you that he's probably Mafia. The quinella. Sheesh."

"Yeah, but I have a new theory. I'll tell you about it later."

"Right. But keep an eye on him." Dante fanned out the bills in his hand and raised his voice. "Looks like everyone's ready to back his woman." Eyebrows lifted, he glanced at Lex.

"Oh, for crying out loud." Lex reached in his back pocket and took out his wallet. "Here." He held out a ten to Dante. After he handed it over, he checked to see if Gillian had seen the exchange.

She was staring straight at him, so obviously she had. He couldn't tell from this distance how she'd reacted to it. He hoped she'd think it was funny.

Jared raised the microphone. "We're ready to start! Music, maestro, please!" The sound of a steel band poured out of the speakers mounted on deck, and the first contestant shimmied under the bar as the crowd began to clap.

Lex evaluated her performance and decided she wouldn't be a contender. He didn't care about his ten bucks, but he wanted Gillian to win. She'd had a tough time, and she deserved this.

Dante nudged him in the ribs. "Here comes BJ." As she wiggled under the bar, Dante whooped and hollered in encouragement.

BJ gave him a big smile when she was finished.

A couple of contestants later, Emily came through and Irwin went crazy yelling for her. Lex was seeing a pattern. Although he wasn't the type to make a public spectacle of himself, he'd better do it in this case, or Gillian might never forgive him.

As it turned out, cheering her on was easy. Once she started under that bar, her back arched to show off her breasts and her body moving to the beat, he not only shouted and clapped, he whistled.

She was laughing by the time she stood upright again, and she waved at him before getting back in line for the next round.

Lex punched Dante on the shoulder. "Did you see that? Did you see how good she looked? Wow! She's something!"

Dante chuckled. "So are you, buddy. It's good to see you in the game."

Lex barely heard him. He was too busy concentrating on the other contestants and looking for weaknesses. By the time the field had been cut down to ten, he was convinced that Gillian had it in the bag.

And he could hardly wait to get her back to the room. She had moves on top of moves. As far as he was concerned, she was the sexiest woman to ever wiggle her way under a limbo stick. And he wanted some of that. Very soon. It was a damned shame they'd have to stop off for condoms on the way.

A couple more rounds, and the field was down to five—Gillian, Cora, BJ, Dorothy, and Emily. Lex was surprised that Nancy was out. She'd had an awkward fall that eliminated her. He'd thought she might be the one to beat, but now that she was gone, he thought Gillian would walk away with it.

On the next round, Dorothy lost her balance and fell, eliminating her chances.

"I hope one of us gets to take home Hector's money," Dante said. "Just for the principle of the thing."

Lex had already decided that if he won the pool, he'd leave the money for Dante. It wasn't much, but added to the value of Lex's car and a few other personal items, it might help the PI agency a little.

He watched as Hector comforted Dorothy, and then the two of them melted into the crowd. "I can't see Hector anymore," he told Dante quietly.

Dante lowered his voice. "He was with Dorothy, though, right?"

"Yeah, but I don't know if that means anything. I suppose they could be working together."

"That doesn't fit," Dante said. "I'm no expert, but I don't think the Mafia guys use women as partners. Anyway, it may not matter. We're out here with a ton of witnesses."

"Good point." Lex did feel better when there was a crowd.

"We can relax, I think. Nothing's going to happen right this minute."

Lex grinned. "Except my girlfriend's going to whip your girlfriend's ass."

"No way."

"You watch how she goes under that pole like she owns it." Lex's grin widened as Gillian leaned back. How she kept her balance in that position he had no clue, but it was giving him ideas for later. He began to cheer her on.

She was nearly under the pole when a funny rumble caught his attention. He wanted to keep watching Gillian, but some instinct told him to find the source of that rumble. He looked up in time to see a large metal drum topple from the catwalk. It was falling straight toward Gillian, and she didn't see it.

Twenty-two

INSPIRED BY LEX'S CHEERS, GILLIAN WAS GIVING THE performance of her life. Closing her eyes, she concentrated on the rhythm of the steel drum band and the delicate business of keeping her balance. She'd forgotten that balance had been one of her talents as a teenager. Recapturing that ability had been easier than she'd expected. She was going to win this limbo contest.

Then Lex's happy cheers changed to a shout of alarm that ruined her concentration. She fell with a thump and her eyes popped open. That's when she saw the barrel heading in her direction. Even without her glasses she could see it was big enough to squish the life out of her.

Before she could react, someone grabbed her arm and dragged her out of the way. The barrel smashed into the deck, splintering the boards as it landed. Gasping for breath, Gillian looked up to see who'd dragged her to safety.

There was Lex, his face drained of all color as he stared at the barrel imbedded in the deck. He was clutching her arm so hard it hurt, but she didn't care. He'd saved her life.

Pandemonium erupted after that. Jared rushed forward, still clutching his live mike, so his wails of concern carried all over the deck. Nancy was right behind him, along with Dante, BJ, Cora, and Little Ben. They crowded around so tightly that Gillian had no room to stand up.

Maybe she shouldn't stand up. She was feeling a little woozy. Her throat constricted when she tried to speak, but finally she cleared it and got some words out. "Lex, I need some air."

Immediately he lifted his head and began to shout orders. "Get back! Everyone step back. She needs to breathe!" Then he helped her up. "That's it. Take a deep breath. Another one." Although he loosened his grip on her arm, he didn't let go of her.

She discovered that was a good thing, because now that she was standing, she was starting to shake. "M-maybe I should sit down."

"Right over here." Lex guided her to a lounge chair. "It's an adrenaline rush. I'm feeling it, too." He made sure she was settled before crouching next to her.

"How about water?" Cora edged closer, as if wanting to do something, anything, to help.

"Thanks, Cora." She managed a smile. "Not right now."

"Anything she wants, she can have." Jared hovered nearby. "I can't imagine what happened. One of the crew members has gone to get the captain. This is horrible. Terrible. All our equipment is inspected thoroughly before we sail. We take no chances with the safety of our passengers, I promise you that."

"Shut up, Jared," Cora said. "We don't need your

blathering to complicate the situation. Have you sent someone up to investigate how that barrel came loose?"

Dante appeared beside Cora. "I just checked it out. The cables were cut."

Everyone gasped except for Gillian, Lex, and Cora.

"Why, that's insane," Nancy said. "I've heard about sore losers, but this is ridiculous. It was only a silly limbo contest."

"No kidding!" BJ said. "You really think somebody's that upset about missing out on a free manicure?"

"You never know," Nancy said. "Some people can't stand to lose, no matter what's at stake."

BJ moved closer to Dante and linked her arm through his. "In that case, we have a sicko on board, and we'd better find out who it is."

Lex continued to concentrate on Gillian, massaging her hand and looking intently into her eyes. "What can I get you?"

"My glasses."

He reached in his shirt pocket and pulled them out. "It's a miracle they didn't break when I dived for you." Opening the earpieces, he put them on with all the finesse of an optometrist.

"Thanks." Her lips felt frozen.

"Anything else? Water?"

"Nothing, thanks." She was afraid to put anything in her mouth for fear she'd choke. "I'll be okay." But she doubted it. She'd thought the theft of her passport was a scary thing. That was baby stuff compared to this.

Someone had tried to kill her. She gazed at Lex. It was good to have him in focus. "Did you . . . see what happened?"

"No. I heard a noise and looked up. The drum was already falling."

Cora glanced around at the circle of passengers. "This is positively maddening. There are a bunch of us out here who witnessed this. *Somebody* must have seen something. There was obviously a person up on that catwalk. Did anyone notice who was up there?"

"I saw some movement up there," Nancy said. "But I couldn't actually see a person, I mean, not well enough to tell if it was a man or a woman."

Gillian's gaze came to rest on Nancy. Something about her wasn't right, and the comment about a man or a woman tickled a thought that had been bothering Gillian ever since she'd met their dinner companion. The limbo contest had caused Nancy to sweat, and the makeup along her jaw had come off.

Because she worked in makeup, Gillian was familiar with the texture of a woman's skin, especially along the jawline where a man had a beard and a woman didn't. Nancy's skin where the makeup was gone had the rougher texture of a man's skin. There was a good chance that Nancy Roth was a man.

That in itself wasn't particularly shocking. Hollywood was full of cross-dressers, and so Gillian shouldn't be surprised to find one on this cruise. Still, she thought Lex and Dante might want to know about this.

As Gillian was contemplating how to make a graceful exit so she could talk to her bodyguards, the captain arrived looking suitably official with his gray hair, mustache, and spanking white uniform.

"Hello, everyone. I'm Captain Hull. My sincere apologies for this terrible incident."

"Wait a minute," Dante said. "Are you saying that you're a ship's captain with the last name of Hull?"

"I'm afraid so." The captain shrugged. "One of life's strange coincidences. And to make things even more unbelievable, my first mate is Mr. Stern."

Dante shook his head. "I'm in the middle of a Monty Python movie."

Irwin raised his hand like a kid in elementary school. "My dentist is Dr. Payne. I thought that was kind of funny."

Emily laughed on cue like a good girlfriend. "It is funny, Irwin."

"That's nothing," BJ said. "I once went to a sex therapist named Lotta Cummings."

"You made that up," Dante said.

"Nope."

Dante stared at her. "You really went to a sex therapist? What's that all about? Do we need to talk about this?"

"We can talk about it later, but I'm all fixed now. And I didn't make up her name. She's well-known in San Jose."

"I'll just bet she is," Dante said.

Gillian felt a smile tugging at her mouth. She hadn't thought she'd ever smile again. "Thanks, BJ," she said. "Whether you made it up or not, that was exactly what I needed." She swung her legs off the chaise. "I'm okay now."

"Rest assured that we'll be looking into this," said Captain Hull. "I have no idea what happened, but we intend to find out. In the meantime, any extra services the ship can offer are yours for the asking at no charge."

"Thank you, but I'll be fine." Gillian's conscience was pricking her something awful. The very nice captain had a damaged deck and suspicious behavior to investigate because of her. She'd brought her problems on board this ship, complicating life for everyone.

Maybe *complicating* wasn't a strong enough word. What if the metal drum had missed her and hit someone else? A killer wasn't always as accurate as they could be.

If she'd been thinking of anyone besides herself, she should have notified the police right after finding Theo. Then she could have gone into the witness protection program and become a stock girl at Wal-Mart. Problem solved.

Except not really. The Mob could find her, no matter where she relocated. Things like that happened all the time. Wherever she went, she could easily put others in danger from stray bullets or exploding bombs. Murder witnesses were like some creepy virus, infecting everyone they touched.

With that cheerful thought, she stood and discovered that her legs were steady enough to take her away from this crowd of people. And away was exactly where she wanted to go. She wished the ship docked in five minutes.

"I'm going back to my stateroom," she said.

"I'll go with you." Cora stepped forward.

"That's okay." She smiled to make sure Cora didn't take her comment as a rejection. "I really want to be alone."

Lex took her arm. "Sorry, but that's not happening."

"No, it certainly isn't." Cora moved to her other side. "Benjamin, walk with me for a while."

"I'm coming, too." Dante hurried after them, dragging BJ by the hand. "BJ, do you mind giving up the rest of the limbo contest?"

"No biggie. The limbo bar was crushed like a matchstick, anyway," BJ said cheerfully.

Gillian moaned.

"Sorry, Gillian." BJ sounded contrite. "I didn't mean to upset you."

"What about the money?" Irwin called after them. "What about the limbo pool?"

"I'll return everybody's money!" Dante called over his shoulder.

"Yeah," BJ said. "What was that with all the money changing hands? Were you betting on us?"

"Sort of," Dante said.

"Were you or weren't you?"

"Dante, I'll handle this." Little Ben hurried to keep up with everyone. "Ladies, each gentleman placed a wager on the woman of his choice. I considered it gallant, like the jousting matches in the days of King Arthur."

"Time out, professor," BJ said. "Those were ladies of the court giving their scarves or whatnot to the knights of their choice. There's a big difference between that and betting who will make it under the limbo stick." She tugged on Dante's hand. "You'd better have bet on me."

"I did."

"How much?"

"Ten bucks."

"That's *all*?" She clicked her tongue in disapproval.

"Come on, everybody." Lex beckoned them to the elevator. "One just arrived."

Once all six of them were in the elevator, Gillian looked around. "You're not all coming to my room, are you?"

Lex pushed the button for C Deck. "I was thinking we should all go to Dante's room."

Gillian remembered the DO NOT DISTURB sign and the mattress leaning against the bed frame. "Good idea. But what I meant was—"

"I know what you meant," Cora said. "And I think it's time we tell Little Ben and BJ what's happening. It's only fair to them."

"I agree," Dante said.

Gillian sagged against the wall of the elevator. "I *hate* that I'm messing up this cruise for everyone!"

"I can't speak for the rest of you," BJ said, "but this cruise is the best thing that's ever happened to me. I don't think you could mess it up now if you tried. Unless you're about to tell me Dante's gay."

"Hey!" Dante frowned. "Just because we haven't had sex yet doesn't mean that I—"

"Kidding!" BJ said. "I'm quite sure you're not gay. You get a boner when we make out."

"Thanks for sharing that with all my friends," Dante said. "I'm sure I'll be hearing about that in the near future."

"I, for one, don't care about that," Lex said. "But we do have to decide if we're going to reveal the situation to two more people. Are we putting them in danger by doing that?"

Little Ben threw out his chest. "If Cora is in any danger, any danger whatsoever, I want to share that with her."

"What he said." BJ gazed at Dante. "Whatever's going on, I would appreciate knowing about it. This guy is very important to me."

The elevator reached C Deck. Lex glanced at Gillian, Dante, and Cora. "So we're telling them everything?"

"I think we should," Dante said.

Cora placed a hand on Little Ben's shoulder. "I agree. You can't build a relationship on false pretenses."

On top of all her other sins, Gillian didn't want to add relationship fraud. "Then I have to agree, too. But I just want to say, I'm through having people taking chances on my behalf. Once we have this discussion, I'm using the ship-to-shore phone to call the cops."

"My goodness!" Little Ben's eyes opened wider. "This sounds exciting!"

"Yeah," Gillian said. "Especially if it's happening to someone else."

NEIL STARED AFTER THE DEPARTING GILLIAN. IF EYES really could shoot daggers, he'd have stabbed her about a hundred times. He couldn't remember the last time he'd felt this frustrated.

The limbo contest had been the perfect venue to eliminate his problem. He'd worked hard to set it up, coaxing Jared to stage a separate competition for the men and women. Gillian had cooperated beautifully by making it into the final five. Neil hadn't wanted to work with a larger group—too chancy.

He still couldn't understand how someone with a figure like hers could be so agile, but it had worked to his advantage. Timing his swan dive perfectly, he'd slipped out of the competition and managed to climb to the catwalk without anyone noticing him. The limbo contest had everyone mesmerized.

He'd partly severed the cables earlier. Working with a pair of manicure scissors instead of a real knife had made that preliminary preparation necessary. A few snips here and there, and one final snip when Gillian had begun to dance under the limbo stick, and Neil could see his future opening like the petals of a rose.

He hadn't counted on the rumble when the metal drum started down, or that the nerdy boyfriend would hear it. Neil had been headed back to the deck by the time the drum hit, prepared to express his great sorrow over the tragedy. Except there had been no tragedy, only a near-miss, thanks to the reflexes of Lex Manchester.

Neil wondered if the nerd had developed those reflexes playing Donkey Kong or something equally ridiculous. In any case, the plan had failed, and Gillian was still walking around breathing the sea air. She'd had the wits scared out of her, which was some satisfaction, but that didn't take care of his problem, now, did it?

After Gillian left with her entourage, Nancy listened to Jared and Captain Hull carry on a pointless conversation about how such a thing could have happened on this cruise. Wouldn't they be surprised. Neil had the urge to pull the manicure scissors out of his sports bra and click them like a pair of castanets under their clueless noses.

But after Captain Hull left, Neil had a better idea. He'd work off his frustration on Jared, who was always good for a few jollies. This time Jared might learn something new, something he'd never suspected about himself. He might discover that he liked boys.

"SO THAT'S THE SITUATION." LEX LEANED AGAINST the dresser in Dante and Cora's room. Gillian sat in the room's only chair, an armless one that had been tucked in the kneehole for the desk. He'd turned it around to face the beds where Dante, BJ, Cora, and Little Ben sat. He wished Gillian didn't look like she was sitting in the witness box.

BJ was the first to speak. "Gillian, that's a really tough break. You were in the wrong place at the wrong time, and that sucks."

"My thoughts, exactly," Little Ben said. "It's terrible when bad things happen to good people."

"And you think Hector Michelangelo might be a Mafia

hit man?" BJ looked worried. "My friend Dorothy's hooked up with him. Is there any way I can warn her?"

Lex shook his head. "I don't see how. Number one, we have no proof he's actually the guy. Number two, if he is the guy, we don't want him to know that we're suspicious of him."

Gillian glanced up at him. Her color was definitely better. "There's always a number two if there's a number one, right?"

He smiled at her. "Right."

"Inside joke, inside joke," Dante said. "You two are so easy to read."

"Like you're not," BJ said. Then she sighed. "I really don't want Hector to be a gangster. I really don't."

"I'm the one who didn't want to jump to conclusions because he's Italian," Dante said. "But that bookie talk was mighty suspect. And did anybody happen to see him around right before the drum fell?"

"If you remember," Lex said. "I told you I'd lost track of him right after Dorothy got eliminated in the limbo contest."

"I do remember that, but he would have had to ditch Dorothy to go up and cut the cables." Dante took off his nerd glasses with a sigh and massaged the bridge of his nose. "Unless she's in cahoots with him."

"Dorothy?" BJ snorted indignantly. "No way. You should have heard her on the cab ride from the airport to the dock. She was so excited about finding her soul mate, and so naïve. Even more naïve than me, and that's saying something."

"You're not naïve." Dante rubbed her arm affectionately. "Let's call you . . . unjaded. Or would it be jade-less? What's the opposite of jaded?"

"Naïve." BJ smiled at him. "But thanks for the effort. And nobody has to worry about Dorothy doing anything wrong. I just hope Hector's not the guy."

"Me, too," Dante said. "She's nice. And by the way, Lex, what was that theory of yours, the one you didn't have time to tell me before?"

"Forget it." Lex wasn't happy with himself. "Thanks to my lamebrained theory, I let myself relax, and you see what happened."

"It was a perfectly reasonable theory," Gillian said. "Don't blame yourself."

"Hell, I blame *myself*," Dante said. "You at least had a theory going. I was just loafing on the job. So tell me the theory."

Lex blew out a breath. "I thought the Mafia might let her go if they thought she was running away instead of planning to tell what she knew. That's why I didn't want her to make the ship-to-shore call, because she might be seen doing it."

"Maybe they bugged your room when they stole the passport, and they heard her talking about doing it," BJ said.

"No, they didn't," Lex said. "I checked that out after the break-in."

"Good man!" Dante looked impressed. "I didn't even think of that. Thank God I have you for a partner."

Lex wondered if Dante had given that comment extra meaning, or if Lex was only imagining it because of his guilty conscience. "Thanks." Then he took a deep breath. "Now that BJ and Little Ben know what's going on, we have to be careful not to let anything slip, like at dinner, for example."

"You mean to my roommate, Nance," BJ said. "She's our only dinner companion who isn't here."

"Uh, BJ?" Gillian turned to her. "Speaking of Nancy . . . I hate to cause you even more problems, but I . . . there's something you should know about your roommate."

Twenty-three

"NANCE IS A *MAN*?" BJ GRIMACED AND WAVED HER hands in front of her face. "Eeeuuuwww."

"That doesn't mean she's a terrible person," Gillian said. "I've known lots of cross-dressers. They can be wonderful friends, and—"

"She *has* been a good friend. Helped me with clothes and makeup. Dorothy, too! I just can't . . . it's freaking me out."

"Nancy is not a man." Dante shifted his weight uncomfortably on the bed. "I don't believe it. I would have been able to tell." He turned to BJ. "She helped you with clothes and makeup?"

"Yes, and if she hadn't, you wouldn't have given me the time of day."

"Yes I would. I think you're hot."

"You should have seen me before."

The discussion made Gillian squirm. It reminded her of how similar her situation was. "I don't mean to ruin your relationship with Nancy, BJ," she said. "But I saw where the makeup had worn off and a hint of beard stubble showed. I don't think I'm wrong."

"You're wrong," Dante said. "I have very good instincts. She's a woman."

"I thought she was, too," Lex said. "But Gillian's the makeup expert. If she says she saw beard stubble, then I'm sure there was beard stubble."

Cora nodded. "Me, too. Gillian's been doing makeup too long to be mistaken about that. And I know exactly what she's talking about. I've been acquainted with a few cross-dressers in my day."

"That's what makes you so fascinating, Cora dear." Little Ben squeezed her hand. "You're the soul of sexual sophistication."

Cora responded with a little purring sound that made Gillian bite her tongue to keep from laughing. Whatever else came out of the cruise, Cora had found herself a hot nerd, and Gillian was thrilled for her.

"I just don't buy it," Dante said. "The way she walks, the way she talks—she's a woman. I'd bet money on it."

BJ patted his knee. "I think you've done enough betting for one day, and besides, you'd lose."

"Come on, BJ." Dante turned to her. "You've slept in the same room with her. Wouldn't you have seen something . . . I don't know . . . dangling?"

"*No,* I most certainly would not. What do you think, I go around staring at people's crotches to see if I can find anything interesting?"

Lex grinned. "You have to realize, Dante, that not everyone does that just because you—"

"I do not! Well, sometimes, maybe. I mean, I'm a guy, okay? And it's women's crotches, before anybody gets any funny ideas. And that's all the more reason why you should believe me when I tell you that Nancy's a woman. There is nothing there. No bulge. Nothing."

BJ stared at him. "You *looked*?"

"She was doing the limbo in a miniskirt! It's not my fault that I'm a red-blooded male who inherited hot Italian blood!"

"Dante," Gillian said gently. "You're not supposed to see anything. They tape themselves. They're very good at it."

"*Tape?*" Dante shuddered. "I'm so grossed out, on many levels. The very idea of taping your . . . well, I don't even want to think about what that must feel like. The putting on is bad enough, but the taking off would be a hundred times worse."

"They shave," Gillian said.

"Well, *duh*. I figured that out, but even so . . . blech! If I've been ogling the taped crotch of a cross-dresser, I'll have to kill myself."

"That won't be necessary," BJ said, putting her arm around his shoulders. "I'll do it for you." Then she leaned in and nipped his ear.

"Ouch." Dante scowled but made no move to pull away.

"You deserve worse than that," BJ murmured. "And just a word to the wise. I don't care who your ancestors were. From now on, the only crotch you ogle is mine. Got that?"

"Got it. I'm turning over a new leaf. I have seen the light. I am taking the pledge. I'm—"

"That's enough," BJ said.

Dante looked quite subdued. "So it's true, then? She is really a he?"

"I'm afraid so," Gillian said.

Dante sighed. "Whatever happened to truth in advertising?"

"Thinking of Nancy as a man makes so much sense," BJ said. "She— I mean *he* was so careful about not getting too close to Dorothy when he was cutting and styling her hair last night."

"That doesn't prove anything," Dante said. "Nancy didn't want to get hair on herself. I don't know how stylists can stand that. Little tiny hairs get on your clothes, and into your eyes, and your nose, and—"

"Shut up, Dante," BJ said. "And it wasn't only that, anyway. When I reached out to touch his silk pajamas, he jumped away like he was scalded. He said something about being ticklish. Maybe he'd taken the tape off before going to bed. Then I brought Dorothy in for a makeover and he had to get out of bed and move around. He was worried we'd discover his secret."

"Very possible," Gillian said.

Dante eyed BJ with suspicion. "Why were you reaching out to touch his silk pajamas?"

"I like silk, okay?"

"I'll accept that answer," Dante said. "But I've come to a conclusion."

Gillian's hopes rose. "You know who's after me?"

"Nope, sure don't. But I do know it's the end of the late, great celibacy plan BJ and I had cooked up. As of this minute, she's switching roommates."

Cora covered her mouth, as if trying to hold back a smile.

"Okay, Cora," Dante said. "I know you didn't think I'd last, but I would have, if I didn't have to save BJ from sleeping in the same room with a cross-dresser in silk pajamas."

"It's not you I was thinking about, Dante, sweetheart. It was Jared Stevenson the Third. He's been panting after

Nancy ever since this cruise began. I wonder if he has any idea what he's latched onto?"

"YOU'RE A *MAN*?" JARED, STARK NAKED AND AROUSED, stood in the middle of his suite and stared at Neil, who had come out of the suite's bathroom wearing nothing but a smile.

"Exciting, isn't it?"

"No!" Jared jumped up and down and flapped his arms like a penguin trying to fly. His penis, which had started to deflate, bobbed up and down with each jump. "No, no, no!"

Neil paused. His eyes narrowed as he took in the deflated condition of Jared's joystick. Could he have misjudged? "I thought you were a player, Jared," he said.

"I am a player! I play with *girls*." He grabbed a pillow from the sofa and held it like a fig leaf. "Get away from me." He backed up. "Get away, get away, get *away*."

"Aw, don't be shy." Neil kept coming, unable to believe he wouldn't win the day. "We could have so much fun. Remember the spanking? Remember the banana? Wouldn't you like—"

"I don't want your banana!" Jared screeched, gawking at Neil's penis. "Keep your banana to yourself!"

"What about the blow job? Wouldn't you like another one?"

"I thought your mouth was a girl's mouth!"

"You won't find a girl who knows as much as I do, Jared. Now put down the pillow and let's have some fun, shall we?"

"No!" Jared stamped his bare foot. "Get out of here!"

This wasn't working out at all the way Neil had envisioned. He had some major frustrations to work off, and Jared was supposed to help him do that. Neil was usually excellent at picking his marks. This whole business with Gillian was throwing him off his game.

He wasn't even sure he had enough material to black-mail Jared. He'd been lazy and hadn't brought his cell phone for the first couple of episodes, but he'd remembered this time and had planned to take compromising pictures of the nerdy cruise director. Without pictures it was his word against Jared's, and Jared could rightly claim that he'd thought he was dealing with a woman.

Damn it, Mercury must be in retrograde. Nothing was going right. Gillian was still very much alive and Jared wasn't queer, after all. Some days it didn't pay to get out of bed.

"I'm very disappointed in you, Jared," he said.

"*You're* disappointed? How do you think I feel? I was falling in love with you."

"And you're going to let a little thing like this come between us?"

Jared's glance swept downward and quickly came up again. "Excuse me, but that's a rather big thing."

"Thank you." At this point, Neil would take his ego strokes any way he could get them. "Sure you wouldn't like to see how it operates?"

"No! Put it away. Immediately. And then leave. It's over, Nancy." He blinked. "That's a funny name for a man."

"It's not my name, you fool." Neil turned and stalked back to the bathroom. At the door, he turned. "I assume you'll keep this information to yourself."

"You think I'd tell? You think I want everyone to laugh at me?"

"Oh, they already laugh at you, but you'd still be wise to keep my little secret." That would truly bite, to be exposed halfway through the trip. But he was reasonably convinced that Jared wouldn't risk his reputation to do that. Neil went into the bathroom and closed the door.

He'd left the tape stuck to the bathroom counter, knowing he'd have to retape before he could navigate his way back to his stateroom after his encounter with Jared. But he'd expected to tape up a happy little dick before making that trip.

Well, that wasn't the case, now, was it? Because Jared was such a dork, Neil was more frustrated than ever. Once he made it back to his room, he intended to plan out exactly how he was going to kill Gillian. Then after they docked in Mexico he'd catch a plane back to L.A. This cruise just wasn't fun anymore.

AS CORA AND THE REST OF THE GROUP DEBATED whether Jared had the slightest idea the person he lusted after was a man, Gillian zoned out on the conversation. She had some thinking to do, and before long she'd come to a couple of conclusions of her own. First of all, she would make the ship-to-shore call.

But she decided not to announce that to the whole group gathered in Dante and Cora's room. Lex had said earlier that if she really wanted to do it, he'd go with her. She intended to take him up on it.

Her second conclusion involved her behavior for the few hours she had left on this cruise. She didn't intend to cower in her room like a scared rabbit. True, Lex would probably stay there with her, and that would have its compensations, but she'd been thinking about her role in all this, and so far she hadn't exactly covered herself with glory.

By taking part in the rest of the cruise activities, she'd show whoever was out to get her that she wasn't afraid.

Of course she was extremely afraid, but she was sick of projecting that image. No matter what happened, her stalker wouldn't have the satisfaction of knowing she was petrified, even if she was. Maybe she had a little of Duke McCormick in her, after all.

She needed to get Lex alone, though, so that she could tell him it was time for her to make that call. Doing that might not be so easy. Their little group of four had grown to six, and nobody seemed ready to leave and get on with the cruise activities.

Because they were all so concerned about her, Gillian didn't feel right asking them to leave and go about their business. But that's essentially what she wanted from them. She was saved by the public address system.

"Sorry this announcement is late." Jared's voice filled the stateroom. *"As some of you know, we had an unfortunate incident during the limbo contest, but the captain and crew inform me that all is under control."*

"Yeah, but what about your girlfriend?" Dante said. "Is she under control, or what?"

"Poor Jared," Gillian said. "First one of his passengers almost gets killed, and now we know his girlfriend's a guy."

"Don't feel too sorry for him," Cora said. "Someday he'll be worth millions."

"At this time," said the future multimillionaire, *"lunch is being served in the dining room, with open seating. Snacks and beverages are available, as always, on A Deck. Don't forget Underwater Charades at two! Meet at the pool for fun and prizes!"*

Everyone in the room sat in silence after the announcement. Finally Little Ben spoke. "It seems inappropriate to go on with the regular activities, under the circumstances."

"I'm glad you brought that up," Gillian said. "Because I've been thinking about that very thing. I'm not going to give whoever's after me the satisfaction of controlling my behavior. I think we should go to lunch."

"I could eat," Dante said.

"Now I'm worried about meeting Nancy," BJ said. "What am I going to say when I run into her?"

"I'll do my best not to run into her," Dante said. "Now."

BJ gave him a withering look. "It sounds as if you were running into her on purpose before."

"I used to run into women on purpose all the time," Dante said. "They're cushy and they feel good. But I've reformed. No more running into women, and especially no running into women who aren't really women. That's creepy." Then he brightened. "So when are you moving your stuff to my room?"

"Right after lunch."

"Then let's hit the dining room," Gillian said. She wasn't the least bit hungry, but she assumed everyone else was. "This is a cruise, which is supposed to be all about the eating."

"And the sex," Cora said. When everyone stared at her, she laughed. "Just wanted to see if you were all paying attention. Okay, we're doing lunch. What next?"

Gillian couldn't believe that she was making a suggestion that involved her wearing a bathing suit, but after almost dying, appearing in spandex didn't seem nearly as frightening. "I can't make the decision for the rest of you, but I'm changing into my suit and heading to the pool for Underwater Charades. Who wants to join me?"

BJ looked doubtful. "Are you sure that's a good idea? If I were you, I'd mostly hang out in the room until the ship docks in Vista Verde."

"That's tempting." Gillian didn't dare glance at Lex and risk giving that comment a sexual meaning. "But I think I'll scare myself worse by hiding away, hoping the bad guys don't show up. I'd rather go out there and act as if nothing's wrong. It might confuse the hell out of them."

"I admire your spirit," Cora said. "And ordinarily I'd be all for that attitude, as you know. But I just watched a heavy metal drum crash down where you almost were. I'm losing my nerve."

Gillian stood and walked over to Cora. Leaning down, she gave her a hug. "Maybe I found it. Come on, everybody. Let's go eat!"

LEX KNEW IT WAS HOPELESS TO TRY AND TALK GILLIAN out of her plan. He'd seen that determined gleam in her eyes before, and it had taken major sexual moves to change her mind. Surrounded by all these people, he didn't have that option. Ironically, he'd wanted her to get more confident, but now that newfound confidence might put her in harm's way.

As they all headed for the dining room, he leaned down to murmur in her ear. "Are you going to let me be your taste-tester?"

She glanced up at him with a smile. "No one will have a chance to poison my food if they have no idea what my plan is. It's only if I stay in one place for too long that they'll be able to mount an offensive. We let everyone know we'd be part of the limbo contest. From now on, I'll try not to telegraph my moves."

"I've been thinking about that. Someone would have had to preplan that, knowing that you were going to be in the limbo contest. I'm trying to think who would have heard it."

"Anyone could have, Lex. We were in an open area, and we weren't guarding what we said. At that point you thought the mob might be willing to let me go."

"And I feel rotten about coming up with that idea."

"Don't you dare blame yourself." She linked her arm through his. "With what had happened so far, it was a perfectly logical thing to consider."

"Maybe I need to stop using logic and start using my gut instincts." Her touch was so warm. If only she hadn't suggested they all go to lunch together, they could be alone right now, satisfying a different kind of hunger.

"That's why I'm planning to do the Underwater Charades. I think the best plan is for me to do the unexpected. Whoever it is would never think that I'd go on with the cruise activities after what happened."

"I don't want you to go on with the cruise activities, but I suppose you already know that." He felt the space between their bodies growing warmer by the second. He wanted to hold her, protect her, and make love to her all at the same time. Instead they were going to lunch with a crowd of people.

"I do." She hugged his arm against her side, as if to make up for what she was about to say. "And there's another thing you're sure not to approve of. Between lunch and the charades, I want to make my ship-to-shore call."

"Oh, God. I should have known that was coming."

"I might as well do it. I couldn't be in any more danger than I am now."

"That's a matter of opinion. Making that call is like waving a red flag in front of a bull."

"You said this morning you'd go with me if I insisted. I insist."

"All right." He would go with her, watch over her, and

make sure the call went through. And then, before they went back to the room to change into bathing suits, he'd ask for a side trip of his own.

Tomorrow was an unknown, a crazy quilt of possibilities that were impossible to predict. But tonight in their room, they should be able to spend hours in each other's arms. He wanted to make certain they had a good supply of condoms.

Twenty-four

THE PHONE CALL TO THE LAPD WAS ALMOST ANTICLI-
mactic. Gillian wasn't sure what she'd expected, but the
detective who took the information hadn't seemed particularly excited by what she was telling him. Maybe they
were trained not to get excited.

He'd asked her where he could reach her for further
information. Although she'd assured him that she had no
further information, she'd given him her address and
phone number in Burbank. No one would ever be able to
reach her there again, but the detective didn't know that.

Finally she hung up, adjusted her glasses, and turned
to Lex. "Guess what? I don't think he believed a word I
said. He thinks I'm some crank caller, maybe high on
something or with an ax to grind."

"It's L.A. They must get a lot of that."

"Somehow it never occurred to me that I wouldn't be
believed."

"Well, you did your civic duty. Let's get the hell out of
this room."

She stood and walked out beside him. Now that the deed was done, she felt a letdown. She'd thought that she'd feel exhilarated and powerful, but instead she wondered if taking the high road like this had been stupid.

He slipped an arm around her waist. "Are you okay?"

"I wish they'd believed me." Tension hummed through her. Lex could help her release that tension, but she'd committed to the Underwater Charades and she intended to follow through. Besides, she was curious to see whether Nancy showed up. She hadn't made an appearance at lunch.

"Whether they believe you or not, they'll have to check it out."

"Yes, but logically, what can they check out? The Mob will have gone over Theo's dressing room and wiped out any prints. The body is probably currently disintegrating in a vat of acid or something equally obnoxious."

"Thanks for that mental image. Ugh."

"Well, am I wrong?"

"Probably not. But they might look into Neil Rucker's whereabouts on the night Theo disappeared."

"And they'll discover that Neil was in Barbados. That was the story he put out to everyone. I was sure that's where he was until I heard him arguing with Theo." She released a gigantic sigh. "I'm so afraid he might get away with this."

"You've done what any reasonable person would do."

"I have not done enough." She thought she caught a glimpse of Hector Michelangelo disappearing around a corner. Or maybe she'd been so worried that Hector would show up that she'd imagined it was him. He and Dorothy hadn't been at lunch, either.

"I say you've done plenty."

"I don't." Maybe she should find Hector and ask him straight-out if he planned to kill her. "You know what I could have done? I just thought of it. I had my cell phone with me when I found Theo. What a dope! I have a camera phone. I could have taken pictures of Theo's dead body. The cops would have paid attention to me, then."

"Gillian, that's hindsight. Most people don't react with that presence of mind in a crisis. How many times in your life have you come upon a dead body?"

"I've come upon a dead body exactly once, and that's more than enough, thank you very much. But I wish I'd been better, braver, more—"

"Cut it out. Ordinary citizens aren't trained to handle witnessing a murder. What you need is something else to think about. Oh, look! We seem to be passing the gift shop."

"You want to buy someone a gift?"

"You must be really agitated if you've forgotten what we were going to buy at the gift shop."

"Oh." Her cheeks grew warm. "Oh, yeah."

"I'd offer to go in alone, but I've promised myself that we'll be joined at the hip for the time being. Actually, I promised Cora that, too, during lunch."

"I know. I heard you."

He glanced down at her, his blue eyes mischievous behind the fake nerd glasses. "So, are you ready to go shopping?"

"I've never bought condoms in my life."

"You're in luck, because you happen to be entering this gift shop with an experienced condom shopper." He walked through the door.

She caught his arm, pulling him back toward her. "Would you mind terribly if I checked out the postcards while you're making your purchase?"

"Chicken." He brushed her nose with the tip of his finger. "They'll still know that you're the woman I'm buying the condoms for."

"I'm sure that's true." She lowered her voice. "But I prefer to stay detached from the point of purchase."

"Then maybe you'd like to tell me your preference in advance."

"My preference?" She blinked at him. "My preference is for birth control that works. No holes. That would be my preference."

"We'll assume that the ship doesn't stock condoms with holes. But there are other considerations. Do you like ribbed or plain?"

She glanced at the woman behind the counter, who was watching them with obvious interest. "Do you think you could keep your voice down?"

"Sorry." He leaned toward her and whispered in her ear. "Ribbed or plain?"

She dipped her head so the clerk wouldn't have the slightest chance of reading her lips. "I don't know. Is one better than the other? I'm not the condom expert. You said you are."

"I'm the one wearing them. You're the one experiencing them. Maybe you never had the ribbed kind, if you don't know the difference."

"That's a good guess."

"So do you want the ribs?"

She glanced up at him. "Oh, why not? You only live once, right?" Then she took a deep breath. "I really wish I'd phrased that differently."

"Gillian, you're going to live to be a very old lady."

"I'd like that."

"I'll be right back. Enjoy your postcards."

She browsed through the rack, paying no attention to the colorful seascapes and quaint Mexican village scenes. Postcards were for people who could send them out, people with normal lives. Tomorrow she'd be on her own, leaving everything and everyone she'd ever known behind. If she lived that long.

"I'm back." He held a bulging plastic bag. "Let's go."

"What else did you get?" She fell into step beside him as they walked back toward the bank of elevators.

"Nothing. Just condoms."

She stared at the bag. "How many did you get?"

"Oh, quite a few." He adjusted his nerd glasses in a very Clark Kentish manner.

"No kidding! I hate to break this to you, but I don't know that I'm capable of handling that many condom experiences in one night. I realize that we need to take advantage of the moment, but there are limits."

He laughed. "Oh, these aren't all for tonight. I don't know how to say the word *condom* in Spanish."

"Huh?" Frowning, she glanced up at him. Then she stopped and stood quite still as his meaning became clear. "Wait a minute."

He met her gaze. "You didn't really think I'd let you go off by yourself tomorrow, did you?" he asked softly.

"You're not going." She'd lost control in so many areas of her life. She wasn't losing control over this. Lex was not going to ruin his life because of her, and that was that.

Lex glanced over her shoulder. "We might want to have this discussion somewhere other than in the middle of the hall."

Gillian turned to find Nancy walking toward them. She did look a *lot* like a woman, especially in a white one-piece bathing suit and a black lace cover-up.

Nancy smiled, her red lipstick perfectly applied. "Hey, you two! Been shopping?"

"Uh, yeah." Lex closed his fist over the neck of the bag.

"You wouldn't be buying any ladies' lingerie, now, would you?" She winked at Lex.

"Why, no, no I wouldn't." He glanced quickly at Gillian.

She shrugged. Unless Dante had blabbed about Lex's Victoria's Secret run, the comment made no sense. Maybe it was time to shift the conversation to another topic. "Looks like you're headed to the pool."

"I am! I'm going to give the Underwater Charades a try."

"Should be fun." Gillian had to hand it to her. Going underwater meant Nancy had to trust her waterproof makeup a *lot*.

"The big news is, I lost my roommate to a man. BJ left me a 'Dear Nancy' letter. She's moving in with Dante." She laughed in obvious delight. "Ain't love grand?"

"I'm happy for them," Gillian said.

"Me, too. Couldn't be more thrilled. And now I have the bathroom to myself! Well, must be off to the pool. Are you two competing in the Underwater Charades?"

"We haven't decided yet," Gillian said.

"Well, I hope to see you there. Bye." With a flutter of her fingers, Nancy continued down the hall and stepped into an elevator.

Lex watched her go. "Did you tell her about Victoria's Secret?"

"I wouldn't do that. I can't even believe Dante did."

"Then I don't get the comment about ladies' lingerie at all. Unless she thinks I'm a potential recruit to her cause, which is really frightening."

"I can't believe that's it. Maybe Dante said something."

Lex blew out a breath. "If he did, he's on my list. Again."

"You know, Nancy reminds me of someone, but I can't think who it is."

"Nicole Kidman, maybe?"

"No, I don't think so. I'll remember who it is, eventually." She faced him again. "Lex, back to what you said before, there's no need for a discussion. Consider that discussion closed."

"Let's go upstairs." He took her arm and started toward the elevators.

"If you think you can convince me with a bag full of condoms, you're wrong. It worked temporarily for the ship-to-shore call, but this is a whole different story."

"I realize that."

The elevator was full, so Gillian and Lex didn't say anything more as they rode up to C Deck. Specifically, the elevator was full of nerds in bathing suits, all of them chattering away, obviously enjoying themselves. After taking a quick inventory of less-than-perfect bodies and ill-fitting suits, Gillian felt better about parading out to the pool in her one-piece.

The message was clear—she'd spent way too much time with Hollywood types who focused entirely on external beauty. All along Cora had been right about taking this cruise together. Too bad the circumstances had turned out to be so crummy.

They were barely inside the room when Lex dropped the bag of condoms to the floor and took Gillian by the shoulders. "Listen to me. I've thought this through very carefully, and I'm going with you."

She pulled away from him and climbed over the

mattress on the floor so she could gaze out the window. Better that than looking into his eyes and discovering that he was falling for her. "How could you think it through carefully? You haven't had nearly enough time to do that. No, Lex. It's out of the question." In the distance she could see a narrow strip of brown across the horizon. Mexico.

"I've had more time than you might imagine." He stepped over the mattress and came up behind her, wrapping his arms around her waist. "This isn't a sudden decision. I never really pictured you going off by yourself."

"That's always been the plan."

"I know, but after our first kiss, I began to consider whether I would go. Last night clinched it for me, but I didn't want to say it yet, because I knew you'd react this way."

She tried to keep her body stiff and resist the temptation of his warm arms around her, but that was a lost cause. Gradually she relaxed against him. "Of course I would react this way. You have a career in L.A. Dante needs you there."

"You need me here." He pulled her tight against him.

Oh, yes, she did, but she couldn't let selfish desires be the deciding factor. "You're basing this on sex." He wanted her right this minute, according to the evidence pressing against her fanny.

"I'd be a liar if I said sex wasn't part of it. I've never had anything this good in my life."

She didn't say anything. She wasn't about to provide him with more ammunition for his insane plan.

He gave her a squeeze. "This is the part where you're supposed to be kind to my ego and tell me that you've never had it better, either."

"I'm taking the Fifth on that."

He leaned down and nuzzled behind her ear. "Then maybe I need to remind you of how good it is. I'll ask you right after I make you come. You might be more inclined to spill the beans with the right timing."

Damn it, she was getting wet, and she had to be stronger than that. Summoning all her willpower, she wiggled away from him, hopped over the mattress, and moved to a far corner of the room. "Lex, there is no way I'm letting you take off for South America and leave your life behind. It's bad enough that I have to do it, but you certainly don't."

"I'm going." He stepped over the mattress and took off his glasses. "And I'm about to convince you it's the right thing to do."

"Stop right there." She held up a hand.

He didn't stop. "I know the problem. It's been too long between orgasms."

She backed toward the door and stumbled over the bag of condoms. Bracing her hands against the door, she managed to keep herself upright.

"Watch out." He reached down and snagged a box out of the bag. "There's condoms on the floor." He kicked the bag away.

"You're making my point for me! This is all about sex."

"It's partly about sex." He opened the box and pulled out a condom packet. "And we need to explore that part some more, so I can soften up your initial resistance to this idea of our mutual travel plans."

"Any day now, my roots will start showing!"

He paused in the act of unzipping his pants and stared at her. "Your roots?"

"Yes." She kept her eyes on his face and tried to ignore the fact he'd started unzipping. "And you might not be so sexually attracted to me then."

He frowned. "Are you saying your ancestors are on the weird side? Because I'm sure I can handle that." He finished unzipping his pants. "Everyone has strange people in their family tree, and it doesn't have to—"

She pulled at her hair. "No, *these* roots. Once I'm down in South America, I won't be dyeing my hair. I don't know if I'll find a place where I can get it colored brown, and if I don't, it'll look really funky for a while, half and half."

Lex started to laugh. "You're talking about your hair?"

"Yes, I am, and if you think that's not important, then think again."

"Okay. I'll think again." He glanced up at the ceiling and tapped his finger against his chin. Then he looked at her. "Nope. Still not important." He took the condom out of the wrapper. "This." He held up the condom. "This is important."

"Do *not* put on that condom."

"You're not suggesting we do it without?"

"I'm suggesting we not do it, period!"

"Bad suggestion." He calmly rolled the condom over his penis.

And she, weak person that she was, watched him. "You're . . . you're living in la-la land."

"No, I used to live there, but now I'm relocating south of the border. Very south."

"You are not! I won't let—"

His kiss ended the sentence and the discussion. By the time he'd slid both hands under her shirt and unhooked the front catch of her bra, she'd forgotten what they'd been talking about.

What happened next was kind of a blur, except that her legs ended up wrapped around his hips and her back firmly braced against the door. Each time he thrust, the door rattled. She could only hope the maid wasn't out in the hall.

She gasped for breath as her climax drew near. "You're . . . crazy."

"And you like it." His hot gaze held hers as he pushed deep.

"So what?"

"So tell me it's good." He shifted the angle slightly, caressing her G-spot with incredible effectiveness.

She moaned. "Okay, it's good."

"The best you're ever had."

She closed her eyes, savoring the pleasure. "Yes . . . the best."

"Gillian, I'm coming."

"So am I. Oh, so am I!" The first spasm rocked through her and she caught her breath.

"I mean I'm coming to South America. Say yes, Gillian."

With the force of a Lex-induced orgasm rolling through her, she'd agree to peddle a tray full of condoms at the county fair. "Yes!" she cried. "Yes!"

"Thanks for letting me . . . come." Groaning, he shuddered in her arms.

Not until later, as they started to change into their bathing suits, did they realize that the curtains had been open the whole time.

Twenty-five

"THAT WASN'T FAIR," GILLIAN SAID AS THEY RODE the elevator up to A Deck where the pool was located.

"No, but it was a hell of a lot of fun." And he'd gotten the response he wanted. No matter what she said, she wanted him and needed him there when she left tomorrow.

"You can't hold me to that answer."

His glance raked over her. "I intend to hold you to anything I can get away with, including me. That red suit should be illegal." He was glad the elevator was empty. The sexual vibes were still so strong between them that they needed this extra moment of privacy.

"I think it's a little tight."

"Want to take it off?" He adjusted the fit of his nerd glasses and tried to look innocent. "We can go back to the room, and you can slip it off so you can be more comfortable. I wouldn't mind. Or you could go back and try on the purple one."

"It's the same size. It would look the same."

He waggled his eyebrows. "I know."

"Do you ever think of anything besides sex?"

"I used to. Then you showed up."

She laughed. "So it's all my fault."

"Pretty much." He loved hearing her laugh like that. After the incident with the metal drum, followed by her call to the police, where she had to rehash the grisly details of Theo's murder, he'd watched her battle fear and disillusionment. Sure, he'd used sex to change her mood, but it had worked, and they'd both reaped the rewards.

"Seriously, Lex, you're not coming to South America with me."

"Seriously, Gillian, I am."

"We don't know if we're compatible enough, and then you'd be stuck down there with someone you didn't even like."

"Oh, now we're back to the Aries and Cancer thing."

"Maybe."

The elevator came to a stop and the doors opened into the hallway on A Deck. A few passengers were in the hall, so Lex decided to postpone any further comments for now.

The area around the pool was crowded with bodies, some white, some pink, but none tanned. Lex wasn't very tanned, either, but he had more color than most everyone except Dante. Apparently nerds weren't sun-worshipers.

Jared stood on a small platform near the pool and directed the charades with a bullhorn. Lex didn't know whether to be horrified or relieved that Jared's bathing suit wasn't any less nerdy looking than the paisley boxer style Lex had been forced to wear. He checked for Hector and found him, Blues Brothers sunglasses shading his eyes, a navy blue bathing suit paired up with an unbuttoned, short-sleeved shirt. He was holding hands with Dorothy.

If Lex thought for sure Hector had engineered the

falling-drum incident, Lex would have no trouble taking the guy on, Mafia or not. But he didn't know. Hector was the guy who looked most like a gangster, but that didn't mean he was the culprit.

Gillian tugged on his arm. "Nancy's coming out of the pool. She must have just finished a round of the charades. Now there's a clue. She has on one of those froufrou bathing caps. If she's wearing a wig, that would make lots of sense."

"That reminds me. I have a bone to pick with Dante. And he's right over there, talking to Cora and Little Ben. Let's go." He caught Gillian's hand and started around to the other side of the pool.

"Hey, buddy!" Dante glanced up, his flip-up shades clipped to his nerd glasses. "You look about as bad as I do. That pink shirt clashes nicely with the paisley. Good work."

"Dante, have you been spreading stories about me shopping in Victoria's Secret?"

"Not me."

Little Ben cleared his throat. "Is this about the time I should go for drinks? I mean, first there's Nancy, and now this."

"No, no," Dante said. "It isn't what you think." He lowered his voice. "Gillian needed underwear for the trip and she couldn't risk going back to her apartment. So Lex did some shopping for her, and I kidded him about it, but I promise I haven't said a word to anybody on this cruise."

Lex gazed at him. "Not even Nancy?"

"Especially not Nancy. Sheesh. Do you think I'd get you into that kind of trouble? Next thing you know she'd be offering you shaving tips." Dante shuddered. "I'm afraid to get in the pool with her. Him. It could be catching."

BJ jabbed him in the ribs. "You are such a homophobe."

"You were the one freaking out when you first heard about it!"

"I know, and I'm not proud of that. But she—he—was really nice to me and Dorothy. I'm cool with everything now."

"Goody for you. You're so evolved. Me, I'm staying out of the charades round she's in."

"Well, she's not in this one," BJ said. "Lex and Gillian? What do you say?"

Lex figured they might as well. "Sure." He turned to Cora and Little Ben. "Are you two playing?"

Cora shook her head. "That chlorine is really hard on my hair. We'll watch you."

"And I'll get us all drinks," Little Ben said. "Name your poison."

Lex felt Gillian tense, and he didn't blame her.

"Uh, let me rephrase that," Little Ben said. "What would you both like to drink?"

"Something virgin," Gillian said. "A mai tai would be great."

"I'll have a virgin, too," Lex said. "Piña colada."

"I can take a hint." Dante rolled his eyes. "Virgin for me, too. Bloody Mary. Maybe I can talk BJ into a real drink."

BJ shook her head. "Mineral water with lime."

"Some cruise this is," Dante muttered.

Little Ben stood. "So that's a mai-tai for Gillian, a piña colada for Lex, a Bloody Mary for Dante, and a mineral water with lime for BJ. I'll be right back."

"Next round!" Jared called out over the bullhorn. "To refresh your memory, one partner gets in the pool, and the other one gets the word from me. Then both partners submerge themselves while the one who knows the word tries to communicate it to the one who doesn't. You can say the word, act out the word, whatever you want. The first partner who leaps up and says the word out loud wins that round for their team."

"I'll get in the pool," Gillian said. "You go get the word."

Lex hesitated. "Get in the shallow end, okay?"

"Are you worried about me drowning?"

"No. I'm . . . uh, the thing is, I can't swim."

Dante stepped up. "But that doesn't mean he's a nerd, or anything."

"Of course it doesn't." Gillian smiled. "The shallow end's fine."

Lex was grateful she was okay with his nonswimming status, but he was also grateful they'd had plenty of sex leading up to his revelation.

"I'll get in the pool with her," Dante said. "Just to make sure she's okay."

Lex gave his partner a sharp glance. "Behave yourself."

"Like you have to say that. Have I ever poached on your territory?"

Lex lifted his eyebrows.

"I mean, recently?"

Gillian laughed. "Let's go, Dante. And don't worry, Lex. I'll keep him in line."

Lex felt certain she would. On the way over to the podium where Jared was giving out the word, he checked to see if Hector was still in his lounge chair. He hadn't moved, and Dorothy was still by his side. Once again, it seemed unlikely that anyone would try something with all these people around. But Lex had thought that before, and then a large metal drum had nearly crushed the woman he loved.

Loved? Where had that come from? Sure, he was planning to go with her to South America, but that was so that nothing horrible would happen to her. That didn't mean he loved her . . . exactly. Then again, that was a fairly drastic move to make for someone else.

"Ready for the word?" Jared asked him.

"Yeah, sure." He took the card that Jared handed him and shielded the contents as he opened the flap. *Commitment.* Son of a bitch.

"Got it?" Jared peered down from his perch atop the podium.

"I've got it." He walked back toward the pool where everyone's head bobbed above the surface, including one particular head, a blonde who kept telling him how ugly she'd look once her roots started to show.

There was nothing particularly significant about that word showing up right now, he told himself. This was a couple's cruise, so of course they'd choose words that had significance for people who were hooking up. *Commitment* was a good word for charades, because it wouldn't be that easy to say underwater.

But he couldn't shake the feeling that the word was meant for him, so that he'd understand what he was about to take on. He'd told Gillian he was coming along, but he hadn't told her why, maybe because he hadn't been clear on that himself. And yet the word *love* had just appeared so naturally in his brain, as if it had been simmering there, waiting for the right moment to shine.

By going with Gillian to South America, was he saying that he wanted to marry her and spend the rest of his life with her? He hadn't been willing to put that kind of weight on the decision, but it wasn't fair to tag along on such a momentous journey without giving her some idea of his intentions. No wonder she hadn't been excited about his announcement. He hadn't framed it right.

Vaguely he remembered some of the points from Little Ben's astrology report. Cancer and Aries were supposed to have problems because Cancer wanted to be romanced and Aries wasn't into that. Judging from his behavior toward Gillian, he'd been a textbook case. All sex, no hearts and flowers.

With luck, he had some time to remedy that.

GILLIAN COULDN'T GUESS THE WORD. WITHOUT HER glasses, all she saw were a mass of bubbles when Lex tried to say it. Then he kept patting his heart, and she was convinced the word was *angina*. But when she leaped up and yelled it out, she was wrong. Then she thought it might have something to do with his lungs and she guessed *congestion*. Dante and BJ were declared the winner before she had even a clue.

"Commitment!" Lex said as they climbed out and grabbed towels.

"Oh." No wonder she hadn't guessed it. Commitment was the last thing on her mind right now. Sex, yes. Despite the paisley trunks, Lex was looking mighty fine. Even those nerdy trunks couldn't spoil the effect of wide shoulders and excellent pecs. Besides, she knew what was under that paisley, and it turned her on.

They agreed to wait out the next round and enjoy the drinks that Little Ben had brought them.

"Nancy was over at the bar," Little Ben said. "We had a chat, and I tried to tell if she was wearing . . . you know . . . falsies. I couldn't tell."

"She has this routine down pat." Gillian glanced over to where Nancy lounged on one of the bar stools. "But you notice she hasn't taken off her bathing cap ever since she put it on. That's because her wig would come off with it."

"Why would she even want to go on a cruise like this?" Dante sipped his Bloody Mary and kept sneaking glances at Nancy. "I don't get it."

"For the same reason I did, maybe," BJ said. "She's looking for someone special. And you never know. One of the nerds might be kinky."

"Not Jared, apparently," Cora said. "That romance is definitely off. He's staying far away from Nancy. My guess is that he found out the truth."

"It must be sad, in a way," Little Ben said. "To be so sexually confused."

Gillian watched Nancy laughing with the bartender. "I don't think she's the least bit confused. She's happy with the way she is. Maybe she'll luck out and find somebody who's happy with the way she is, too."

"Hey, there's another charades round starting, Dante," BJ said. "Let's go rack up some points."

"We're going to give you some competition this time." Gillian turned to Lex. "You go in the water and I'll get the word."

"Yeah, we'll switch around, too," Dante said. "That way one of us is always with Gillian."

She appreciated that. Although she was determined to spend this last day of the cruise having a good time, it was nice to know that several people were watching her back. She got the word from Jared.

This time it was *aphrodisiac*. She wondered if Lex ever needed anything other than visual stimulation. He might not think aphrodisiacs made any sense, which would make it tough to communicate the concept.

She shouldn't care whether they won or not, but as she

hopped into the pool next to him, she felt her competitive urges rising to the surface. She caught him looking at her with an odd expression on his face.

She sighed. "My hair's a mess, huh?"

"No. I like it all wet like that. I was thinking you look great, so excited and happy. I wish we were on the cruise to have fun and play games, enjoy sex and great food."

"I wish that, too."

"Contestants, duck under!" Jared announced over the bullhorn.

"Here goes." Gillian submerged and began mouthing the word. It had so many syllables, and the more she tried to say it, the fuzzier her brain became.

Lex popped to the surface, and she rose with him. Wow, she was really dizzy. Maybe she'd held her breath too long.

"Androgynous!" Lex shouted.

"Wrong!" Jared shouted back.

Gillian couldn't see well without her glasses, but she could swear that Jared blushed. Poor Jared. His sweetie had turned out to have extra body parts he hadn't counted on.

"Let's try again." Lex sank beneath the water.

Gillian sank, too, but she was having trouble with her coordination. She kept drifting sideways, and she couldn't seem to hold her breath. Somehow she made the mistake of breathing in, and then she couldn't figure out what to do about it.

Lex's face came close, and then he lifted her out of the water. She couldn't get her breath, and the blue sky above her seemed to shimmer and pop. Pretty colors, but she was afraid she might pass out, and that would be embarrassing. She began to shiver. And then she couldn't breathe at all.

Someone stuck a finger down her throat. How icky. She tried to pull it back out, but her arms and hands wouldn't work right. Then she threw up. That was not what she'd been going for. Someone had made her do that, and they'd pay the consequences.

Throughout it all she heard Lex's voice, soothing her, telling her it was okay. She would be fine. He was right there, and he would protect her. Yeah, but he hadn't stopped that maniac from putting a finger down her throat and making her throw up.

Finally, the haze cleared a little bit and she looked up to find Lex, Dante, Cora, BJ, and Little Ben leaning over her. There was bustling in the background, and soon someone in an official-looking uniform shouldered his way into the group and leaned over her, too. She felt like the camera person inside a football huddle.

"I'm Mr. Stern," the man said. "Maybe we should have the ship's doctor take a look at her."

Don't talk about me in the third person, like I'm dying! She wanted to shout that, but she couldn't seem to say anything, let alone shout.

"I don't think that will be necessary," Lex said. "Gillian, are you feeling better?"

She drew on what little energy she had and managed to nod. No matter what, she didn't want to lose contact with Lex, and going to see the ship's doctor could threaten her contact with her bodyguard.

"Sun and alcohol can be a wicked combination," said Mr. Stern.

"True." Lex's jaw was tight. "We'll be careful about that from now on."

"Keep an eye on her." Mr. Stern moved back. "Let me know immediately if her condition gets worse."

"Let's get her to her stateroom," Dante said.

Cora looked grim. "Good idea."

Gillian didn't remember a whole lot about the trip. There was some comment about the mattress that was still lying on the floor, and then she was laid carefully on her bed. Conversation went on above her, and she only caught snatches. It was all about the drinks and who had access.

She figured out the general content. Someone had tried to poison her by putting something in her drink. Someone else, probably Lex, had stuck his finger down her throat and made her throw it all up again. So he was the maniac she'd planned to settle a score with.

A person couldn't very well be upset if another person made her throw up in order to get poison out of her stomach. But the total effect must have been less than lovely. Not exactly a sexual turn-on.

One statement came through loud and clear. Lex's voice, filled with fury, said quite clearly, "I'm not letting her out of this room again."

She tried to protest, but she was still too weak to talk. She'd planned to wear the silver dress to dinner tonight. The dress would go back to L.A. with Cora tomorrow, so this was Gillian's last chance to appear in Marilyn's gown.

"I don't care what she thinks," Lex said, as if he'd tuned in to her thoughts. "If she feels like eating, one of you can bring food in after you've made absolutely sure no one has tampered with it. We have our walkie-talkies. We'll communicate that way."

"I'll go into the kitchen and stand over them while they dish it out," Cora said.

"And I'll go with you," Little Ben said. "I feel awful, thinking that someone used the drink I bought her to do this thing."

"It wasn't your fault," Lex said. "If anything, I blame myself."

"Don't," Dante said. "We all kept an eye on Hector, and he didn't get anywhere near that drink."

"Which means it's someone else," Lex said. "Or maybe there's more than one of them. In any case, she's not leaving this room."

So that was that, Gillian thought. It seemed that she was a prisoner, but at least she was on intimate terms with the jailor. That was her last conscious thought before she drifted off to sleep.

Twenty-six

AFTER EVERYONE LEFT, LEX CLOSED THE DRAPES AND turned on one lamp across the room from the bed, so Gillian wouldn't wake up in the dark and be scared and disoriented. Then he settled down on the desk chair and got his own adrenaline rush under control.

He probably should have taken off her bathing suit, which was still damp, but that might wake her up, and he thought she needed to sleep. Picking up the spread lying on the floor, he shook it out and covered her. Hesitating by her bed, he gave in to the urge to lean down and place a soft kiss on her cheek. Then he closed his eyes and said a little prayer of thanks that she was okay.

He'd had enough close calls to last him forever. Glancing at the door, he thought about the key access someone on board had. Might as well drag the mattress over there and at least lean it sideways in the entry area. That way the bathroom was available but no one could get in the door without banging against the mattress.

Once he'd accomplished that, he sat on the desk chair

again. His brain kept playing with what had happened and trying to come up with some answers. He couldn't believe that anyone had wandered by and tossed something in her drink while it was sitting on the table with Cora and Little Ben right there. That meant it had been doctored before it arrived at the table.

That didn't help much, though. Several people had been over there, and then there was the bartender, himself. Hector could have bribed him. But how would anyone have known which drink was Gillian's?

Then he knew exactly how. Picking up his walkie-talkie, he stepped into the entryway, hoping that would muffle the conversation enough so he wouldn't disturb Gillian.

Dante answered immediately. "What's up? Over."

"I figured out how someone knew which drink to poison. Are Little Ben and Cora right there with you?"

"Negative. Over."

"Good. I don't want Little Ben to get upset, but remember how he recited our orders before he left the table? I'll bet he recited them again when he got to the bar, just to make sure he got them straight Anybody listening would have known the mai tai was Gillian's. Over."

"I'm sure you're right, buddy. Damn. And there were a bunch of people at the bar, too. Over."

"I know. And we have no idea if someone's been bribed to be a part of this operation. I've been thinking about dinner, and I'll bet Gillian will want something to eat by then. So will I. But we can't have Cora or Little Ben making the same mistake of saying who the meal is for. Over."

"BJ and I will handle the food. We'll give Cora and

Little Ben something else to do. Don't worry. I'll take care of it. Over."

"Thanks. Over and out." Lex gazed at the walkie-talkie. Dante was a good guy, and Lex hadn't warned him yet that he'd be leaving with Gillian in the morning. He needed to do that, but he couldn't picture saying it to his best friend over a damned walkie-talkie.

So much had changed so fast. Originally he'd been hired to protect Gillian during the cruise. Now he intended to protect her for the rest of her life, if she'd have him. He had no idea where they'd live or how they'd live, but they would be together.

He thought about that for some time, daydreaming about how it would be living with Gillian. The daydream was going along fine until he remembered her chief complaint, that he was the wrong astrological sign for her. He wasn't romantic enough.

After stewing about that for another long while, he began to come up with some ideas that might impress her right now. For starters, the lamp he'd turned on could be decorated with some of her Victoria's Secret underwear. He headed for the drawer. Handling the underwear got him hot and bothered, but he forced himself to settle down. This was about romance, not sex.

His major problem was trying to separate the two. In his mind, sex and romance went together. He couldn't envision one without the other. When he was enjoying sex, he was also feeling romantic, or what he thought of as romantic. Wasn't it all about wanting to spend more time with that person? Like a lifetime? With lots of sex thrown in?

In any case, the room now glowed pink from the bra and panties he'd arranged over the lampshade. He'd never been in a brothel, but he imagined the lighting would be like this, and brothels were about sex, not romance. It was all so confusing.

What else? Romantic music would be nice. He tried the intercom music, but it was currently broadcasting mariachi tunes. He tried turning it down low, and that was a little better. Maybe some music, even trumpets, was a step up from no music at all.

Flowers would be good, but he couldn't figure out any way to add flowers to this scene. There was a complimentary magazine, a tourist's guide to Mexico, on the desk. He flipped through it and found a picture of a Mexican woman holding a basket of flowers. Close enough. Tearing out the picture, he propped it up on the nightstand next to Gillian's bed.

Then he settled down on the desk chair and started going through the rest of the magazine. He found a few more pictures that included flowers, so he tore those out, too, and placed them in various spots around the room. The area was looking quite festive and romantic, if he did say so himself.

He was reading an article about sport fishing in Mexico and wondering if he should consider getting into that when Gillian moaned softly. Putting down the magazine, he got up and walked over to her bed.

She turned on her back, dislodging the covers, and her eyes fluttered open. "Am I dying?"

"I hope not."

"I was dreaming that I heard trumpets, and I think they have trumpets in heaven."

"I wouldn't know about that." But she looked like an angel to him, with her hair all fluffy around her head, like a halo. He'd never seen a picture of an angel in a red bathing suit, though.

"I can still hear the trumpets."

"Oh." He'd been so involved in looking at her that he'd forgotten about the music. "It's the intercom. Mariachis. I kept it low, hoping that it might be . . ." He couldn't bring himself to say *romantic,* because he was afraid he might have goofed that up.

"Why is it so pink in here?"

Yep, he'd definitely goofed it up. "I, uh, thought pink lighting would be more soothing to your eyes."

She sat up slowly and looked around.

"Are you feeling okay? Maybe you shouldn't sit up yet."

"I'm feeling a little weird, but mostly I feel normal." She gazed at the pictures propped up around the room. "Nice pictures. They're a little blurry, but I can tell they have good color. Where'd they come from?"

"A magazine I found on the desk."

She glanced up at him. "You tore them out?"

"It was a complimentary issue. I don't think anybody will care."

"I didn't mean that. I just . . ." She focused on the lamp across the room. "So that's how come it's so pink in here." She squinted at it. "What's that hanging on the lampshade?"

"Your underwear." He braced himself for her to start laughing. He was a washout at this romantic stuff, and he might as well face it. If she didn't want to spend the rest of her life with him, he'd convince her to spend a few months, until she was settled and safe in South America.

Instead of laughter, he heard a sniff. Then another one. Then a gulp. He crouched beside the bed. "Gillian, are you *crying*?" That was so not what he'd been going for.

"Y-yes."

Oh, God. He'd done such a bad job of it that he'd made her cry. "I'm sorry." He felt a little like crying himself, except that guys didn't do that. They punched things, instead. "I probably shouldn't have tried, considering that I don't have a romantic bone in my body, but I thought that—"

"Lex, come here." She held out her arms.

He climbed into bed with her, because that was the only option, and he held her while she cried. "I'm sorry," he murmured about a hundred times.

"No, no!" She shook her head so hard she bashed him in the chin. "Don't be sorry. I *love* what you did. It's the sweetest thing anyone has ever done for me." She continued to sob.

"Yeah, but it's not romantic."

"Yes it is," she wailed. "It's romantic, and crazy, and creative, and you still can't go to South America!"

He held her tight. "Just try and stop me."

GILLIAN KNEW SHE WOULD STOP HIM, AND SHE'D FIG-ured out exactly how to do it. She'd figured out something else, too, and now she had to decide what to do about that.

As she'd hovered between sleep and consciousness, images had danced through her head, images of Theo and Neil. And then, interspersed with those images had been flashes of someone else . . . Nancy Roth. Gillian's subconscious had been wrestling with the question of Nancy, and who she looked like.

Gillian woke up knowing the answer. Now she needed a plan. But she couldn't think with Lex holding her close. When he did that, she wanted to have sex, especially after his endearing attempts to be romantic.

Knowing how hard he'd tried had opened the floodgates, but she was getting control of her tears. And if she didn't put a little distance between them right now, he'd soon have control of her. She couldn't think and have orgasms at the same time.

"Lex." She pushed gently at his chest. "I need . . . to go into the. . . ."

"Oh. Sure." He let her up immediately. "Do you feel like you're going to throw up?"

"No. In fact, I'm sort of hungry." She started toward the bathroom.

"I don't think you should leave the room until tomorrow morning. If you want something to eat, I'll have Dante get it."

She turned back to him. "I thought I remembered a dinner plan being discussed before I went to sleep. You're keeping me locked up here all night, aren't you?"

He looked wary, as if he expected an argument. "It's the best way to keep you safe. I realize that means you can't take advantage of the couples massage, but—"

"That's okay."

"I'm glad to hear you say that. I can't control the whole ship, but I can control what happens in this room."

She arched her eyebrows. "Is that right?"

"Well, in a manner of speaking." He flushed. "I meant safetywise, not sexually."

"Oh."

"You're all right with staying put?"

"Yes. I've had enough excitement for now." She gave him the once-over. This would be their last night together, and she planned to enjoy it. "At least, *that* kind of excitement."

His gaze warmed. "Look, I'm not suggesting we stay here just so we can have sex all night."

"You're not? That's too bad."

His breathing changed. "Uh . . . then do you want food now . . . or later?"

"Now. Then we won't have to be interrupted."

"Okay." He swallowed. "What would you like?"

She was touched by his eagerness to please her. Leaving him tomorrow would be awful, but she had to. It was for his own good. She paused in the bathroom doorway. "Whatever Dante can get us would be fine. I'm not fussy."

"I'll call him." Lex picked up the walkie-talkie.

"You know what? While we're waiting for the food, I'm going to take a shower and change into my nightgown."

"Your . . . your nightgown?"

"Uh-huh. Maybe I'll wear the white one tonight."

He looked worried. "But Dante will be coming with the food."

"Then how about if I stay in the bathroom until he leaves?" That would give her plenty of planning time.

"Good." Lex's shoulders relaxed. "Good idea."

Moments later, Gillian was standing under the hot shower spray, which was where she often came up with her best ideas. She had to remember that she was dealing with the Mafia, and the Mafia could be tricky. Lex and Dante weren't equipped to handle gangsters, but they would try. They could bring a vendetta down on themselves by acting rashly.

If Gillian could be the first one off the boat when they docked in the morning, she could go straight into town and find a telephone. Vista Verde might be on the small side, but surely they'd have a telephone. She'd call the LAPD and tell them that Neil Rucker was on board the *Sea Goddess* disguised as a woman named Nancy Roth. They could quietly pick Neil/Nancy up when the ship docked again in L.A.

Once Gillian had made her phone call, she could hire someone to drive her far, far away. With luck she'd be miles down the road before anyone else made it off the ship. Lex and Dante couldn't be blamed by the Mafia for having anything to do with Neil's capture, because they wouldn't have the information about Nancy. Therefore, no reprisals.

There was a small chance the LAPD wouldn't believe her story, but if they'd at least meet the *Sea Goddess* when it came into port and question Nancy, any decent detective would soon figure out she wasn't who she seemed to be. Then it was a matter of getting a confession.

That was where Gillian came up against her conscience. If she agreed to go back to L.A. and testify, it wouldn't matter whether Neil confessed or not. She was an eyewitness to the murder.

Well, she'd cross that bridge when she came to it. First the police had to nab Neil. And it couldn't be connected in any way to Lex or Dante. She wasn't about to have those guys pay the price.

LEX THOUGHT GILLIAN WAS UP TO SOMETHING, BUT he'd be damned if he knew what. She was being too cooperative, too willing to stay put in the room until tomorrow morning. He'd been around her long enough to suspect that meant she had something up her sleeve.

But she couldn't leave while he was awake, and he'd decided they'd sleep with the mattress up against the door again tonight. It would keep intruders out, but it would also keep Gillian in. Maybe she had no plans to go wandering around the ship. But she was definitely plotting mischief. He could see it in her big brown eyes.

Dante arrived sooner than he'd expected, and he had to

haul the mattress out of the way before he could open the door. At the last minute he ran back and pulled the pink underwear off the lampshade and stuck it under Gillian's pillow.

Finally he answered the door. "That was quick."

"You, on the other hand, were incredibly slow," Dante said. "Did I interrupt something?"

"No. I had to pull the blockade away from the door. I would have done it sooner, but I thought you'd be a while."

"One thing about cruise ships, there's always food around somewhere." Dante wheeled a cart covered with a white tablecloth into the room. The cart held two plates covered with metal domes, two salads, two dishes of chocolate mousse with whipped cream and shaved chocolate on top, two wine glasses, a bottle of red wine, two candles in candleholders, and a rose in a bud vase.

Lex closed the door and stared at the display. "How'd you do all this?"

"Cora ordered room service for her and Little Ben in his room." Dante picked up a book of matches and lit the candles. "She told the cruise staff that they were celebrating their engagement."

"That's outrageous!"

Dante blew out the match and glanced at him. "Actually, it's true. But they're going to make do with snacks in the bar and a couple of really big margaritas instead."

"They're engaged? Already?" Lex wasn't sure he approved. "But she barely knows the guy."

"She knows him about as well as you know Gillian, and you're planning to run off to South America together."

Lex's jaw dropped. "How'd you know that?"

"I didn't, for sure, but I had a feeling. Now I know."

Lex's conscience bashed him over the head. "I should have told you earlier. I was afraid to, because I thought you'd go ballistic, and I . . ." He paused. "How come you're not going ballistic?"

Dante shrugged. "What's the point? You've met the woman of your dreams, and she has to leave the country. I can't expect you to do anything else. In fact, I'm not sure where I'll be in a few months. BJ's job is in San Jose, and she really likes where she works. She might be able to transfer, but if she can't, I'll have to move up there."

"You'd leave me?"

"Hey, you're the one leaving *me*, remember?"

"I meant, if I didn't have this South America deal. You'd just up and go to San Jose and desert me?"

"I might."

"But you've never let a woman call the shots."

Dante smiled at him. "That's because I've never found the right one." He pointed a finger at Lex. "And you know exactly what I'm talking about, too. Oh, here's the info for Cora's lawyer." Dante dug in his pocket, pulled out a business card, and handed it to Lex. "Cora wants Gillian to have it as a contact point."

"Thanks. I'll give it to her."

"So, are you going to tip your waiter?"

"Yeah." Lex was still blown away by Dante's dedication to this relationship with BJ. "Yeah, I am. I'm giving you Cora's fee, and my car, and anything in my apartment you can use or sell."

"Wow." Dante blinked. "Thanks. I wouldn't have done that for you if I'd gone to San Jose and left you in the lurch."

"South America is a little different proposition."

"I suppose. So I get it all, huh? Even your baseball card collection?"

"How do you know I still have that collection?" It was his guilty little secret. He was too old and too cool to have something like that, but he hadn't been able to give it up.

"Again, good guess. You're a nerd at heart, Lex. I guess that's why I like you. I've discovered I have a real fondness for nerds."

"I'm not a nerd."

"Yes you are, and that's a good thing." Dante rocked back on his heels. "So, what's the plan for tomorrow?"

"We don't have one. I'll have to call you on the walkie-talkie when I know more. The thing is, Gillian doesn't want me to go with her. She thinks I'm throwing my life away, and then there's this thing about her roots."

"Her roots?" Dante stared at him. "I don't get it."

"Me, either. It's some female hang-up having to do with how she looks. She's afraid that if she doesn't keep her hair blond and wear makeup and stuff, I won't think she's sexy. Is that stupid or what?"

"It's stupid, all right, but I know what you're dealing with. BJ is convinced if she hadn't had a makeover I wouldn't have noticed her. Don't women understand that all we care about is their naked bodies?"

"And their intelligent minds," Lex said quickly, in case any of this discussion was filtering through the bathroom door. He tilted his head in that direction, to tip off Dante.

"Oh, well, yeah." Dante choked back a laugh. "Of course I mostly care about BJ's intelligent mind. That's it. Her mind." Then he grinned and rolled his eyes. "Good luck convincing her, buddy. Hope the engagement dinner helps."

"I feel sort of guilty, taking it away from Cora and Little Ben."

"Don't be. Cora's already said yes." He lowered his voice. "You, on the other hand, still have some work to do." Then he waggled his eyebrows and walked out the door.

Twenty-seven

GILLIAN HAD CAUGHT BITS AND PIECES OF LEX'S CON-
versation. When she'd heard something about Cora getting engaged, she'd longed to rush out and ask for details,
but she'd promised Lex she wouldn't appear in front of
Dante in the white nightgown. And once she'd put it on,
she had to agree that was the wise choice.

It was looser than the black stretch lace, but the neckline dipped much lower, so that her breasts were barely
covered by the filmy material. It hung to mid-thigh and
had a matching pair of skimpy panties. She decided to put
those on, although they didn't make her feel much more
dressed.

As for makeup, she'd put on a little. The nightgown
seemed to call for it. But she hadn't created the red-lipped
Marilyn look, instead going for a nude shade of lipstick
and very subtle mascara and blush.

She'd never eaten a meal looking this sexy. Maybe
they wouldn't make it through the whole meal, considering how Lex usually responded to visual stimulation. And

that was okay. He didn't know this was their last night together, and because of that, she'd go along with whatever he wanted.

Taking a deep breath, she opened the bathroom door and stepped into a room that was no longer pink. The glow of candles beckoned her, instead. As she walked more fully into the room, she found a room service cart with the leaves up, and as romantic a table setting as she could ever ask for.

Lex had positioned the cart at the end of her bed, so that one of them could sit on the bed and the other could take the desk chair on the far side. He stood waiting in the little aisle between the beds, and when he saw her, he gasped.

She remembered that she'd made that happen the first time they'd met, when she'd worn the silver Marilyn dress. The thrill hadn't worn off for him, and she would be gone before there was even the remotest chance of that happening.

"You look . . . amazing."

"Thanks." She gestured toward the table. "This is beautiful."

"I can't take credit for it. I don't know if you could hear any of what Dante said, but—"

"Cora and Little Ben are engaged. I gathered that much." She was almost afraid to breathe in this nightgown. Something important might slip out. Once that happened, the meal would be over, and the food smelled delicious.

On the other hand, Lex looked damned good, too. After another near-death experience, she wouldn't mind celebrating life by getting it on with her resident bodyguard. Fortunately, she'd decided to leave the choice up to him, and he couldn't make a bad decision.

"Here's the card for Cora's lawyer."

"Thanks." She took it from him. "Where would you like me to sit?" If he told her to lie down, instead, she'd know his choice.

"In the chair." He came over and held it for her.

"Thank you." She placed the business card beside her plate before she sat down.

Lex scooted the chair in. "Just so you know, from this angle I can see just about everything."

The tremble in his voice made her reconsider whether they should start with the meal. "Is that so?"

"I wanted you to know, because I can't take credit for this meal, but I can take credit for enjoying it with you, all the way through, including the mousse, and not . . . not attacking you."

She thought about telling him that he could attack at will, but she sensed this was a self-imposed test, and he'd like himself better if he passed it. "Then I'm giving you all kinds of credit."

"I appreciate that. Because right now I want to rip off that white deal you're wearing and suck on your breasts." He walked around the table and eased onto the other side with a slight wince. "And I have an erection the size of the Coit Tower."

She decided to help him out by changing the topic. Placing her napkin in her lap, she glanced at him. "When's the wedding?"

"Do you want one? I'm sure we could arrange it, although most of South America is Catholic, I think. Are you Catholic? I never thought to ask something like that. There are a lot of things we haven't discussed, and I'm sure that you—"

"I meant for Cora and Little Ben," she said. But the

comments about a wedding involving her and Lex had been telling . . . and poignant. He was willing to marry her, and yet he'd known her such a short time. With Cora and Little Ben it was more understandable. At their age, they wouldn't want a long courtship.

But, at least potentially, Lex had decades ahead of him. How could he suggest marrying her when he still hadn't seen the real Gillian McCormick? She had to believe it was all about sex, and for him, that was a powerful motivator. She had to save him from himself.

"Oh. Right. Cora and Little Ben. I don't know." He became very busy uncorking the wine and pouring her a glass. "Sorry. I got ahead of myself, I guess." He poured himself a glass, set down the bottle, and picked up his glass. "Here's to . . . the future."

"I'll drink to that." A separate future, but one where each of them flourished. She clinked her glass against his and her nipple almost popped out of her nightgown.

Lex stared at her chest. "This is going to be tough."

"Do you want to just—"

"No." He tossed back a mouthful of wine. "We're going to have a romantic candlelit dinner, damn it."

She pressed her lips together so she wouldn't laugh. "Most couples don't have a dinner together while the woman in question is wearing a nightgown and a bed is in the immediate vicinity."

"Doesn't matter. You think this is all about sex, and I'm determined to prove to you that's not true."

"It is about sex, and you know it."

"Not completely. There's other . . . stuff."

She didn't want to press him to name that stuff, because he might get into areas they shouldn't talk about, especially knowing that he expected them to leave together tomorrow, and she knew it wouldn't be happening.

"The food smells great." Lifting off the dome covering her plate, she discovered filet mignon, steamed veggies, and rice pilaf. "Yum."

Lex took off the cover on his identical plate. "This is risky."

"Risky?" She paused with her fork and knife in midair. "You think it could be poisoned?"

"No, I think we have no idea if the steak is how we'd order it."

"Let's see." Gillian cut into hers. "Looks like medium to me. That would have been a safe choice. I suppose yours is the same." She glanced up when he moaned.

He was staring at her chest, and his eyes had glazed over.

She checked her nightgown, and the act of cutting her steak had partially exposed one nipple. "Sorry." She pulled the material back into place.

He cleared his throat. "When you cut your steak, everything . . . wiggled."

Laying down her knife and fork, she pushed back her chair. "This isn't going to work. Either I have to put on more clothes, or we have to have sex."

"Uh-huh."

She stood, her heart pounding. "Which?"

He pushed the table aside. "I thought I'd be stronger."

"You don't have to be strong." Stepping in front of him, she moved between his outstretched knees. "Take whatever you want."

He gazed up at her. "Ah, Gillian, forgive me." He eased the spaghetti straps down over her arms. "But I need . . ."

"I know." As the nightgown slipped over her hips and fell to the floor, she cupped her breasts and leaned forward. "So do I."

Because he took such pleasure in her body, she could be more uninhibited than she'd ever been in her life. She could offer herself in this way, and thrill to his grateful response. His hot mouth stirred her blood and made her bold. She pushed him back onto the mattress and sat astride. Then she leaned forward and teased him with gentle shimmies that drove him wild.

Laughing, she began to undress him, stroking him with her breasts until he was gasping for breath. Once she'd gotten rid of his clothes, she made love to his penis. This would be her gift to him, to take him all the way. He seemed willing to go along.

But just when she imagined she was in control and he was her helpless slave, he clamped both hands around her waist and rolled her to her back. "No." He struggled for air. "No."

She gazed up at him. "You were having fun."

"You'd better believe it."

"So why not let me?"

"Because . . . I want . . . more." Holding her down with his body, he fumbled on the nightstand and came up with a condom packet.

"More than a climax?"

"Yes. Stay right there."

"I'm not leaving." *Yet.*

"Good." He rolled away from her and put on the condom. Then he stripped off the flimsy panties she wore and moved between her thighs. "It's more than sex." Holding her gaze, he eased slowly inside. "And you know it is."

As he slid gently home, all the while looking into her eyes, she wanted somewhere to hide. She could deal with wild, boisterous sex. She couldn't deal with this.

"I know you're worried about whether we'll be good together." He began to move within her, but his breathing had steadied and the urgency was gone. "Don't worry about that. We'll take it one day at a time."

"It's not only that."

"I know. You think I'm crazy to give up all I have in L.A." His stroke was gentle, and oh, so persuasive.

"Yes." She knew what was right, but it was so hard to remember when he was loving her like this.

"That's my choice. It's what I want to do." His blue eyes searched her expression. "And it's what you want, too."

"It's not . . . about wanting." Her resistance was crumbling. He would make her come, and then she'd agree to let him throw away his life for her.

"It's all about wanting." He'd found that delicious spot that turned her into a quivering mass of acceptance. "Tell me you don't want me."

"I . . . can't."

"I know." He used just enough force to bring her unbelievable pleasure. "Because you do. You want me, and I want you. It's all so simple. Now come for me, Gillian."

She did, arching her back and crying out with the joy of it. Tears streamed down her cheeks.

He kissed them away. "It's so good. So very good." Then, with one smooth thrust, he climaxed, his body quaking against hers.

She held him as they both quivered with the aftershocks. Tears of a different kind leaked from beneath her closed eyes. She would still leave him, but he'd just made it a thousand times harder.

◆ ◆ ◆

LEX THOUGHT THE DINNER TASTED FINE COLD. FROM the way Gillian kept looking at him during the meal, he must have made the impression he'd been after. He wasn't planning to tell her he loved her . . . yet. She might not be willing to believe it now.

But after they'd weathered the excitement of plunging into unknown territory together, after he'd proved himself a worthy traveling companion as they navigated their way down to South America, then she might be ready to accept the truth. She might even be in love with him by then.

If she'd only trust that he was capable of making this decision for himself, then they'd have days to work through their differences, whatever they might be. He didn't think they'd be significant. They had shared values, similar intelligence levels, and incredible sex. She might want to minimize the importance of that last thing, but he didn't, not for a minute.

She certainly didn't object to the idea of making love again after dinner. And she didn't seem to mind indulging again once they'd positioned the mattress in front of the door for the night. Once he'd accomplished that, he was able to finally go to sleep. The next morning they'd be docked at Vista Verde, and when she left, he'd go with her. There was really no way that she could stop him.

GILLIAN SLEPT VERY LITTLE. TOMORROW WAS THE most important day of her life. She hoped it didn't turn out to be the last day of her life. Her tummy churned every time she thought about what she had to do.

Then she'd think about leaving the man who slept so peacefully beside her, and her heart would start to hurt. On one hand she wanted to get this over with. On the other she wished the night would go on forever, so she'd never have to leave the man she loved so desperately.

Eventually light began to trim the edges of the curtains, although the ship's engines continued to thrum steadily. Gillian climbed out of bed and walked over to the window to peer out. The ship cruised quite close to land, and she could see volcanic outcroppings and crescents of sandy beach. Birds wheeled in the bright blue sky.

"Are we almost there?"

She turned to find Lex sitting up and watching her. "Looks like it."

"Then we'd better get ready. I think we should plan to be the first ones off the ship."

"Right." She would be, but he wouldn't.

"I've been trying to decide if it would be better to hire somebody to drive us, or see if we could buy a car."

"I'm not sure." She'd decided not to lie if she absolutely didn't have to, but she might neglect to say a few things.

"Me, either, but I'm thinking hiring someone might make the most sense. That keeps things more flexible." He stood, magnificent in his nakedness. "So is that the plan? Skip breakfast and get off the ship ASAP?"

"Sounds good to me."

"Okay, then." He leaned down and tipped the mattress up against the closet. "Let's get ready."

"Yes, we need to." She wasn't sure when her opportunity would come. She only knew her timing had to be perfect.

As they shared the bathroom and got dressed, Lex talked about what he should take in his backpack. "I don't want to make it look too bulky, because then someone might get suspicious. I can take a few things of yours, though, because I'm sure you can't cram very much in your purse."

She couldn't, indeed. Mostly she was counting on the money that Cora had given her, plus some essentials like a toothbrush, deodorant, and some basic makeup. A change of underwear, one extra blouse—and that was about it for her. She would love to have her passport, but that was gone. The business card for Cora's lawyer was tucked in her purse, though, so she could get her duplicate from Cora eventually.

The ship's engines slowed, and a series of thumps and scraping noises told her they were docking at Vista Verde.

"We're here," Lex said. "Don't forget your nametag. We'll need that to disembark."

"Got it." She lifted the cord over her head and settled it around her neck.

"Are you about ready?"

"Close." Bustling around as if she had more to accomplish, she tried not to seem as if she were watching Lex, although she was aware of his every move.

"Me, too. I wonder if I should take my shaving stuff. Ah, I'll just buy it later on. Or maybe I'll let my beard grow. Do you like beards?"

"Sure." She picked up his walkie-talkie from the nightstand. While he was taking his razor and shaving cream out of his backpack, she was able to set her trap without him noticing a thing.

"Are you going to call Dante?" she asked. Her heart twisted as he looked at her with such an open expression of gratitude.

"Damn, I almost forgot. Thank you for reminding me.

That would be crummy, if I didn't let him know we were leaving." He glanced around. "Have you seen my walkie-talkie? I thought I left it on the nightstand."

"Believe it or not, I think it's in the bathroom."

"Huh. I must be really distracted if I put it in there."

She held her breath as he stepped over the sill into the tiny bathroom. How she loved him. And she would never see him again. She closed the door quickly, and as he yelled in surprise, she flopped the mattress down, blocking the bathroom door, but not her exit.

"Gillian!" He threw his weight against the door, but it held. *"Gillian!"*

"I love you," she whispered as she grabbed her purse, opened the door, and fled down the hall.

The crew was just lowering the gangplank as she arrived at the double doors leading off the ship.

A young crew member smiled at her. "You're up early."

"Lots of shopping to do." She gave him her nametag to swipe.

"Have fun." He handed it back to her. "Don't lose that. It's your entry back on board. We sail at four-thirty this afternoon."

"Thanks." She hurried down the gangplank. By four-thirty she'd be far away from this ship . . . far away from Lex. Her chest hurt as she walked quickly along the wooden dock toward the tiny cluster of buildings and shacks that made up Vista Verde.

As she walked, she took her own walkie-talkie out of her purse and punched in Cora's code.

Cora didn't answer. Gillian remembered the morning before, when she and Lex had found Cora and Little Ben snoring away in a couple of deck chairs, oblivious to everything. That seemed like years ago.

She'd wanted to tell Cora good-bye and thank her for all her help. So much for that idea. Turning off the walkie-talkie, she took aim and threw it into the water.

So that was it, her last contact. The cruise had been a piece of cake compared to this. Now she was officially on the run. Alone.

Twenty-eight

LEX GULPED IN AIR AND GRABBED THE WALKIE-talkie. At least she'd left him that. Cora had a key to the room. But Cora wasn't answering her walkie-talkie. *Shit.* Lex pictured both Cora and Little Ben dead to the world after a night of margaritas and other activities he didn't want to think about. Starting to sweat, he punched in Dante's code.

He should have seen this coming, should have known she'd figure out a way to keep him from following her. Damn it! Why wasn't Dante answering?

Finally Dante responded, sounding very sleepy. "Italian Stallion, here." In the background, someone giggled.

"Dante, she trapped me in the bathroom and left! Over!"

"Yikes!" Dante sounded wide awake, now. "How'd she do that? Over."

"Who cares? Cora's got a key, but she's not answering her walkie-talkie! Hello? Are you there?"

"Yeah! You're supposed to say *over*. Over."

"To hell with that. Do you understand? She's gone and I'm stuck! Over, damn it!"

"Okay, okay. Calm down, buddy. I'll get the key from Cora. I'll be there in two shakes of a lamb's tail. Don't worry. We'll find Gillian. Over and out." The walkie-talkie went dead.

Lex stared at himself in the bathroom mirror. A complete idiot stared back. He'd known Gillian was smart, had known that she was determined not to let him sacrifice himself for her cause. But it was no sacrifice. Without her, life would be one miserable day after another, filled with regrets for what might have been.

He should have told her he loved her. Whether she'd believed him or not, she might have realized how serious he was about going with her. She would have had to deal with a declaration of love. But he'd let her off the hook on that one, and now . . . now she was out there, alone and unprotected.

Picking up the walkie-talkie, he tried Cora again. Still no answer. With nothing else to do, he kept trying her over and over. He could easily go crazy trapped in here, knowing that Gillian was wandering around some unfamiliar village looking for the best way to escape into the countryside.

She needed someone with her. Lex wasn't convinced he was her best bet, but he was currently available, or he had been until she'd shut him into the bathroom. He'd made it so easy for her with his mattress program. Then he'd walked right into the trap she'd laid. She'd put his walkie-talkie in here to lure him inside.

If he weren't consumed with worry, he'd admire the way she did it. He wondered when she'd come up with the plan, but he suspected she'd had it for quite some time. She'd made love to him all night long, allowing him to believe that she'd been lulled into an agreement that had existed only in his sex-besotted brain. All along she'd meant to leave him. That had taken nerve.

After what seemed like hours, the stateroom door opened. "Lex, buddy! The cavalry has arrived!"

"Cut the drama, Dante! Just move the damned mattress, okay?"

"You got it." Some scuffling ensued. Then Dante opened the door. He was unshaven and dressed in wrinkled shorts and a plaid shirt that was buttoned up wrong. "Let's go."

"I want to go, too." BJ came through the door, looking as disheveled as her sweetheart.

"We want to go, too." Cora, uncharacteristically rumpled, crowded into the room, followed by Little Ben.

Lex stared at the group with growing horror. "No. You can't all go. There's no telling what will happen. We're dealing with the Mafia. They could have accomplices here in Vista Verde, for all I know."

Dante shivered. "You never brought that up before."

"I didn't think it mattered. I was going to be the only one dealing with them." He stared hard at BJ, Cora, and Little Ben. "I mean it. Don't follow us. You'll only slow us down, and we'll have to worry about your safety."

"He's right," Dante said. "Stay here."

BJ lifted her chin. "I'm going. You need me. I'll bet I can guess how she's thinking. I'll help you find her."

"BJ could be right about that," Dante said. "She's magna cum laude."

"So am I," Lex said.

"You are?" Dante's eyebrows lifted. "How'd I miss that?"

"I don't go around with it on a T-shirt." Lex was out of

patience. In other circumstances, he might have worked harder to make certain everyone stayed safe, but right now, the only person he cared about was Gillian. Short of locking everyone in the bathroom, he didn't know how to keep them from following him.

"Okay, I'm leaving," he said. "I can't stop you from coming along, but I'm not waiting for anyone. Either keep up or get left behind." Pushing past the bodies clogging the door, he started down the hallway at a trot.

"I'm right on your tail, buddy!" Dante caught up with him before he got to the elevator, and BJ joined them a second later.

"You young people go ahead," Cora called after them. "We'll cover your flank!"

Lex groaned and plunged into the elevator. This was going from really bad to absolutely disastrous.

VISTA VERDE WAS SMALLER THAN GILLIAN HAD EX-pected. One unpaved street ran past a group of open-air stalls that were more temporary shacks than permanent structures. Each merchant had cleared away a section of prickly pear and cholla cactus, nailed together some boards and plywood, and declared themselves in the tourist business. A few vendors were starting to take down the front panels in order to sell the wares stored inside to the cruise ship full of passengers.

The only substantial building in town seemed to be the cantina, an adobe building located at the far end of the dusty street. The scent of fried tortillas hung in the air, and a couple of chickens ran squawking across in front of Gillian as she walked briskly toward the cantina. That looked like the only logical place to find a telephone and someone with a car.

She fought panic at the rural character of the town. She'd expected more of an infrastructure—a train station, maybe, or even a bus depot. This looked like little more than a byway to satisfy the tourists on the cruise ships.

A few rickety-looking houses painted in pinks and blues sat up on a hillside at the far end of the street. A couple of them had rusty trucks parked next to the house under the shade of scraggly mesquite trees. The trucks didn't look as if they'd make it down the street, let alone to a village with more options.

On her way into town, she'd passed a few fishing boats moored at the dock, and she supposed leaving by sea was always a possibility. But she hated the idea of going back in that direction. She'd made it to town ahead of the other passengers, and that's the way she wanted to keep it.

A vendor called out to her as she walked past. "Señorita! Come look! I give you good price!"

Turning, she waved at the man who was selling serapes and large straw hats with MEXICO stitched on the crown. "Maybe later!" Then she glanced up at the banner strung across the front of the cantina and wondered if the passengers would be insulted by a sign that read WEL-COME, GEEKS!

The door to the cantina stood open, and she walked into the dim interior. "Anybody here?" The place smelled of cigarettes, beer, and refried beans. She'd bet they served good ones here, but she'd never have the chance to find out.

Empty tables and chairs were scattered about, some made of wood, some made of slats and oiled pigskin. She imagined by noon the place would be jumping with tourists eager to down as much blue agave tequila as they could hold.

"Can I help you?" A short woman with her dark hair in

a bun came through a curtained doorway. She dusted flour from her hands. "We're not open yet."

Gillian was grateful the woman spoke good English, but she shouldn't be surprised. Obviously this town existed because of the cruise lines. They would need to understand the language of those bringing the money. "I know. I need . . . a telephone." She'd start with the first order of the day and move on from there."

The woman gazed at her. "You have a calling card?"

"Yes."

"This way." The woman beckoned her back behind the battered wooden bar and pointed to a black phone that looked like it had been manufactured fifty years ago. It had a rotary dial.

Beggars couldn't be choosers. Gillian smiled at the woman. "Thanks. I won't be long."

"Take your time." The woman waved at the phone. "Nobody ever calls." Then she disappeared into the kitchen.

Gillian had her calling card ready and the receiver in her hand when she noticed a movement by the door of the cantina. She ducked down. It was probably only one of the vendors, but she didn't want to take chances.

Then she heard footsteps on the wood floor of the cantina. She wondered if a hunted person developed special instincts, because she knew without looking that the person standing in the cantina was searching for her. She was just as sure it wasn't Lex. Lex would have called out her name.

Whoever it was walked out again. Gillian peeked over the edge of the bar and saw a man with his back to her standing in the arched doorway of the cantina. She began to shake. Hector Michelangelo.

Crouched there gripping the edge of the bar, she waited for what seemed like a lifetime until Hector moved away and started back down the street. But he was sauntering, not walking as if he intended to return to the ship. He must have seen her walk into town and had followed. It didn't take much imagination to figure out why.

Slowly she replaced the receiver of the phone. She could call later, once she was away from this place. One day wouldn't make a difference, and she'd probably been foolish to think she had to call right away. Either foolish or unsure how long she'd be alive to accomplish that. She'd go with foolish.

Quietly she slipped through the curtained doorway. Obviously startled, the woman in the bun looked up from the table where she was making tortillas. The kitchen smelled of onions and chili peppers, and Gillian wished she could be just a tourist looking forward to lunch at the cantina.

"Did you make your call?" the woman asked.

"Yes." Gillian decided she needed to get used to telling lies. No matter how she disliked doing that, it would help her survive. "I'm trying to meet up with a friend. Is there anyone around here who could drive me somewhere?"

The woman gazed at her with suspicion. "Where?"

"To the next village."

"That's three hours away. Your ship sails at four-thirty. You might miss it."

"I know." Gillian reached in her purse and pulled out her wallet. "I can pay."

The woman studied her for a long, agonizing moment. "Wait in the cantina. I'll see what I can do."

"But couldn't I wait here?"

"No." The woman didn't seem to want Gillian and her problems invading this kitchen. "In the cantina."

Left with no choice, Gillian walked back through the curtained doorway. Then she peered out into the street looking for Hector. He'd stopped by the vendor selling serapes and large straw hats. Maybe he was planning to take home a souvenir to commemorate getting rid of her.

LEX, DANTE, AND BJ HAD STARTED DOWN THE GANG-plank when Dante pointed at someone walking along the dock toward town. "Isn't that Nancy teetering along on a pair of stilettos?"

"Looks like it." Lex continued at a brisk pace down the dock, which creaked as the waves rolled underneath. The air smelled of fish and rotting wood.

He didn't like this place. It was too remote. People could be eliminated here, and there would be no trace. Number one, there was the ocean for hiding evidence, and number two, there was all the open desert. God, why hadn't he figured out Gillian's trap and stopped her from taking such a foolish risk in such alien territory?

"I wonder what Nancy's doing out here so early?" Dante said. "You'd think a party girl would wait until the cantina opened for business."

"Call me paranoid," Lex said, "but I'm suspicious of anyone who's out here right now, considering that Gillian's already left the ship."

"Right," Dante said. "A cross-dresser isn't going into town to stock up on serapes and straw hats."

"She has something to do with this trouble with Gillian," BJ said. "I have a gut feeling about it."

Lex didn't want to hear that, but he wasn't going to dismiss any possibility. Too much was at stake. "I wondered that, too, but Mafia guys are about as macho as you can get."

"You're stereotyping again," Dante said.

"Maybe." Lex kept his eyes open as he moved quickly down the dock. He didn't think Gillian would have taken refuge in a fishing boat, but he looked them over, all the same. "But consider the Sicilian mind-set. Isn't masculinity a big deal in that culture?"

"It is now," BJ said. "But you go back to early Rome, and you had all sorts of interesting things going on, sexually speaking. Maybe Nancy's a throwback."

"I'm sorry." Lex shook his head. "I don't picture some godfather type sending a cross-dresser out to handle a job. It makes no sense."

"We're going to overtake her," Dante said. "Are we planning to make pleasant conversation or what?"

"I'll make the conversation," Lex said. "She got out here ahead of us, and right now we need information. She happens to be the only source of it in sight."

Dante leaned close to BJ. "Lex has more investigative experience than I have, so I let him handle this kind of work. I just deal with the more physical parts of the job."

"Watch yourself, Dante," Lex said. "Don't be getting into trouble by bragging about yourself."

"What? I had a course in karate once."

"In high school."

"You don't forget that stuff," Dante said. "It's like falling off a bike. Wait. That didn't come out right."

"It came out perfectly," Lex said. "Now be quiet and let me see what Nancy has to say for herself. Hey, Nancy! Wait up!"

Nancy turned and shaded her eyes. "Why, if it isn't my old roommate, BJ, and her new roommate, Dante! And Lex, who used to be my dinner companion, except you didn't show up at the table last night, and neither did Norma Jean. What happened to you two?"

"Norma Jean wasn't feeling well," Lex said.

"Is she still under the weather?" Nancy was dressed in

a bright yellow sundress that barely covered her ass. The stiletto heels matched perfectly.

"She's feeling better, thanks." Lex wished Nancy weren't wearing sunglasses. He'd like to read her expression better. "You're up bright and early this morning."

"Goodness, yes! I'm always ready for a bargain. These quaint little stalls sometimes have the most marvelous leather items." She smiled at Lex. "Are you into leather?"

"Not especially." Nancy gave him the creeps, and he supposed that was his homophobia kicking in. But maybe it was something more. He just couldn't imagine how she could be part of a plot to take out Gillian. "Looks like we're the only ones up and about this early, though."

"Not quite."

"Oh?" Lex didn't dare hope that she'd mention seeing Gillian.

"I noticed that dark-haired guy Hector had a head start on me as I was walking down the dock. I thought he might be with Dorothy, but maybe he's decided to head out early and surprise her with a souvenir."

Lex tried to control his reaction and wasn't sure if he succeeded or not. "Hector, huh?" He looked at Dante. "You know, we haven't gotten much exercise on this trip."

"Speak for yourself."

"How about a race into town?"

"You're on. Go!"

Lex took off with Dante right by his side.

"Hey, wait for me!" BJ called. Soon she was sprinting right beside them.

"Hey!" Dante glanced sideways at BJ. "Where'd you learn how to run?"

"Cross-country champ, senior year." She pulled slightly ahead of them.

"Damn." Dante dragged in air. "Smarter than me and faster than me."

Lex put on a burst of speed. "Just what you need as my replacement."

Dante gasped for breath. "Considering my relationship with BJ, you might want to rephrase that."

Lex and BJ reached the outskirts of town slightly ahead of Dante. Lex and BJ slowed to a walk, and Dante nearly ran them over.

He stopped and braced his hands on his knees as he struggled to breathe. "I thought we were in a hurry."

"We don't want to go racing down main street, now, do we?" Lex said. "From this point on, we have to be stealthy." He gazed at Dante and shook his head. "As if."

"I can be stealthy. Just as soon as I catch my breath."

"Ready?" Lex looked back and saw Nancy hurrying down the dock as fast as her high heels would let her.

"Let's find Gillian," BJ said.

"Right." Dante fell into step beside them.

They turned the corner and gazed down the dirt road.

Dante cleared his throat. "Does anybody else feel an OK Corral moment coming on?"

"Let's hope not." He searched the street, not expecting to find Gillian, but hoping she might be there, somewhere. "Hector's over by that stall," he said quietly. He was relieved to see the guy out in plain sight. It seemed likely Hector hadn't located Gillian yet, either.

"Okay, here's the plan," BJ said. "We go over and talk to Hector about souvenirs and stuff. Then I say I have to go to the bathroom. I'm sure the only bathroom in this town is in that cantina. And if Gillian's looking for a way out of town, she would have gone there first."

"Good," Lex said. "That way we can keep Hector

occupied while you check out the cantina and ask if anybody's seen Gillian."

"And the story makes sense," Dante said. "Women are always having to go to the bathroom."

BJ glared at him. "We'll take that up later. Okay, let's roll."

Hector looked up from the serape he was examining as the three of them approached. In his Blues Brothers sunglasses and holding a cigarette, he looked very much like a Mafia guy to Lex. But there was no proof. Hector could be simply buying a souvenir for Dorothy.

"Hi," Hector said. "You three must have been up at the crack of dawn."

"You know what they say." Dante walked over to a display of painted gourds. "The early bird gets the maracas. Check these out, BJ."

Lex took a deep breath and stretched. "Feels good to get here ahead of the crowd, you know?"

Hector nodded. "Yeah." He studied Lex. "So, want a cigarette?"

That was all he needed, to choke himself to death on a cancer stick when he needed to be alert and ready for anything. "Thanks, but I don't dare. I caught hell for the last one."

"Norma Jean's right about that. Smoking's bad for you. Where is she, by the way?"

"Under the weather," Lex said.

"Hm." Hector looked unconvinced.

"You guys, I really, really have to go to the bathroom," BJ said. "I'm heading over to the cantina to see if they have one there."

"Oh." Dante looked at her. "Good idea. We'll be right here. Hector, what do you know about maracas?"

"Not much." Hector watched BJ walk across the street toward the cantina. "I was thinking Dorothy might go for a serape, though. She was talking about getting one to hang on her wall." He turned to Lex. "You should get something to take back to Norma Jean. I'll bet she'd like that."

"I'm sure she would." Lex tried to convince himself that Hector was just a guy out buying a surprise gift for his girlfriend. But he couldn't make himself believe that.

"Whew!" Nancy hurried over to them, her heels sinking into the ruts in the road. "That was quite a trip. You boys shopping?"

"*Sí,*" the vendor said, smiling. "They buy many things. I make them good price. You, too, pretty lady."

Nancy batted her eyelashes at him. "I'm sure I need one of everything you've got, señor." She glanced at Dante. "Where's my old roommate? Drinking in the cantina already?"

"The señorita, she's in the bathroom," the vendor said.

"Oh." Nancy surveyed the dusty street. "In the cantina, I assume?"

"Only one we got," the vendor said.

"Well, I need to go myself. If you boys will excuse me, I'll be right back."

Twenty-nine

WHEN GILLIAN HEARD FOOTSTEPS CRUNCHING ON the dry dirt of the street, she left her seat at a table and crouched behind the bar. Whoever it was walked into the cantina, but the footsteps sounded lighter than Hector's.

"Gillian?" someone called softly. "You in here? It's BJ."

Gillian closed her eyes in frustration. This wasn't working out the way she'd hoped at all. But maybe, with a little bit of luck, she could hide from BJ.

"Okay, maybe you're not in here," BJ said. "But in case you're hiding somewhere and can hear me, I just want to say that Lex is totally in love with you. I know you're trying to protect him, and I understand that. I'm thinking you must love him, too."

Yes. More than I realized.

"Anyway, he wants to help you," BJ said. "He's out on the street right now with Dante. They're talking to Hector. We still don't know if Hector's Mafia or not, but the two guys are keeping an eye on him. If you'd like to get a message to Lex, I could take it to him. Hector wouldn't have to know you're in here. If you are in here."

Gillian tried to breathe very quietly. It didn't really matter whether Lex was motivated by sex or love. In the long run, he'd still be making an unacceptable sacrifice to run away with her. She couldn't allow it.

"I had the feeling you would be hiding in here until you can get a way out of town," BJ said. "Maybe I was wrong."

"You weren't wrong." The short woman with the bun came through the curtained doorway. "She's right there, hiding behind the bar. What's this about Mafia, anyway?"

Ratted out. With a sigh, Gillian stood. She couldn't blame the woman. Who wanted to get involved with gangsters when all you wanted was to earn a few pesos from the tourists?

"Gillian!" BJ's gaze darted from her to the woman in the kitchen doorway. "We don't know that the Mafia's involved with this, ma'am. I was just looking for my friend."

"She wanted a car to get away." The woman turned to Gillian. "No car. Sorry."

"I'll pay more money," Gillian said.

"No. No car."

"What's this about a car?" Nancy walked into the cantina. "Oh, my goodness. If it isn't Norma Jean. Lex told me you were under the weather, and I have to say, you do look a little pale, darling."

Gillian's heart slammed against her ribs, but she forced herself to breathe and think carefully. She had to get BJ out of harm's way. "Nancy! Just the person I wanted to see."

"Is that right? Funny, because I was hoping to run into you, too."

Gillian glanced over to where BJ stood looking confused. "BJ, I have to ask you, as a friend, to go back to the guys and not say you found me in here."

"But what about Nancy? She'll tell them."

"I don't think she will. Will you, Nancy?"

"No, I most certainly won't. I'll keep your little secret."

BJ frowned. "I don't get this."

"It's simple," Gillian said. "Nancy's going to help me get away. Right, Nancy?"

"Absolutely, honey bunch. That's the plan. That was the plan all along. In another hour or so, we'll both be gone. I'll take care of everything."

"So you're running off with a cross-dresser." BJ shook her head. "That's pitiful, Gillian. And poor Lex. And you don't have to worry about me telling him anything. I'd rather he didn't know." BJ turned and stalked out of the cantina.

"Nice work." Nancy advanced toward her.

"This is between you and me." Gillian searched the bar for a weapon and found a small paring knife that was probably used for slicing limes. She picked it up and stuck it behind her back.

"I don't want any trouble!" the woman said from the kitchen doorway.

"No problem," Gillian edged away from the bar. "We'll go out behind the cantina. We just have to make a detour through your kitchen."

"Suits me," Nancy said.

Keeping her gaze fixed on Nancy, Gillian backed through the tiny kitchen filled with the scent of onions, garlic, and hot oil. Nancy followed, her heels tapping deliberately and surely on the wooden floor as she navigated the small space.

With a quick glance over her shoulder, Gillian located the rickety screen door. She backed through it into a dusty yard shaded by a mesquite tree. She heard the sound of chickens clucking.

"I hope you're not planning to run," Nancy said.

"No." Gillian's heart hammered, but her head was clear. She was the only one who could stop Neil, the only one who would take the blame for it. "Not this time."

HECTOR GAZED AFTER NANCY AS SHE TEETERED OVER toward the cantina and walked through the door. "Stupid shoes for this place."

"Yeah," Lex said. Then, on impulse, he decided to see what Hector's reaction would be to some news about Nancy. "We have a theory about her," he said.

Hector glanced at him. "What's that?"

"That she's a man dressed as a woman."

Behind Hector's sunglasses, his eyebrows lifted. As he stood there with a serape dangling from one hand, he uttered a soft, Sicilian-sounding curse. "I should have known."

Then he turned toward the cantina. "She can't go in there!" He dropped the serape in the dirt and started off at a run.

He collided with BJ, spun around, and hurled himself through the cantina door.

Lex took one look at Dante and they both ran after him.

"Wait!" BJ tried to block their progress. "Don't go in there!"

"We have to." Heart pounding, Lex brushed her aside.

"No, Lex!" BJ caught his arm. "It's not how you think it is!"

"BJ, don't try to stop me." He shook her off and kept going.

"But . . . but . . . Gillian's running off with Nancy!"

"The hell you say." Lex dashed through the cantina door with Dante right behind him. Gillian might have tried to give him the slip this morning, but no way was she running away with a cross-dresser. She was in love with *him*, damn it.

ONCE THEY WERE OUTSIDE, GILLIAN CROUCHED LOW and brought out the knife. She wasn't planning to kill him, but if she could disable him, that would be good enough. She'd never used a knife as a weapon in her life, though. Her odds weren't very good in this fight, but she was the only one standing between Neil Rucker and his freedom.

"Ah, I see you're armed." Neil took off both shoes, but he held on to one. "So am I." He began to circle her.

"I suppose you have a stiletto and you know how to use it."

"You caught that line, did you? Then you must know what happened after that."

"I'm not Theo."

"No, you're certainly not. But you're a bigger threat to me than he was. So I'm afraid you'll have to—" He paused and lifted his head. "I hear shouting."

Gillian did, too. Maybe BJ had said something, after all. The last thing Gillian wanted was Lex riding to the rescue and bringing the wrath of the mob down on himself. And yet she'd run out of ways to protect him.

When Hector came through the screen door, she lost all hope. So she was really and truly dead. She might be able to fight off Neil, maybe even subdue him, but she was no match for both Neil and Hector.

Neil glanced at Hector. "I thought so. My stepfather sent you to help, didn't he?"

"Yeah, he sent me."

Gillian moaned softly.

"But not to help you. To watch out for her."

Neil shot him a quick glance. "That's a joke."

"No it's not. You have orders to leave her alone and come with me. If you do that, you won't get hurt. Drop the stiletto."

"Okay. Sure." Neil let the shoe slip from his hand.

Gillian couldn't believe he'd give in so fast. Then again, Phil Adamo was a scary guy. As she started to relax, Neil leaped. In one smooth motion he'd twisted her arm behind her back and had the knife she'd meant for him pressed against her throat.

"Sorry," he said to Hector, "but that program doesn't work for me. My stepdaddy's trying to ruin my life, and I don't care for that."

"You'll live to regret this decision," Hector said.

Gillian hoped she lived, period.

"I doubt it," Neil said. "Gillian and I will simply disappear from this little burg." He started backing away from Hector. "If anybody tries to stop us, I'll kill her. Simple as that."

"What difference does it make?" Hector said. "You'll kill her anyway."

"True, but if you let me go you won't have to watch. And you can tell my stepfather that so far as you know, Gillian's still alive. It won't be a lie. And he might spare your worthless hide."

Gillian shuddered.

Hector's voice was steady, as if he were discussing the weather. "You'll have no transportation."

"Sure I will. Thanks to all the training I got growing up, I can hot-wire anything with an engine. Those trucks on the hill wouldn't be my first choice of a vehicle, but they'll get me to something better."

Dante came through the screen door. "I see we have a little party going on here. Hector, it seems we misjudged you."

"Nah, you had it right. I work for Phil Adamo. Just not for Neil Rucker. I should have figured that one out sooner."

Gillian watched the screen door. Lex should be stepping out any minute now, but there wasn't a thing he or anyone could do. She would try to get away, of course, and maybe she'd even succeed before Neil slit her throat. But she couldn't count on it.

"Say, Neil," Dante said. "You might want to watch where you're going. Lots of cactus around here. I'd hate to see you back into one, you being barefoot and all."

"Nice try. There's no cactus in the street, which is how I plan to get up to that rusty old truck I spotted earlier." He backed away faster. "I probably shouldn't have worn the stilettos, but I thought it would be such a nice touch if I dispatched Gillian the same way I did Theo. I love drama."

"I don't know if you're making a wise move," Dante said. "It could get prickly on that street."

"There's no cactus, I tell you! They drive their trucks down that street. They wouldn't want to blow a tire on—" Then he screeched like a banshee, and, for one brief moment, loosened his grip on Gillian.

BJ came out of nowhere and grabbed her, pulling her to safety as Lex appeared and hurled himself at Neil, knocking him backward onto the pieces of cactus scattered behind him all along the dirt road.

Gillian winced as the two rolled in the dirt and some of the cactus ended up stuck on Lex. Then Dante and Hector moved in. They both sustained cactus damage, too, but Neil in his miniskirt took the worst of it.

BJ went in search of rope while the men held Neil pinned to the ground. She was back in no time, and Hector did the honors of tying him up securely. Neil sat in the dust, covered in cactus and moaning.

Gillian ran to Lex, desperate to hold him.

"Stop!" He held up a bleeding hand. He gazed at her with longing. "Wait until I'm dethorned."

"Oh, Lex. Your hands . . ."

"There wasn't time to get gloves."

Her heart twisted at the pain he'd suffered to save her. "I love you so much."

"I love you, too. But stay away until I'm safe to touch."

"Let me see what's available in the kitchen." She hurried inside to find the cantina owner working doggedly away on her tortillas, as if she had no interest in the goings-on outside her screen door.

"Excuse me," Gillian said. "I need something to take out cactus needles."

The woman rolled her eyes and sighed. "You gringos. Don't you know enough to stay out of the cactus?"

"I guess not. Can you help?"

"Leave it to me." The woman rummaged through a drawer and came up with several utensils. Then she marched outside, shaking her head. "Gringos."

❖ ❖ ❖

EVENTUALLY THE WORST OF THE THORNS HAD BEEN extracted, although Lex thought he might be pulling cactus out of himself for weeks. It didn't matter. He was sitting in the cantina next to Gillian sipping a most excellent blue agave margarita. They were holding hands . . . carefully, but still holding hands.

Crowded around the table were Dante, BJ, Cora, and Little Ben. Hector was still out in back with Neil. He'd radioed for a boat to come and pick them both up.

"I have one little problem," Gillian said. "I tossed my nametag into the ocean."

"Omigod." BJ started to laugh. "Jared will have a conniption."

"You could borrow Nancy's wig and use her nametag," Dante said. "She won't be needing it."

"That won't be necessary." Cora sipped her margarita. "I will talk with Jared. Unless he wants me to tattle on him to his grandparents about his rendezvous with a cross-dresser, he'll be happy to let you back on board and make you a new nametag."

"That sounds better to me," Lex said. "I'd rather not spend the rest of the cruise with Nancy Roth, thank you very much."

"I'm still uneasy about what will happen to her . . . I mean, him," Gillian said. "I think Hector should let us call the LAPD. I want to make sure Neil pays for what he's done."

Lex glanced at her. "Ever hear of Mob justice?"

"Yes, but—"

"With apologies to our criminal justice system," Lex said, "I think Neil's in for a much worse time than if we turned him over to the LAPD. Our prisons are pretty cushy compared to what he's in for. And our system includes parole. Neil will never be free again."

"It did sound very grim," Dante said. "Did you hear the details, Gillian?"

"Hector's taking him off to some island, but for all I know it could be a tropical paradise."

Lex pushed back his chair. "Come on. I think you need to have Hector explain it more fully. I'm not sure you were listening closely enough." As they walked out the front door of the cantina, he leaned close. "Plus I want to get you alone and have my way with you."

She smiled at him. "You keep telling me that won't happen for weeks, until you're cactusfree."

"I don't have any cactus in my tongue."

"Oh, I *see*."

"Yes, you will. Shortly."

They rounded the building and found Hector sitting propped against the wall having a cigarette. Neil, although he had most of the cactus removed, was still tied up. The mesquite tree had been shading him, but the shade had shifted. Hector didn't seem concerned that Neil was beginning to burn.

Hector stood when they arrived. "Hi."

"I brought Gillian back out here because she's concerned that Neil isn't going to get what's coming to him."

Hector's laugh had zero humor. "I wouldn't wish his fate on my worst enemy."

"I don't want to hear about it!" Neil bellowed. "Not again!"

"Too bad." Hector turned to Gillian. "Phil Adamo owns an island not far from here. The terrain is about like this— volcanic rock and cactus. There's no indoor plumbing and nothing but a wooden shack with a cot and a table inside. Once a week, there will be a food drop, but it'll be mostly rations from army surplus, nothing you or I would want to eat. Every six months he'll get a new pair of pants and a shirt."

Gillian had to admit that sounded bad, especially for someone like Neil, who was used to the good life. "Is anyone else on the island?"

"Nope. I think Phil bought the place because he envisioned having to put this guy on it someday. He's been a problem for years."

Neil glared at them. "I have not."

Hector continued as if he hadn't heard him. "Neil's mother will get a slightly sanitized version of where her son is spending his time. She'll think he's off making movies in Europe and that he's upset with her over some petty thing. That should hold her off for a while. Phil can invent something else if he needs to. You don't want to get Phil Adamo mad at you. It's no fun."

Gillian nodded. "I can see that. Thanks, Hector." She started to shake his hand, but he pulled back.

"Sorry. Still a few thorns in there."

"I understand. So I guess I won't see you again."

"Nope." Hector glanced at his watch. "I got through to the boss. The guys should arrive any time now to take us both to the boat. We'll head straight to the island from here, and then I'll go on back to L.A."

"What about Dorothy?"

"Give her my regards. Tell her . . . tell her I had urgent business."

"You won't see her again, either, will you?"

"No." Hector looked sad for a moment. "But that's for the best."

"Thanks again, Hector," Lex said.

"Hey, I should be thanking you. I wasn't sure how to handle this situation without the use of a gun, and with security these days, that was too risky to bring on board. I wasn't allowed to kill him, anyway. Your cactus trick saved the day for me."

"And me," said Gillian, smiling at him.

Lex had a sudden urge to make her smile some more. "Ready to go back?"

"Uh-huh."

With a hand on her shoulder, he guided her around to the front of the building. "Let's walk a little."

"Suits me."

They wandered down the row of vendor stalls. "So you won't be running off to South America," he said.

"Doesn't look like it."

"I was wondering if I could interest you in a different plan." His heart beat faster. She could reject him, and he was prepared for that. They'd known each other a short time, but it had been packed with enough experiences to make him sure. Still, she might not be.

"Such as?"

"It's not quite as wild and crazy, but almost. I thought maybe . . . instead of running off to South America . . . we could get married."

She stopped walking and turned, her expression stunned. "But . . . but you don't really know me."

"What do you mean, I don't know you? I've shared a room with you two nights in a row. Number one, I know you're a mattress hog. Number two, I know you get makeup on the towels. I love you, anyway."

"I'm . . . I'm sort of a nerd."

"So what? Me, too. Sort of."

A smile tugged at the corners of her mouth. "There's the issue of my roots."

"To hell with your roots! I know what the real color of your hair is, in case you've forgotten, and I like it just fine. I love it, in fact. I can hardly wait to see it again."

That made her blush. "Lex, really."

"Yes, really. I want to spend the rest of my life getting naked with you, but that's just me. You have to speak for yourself."

Her face was bright red as she glanced around at the street filled with cruise ship passengers. "Okay," she said quickly. "I'll marry you. But let's lower the volume on the naked part of the conversation."

"I can do that." His heart had turned into a Mexican jumping bean. He'd just proposed and she'd just accepted. This was huge. He needed to tell . . . somebody.

He caught the eye of a tall geekish guy wearing a sombrero he'd obviously just bought. "We're getting married," Lex said. He couldn't stop grinning as he thought about that.

"Cool." The geek smiled back. "Apparently the cruise produced the optimal result for you."

"What result?" A redhead with freckles and a painful-looking sunburn walked over to peer at the guy with the sombrero. "What on earth are you talking about, Stephen?"

"Them." Stephen pointed to Gillian and Lex. "They're getting married."

The woman's eyes widened as she looked in their direction. "Now?"

"Well, not right this minute." Lex discovered he wouldn't mind that, though. Marriage was fine, but the thought of elaborate wedding preparations gave him hives.

"Definitely not now," Gillian said. "There's no . . ."

She surveyed the area. "There's no place, and we have to . . . we have to get a license and plan . . . stuff."

"You could do it on the ship," Stephen said. "Ship captains can marry people and you could cut through all the red tape. I researched it."

"Did you?" The redhead looked at Stephen with more interest. "And why would that be?"

Stephen launched into an explanation about contingency plans, but Lex wasn't paying attention. He was too busy concentrating on Gillian, who seemed either very scared or very excited by the prospect of a shipboard wedding. He needed to find out which, because he loved the idea.

"We could do that, get Captain Hull to marry us." He made the statement sound as casual as possible.

She swallowed. "And it would be legal?"

"You'd question Stephen?"

"Guess not. But . . . I don't have anything to wear."

"Wrong."

"Marilyn's dress?"

"Perfect."

She hesitated. "Do you want to?"

"More than you know."

"Why?"

"Because it would be very—" Just in time, he caught himself before he said the word *efficient.* "Romantic."

Her eyes glowed. "Oh, Lex. You understand, after all."

"Of course." As he took her into his arms, being very careful of the cactus thorns, he mentally crossed his fingers. He didn't understand squat, but he'd just negotiated a deal that would give him a lifetime to study up. He was excellent at studying up, because, as Dante had sensed all along, Lex was basically . . . no, *predominantly,* a nerd. But then again, so was the woman he loved.

She's an aspiring psychologist with her very own PERSONAL stalker.

He's a sexy, successful businessman who wants to be her very, very PERSONAL bodyguard....

February 14^(th) is the hottest day of the year for these two Cupid-struck souls in

MY NERDY VALENTINE

Don't miss the next novel from beloved *New York Times* bestselling author

Vicki Lewis Thompson

Coming in January 2007 from St. Martin's Paperbacks

ISBN: 0-312-93909-4